Special Thanks to our Indy Writes Books Sponsors

PUBLISHING SPONSOR

Margot L. Eccles Arts and Cultural Fund at CICF

★

FIRST EDITION SPONSORS

Bibliophilopolis
Larry B. Gregerson
Nancy C. Lilly
John and Sandy Masengale
Quirk Books
Cheryl and Jim Strain
Well Done Marketing
Quentin and Diane Young

★

FIRST READER SPONSORS

Stephanie Croaning
Beth Thomas and Dennis Dawes
Pam and Bob DiNicola
Homespun: Modern Handmade
Geoffrey Lamb
Mango Saxman Dann
Anne and Tim Need
Gigi and Mike Nicholas

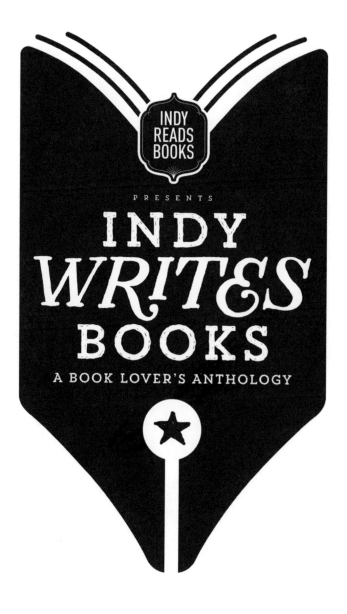

INDY
READS
BOOKS

PRESENTS

INDY *WRITES* BOOKS

A BOOK LOVER'S ANTHOLOGY

Published in 2014 by Indy Reads Books
Cover Design by Amy McAdams *www.amymcadams.com*
Book Design by Zachary Roth (*@compactdiscs*) of the Butler Pub Lab.
Set in Crimson Text; titling in Herschel, Trend, and IM Fell DW Pica

First edition November 2014

ISBN: 978-0-692-30029-9

Manufactured in the United States of America

911 Massachusetts Ave
Indianapolis, IN 46202
indyreadsbooks.org

INDY
WRITES
BOOKS

A BOOK LOVER'S ANTHOLOGY

★

edited by

M. TRAVIS DiNICOLA
& ZACHARY ROTH

with an introduction by

DAN WAKEFIELD

CONTENTS

Before We Begin

Drama

Fiction

Puzzles

Translations

PREFACE

M. TRAVIS DiNICOLA

Executive Director, Indy Reads
Founder of Indy Reads Books

Welcome to *Indy Writes Books*!

If you bought this book, thank you so very much. If it was a gift, then congratulations on having someone in your life who cares enough about you to buy you a pretty cool gift!

Indiana has some amazing authors. I believe that right now is one of the most important times for authors in our community. We are very fortunate to have so many incredible best-selling authors and emerging authors living and working here today. Indy Reads Books wants to draw attention to this, to celebrate them, and to share these authors with the public through this collection. It is my hope that you, the reader of this anthology, will find some old friends and discover some fantastic authors whom you may not have read otherwise.

This book is also a "fundraiser" for the non-profit organization Indy Reads. Our mission is to promote and improve the literacy of adults and families in Central Indiana. Indy Reads Books is a project of Indy Reads, and all proceeds from the store benefit Indy Reads. (If you haven't yet visited Indy Reads Books, I hope you do so soon. We sell both used and new books, and are the only independent bookstore in downtown Indianapolis.) All the proceeds from this book also go directly to supporting the work our students and tutors do. Some students come to us so that they can get a high school diploma, others because they want to get a driver's license, or vote. Many struggle with reading their medication labels or understanding their bank accounts. Some are parents who want to be able to read to their kids. And others want to be able read a recipe so they can cook for themselves.

Our students do not come to us to learn how to read for pleasure; that is a luxury they don't have yet, though many of them will discover it. They come to us to learn how to read for survival.

In 2013 more than 800 volunteer tutors helped over 1,600 adult students take a big step on their path to self-sufficiency. This would not be possible without the generous support of people like you. Every $5 we raise provides one hour of free tutoring to an adult student who is trying to improve their reading and writing skills for a better life. So, each copy of this $25 book will support 5 hours of tutoring! You can always learn more about our programs at *indyreads.org*.

Publishing this book is something we wanted to do almost from the first day we opened the bookstore in 2012, especially once we started experiencing the great support that local authors were giving to Indy Reads Books. We've hosted hundreds of author readings and signings at the store in the past two years. "I remember listening to Cathy Day read an unpublished work at one of our first author events and thought, "we should put this in a book!"

There is a great tradition of bookstores publishing books. If not for Sylvia Beach and her Shakespeare & Co. bookstore in Paris, we might have never had James Joyce's *Ulysses*. Lawrence Ferlinghetti's City Lights bookstore in San Francisco has over 200 books in print, including Allen Ginsburg's *HOWL*, which they first published in 1956 as part of their Pocket Poets series. More recently, and locally, Jim Huang's The Mystery Company bookstore in Carmel, Indiana has closed, but still continues to publish award-winning mystery series and anthologies as Crum Creek Press. I hope that Indy Reads Books will become a part of this tradition with the release of its first publication, *Indy Writes Books: A Book Lover's Anthology*. It is our hope that it is just the first of many books to be published by Indy Reads Books.

The 29 authors, poets, essayists, puzzle-makers, and artists featured in the book have all been supporters of the store, and have generously donated their works for this publication. We asked them to contribute work that had "something to do with reading, writing, literacy, books, or bookstores." Almost all of the works were created specifically for this publication, and only a handful have been previously published. It is truly a booklover's anthology published by a store made for booklovers.

On the day we opened the bookstore, we were fortunate enough to have the now world-famous John Green be the first author to read at Indy Reads Books. He had just come home from a national tour promoting *The Fault in Our Stars* and told the large crowd of his fans, "I'm so proud to be living in a city that is opening a bookstore instead of closing one." This was a glorious moment. That statement, and the encouragement he has given the store, has given me inspiration every day since. John was the first author we asked to be a part of *Indy Writes Books.* He agreed immediately and contributed three pieces that were originally produced for Chicago Public Radio, and are being printed here in a book for the first time.

Other works, like Lou Harry's new play, or John David Anderson and Larry Sweazy's new short stories, are set in bookstores that remind me a lot of Indy Reads Books.

Barb Shoup's essay is about the power of experiencing other people's worlds through the teaching of literature, while Susan Neville's essay about a gathering of literature professors is really an homage to James Joyce.

Ben Winters' story imagines a new technology where people can literally disappear into the world of a book.

There are two historical pieces by Ray Boomhower, a travel essay by Carol Faenzi, and a mystery by Terry Faherty.

The book contains a puzzle from "NPR Puzzlemaster" Will Shortz. Even the JUMBLE creators, Jeff Knurek & David Hoyt, submitted a version of their illustrated word puzzle that features Indy Reads Books, and yours truly as a cartoon character.

There is work from former state Poets Laureate Karen Kovacik and Norbert Krapf, as well as poems from Liza Hyatt and Bonnie Maurer.

Victoria Barrett, Michael Dahlie, and Frank Bill share stories, as do Lorene Burkhart, Mary Susan Buhner, Amy Sorrells, and Angela Jackson-Brown.

Lyn Jones contributed an essay, and Gordon Strain & Dianne Moneypenny submitted stories with illustrations *and* translations!

And Cathy Day, who first got me thinking about creating this anthology, has a piece too. I am grateful to all of them for their work and support.

Along with including a short memoir about his god-daughter, the legendary author Dan Wakefield was also generous enough to write an introduction for the book that takes a look at the great tradition of Indiana authors. Over the past few years, after moving back to Indianapolis, Dan has become one of the greatest supporters of Indy Reads Books. We joke with him that he has become the "patron saint" of the bookstore. He has read and spoken at the store more than any other author, sends authors and customers to us regularly, and is also one of our best customers! I am very lucky to call this icon of Indiana literature a close friend. Dan and I have spent many hours at either the Chatterbox Jazz Club on Mass. Ave. or the Red Key in Broadripple (the former being my favorite watering hole, the latter his, and both are great gathering places for writers and readers) talking about literature, and authors, and planning this book. I have learned so much from him, and have gained so much from our friendship. It is an honor to have him be a part of this book.

Butler University's Pub Lab, and Pressgang, a small publishing house affiliated with the MFA Program in Creative Writing, is assisting with editing, typesetting, and other publishing logistics. Zach Roth, a graduate of the program, is the co-editor of the book along with myself. His work has been extraordinary. So much of the look and feel of this book is because of his great sense of style and love of literature. It looks and feels like a book that wants to be read. He is to be commended.

Indy Writes Books is also fortunate to have designer Amy McAdams, who designed the original logo for Indy Reads Books, as our cover designer. I love the image of the pen nib, which also doubles as a book, and suggests the Indianapolis city flag. When we asked Amy for a design that celebrates Indianapolis authors, she nailed it!

The amazing Indy Reads Board of Directors, our dedicated staff (in the office and at the bookstore), and our incredible volunteers and students also deserve much thanks for their ongoing work, which makes all this possible. Special thanks to Alyssa Newerth, our Director of Advancement, and Jenny Dwenger, our bookstore manager.

Credit for this book, and the bookstore, also needs to be given to Michael Svoboda. When I was in college and graduate school at Penn State, I worked for Michael at his bookstore, Svoboda's Books. It was there that I first learned that operating a bookstore is so much more than just selling books. The best bookstores bring together readers and writers, books and ideas, families and strangers. And they aren't afraid of free speech. They are an essential part of a community's cultural identity. They are celebrations of literacy. Svoboda's Books was the inspiration for everything we do at Indy Reads Books, and for *Indy Writes Books.*

I also want to thank all of our First Edition and First Reader sponsors who believed in this project enough to contribute generously to ensure its publication. It is creative philanthropy of this nature that makes a thriving arts and cultural community possible. Their names are listed on the very first page.

As was the case with the founding of Indy Reads Books, *Indy Writes Books* would not have been possible without the support of the late Margot Lacy Eccles. Thanks to the original financial investment by Mrs. Eccles, Indy Reads opened Indy Reads Books, a community bookstore selling used and new books in downtown

Indianapolis, along the Cultural Trail on Mass. Ave. First on a napkin, and then later in a full proposal, the original plan for the store was created under her direction and guidance. Key elements of this plan she championed are: all used books are donated and sold at a very affordable price; the store is run by a combination of a few paid staff with dozens of volunteers; the store provides space for Indy Reads students and tutors to work; and all proceeds from the store go back to support Indy Reads adult literacy programs. Mrs. Eccles wanted the store to serve the community. And with Mrs. Eccles's support, Indy Reads Books was also able to attain the additional funding from the Efroymson Family Fund, the Glick Fund, and Giving Sum which made the store possible.

"Mrs. E.," as many of us in the Stanley K. Lacy Executive Leadership program called her, was my mentor. As part of her legacy, she also created a very special fund to support the "big dreams" of arts and cultural organizations she cared about in her lifetime. Indy Reads is very fortunate to be one of these organizations. With support from the Margot L. Eccles Arts and Cultural Fund at CICF, Indy Reads Books has become a publisher, and joined a great tradition. I believe she would have been proud of what she made possible. She is greatly missed by all of us.

And finally, to you, the reader, thank you. You are the reason we do this. Read on!

CORN, LIMESTONE, HORSEWEED AND WRITERS

DAN WAKEFIELD

The late Jim Goode, a friend from Shortridge, told me he wrote a paper at Wabash on Indiana writers, and found there was a time when five of the ten books on the *New York Times* Best Seller List were written by Hoosiers. He said when he told a colleague at *Life* magazine about this phenomenon, he was asked "Is there something in the water there?"

There must be.

Whatever is "in the water" here not only produces writers, it produces writers who write good books—books that readers enjoy. From reports on best-selling books by Indiana authors, the "phenomenon" Jim Goode told me about may easily have occurred more than once. In "What Made Hoosiers Write," an article in *American Heritage* (1960), Howard H. Peckham, Director of the

Indiana Historical Bureau, points out that "...it was not simply that so many Hoosiers wrote that gave the state its [literary] reputation; it is the indisputable fact that a score of those writers produced one bestseller after another which compelled national attention to Indiana."

John Moriarity, a librarian with the objectivity of an "Eastern outsider" (he came from Connecticut), took over the libraries at Purdue during WWII, and was so impressed by the sheer number of Indiana writers that he decided to see how they fared with readers throughout the nation. Using formulas based on national rankings such as Alice Payne Hackett's *50 Years of Best-Sellers*, Moriarity wrote, in his 1947 article "Hoosiers Sell Best" in *The Indiana Quarterly for Bookmen*, that the states whose writers had the most bestsellers were: 1, Indiana; 2, New York; and 3, Virginia.

Updating rankings and enlarging them to include authors from other countries who were popular in America, IUPUI librarian Steven J. Schmidt found in his 1990 study ("Do Hoosiers Sell Best?") that the state or country with the most bestselling authors were: 1, England; 2, New York; 3, Indiana.

Indiana has been producing writers "nearly as regularly as corn and limestone," according to Arthur Shumaker, in *A History of Indiana Literature*, or, in another homey phrase, Hoosier writers "grew as naturally and as luxuriantly as the horseweed along the banks of the quiet Indiana streams," as R.E. Banta wrote in "A Word About Indiana Authors" in 1949.

It's still happening.

Here is my hot news: "The Golden Age of Indiana Literature" never ended, and is still in full swing.

The term is usually said to cover the years from 1880-1920, or from Lew Wallace's *Ben Hur* in 1880, to Booth Tarkington's *Alice Adams* in 1921.

There were many best-selling Hoosier authors in that era whose names I never knew (but that figures—some of the writers who were famous in the 1950s are already forgotten). I did know about the book that kicked off the era with a bang that is still ringing in the ears of readers—*Ben Hur: A Tale of The Christ* was in my father's bookshelf. I have to admit I didn't read the novel by Lew Wallace of Gary (who was also a General in the Union Army), but I saw the big hit movie with Charlton Heston in 1959. Both the novel and the movie set records: *Ben Hur* outsold every book but *The Bible* and *Uncle Tom's Cabin* from 1880 until *Gone with the Wind* came out in 1936. After *Ben Hur* became the highest grossing movie of 1959 and won a record eleven Oscars, the novel soared back to the top of the best-seller list, and has never been out of print.

The "Golden Age" seems to have been declared for its turn of the century stars who were photographed together like a Mt. Rushmore of Indiana authors of the era: Booth Tarkington, who won the Pulitzer Prize for both *Alice Adams* and *The Magnificent Ambersons* (Orson Welles produced and starred in a movie version); James Whitcomb Riley, "The Hoosier Poet," author of nationally best-selling books whose title poems I memorized at School #80 (*When The Frost Is on the Punkin*, and *Little Orphant Annie*); Meredith Nicholson, whose *House of a Thousand Candles*, a bestseller in 1905, is now reprinted as a "Classic" in a series called "Forgotten Books" (Nicholson's house where he wrote the book is now a historic site at 1500 N. Delaware); and George Ade, known as "The Aesop of Indiana" for his best-selling *Fables in Slang*, as well as acclaimed plays and musicals including the Broadway hit "The College Widow," made twice as a movie.

And that doesn't even include Gene Stratton (Mrs. Charles Darwin) Porter, *nee* Geneva, whose wildlife stories like *Girl of the Limberlost* sold millions. The literary critic Willam Lyons Phelps called her "a national institution, like Yellowstone Park." One thing is sure in writing any account of Indiana authors: you are certain to leave out dozens—nay, *hundreds*—of worthy names.

The problem of accounting for the overgrowth of corn, limestone, horseweed and writers that continue to luxuriate here along the "Banks of the Wabash"—as well as The Ohio, White River, The Canal, Lake Maxincuckee, Wawasea and the gravel pits poetically transformed into "lakes"—was summed up long ago in a tale attributed to Opie Read, an "Eastern" lecturer from The Chattauqua circuit who came to speak in Indiana. He began an address here by saying he was aware of the great literary reputation of the state, and asked any writers in the audience to come and join him on the stage. Everyone present headed for the stage except for one man in the front row. It was explained to the speaker that "He writes too but he's deaf and didn't hear what you said."

Already I've forgotten one of Kurt Vonnegut's favorites, Frank McKinney "Kin" Hubbard, whose "Abe Martin" character with his sly satiric sayings for *The Indianapolis News* was syndicated in three hundred papers nationwide. Vonnegut often quoted "Abe Martin" wisdom in his talks. In a commencement address at Butler, he passed on these sayings of "Abe":

"It's no disgrace to be poor, but it might as well be."

"I don't know anybody who'd be willing to work for what he's worth."

★

To qualify as an "Indiana writer" in *The History of Indiana Literature*, an author must have lived here at some time or other and show "evidence in his life or in his works of the influence of an Indiana environment—one whose residence here has really affected him." For that reason, the drama critic George Jean Nathan "does not show any Hoosier influence in his work and is therefore out." By the same standard, Theodore Dreiser "very reluctantly" has been excluded because of "insufficient residence and Indiana influences."

Since Dreiser was born and grew up in Terre Haute, and went to Indiana University for a year, he fulfills the residency requirement (more than some others who are included), so he must be lacking in "Indiana influences." One might surmise that his joining the Communist Party just before his death may have been the factor that disqualified the author of such novels as *An American Tragedy* (1925) and *Sister Carrie* (1900) as an "Indiana writer." H.L. Mencken called Dreiser "a great artist," and wrote that "no other American of his generation left so wide and handsome a mark upon the national letters," while the literary critic Irving Howe called him "one of the few American giants we have had."

In an effort to reclaim Dreiser as an "Indiana writer," I would like to suggest that his becoming a Communist shortly before his death be balanced—and perhaps offset—by the fact that his brother Paul Dresser wrote "On the Banks of the Wabash," an Indiana anthem that became the top sheet music bestseller of its era, and is still sung proudly and nostalgically by Hoosiers today.

★

At the very end of "The Golden Age" in 1925, another Indianapolis-born writer started a distinguished literary career, but she is not mentioned, perhaps because in a different way than Dreiser, she failed to show the proper "Indiana influences." Janet Flanner was the daughter of Frank Flanner, co-owner of the local mortuary, and after two years at The University of Chicago, she served as the first movie critic of *The Star*. She married briefly and left Indianapolis, spending most of her life living with women, primarily Solita Solana, who she met in Greenwich Village. According to *The History of Indiana Literature*, one of the "concrete reasons" for the success of Hoosier authors is that "They had no use for any cult of obscurity, and they developed nothing in the way of synthetic intellectual centers such as Greenwich Village."

As if meeting her female companion in Greenwich Village weren't enough, Ms. Flanner moved to Paris (an even more notorious "synthetic intellectual community"), where she became a correspondent for *The New Yorker* magazine, writing "Letter from Paris" under the pen name "Genet." She hung out with such non-Hoosiers as Gertrude Stein and Alice B. Toklas, Ernest Hemingway, Djuna Barnes, e.e. cummings and F. Scott Fitzgerald, and was made a knight of the *Legion d'Honneur*. She won The National Book Award for her *Paris Journal-1944-1965*.

The main part of *The History of Indiana Literature* is limited to fiction writers, but in a paragraph on other well-known Hoosier authors that came after "The Golden Age," the author cites WWII war correspondent Ernie Pyle, a category in which Flanner might qualify for her three-part profile of Adolf Hitler, coverage of The Nuremberg Trials, the Suez Crisis, and the Soviet invasion of Hungary.

It is only fair to report, however, that in a final farewell to Indiana, rather than joining her famous fellow Hoosiers such as James Whitcomb Riley and John Dillinger in Crown Hill, Flanner chose to have her ashes scattered over Cherry Grove on Fire Island. R.I.P. "Genet."

★

If you thought "The Golden Age" of huge bestsellers from Indiana authors ended with *Ben Hur* riding his chariot into eternity, you had best think again. Hardly had the dust settled on "Little Orphant Annie" and other Golden Oldies, when in 1929 a minister from Columbia City published his first novel—*Magnificent Obsession*—that was not only written in the religious fiction tradition of *Ben Hur*, but rivaled its success. Author Lloyd C. Douglas left the pulpit for the pen, and followed this with other bestsellers, most notably *The Robe*, which stayed on the best-seller list for three years after it was published in 1942, and returned when it became the first movie made in "CinemaScope," starring Richard Burton. (*The Robe* was my mother's favorite book, so with that and my father's copy of *Ben Hur* in the house, I had a best-seller school right there at Sixty-First and Winthrop, had I not neglected them.

Topping off the era of Indiana writers' bestsellers in the '40s that became hit movies in the '50s is Ross Lockridge's *Raintree County*, which was published in '48 and hit the screen in '57 with Elizabeth Taylor and Montgomery Clift. The novel not only was a big bestseller, but its author was celebrated in a poem by Nobel Laureate Pablo Neruda along with such "American giants" of literature as Melville, Whitman, Poe, Dreiser and Wolfe. Some purists may wonder if Lockridge's tragic suicide at the height of his fame indicated a failure to show "evidence in his life" of "the influences of an Indiana environment," but surely the creation of a fictional Indiana country for the setting of his novel is enough to redeem his status as a Hoosier writer.

While these hit movies based on books by Indiana authors were dazzling multitudes all over America in the fifties, a '42

Shortridge High School graduate (and columnist for *The Daily Echo*) was toiling away in literary obscurity in a small town on Cape Cod. It was not until his novel *Slaughterhouse Five* was published in 1969 that Kurt Vonnegut found fame and fortune. Based on his experience surviving the fire-bombing of Dresden as a prisoner of war in an underground meat locker, the novel became an overnight best-seller. Fans formed lines that snaked around the blocks of bookstores wanting his autograph—er, except in his Hoosier hometown. I received a letter from Vonnegut on May 9, 1969 that read as follows:

> Dear Dan:
> At the request of Ayres [department store], I went to Indianapolis last week, appeared on a TV show and a radio show, then signed books in the [L.S. Ayres] bookstore. I sold thirteen books in two hours, every one of them to a relative. Word of honor... Peace,
> Kurt

It wasn't until 2007 that the city officially recognized him by proclaiming "The Year of Vonnegut," but he died sixteen days before he was scheduled to give the "acceptance speech" at Clowes Hall. The talk he had written was read there by his son Mark, a doctor in Boston who is also a writer (author of two fine memoirs.) Now there is a Vonnegut Museum and Library in the city, and a larger-than-life portrait of him on the side of a downtown building. Vonnegut remains a national treasure, his work translated in all the major languages of the world, and all of his books still in print.

★

John Green is ushering in a new age of social media-powered literature that could well make *Ben Hur*'s popularity seem like a chariot compared to a rocket.

Already a hero to millions of young adults, Green's novel *The Fault In Our Stars*, a realistic tale of two teenagers battling cancer, was a best-seller before it was published and opened at the top of the best-seller list; the novel's faithful movie translation helped power its reach to adult audiences of all ages.

Green was born in Indianapolis but his parents whisked him off to Michigan three weeks later; his Hoosier karma brought him back when his wife took a job as Curator of Contemporary Art at The IMA. He set up shop in Broad Ripple, where he not only writes best-selling novels, but also teams with brother Hank to produce the Vlogbrothers channel on YouTube, and with Hank and wife Sarah he turns out educational videos on literature, science and art. John Green is not only a best-selling author, he is a walking multi-media corporation. *Time* magazine named him on their 2014 list of the 100 most influential people in the world. Since Green is thirty-seven, Indiana's "Golden"—or maybe now, in record business terminology, "Platinum"—Age of Literature, seems insured for a long time to come.

As "Abe Martin" might say: "This ain't just corn and horseweed."

★

I know I run the risk of alienating hundreds of writers who probably live within a few square miles of me, and a half dozen good writer friends here whose work I genuinely admire, by mentioning the work of one among so many. (Oh well, it won't be the first time I've offended fellow Hoosiers of all occupations, ages and backgrounds.) Still, I can't resist quoting the writer who, more than any other, brings back to me the place where I grew up, the place I love, the place that is conjured up so powerfully for me by Susan Neville in her *Indiana Winter*:

> "And still we float so gently on this gloom in the graying yellow October daylight, in the night lit with candles, in the strong wood houses and barns, in the orchards where the apples fall into our hands and the leaves twist down. We sail on the land as though it's real, our compasses pointing north, as though we know where we are. We eat sugar pears and watch the sugar maples blaze and we suck on sweet candy and smell the damp decaying leaves, and we hold tight as the boat heaves and the land pitches."

Bless us all, us Indiana writers—and bless those Hoosiers who don't rush forward when all the writers in the audience are called to join the speaker on the stage. Hopefully, there are some left in the audience (as well as the deaf man who didn't hear the call), who are willing to stay in their seat as we pour out our words. Bless those most of all—the readers.

Dan Wakefield would like to thank Indy Reads intern Meredith Deem for her excellent research assistance.

INDY
WRITES
BOOKS

A BOOK LOVER'S ANTHOLOGY

LIZA HYATT

HOUSEHOLD GODS

Loved and passed from hand to hand for generations,
given as my birthright, they fill my house with silence
and intimate conversation that is spiritual.
They need solitude, demand it, but in it with them,
I am never alone and they welcome visitors
who enter my house and go to them first,
reverently touch their spines and call out,
"I love this one!" and "This changed my life!"

They love us too and need us to reach out,
hold them and ask questions. They are teachers,
healers, singers, mothers and fathers to us.
They are weavers who fill open minds
with the most generously composed
tapestries that can be spun from language,
wefting ideas together for as many hours
as we can pay attention, including us
in the dialogue they have kept alive for centuries,
and inviting us to respond in kind
by putting pen to paper and mapping
our way out of the cave, toward
fever and remembered wings and enlightenment.

When I am tired and trapped in a too small life,
I find them rallied side by side, shoulder to shoulder,
warriors ready for battle with not a sword among them,
only words, only bodies pressed from wood pulp,
bodies tattooed with black ink,
some with yellow, brittle old skin,
some scribbled on in childhood
or scored and marked in study
or new, white virgins,
all ready to fight for what is true and wise.

If they survive fire and flood, they will be destroyed
by time's slow acid. I keep them immortal
by spending time at their hearth, learning by heart,
giving them to students and children,
everyone in pain, in wonder.

Liza Hyatt is the author of *The Mother Poems* (Chatter House Press, 2014), *Under My Skin*, (WordTech Editions, 2012), *Seasons of the Star Planted Garden* (Stonework Press, 1999), and *Stories Made of World* (Finishing Line Press, 2013). She has been published in various regional, national, and international journals and anthologies. In 2006, Hyatt received an Individual Artist Project Grant from the Indiana Arts Commission.

Liza is an art therapist (ATR-BC, LMHC) and adjunct professor at both St. Mary of the Woods College and Herron School of Art and Design. She hosts a monthly poetry reading at the Lawrence Art Center. She is the author of *Art of the Earth: Ancient Art for a Green Future* (Authorhouse, 2007) an art-based eco-psychology workbook. For more information, visit *lizahyatt.wordpress.com*

BETWEEN THE LINES

BEN H. WINTERS

"Outside of a dog, a book is a man's best friend. Inside of a dog, it's too dark to read." — *Groucho Marx*

1

When the company announced that they would be making an announcement, everybody flipped out.

The stock price jumped. Bloggers blogged furiously. Website reporters and newspaper reporters and on-air reporters all reported feverishly on each other's reports. For those wild three weeks, between the announcement of a forthcoming announcement and the announcement itself, people all over the country and all over the world were whipped into a great froth of anticipation.

All, of course, exactly as the company had intended!

They had been known as much for their products as for the reveal of those products. Their gadgets were more than useful, more than fun: They were game-changing. Paradigm-shifting. Life-altering.

And so what would it be this time?

Time-travel, perhaps? A personalized handheld device for transporting amongst the eras of humanity. A wristwatch, maybe, that when properly dialed zaps its wearer through the eons.

Or maybe teleportation, a push-button atomic dematerializing and rematerializing machine, so the consumer might on a whim leave his home in Duluth and spend the afternoon on the Champs-Élysées.

Maybe x-ray vision, other people speculated hopefully. Maybe telepathy! Maybe jet packs—people *always* think it's going to be jet packs.

Others cautioned that the announcement might be something more prosaic. Something dull but useful. A machine to conserve one's household energy usage, or a workplace utility to maximize employee output. A product no one would totally understand, but everyone would nevertheless be expected to enthuse over.

How incredible, then—how *delightful*—that when at last the three weeks had elapsed and the announcement came, the new device turned out to be one that allowed human beings to enter into works of fiction.

Not just "virtually," either. The company spokesmen and spokeswomen were very clear about that. This was no cheap digital sensorium, no dolled-up video game—this was real. The user of the new device would literally, actually *go into* their favorite works of literature and become part of the story, interacting with the characters and walking with them through the world of the book.

Incredible? Beyond incredible! Delightful? Past delightful—sublime!

This remarkable device was born from many years of top-secret collaboration from all departments of the company: Artificial intelligence folks; hardware designers; software engineers; professors of comparative literature.

The product was called Between the Lines, and sales were through the roof.

First of all, a person had to buy a Between the Lines: that was the slim, handsomely constructed black box into which you inserted an OpenBook—that being a book retroactively engineered to be "opened" by the Between the Lines to allow access to the "reader." Once you owned an OpenBook you could "enter in" at any time, and go where you wished inside the universe of the story. After a period of one hour, the "reader" would be automatically ejected from the OpenBook, and the story would reset itself for her next entry.

OpenBooks were of course to be sold separately, and licensing arrangements had been made, before the announcement, with all of the major publishers and most of the smaller ones, for their creation. Nearly every title was available, and people snapped them up. *A Tale of Two Cities* was an early best-seller, as was *Tarzan*. Middle-aged adult men were found to be partial to *Treasure Island*, while certain works of *Jane Austen* proved irresistible to a certain demographic.

There was almost no novel that wasn't translated to an OpenBook version, and many were instant bestsellers: from obvious visceral attractions like *Dracula*, to more cerebral fare, like *The Golden Notebook* or *Bleak House*.

On the day that Ayn Rand's *The Fountainhead* was released as an OpenBook, many, many people purchased it.

OpenBooks, though very expensive, made popular presents: what better anniversary gift could there be than the gift of solving the mystery of the Baskervilles alongside Holmes, or wandering for an hour through the forking paths of a Borgesian puzzle?

Some authors righteously opted out of the licensing deals. There would be no OpenBook edition of *The Corrections*, at Jonathan Franzen's irritated insistence. *To Kill a Mockingbird* remained closed, despite a fevered campaign to get Harper Lee to change her mind. Beckett's estate would not grant access to *Nausea*, although Joyce's surprised the world by allowing an OpenBook *Ulysses*, which proved a smash hit.

New authors, inevitably, began to craft tales explicitly for the OpenBook market, and "immersivity" became the new watchword in publishing seminars and MFA programs. Novels appeared by the score featuring inviting seaside locations, challenging mountains begging to be climbed, and all manner of beguiling erotic scenarios.

Children, of course, were a huge market. Parents were assured over and over how safe the machine was for even the littlest readers, and they thrilled at the experience of saving Wilbur from Mr. Arable's axe, or watching the emperor prance past and loudly pointing out his ridiculous nakedness.

And the thing about the children was that they felt none of the anxious twinges that troubled some older users of the Between the Lines—those adults who, even as they embraced the new technology, even as they so enjoyed dancing the mazurka alongside Anna Karenina, or trading quips with Wodehouse's Jeeves, sometimes longed for the time when books were closed affairs, to be "entered into" only figuratively.

"Oh, mom!" their little readers would say, disappearing with a giggle for another hour of cavorting with Elephant and Piggy. "Oh, dad!"

2

Caitlin Sutter had always, always, always loved to read.

As an infant she had never wanted anything but to sit in someone's lap and be read to. There was nothing she so adored, from the day she began to puzzle out words on her own, than to sit in some sunlit corner of the apartment turning pages. If ever her parents didn't know where she was, that's where they would find her: body curled up around a long pillow, eyes wide with interest or astonishment, one finger idly curling and uncurling a single strand of her thick dark hair. Reading.

Her mother Mrs. Sutter would say to her little girl, when she could capture her attention for a moment, "You have such big eyes, my love. Do you know why you have such big eyes?"

And Caitlin would look up dreamily and say "why?" and Mrs. Sutter would stroke her hair and say "so you can read twice as fast as everyone else."

And little Cait would smile, and allow herself to be hugged, and then go back to whatever it was she was reading.

Despite this deep love, eighteen months after Between the Lines was invented, Caitlin had never "entered in" to a book. The reason was simple: money. Between the Lines cost a great deal, and each individual OpenBook cost a great deal also, and the Sutters—while not poor—simply could not afford such luxuries.

Caitlin, for all her deep focus on her books, was aware of her parents' constant low-level anxiety about finances and the future and "making ends meet." When she came down at night because she couldn't sleep, asking to read for ten more minutes, she would find them huddled at the kitchen table, poring over the bills.

So though of course she wanted a Between the Lines badly, though she heard from better-off friends at school of the marvel of the thing (friends who didn't even like to read, in particular, who hadn't cared about books at all, before this new fad)—she would never have been so inconsiderate, so *selfish*, as to ask her parents to get one.

But they were going to get her one anyway.

They were saving up, in secret, so they could get her one on her birthday.

She was going to be twelve, and her parents could no longer bear the idea of their darling and book-obsessed little girl being without this miraculous thing that had changed the face of books. They had been scrimping; skipping breakfasts; going without new clothes. Mr. Sutter had stopped buying his monthly Travel System card, and had instead been getting up before sunrise every day and walking to work.

★

Wolcott & Lombe was a small bookshop downtown, and Mr. Sutter arrived there just before closing on a Tuesday night, the night before Caitlin's birthday.

He very nearly didn't make it; the store's posted closing hour was 7:00, and since he didn't get off work until five and since he was walking, he had to race the last three blocks, sprinting furiously in his work suit and heavy black work shoes to get there in time.

In retrospect, of course, it might have been better if he *hadn't* made it, but he did—Mr. Sutter burst into the store just before closing and caught his breath, looking with amazement around the small and brightly furnished establishment. W&L had a bright pink awning and sleek violet furnishings, along with the traditional hardwood furniture and framed author posters, as if to announce: Yes, we have the latest magic, but we're *still* a book shop.

Once there had hardly been any bookstores , but in the year and a half since Between the Lines many new ones had opened, and W&L was one of the finest. It sold Between the Lines, and decorative tags for your Between the Lines, and special branded Experience Journals to write in each time you emerged from your OpenBook. Oh, and books, too—the old kind—a few racks of them, toward the back, by the restrooms, which were only open to customers.

Mr. Sutter selected a Between the Lines and a case, and found the OpenBook he was looking for right away. He held it up lovingly and smiled at the cover illustration: the elusively smiling cat, the Mad Hatter, the pretty little girl. He thought pleasantly as he approached the checkout that the heroine looked just like his daughter.

She's going to love it, he thought, with that special flush of satisfaction that all parents get when doing something they know will bring pleasure to their child. *My goodness, she's going to love it!*

He hesitated only slightly as he handed the Between the Lines and the OpenBook to the sullen young man behind the counter.

"I just wondered..." said Mr. Sutter, furrowing his brow. "Is there any danger?"

"No, sir."

"In *Alice in Wonderland*? The rabbit hole—the potions—and, you know. 'Off with 'er head' and everything?"

"There is no danger in any of these books, sir," huffed the man behind the counter. "That's the whole *point.* You go in to the book and you experience the book, but you can't change the story, and the story can't change you. But the memories? The memories last a lifetime." The man said all of this very quickly and totally without affect, and Mr. Sutter recognized everything he said from the advertisements.

"Okay," he said. "Thank you."

"So you'll take it?"

"Yes, please."

Mr. Sutter signed the credit card slip and watched as the clerk wrapped the OpenBook with brisk efficiency in layers of violet tissue and placed it at the bottom of a violet bag. Watching the present be wrapped he smiled to imagine the delight that Caitlin would have on unwrapping the gift; imagining her leaping, with two feet, into the opened world of *Alice in Wonderland.*

He thanked the disinterested clerk one more time, and held the package tightly as he turned to leave the shop...and saw one more OpenBook, displayed on the corner of the Classic Favorites table.

He stopped.

He shouldn't have. He should have marched right out of there. He should have obeyed the unspoken exhortation of the clerk, who was clearing his throat loudly and staring at his watch, which now read seven o'clock.

But Mr. Sutter felt so proud of himself, and felt so proud of his wife for having thought of the gift, and for all their sacrifices made to get it. He lifted the second OpenBook and turned it over in his hands. He and his wife so rarely got gifts for each other. And what he hadn't told her was that he wasn't just skipping breakfast, but lunch too, in case they raised the prices of the Between the Lines, or of the OpenBooks, before Caitlin's birthday.

He had extra money. And she would love the OpenBook—Mrs. Sutter. How she would love it. She would be startled that he did it, and would scold him for it, but she would love it so.

Mr. Sutter turned back to the counter and took out his credit card one more time.

★

Caitlin Sutter—to employ a cliché that the bookish girl would surely recognize as such—did not have a rebellious bone in her body. She always did as she was told, always made her bed and washed her hands and tidied up her room. If on occasion she had to be called more than once to the dinner table, it was only because her attention was so deeply focused on *Charlie and the Chocolate Factory* or *Harriet the Spy*, or whatever book had gathered her attention on that particular evening.

But on the morning of her twelfth birthday, when she woke up before her parents and came down the stairs, and spotted that small violet gift bag with the black handles, and she knew immediately what it was—well, it was irresistible. Though properly she should have waited for her parents to wake up and present her with the gift, Caitlin simply could *not* wait.

She reached into the bag, already knowing what was in there, not quite believing it was real—until she touched it, until she felt the smooth plastic, magical surface of the Between the Lines. She closed her eyes and sighed with pleasure, just from the feel of it, and all the possibilities it held.

We must forgive Caitlin her impatience. We must forgive her excitement.

She sat down and opened the bag and took out the Between the Lines, and all of us would have done the same. We've all known the keen anticipatory pleasure, after all, of a new book. The glossy surface and the uncreased spine, all those words waiting to be read, all that story waiting to be rolled out before us like a red carpet. Now imagine Caitlin's feeling, knowing the experience awaiting her was not just reading a new book, but entering into one. Feeling it, from the inside out. Holding the Between the Lines and reaching in for the OpenBook that lay below it, she felt what she would come to recognize, many years later, as *passion*—it might be too crude to call it lust, but that's what it was, wasn't it? It was the lust of a bookish and sensitive girl holding in her hand a newly physical way of loving what she loved the most.

Caitlin's excitement was so keen, in fact, that she didn't even stop to see what the OpenBook was as she inserted it into the machine. She saw that there were two OpenBooks in the bag, and thought without thinking that both were for her. Why else would they be in the bag? It wouldn't have occurred to her that her father had on impulse bought one for her mother, too, and had absentmindedly left both in the bag.

And so it was that by the time the Sutters awoke and came downstairs, their daughter was gone. She had disappeared into a book. Alas, *Alice in Wonderland* sat still wrapped in the violet tissue-paper packaging at the bottom of the violet bag. She was in *A Clockwork Orange* instead.

★

The CUSTOMER SUPPORT information on the side of the Between the Lines directed consumers to a website address. The phone number listed on the website address was answered by an automated system directing people to the website.

At last, while Mrs. Sutter paced the room, rubbing her eyes, chewing her nails, Mr. Sutter instant-messaged with a faceless company employee, explaining as fast as his fingers could type what had happened: his young and defenseless twelve year old had accidentally entered into a world of violence and drug abuse and hatred.

WHOOPS! came the response, followed by a smiling emoticon that made Mr. Sutter howl in anger.

The faceless person on the other end typed quickly. He or she or it explained to the horrified Sutters that there was nothing to be done. Caitlin would be fine. To follow someone else into a book was impossible, except of course in the Beta version which was not yet available. Don't worry, the person typed at last, You can't change the story, and the story can't change you. But the memories? The memories last a lifetime!

Mr. and Mrs. Sutter sat together on the floor of the living room, her hand clasped tightly in his, counting the minutes until their daughter emerged.

★

Which she did.

Exactly as promised, at exactly the hour mark Caitlin was back.

She rematerialized in the Sutters' living room, screaming and screaming.

Her mouth was frozen open in a deranged rictus of horror and despair, and her screams only accelerated when she saw her parents rushing toward her. She fell into their arms, taking heaving breaths, pushing her head into her mother's chest like a small animal, drooling and muttering "oh oh oh." Mr. and Mrs. Sutter clutched her and held her and said all the small useless things that parents say in the face of a child's distress.

"It's okay."

"It's going to be okay."

"Oh honey...oh honey my love..."

Soon Caitlin's body unclenched, and she stopped crying. She was pale, and her eyes twitched, as if replaying frightful scenes. Mrs. Sutter settled into a chair with the girl on her lap. Mr. Sutter went into the kitchen to make tea.

Caitlin would not describe what had happened. She would not speak at all. By the time Mr. Sutter returned with the steaming teapot, Caitlin had climbed out of her mother's lap and was standing with crossed arms in one corner of the living room, looking warily around the room like an injured animal.

Gently they asked, but Caitlin refused, quietly but adamantly, to describe what she had seen.

Her parents looked at each other, helpless. Both knew Burgess's novella well, knew exactly what went on in there.

"Honey?" they said to her.

"Sweetheart? Are you okay?"

Mr. and Mrs. Sutter stood clutching each other, staring at their daughter, who looked back at them blankly from the place she had taken on the wall. As if looking past them—looking *through* them.

"I am fine," she said flatly. "I am fine."

"Honey—" said Mr. Sutter again, rising, placing one arm on his precious daughter's shoulder. She shook it off, an immediate and fierce gesture, like a lion shaking off an insect. "I'm *fine*," she said again—and that was it. She walked slowly up the stairs, back to her room.

The tea went cold on the tray.

Mrs. Sutter buried her head in her husband's chest, and began to weep.

★

Caitlin's parents watched her closely over the following week. In truth, the Sutters watched Caitlin closely over the months and then the years to come.

There were, as promised, no physical signs of her adventure inside *A Clockwork Orange*. If Caitlin had suffered directly any of the ultraviolence that runs in tangled red lines through that novel, she bore no traces of it: no scabbing, no lacerations, no bruises, no limp. Her face was the same red-cheeked round child's face, her body the same coltish small body, not a scratch on her.

And yet she had been changed. There were the words, of course, the occasional words—as the week progressed, occasionally in her speech some the novel's bizarre neo-Russian patois would surface: she would refer to her parents as "me droogs," or ask for a glass of "milk-plus," and then wrinkle her nose, give a tight little shake of the head, as if confused and irritated by something someone else had said.

Never would she discuss what and happened. Indeed, Caitlin rebuffed any suggestion that there was anything to discuss.

They celebrated her birthday that weekend with a small circle of family and friends, as they had planned, and gifts were exchanged. Her best friend Martha presented Caitlin with a cloak like the one worn by Harry Potter, in recognition of their mutual affection for that celebrated series. Caitlin accepted this gift with tightlipped politeness, and even draped the cape over her shoulders for a photograph. But her eyes never lightened. She took no pleasure in it.

Mrs. Sutter, looking at the picture later, could tell that her smile was an empty and tired smile. *She's done with all that*, thought Mrs. Sutter. *Kids books and kids things. Done with it all.*

Late that night, Mr. Sutter discovered the OpenBook of *Alice in Wonderland*, still wrapped in its violet packaging, where it had fallen behind the living room table. He threw it in the garbage.

3

Time went on. Life went on.

There were other incidents, other notable malfunctions or misuses of the Between the Lines system. In another unfortunate and widely reported case, a fifteen year old boy entered his mother's copy of *Fifty Shades of Grey*, and in that case the company agreed to send help. After twenty minutes they found the lad, although he had to be removed forcefully, with a net. This boy's case was much discussed in the media, and so was Caitlin's, and so were some others. There were grand jury investigations, Senate hearings, calls for boycotts and counter-calls for rallies in celebration of the First Amendment.

The excitement over Between the Lines, in any case, was eventually superseded by new excitement, over new and still-more-disruptive technologies, new forms of distraction. Between the Lines changed from being the thing that everyone was doing to just one more distraction on the menu. Many people who had been early devotees tired of the novelty and stopped buying OpenBooks entirely; others indulged on occasion, when the mood struck; others became lifelong devotees, discussing their experiences on forums and at conventions, and expressing astonishment that anyone still read books "the old way."

★

Some years later, when Caitlin was in her early twenties and working as an assistant teacher at an elementary school, she met a young man named Richard who was a child psychologist, and the two of them recognized a certain specialness in each other, and began to spend a lot of time in one another's company.

They would go for walks, and together haunt the actual-physical book stores that had come back into fashion when the vogue for Between the Lines had faded. They talked about favorite novels, and he got her to read *World War Z* and she got him to read *Silas Marner*, and they fell in love in the way that two bookish people do: sitting on a blanket in a park, reading paperbacks together, occasionally looking up at the same moment to share a smile.

Richard knew, of course, what had happened to her—he remembered it from the newspapers, from growing up. But he waited until she mentioned it, which she did after six or seven months of dating.

"So..." she said one afternoon. They were on their picnic blanket, in their favorite corner of the park. "I've never really told you, about this—this crazy thing that happened to me—when I was a kid..."

Richard, being the kind and sensitive young man that he was, slid a bookmark into his novel and let her tell her story without interruption. When she was done he nodded thoughtfully, rubbed his chin. Caitlin thought in that moment he looked like David Copperfield: handsome, earnest, sensitive, bright.

"Well, that's awful," Richard said. "I'm really sorry."

"It *was*," Caitlin said, and laughed, just a little. "It was awful." She tilted her head back, for a moment, and studied the clouds. "But worth it."

Ben H. Winters is a New York Times bestselling author and the winner of both the Edgar Award from the Mystery Writers of America and the Phillip K. Dick Award for Distinguished Science Fiction. His most recent book is *World of Trouble*, the last volume in the Last Policeman trilogy. He lives in Indianapolis with his wife and three kids.

NORBERT KRAPF

THE SECRET SOCIETY OF BOOK LOVERS

To love a book
is to leave your
public self behind
and enter into
the multiple selves
of another who
gives you the capacity
to see, feel, and touch
the lives of others

and become one
with strangers as
they journey forth
into a territory where
sunshine and shadow
kiss at the crossroads

and come back
to your old self
enlarged in a way
not visible to passersby
who have never left
where they've always lived

but noticeable to
other lovers who
smile knowingly
when they read
hints of where
you have been
in your latest affair
of head and heart

and nod in silent
approval as they
yearn for the renewal
you have brought back
from that other country
to your known address.

Norbert Krapf, Indiana Poet Laureate 2008-10, is a Jasper, IN native and emeritus professor of English at Long Island University, where he taught for over thirty years. He lives in downtown Indy, within walking distance of Indy Reads Books, to which he gives the books that do not fit on his shelves, and the Indy Marion County Public Library, which he enjoys visiting. He loves to collaborate with musicians such as jazz pianist and composer Monika Herzig, with whom he released a jazz and poetry CD, and Gordon Bonham, with whom he combines poetry and blues and from whom he takes guitar lessons. He recently held a Creative Renewal Fellowship from the Arts of Indianapolis to combine poetry and blues, and the most recent of his poetry collections is *Catholic Boy Blues: A Poet's Journal of Healing* (2014).

MOVING AGAIN

JOHN GREEN

Until last week, when I moved for the second time in a year, I really loved my job. I worked for a magazine in Chicago, and my job involved reviewing a lot of books. I had two specialties as a book critic: I reviewed many books about the Islamic world, and I also reviewed most every book that was published about conjoined twins. That may not seem like a big task, but the Conjoined Twin as literary archetype is huge right now, and I'm pretty sure that last year more books about conjoined twins were published than there are actual conjoined twins.

One of the first things I realized when I started working at *Booklist* is that my mother was wrong when she told me "You can never have too many books." For instance, I own too many books—eleven—about or featuring conjoined twins, and too many—147—about terrorism. Until recently, these books were displayed prominently in our library, which for the record was also our dining room and our kitchen, in hopes that visiting young women would find them impressive and think I was smart and want to lay in bed with me and read about conjoined terrorists.

But recently we had to move (which is a long and familiar story involving my lying, Hummer-driving landlord, who has single-handedly turned me on to the idea of Class Warfare), so I had to put the couple thousand books I've acquired over the years into boxes.

After I'd packed them, I remembered what I learned the last time I moved: the one unassailable fact about literature is that books are heavy. So I unpacked the books and tried to weed out the losers.

Surely, I thought, I don't need to keep *Booty Killer*, a novel that tries to be Bridget-Jones-for-guys but succeeds only in being almost breathtakingly awful. No woman is going to see *Booty Killer* on my bookshelf and want to make out with me. But then I got to thinking about that one part where the narrator's best friend tries to seduce goth girls over the Internet, and I thought maybe I'd want to re-read that scene one day, because A. it was pretty funny and B. it had some pretty good tips on how to seduce goth girls over the Internet.

And so it went for hours, as I found reasons to keep books devoted to the premise that Saddam Hussein would unleash mustard gas on the world by the end of 2002, and books I know full well I'll never read, like *The Creation of Psychopharmacology*. In the end, I threw away a single volume: the Owner's Manual to my long-deceased Volvo 240, and even that hurt almost too much.

There comes a time in all our lives when we realize we aren't as young as we used to be, that we can't just go begging our friends to help us move thousands of books and one pull-out couch that judging from its weight contains somewhere within its recesses a fortune in pure gold. We all reach the point where we give in to the onslaught of aging and just call professional movers. But darn it, I'm not that old yet, so my roommates and I enlisted our friends and acquaintances, and we did it. From the 147 terrorism books to a bed frame that seemed tailor-designed not to fit through a doorway, we moved it all.

Well, actually, I had to review this great new novel about a love square featuring two sets of conjoined twins, so mostly I just sat in the U-Haul and read, regretting the loss of that lovely and informative *Volvo Owner's Manual*, which my moving pals could have easily carried. So maybe mom was right: I guess you can't have too many books, provided you also have plenty of friends who will work for beer.

John Green is the author of four novels, including the #1 *New York Times* bestseller *The Fault in Our Stars*, which *Time Magazine* named the best novel of 2012. He's also the cocreator with his brother Hank of the popular YouTube channels vlogbrothers and crashcourse, which have been viewed more than 400 million times. He lives in Indianapolis, Indiana.

IMAGINE BEING
JOYCE CAROL OATES' AUNT,
JUST FOR A MINUTE

LOU HARRY

Setting: A bookstore fiction section.

Lights up on **CARRIE** *and* **KAREN**, *both in their 30s, facing an invisible fourth wall of books. Karen is scanning titles. Carrie has taken a Joyce Carol Oates book off of the shelf. They do not know each other.*

CARRIE
(to herself) Can you imagine. . . ?

KAREN
What?

CARRIE
Oh, sorry.

KAREN

I thought you were. . .never mind.

CARRIE

Sorry, I was just. . .well. . .I mean, can you imagine what it would be like to be Joyce Carol Oates' aunt?

KAREN

Excuse me?

CARRIE

Being Joyce Carol Oates' aunt. *(silence)* The writer. Joyce Carol Oates, the writer.

KAREN

I know who Joyce Carol Oates is.

CARRIE

I didn't mean to insult you.

KAREN

You didn't insult me.

CARRIE

Good. If I did, I'm sorry. *(silence)* I mean, I can't imagine. *(silence)* The obligation must be overwhelming.

KAREN

Obligation?

CARRIE

The obligation of being her aunt. Of being Joyce Carol Oates' aunt.

KAREN

She's a grown woman, right?

CARRIE

So?

KAREN

She can take care of herself, I presume. Drive. Lift things.

CARRIE

That's not what I'm saying. *(pause)*

KAREN

Then what are you saying?

CARRIE

Never mind *(pause)* Let's say it's Thanksgiving and the family is gathered around the table.

KAREN

The Oates family?

CARRIE

Yes. So you're Joyce Carol Oates' aunt. What do you say?

KAREN

Er...grace, maybe? I'm guessing.

CARRIE

Not about that. About her books.

KAREN

Her books?

CARRIE

Yes, she's a writer.

KAREN

I know that. I told you I know that.

CARRIE

A very prolific writer.

KAREN

Yes, I know.

CARRIE

I mean, a crazily prolific writer. Like a couple of books a year prolific.

KAREN

So?

CARRIE

You can't keep up.

KAREN

Do I have to?

CARRIE

You're her aunt. Don't you think there's an expectation?

KAREN

An expectation?

CARRIE

Yes, an expectation. Your niece is Joyce Carol Oates. Shouldn't you have read her latest book?

KAREN

Okay.

CARRIE

But it's not okay. How many books do you think the average person reads a year? Not like you or me. We probably read more than average. But think about it. Think about the average reader. What? Maybe 15 books? Ten if they have some heft to them.

KAREN

Heft?

CARRIE

Hefty books. Not, like, you know, quick reads. Joyce Carol Oates' books usually have heft.

KAREN

Okay.

CARRIE

That means, as her aunt, you are obligating something like a third of your reading to the books of one author. Just by being her aunt. She monopolizes your reading life. Do you want anyone monopolizing your reading life like that? I don't care if she is your Dad's sister.

KAREN

Or my Mom's sister.

CARRIE

Whatever. Besides, any of her books might have something about you in there. Fictionalized, of course.

KAREN

I've got nothing to hide from my darling niece Joyce. *(pause)* Wouldn't it be worse if you were Stephen King's brother-in-law? I mean, that's what you call hefty.

CARRIE

That's different. For one, Stephen King writes page-turners. They move. For another, I don't think Stephen King would give a damn if his relatives didn't read every one of his books. Or any.

KAREN

If they can read at all.

CARRIE
That's kind of insulting. Do you know them?

KAREN
Wait. Why would Stephen King care less than Joyce Carol Oates? Don't you think that's a bit sexist?

CARRIE
Well, she seems...fragile.

KAREN
Unbelievably sexist.

CARRIE
No.

KAREN
You're saying that, because she's a woman, she's going to have expectations. She's going to be so needy that she requires those in her family, even a distant aunt...

CARRIE
Who said anything about distant. I'm thinking you're fairly close.

KAREN
If we were close, she'd know if I was reading her books. I'd tell her when I finished one. Thanksgiving dinner would carry no more expectations for literary conversation from me than any other meal. I could mention her latest book when she met me for lunch at Quizno's.

CARRIE

Okay, so you're not so close.

KAREN

Used to be. But ever since the divorce...

CARRIE

Who's?

KAREN

Never mind. We just haven't been that close. Really, Thanksgiving is the only time we see each other.

CARRIE

You haven't friended her?

KAREN

She doesn't have Facebook. That's how she gets so much writing done.

CARRIE

That makes sense.

KAREN

I don't even know if I'm going to Thanksgiving this year. It's never what you hope. What you expect. And spending the week before trying to cram the rest of her novel. Reading *American Appetites* or *Blonde* or *I'll Take You There* or *Daddy Love* or *A Fair Maiden* or *By the North Gate* or *Carthage* or *Them* or *Mudwoman* or *Wonderland* or *Freaky Green Eyes* or *Missing Mom* or *With Shuddering Fall* or

Zombie or *My Heart Laid Bare* or *We Were the Mulvaneys* in the car while my husband drives. He always talks when I'm reading in the car, like reading isn't really actually doing anything. Like his inane comments fit comfortably with whatever I'm reading.

CARRIE

Books on tape?

KAREN

We tried that. *With Because It Is Bitter and Because It Is My Heart.* Got about halfway through. Had to keep going back every time he interrupted. Worst drive ever. Never finished that one. Had to fake it.

CARRIE

Fake it?

KAREN

Joyce was in a particularly questioning mood that year. Needy? It was like she was still mentally rewriting the book even after it was out. Like there was something she wasn't satisfied with. Something she wanted us to solve for her. And, sorry, that's not what I'm at Thanksgiving to do. I have my own life, thank you very much. Jim and I were having some serious problems that year and I thought...thought...that maybe I would find some support from the family. But, no, it was all about Joyce and the book and the reviews and playing the stupid game of trying to get her to talk about the next book or any of the seventeen that she's in the middle of writing at any given moment, even though we all know that she won't say a word about it. Them. Of any of them. Like it's some state secret. Like it would rip the fabric of time and space for high-and-mighty Joyce to let slip a hint of what's coming out of her brilliant literary brain. Seriously, I just want to kick her sometimes. *(pause)* So are you going to buy it?

CARRIE
What?

KAREN
The Joyce Carol Oates book. In your hand.

CARRIE
I feel like I should.

KAREN
She is good.

CARRIE
I've heard.

BLACKOUT
END OF PLAY

Lou Harry, Arts & Entertainment Editor for the *Indianapolis Business Journal,* is the author or co-author of more than 25 books including *Creative Block* (Running Press), *The High-Impact Infidelity Diet: a Novel* (Random House) and *Kid Culture* (Cider Mill Press). Co-creator of the long-running interactive show "Going…Going…Gone," his produced plays include "Lightning and Jellyfish," "The Pied Piper of Hoboken," "Beer Can Raft," and "Midwestern Hemisphere." He is honored to have served as emcee for many an Indy Reads benefit event and is co-producer of Indy Actors' Playground, held monthly at Indy Reads Books.

YOUR BOOK
A NOVEL IN STORIES

CATHY DAY

PROLOGUE

You write a book. The manuscript is 241 pages long. Devotedly, you mother each of its 64,739 words, especially Fred, Helen, escape, snow, vaudeville, never, Indianapolis, time, bed, father, night.

How do you know this? These are the biggest words in your word cloud.

What the hell is a word cloud? A visualization of your word frequency.

Where do these clouds come from? That is a very good question.

How do you make one of these things? The same way you Obama-fied a picture of your cat—you go to a website, upload a file, click "Go," and abracadabra! Your cat is red, white, and blue, ordering you to CHILL instead of HOPE.

Why make a word cloud? Because you have just finished the 245th and final draft of the book. You've just had three martinis and you're feeling giddy, emailing your word cloud to all your friends—until you realize that it's possible to extrapolate the entire plot of your book based solely on a 75-word cloud.

But this story isn't really a story about words, which is surprising, considering it's a story about a book and what happens once you've decided that it's time. You've done all you can do, and so you wrap a scarf around its neck, kiss the book on the forehead, and push it into a cold, gray afternoon at the dawn of the twenty-first century.

THE BIG PUSH

Once upon a time, there lived an editor with the Midas touch. Every book he liked turned to gold. Back then, he had a twenty-something assistant who chewed sunflower seeds at her desk ("bird food," he called it). He dubbed her "Bird Brain," then "Birdie." At first he used these terms with endearment, but once she began moving up—toward, then past him—he used them sparingly, usually before contentious editorial meetings.

This morning, for example, when she walks into the window-walled conference room, he says, "It's not like the old days, is it Birdie? We used to sit in this room and argue about which book showed the most talent. Now we argue about which book will sell." He waves his hand toward the marketing types who all stiffen in their chairs, as if he's just told an inappropriate joke.

She lets the Birdie crack go, as she always does. She isn't that girl anymore. Now, she's the one with the Midas touch. She's YOUR EDITOR, which is why your ambitious-but-as-yet-

unknown-and-so-still-lowercased agent called her every Friday
for six months to schedule a lunch, and she finally agreed for no
other reason than his impending call was beginning to taint her
Friday afternoons. When it's time, she makes her pitch to the
crowded room. "*This* is the book we should push next summer."
She observes the marketing types: the more YOUR EDITOR
talks, they lean forward in their chairs, tapping their pens. When
her former boss pitches his author, the marketing folks cross
their arms like a gauntlet of high school principals. Even before
the decision is made, YOUR EDITOR knows she has won. More
money will be spent promoting or "working" your book than other
books published by this company. A full page in the catalogue. A
senior publicist, not a junior one. One thousand advance review
copies sent to magazines and newspapers. The best in-house
designer will do the cover.

In a celebratory mood, YOUR EDITOR decides to take the
rest of the afternoon off. She loads two manuscripts that needed
to be read a week ago into her bag, turns off the lamp on her desk,
and says goodbye to her assistant. She passes the doorway of her
former boss. "Goodnight!" she calls out, emphasizing the fact that
it's only three o'clock, and she is going home. He doesn't wave
back, only glowers at her over his reading glasses.

YOUR EDITOR loves this office, this work, putting books
into the world. She loves the bag of stories on her shoulder, the
political labyrinth of meetings, the clack of copy machines, books
standing on the shelves like trophies, each one with a story to
tell. She loves the stories inside the books, yes, of course, but
she also loves the stories outside the books, which is the story
of how a story travels from the author's imagination into the
reader's imagination. To do so, it must travel through a vast maze

called commerce, and YOUR EDITOR has devoted her adult life to understanding that maze, which is why she lives inside it and inside this office, even when she isn't physically here. As she walks to the elevator, she recalls those humbling Bird Brain days, and then she hears the buzz of all the assistants in cubicle row talking about YOUR BOOK—a beautiful, triumphant sound.

FIVE POPS

Your in-house designer is charged with creating the perfect cover for YOUR BOOK. Luckily, your designer majored in Marketing and Design in college, and the most important thing he learned is this: it takes five pops to move customers to buy a book—or anything for that matter. Five pops on their radar. Blip. Blip. Boom. Baddabing. Baddaboom.

He flips through the pages of your manuscript, reads the jacket copy written by YOUR EDITOR. He feeds that jacket copy into www.cloudofwords.com. *Aha*, he thinks. *Nostalgia. Midwest. Old-timey times.* He plugs "black white photograph couple" into a stock photo search engine. Too many results. He adds "holding hands." Ten results. He narrows it down to one in particular: a sepia-toned photograph, circa 1940-ish. A couple stands outside a clapboard house. The man—for some reason your designer thinks of him as "Byron"—wears a clean white shirt and tie, but surely he doesn't dress this nice every day. It's the haircut, maybe, like something you get at home in the kitchen. Byron holds a shy woman's hand. Betty? No, Madeline. Maddie May. But she's looking at something else—not down at her hand, not at Byron, and not at the camera, but rather into the black-and-white distance. *It's an engagement day picture*, the book designer thinks to himself. *This kind of photo—isn't it ground zero for every family, even mine?*

Once he's selected the image, he considers a variety of fonts: Bookman? No. Antiqua? No. Baskerville? Not quite. Finally, he selects Meridien, designed by Adrian Frutiger (based on the sixteenth-century characters of Jenson) who says that "type design, in its restraint, should be only felt but not perceived by the reader." He types YOUR NAME over the couples' heads, and the title below their feet: YOUR BOOK: A NOVEL IN STORIES.

THE STARTLING POWER OF SIMPLE THINGS

YOUR EDITOR says everyone absolutely loves this haunting, nostalgic cover. On the phone, she says, "We'd like to send out review copies with some sort of promotional item."

"You mean like a key chain or a water bottle?"

"Yes, but something much more clever." You think a minute. "A thimble. A silver thimble."

YOUR EDITOR loves this idea. It will accentuate YOUR BOOK's old timey-ness. Plus thimbles are cheap.

And it works. One thousand weary book reviewers, sitting at one thousand desks—with books stacked on and under the desk, on the shelves, on the floor—grudgingly open the package that contains YOUR BOOK. Out falls the thimble, and those one thousand weary people are transported to a time long ago—a mother darning socks or a grandmother sewing curtains or an old uncle hemming a pair of trousers—and in this moment of wistful reverie, they open YOUR BOOK and begin to read.

A STRONG LITERARY DEBUT

A review copy of YOUR BOOK (and the enclosed thimble) is sent to the corporate office of BIG CHAIN BOOKSTORE to be considered for the *You've Got to Read This!* Prize.

Any book the publisher feels is making a "strong literary debut" is eligible for consideration. A volunteer reading committee comprised of BIG CHAIN BOOKSTORE employees and corporate staff reads the submitted review copies and chooses fifteen books for the prize.

YOUR BOOK is one of those chosen. BIG CHAIN BOOKSTORE sends a bill to your publisher so that you can collect your prize. This is what you win:

1. Prime placement in high-traffic areas of BIG CHAIN BOOKSTORE.

2. A display underneath YOUR BOOK, what they call in the business an "individual shelf-talker," with the teaser line: "*YOUR NAME mines her rich family history, melding it with the transformative power of her brilliant imagination to create a powerful book.*"

3. 30 percent off YOUR BOOK, increasing the likelihood that people will pay for it in hardcover.

4. An individual review of YOUR BOOK in a promotional brochure, available free to customers on the *You've Got to Read This!* shelf and in "strategic" store locations.

5. Promotion on www.bigchainbookstore.com and targeted e-mail blasts to subscribers.

6. Invitations to read at BIG CHAIN BOOKSTORE locations in major metropolitan areas.

7. Direct mailings plugging YOUR BOOK to book group discussion leaders.

THE NIGHT BEFORE PUB DATE

Two years have passed since you said goodbye to YOUR BOOK. Tomorrow is your official publication day, or pub date, but somehow used copies of YOUR BOOK are already for sale online. How can this be? You don't understand. My God, there are so many things you don't understand. You picture YOUR BOOK inside an enormous factory, rolling down a conveyor belt from station to station. Not the *physical* book, which has already been printed somewhere in Missouri at a book bindery, a real factory. This you know. Factories you understand. Your father worked in one all his life. But something else is moving through that imaginary factory, not the book itself but how people feel about the book, which you're just beginning to understand is also a made thing. Your computer dings with new messages, but you're in sitting in front of the television, caught in an endless loop of *Law & Order*, folding origami cranes. One after another after another. Your friends ask, "Why are you folding birds?" and you tell them that it's a Japanese tradition, a blessing for your book, but the truth is you don't know what else to do with yourself. The phone is ringing again. Birds flock around you, one every two minutes, all night long.

LOCATION, LOCATION, LOCATION

A week later, a man named Adam walks into a bookstore. YOUR BOOK sits face-out on a shelf just inside the store. He sees it kinda sorta out of the corner of his eye. The image on the cover of YOUR BOOK (pop) registers with Adam, but on the subliminal level, along with hundreds of other product images fighting for his attention in that split second. THIS CD. THAT MAGAZINE. THIS DVD. THAT TIN OF BREATH MINTS. The problem is that Adam entered the store with an image already in his head, the gingerbread cookie couple, a brand that signifies relief of unbearable urges.

In the restroom, Adam scans an in-store promotional brochure posted above the urinal, which features that season's winners of the *You've Got to Read This!* Prize. As promised, YOUR BOOK is being featured in strategic store locations. Pop.

A month passes. A magazine reviews YOUR BOOK. This magazine has a circulation of one million, including Adam. He keeps the magazine next to the toilet. He doesn't read the review of YOUR BOOK, but he does notice the cover (pop), which briefly reminds him of his great grandparents, a mythic couple who ran a mercantile business in Kansas City, or so the story goes. He thinks about them for a full twenty-four seconds and then turns the page.

Four and a half months pass. At work, Adam notices that Harriet, the woman with Tina Fey glasses who works in the cubicle next to him, is reading YOUR BOOK (pop). He's been thinking about asking her out. "I heard about that book," he says half truthfully. "Do you like it?" Harriet says she loves YOUR BOOK.

A month later, Adam walks into the bookstore and stops to check out the books on display. He sees YOUR BOOK (pop), and puts it under his arm. He remembers his first and only date with Harriet, sitting together at a café table, clutching his beer for dear life when she asked, "Who do you read?"

IF YOU LIKE THAT, YOU'LL *LOVE* THIS!

Brit downloads a song from an online bookstore. Before she checks out, the online bookseller tells Brit that many customers who bought songs by THAT ARTIST also bought YOUR BOOK. She clicks on the link, quickly scans some reviews, one from THAT NEWSPAPER, which is mixed, and five from readers, which are glowing. Brit doesn't know that these reader reviews were written by old friends of yours. "What the hell," she decides. "I need a book to read on the bus anyway." She clicks "Add to cart," and buys YOUR BOOK.

HONEY DO THIS, HONEY DO THAT

A newspaper in a mid-sized city reviews YOUR BOOK, and Constance reads it one Sunday. Yes. She still reads the newspaper. Yes. This newspaper still reviews books. But Constance doesn't buy YOUR BOOK.

The next day, Constance needs to go to the doctor, and her husband Ronald isn't feeling up to it. So, she takes the bus and sits down next to a young girl (Brit) who's reading something very intently. It's YOUR BOOK. Constance remembers the cover from the Sunday paper, the black-and-white photo of the couple holding hands. She remembers the words in the review, "rich family history." As the bus lurches along, she closes her eyes and pictures her parents on their wedding day. They're standing in front of her granddaddy's house in Lexington, Kentucky, dressed in traveling clothes. It's one last pop of the flash before they jump in the soaped-up car to drag tin cans all the way to Florida, or so the story goes. She remembers this moment before her birth because of the photograph, which always rested in a silver frame on her mother's dressing table. As a girl, Constance studied the picture watchfully, hoping she might materialize at their feet or from behind a bush. For a long time, she couldn't conceive of her parents living in the world without her, and sometimes she still can't. That photograph taught her what time meant, and as the automated voice announces her stop, "Parkview Memorial Hospital," Constance wonders how long it's been since she thought about her mother's dressing table: the pearled mirror and brush, the crystal earring dish, the perfume atomizer that sprayed a scented cloud of mist, two tubes of lipstick standing at attention—red for night, coral for day. Constance rises to her feet amid the backpacks and shopping bags, grips the metal handrails trying hard not to lose her balance and fall. Why is she on the bus? Then she sees the hospital—yes, of course, her doctor's office is in the professional wing. Right.

Later at home, Constance goes through the recycling bin, looking for the review of YOUR BOOK. *I'll clip it,* she thinks, *and put it in my purse so the next time I'm out by the mall, I can buy the book at that big fancy bookstore that smells like coffee.* Unfortunately, Ronald took out the recycling that morning, so she can't read or clip the review. Constance writes, "Your Something? Old photo?" on her Honey Do List, a green pad of paper shaped like a slice of melon. Before bed, she gives Ronald the Honey Do List. "Get me this book. There's a picture on the front of a couple back in the old days, and it looks just like that one photograph of my folks. You know, the one that sat on my mother's dressing table?"

Truth be told, Ronald has never seen this dressing table, never even met the woman, but he doesn't let on. Instead, he says, "Sure, sweetie," and puts Constance to bed. He puts her list in the cigar box he keeps in his sock drawer. The box overflows with melon slices that say: RX. Apple fritters. Cast on 30 stitches. Get right with God. Underwear.

FRESH AIR

A radio station interviews you about YOUR BOOK, and Delores, who is driving home from work thinking about what to make for dinner, half listens to your voice. A few days later, Delores is in a bookstore with her kids who need the new Harry Potter and YOUR BOOK cover catches her eye. *I think I've heard about this one...* she thinks. Delores wanders over to the books on tape section, but YOUR BOOK isn't available. Oh well, she thinks and treats herself to a women's magazine instead.

BOOK REVIEWING 2.0

Ephraim mentions in his blog that he loves YOUR BOOK, and Frances, who has a crush on Ephraim and eagerly follows his blog, buys YOUR BOOK, too.

Upon finishing YOUR BOOK, Frances writes a great Goodreads review of YOUR BOOK. She goes back to Ephraim's blog entry about YOUR BOOK and comments, cutting and pasting her review into the comment field. She waits a week. Then two. There's no response from Ephraim, but Frances doesn't mind. She knows Ephraim gets a lot of comments on his blog and doesn't have time to individually respond to all of them.

Which brings us to Gus.

Gus is very attracted to Frances, and he doesn't understand what she sees in Ephraim. He follows Ephraim's blog, trying to learn what it is about this man that has so transfixed Frances. About a week after Ephraim posts his review of YOUR BOOK, Gus gets an email that Frances has posted a new book review on Goodreads. He logs in to find out what Frances is reading, and when he sees that it is YOUR BOOK, he laughs out loud. *Fine then*, he thinks. *I'll read YOUR BOOK, and I'll bet the only reason Frances likes it is because that dickhead Ephraim liked it.* In this frame of mind, Gus purchases YOUR BOOK and reads it. *I was right*, he thinks. *This book blows.* He logs into Goodreads to write a scathing review, but changes his mind when he realizes that Frances will never, ever sleep with a man whose taste in books runs counter to her own. Instead, Gus simply lists YOUR BOOK as one he has read, wondering if Frances will notice. Gus has twenty-five friends on Goodreads.

Which brings us to Harriet.

Harriet (who works in the cubicle next to Adam) is friends with Frances. One Sunday afternoon, Harriet picks up Frances for brunch and notices YOUR BOOK sitting on the coffee table. Harriet asks, "Can I borrow this?" and Frances says sure. Harriet loves YOUR BOOK and takes it to work, where Adam sees it and eventually asks her out. She also adds it to her virtual bookshelf on Facebook. Harriet has fifty friends on Facebook.

Which brings us to Inez.

She is one of Harriet's fifty friends. They went to the same college, had the same major, but honestly, if it wasn't for Facebook,

Harriet would have lived a full and happy life never once thinking about Inez. But Inez collects friends on Facebook like women used to collect locks of hair from loved ones and weave them into jewelry—because she is sentimental, because seeing the little pictures of her 454 friends makes her feel not so completely alone on the face of the earth.

When Inez sees on Facebook that Harriet read YOUR BOOK, she decides to check it out of the library. It's another empty weekend, and Inez changes her Facebook status to say, "Inez is reading YOUR BOOK." Most of Inez' Facebook friends are fellow lonely people who stay in and read a lot. Of those 454 people who see YOUR BOOK mentioned in her status update, 203 eventually buy your book, which bumps your Amazon.com rating to a heady #329.

"How did this happen?" you ask, and YOUR EDITOR says, "It's the review in THAT MAGAZINE EVERYONE KEEPS BY THE TOILET. I'm sure of it."

IT'S AN HONOR TO BE NOMINATED

Jim nominates YOUR BOOK for a prize, which is announced in THAT NEWSPAPER. He is quoted as saying, "YOUR NAME is making one of the strongest literary debuts I've seen in many years." You don't win the prize, but you go to the ceremony, drink free Manhattans, and have a really fun time.

THE FIRST RULE OF BOOK CLUB

Karla is scanning THAT NEWSPAPER. She has to suggest something for her book club. She's supposed to have read the book before suggesting it, but Karla has zero time to read these days. She needs a sure-fire crowd pleaser. Karla sees that YOUR BOOK was nominated for a prize, but didn't win. She picks the book that won the prize, which is NOT YOUR BOOK. On the appointed night, the members drink a lot of wine and shrug their collective shoulders, saying "Sorry, Karla. We just couldn't get into it." Karla says, "Really? I just fell in love with it." In truth, Karla is secretly thankful no one wants to talk, because she hasn't read NOT YOUR BOOK either.

YOURTUBE

Your nephew Monty is in film school, and he makes a funny book trailer for YOUR BOOK and puts it on YouTube. You send the link to ten friends. Within two weeks, YOUR BOOK TRAILER has gone viral and has been viewed one million times. Unfortunately, the only people who actually buy YOUR BOOK are the ten friends you sent the initial link to.

PLAN B

YOUR EDITOR calls. "BIG CHAIN BOOKSTORE says they won't buy more than 10,000 copies of YOUR BOOK in paperback unless we do a total cover redesign." They send the new cover by email, but it's pretty much the same, except the old couple's heads have been cut off. YOUR EDITOR explains that the reason headless torsos work so well for book covers is that it allows readers to "become" the characters or to imaginatively top those torsos with the faces of loved ones. You tell your editor that it's not necessary to decapitate people to achieve this effect. You say, "Look, if you really want to change the cover, change the cover." They send it to you via email. The color image startles you at first, like austere Kansas giving way to Technicolor Oz. A smiling woman with crow's feet and red lipstick stands on a sandy beach wearing a turquoise swimsuit (the same hue as the ocean behind her shoulder and the font in which YOUR NAME appears) and a swimming cap adorned with white flower petals. Why is Esther Williams on the cover of YOUR BOOK?

You ask, "Can we go back to the Headless Torsos? I like that better than Esther Williams. Besides, nobody in my book even goes swimming. It's Indianapolis." But you are outvoted. You know this cover will win because it says, "Ladies, read me on the beach this summer. You'll enjoy your down time more if you read this book." And this—you have learned—is perhaps the most powerful message of all.

SOPHOMORE EFFORT

Maybe it's time to start YOUR NEXT BOOK. You miss the high of those early days, how your inbox was like a Christmas tree with an infinite number of gifts underneath, waiting to be opened. You miss everyone saying how much they love YOUR BOOK. You want this feeling back. But the only way to get it back is to write YOUR NEXT BOOK, and every time you write a paragraph, you read it as you imagine YOUR EDITOR will read it, and the book reviewer at THAT NEWSPAPER, and that snarky book blogger in Seattle. They aren't going to like that paragraph at all. You're sure of it. So you rewrite it. Then you rewrite it again. Then you close your laptop and pour yourself a tall glass of something.

LONG LEGS

A few years go by. Ned sees YOUR BOOK on a flyer posted on a bulletin board at a branch of the city library, announcing that you will appear to talk about what they call "the writing life." Ned makes a note to himself to attend your event. He goes to all events at the library; they serve free cookies and coffee. Ned sits in the front row at your talk, chewing his cookie. He asks, "Why did you write YOUR BOOK," and you tell him, which is the story of who you are as a human being. People think the story you told in YOUR BOOK is the story of who you are as a human being, but this isn't true, and you are pleased that the rumpled fellow in the front row eating a cookie seems to understand this. Ned asks, "What did you do the first time you saw YOUR BOOK, held it right there in your hands" and you confess that you wept tears of joy and thankfulness. Afterwards, Ned doesn't buy YOUR BOOK, because he has no money, of course, but you shake his hand and thank him for coming.

A few days later, he rides the bus to a different branch of the library to attend another talk about the writing life and eat free cookies. Ned asks the writer, "Why did you write NOT YOUR BOOK?" and she says, "Why does anybody do anything?" Ned does not try to shake her hand. Afterwards, he tells the librarian about you and YOUR BOOK, and the librarian orders YOUR BOOK for their collection. Over the next few months, Ned rides the bus all over the city, attending all the writing life talks, eating all the free cookies, and at every library, he tells the librarian on duty about you and YOUR BOOK.

Two years later, a committee of local librarians nominates YOUR BOOK for the One City, One Book program. You email

YOUR EDITOR, and she says YOUR BOOK has what they call "long legs," but how is YOUR NEXT BOOK coming along? Your mother says, "Wow! Everyone in your city is supposed to read it? That's a lot of people! That's..." She pauses, "...potentially 320,000 books."

"How do you know that, Mom?"

"I SEARCH ENGINED it. I SEARCH ENGINE everything these days."

On the appointed day, you show up at the library. You answer questions, give a reading, but unfortunately, the library only sells eleven copies. Ned is there, of course, in the front row, but he still doesn't buy YOUR BOOK. Feeling bold, you decide to tease him about this. He laughs and points to Esther Williams. "I read on the bus. I can't read a book that looks like that on the bus."

DOCTOR, DOCTOR

A few more years go by. Finally, you write YOUR NEXT BOOK. The manuscript is 435 pages long. But the story of the book doesn't turn out anything like YOUR FIRST BOOK. When you compare the two experiences—which you do—it's apples and orangutans. If the story outside YOUR FIRST BOOK was "Everything Goes Right," the story outside YOUR NEXT BOOK is "Nothing Goes Right."

You go see your doctor because you can't stop weeping. She stands there, waiting patiently for you to catch your breath. "I wrote a b-b-book," you say.

"Congratulations," the doctor says.

"N-n-nobody likes it."

The doctor stares at the snow falling outside the window. "I went to Princeton and applied to get into their writing classes, but I didn't make the cut. So I switched to premed and here I am." The doctor smiles ruefully.

You hear stories like this a lot. What you want to say is, *Well, then I guess you didn't really want to be a writer if you stopped the first time someone told you, "Thank you, but no."* But you don't. Instead, you say, "I'm sorry they turned you down, but I'm also glad because it means right now you're my doctor, and I need help."

There's a long pause, and then the doctor clicks her pen. "I'm going to write you a prescription for anti-anxiety meds. It should help until you come to terms with this." While she scribbles on the prescription pad, you remember the opposite of this day, the day you finished YOUR NEXT BOOK, how your body glowed and hummed with joy. Holy crap, you felt so good. So why do you feel so ashamed today? Stepping off the crinkly-papered table, you take the prescription, shake the doctor's hand, and drive straight to the drugstore. Do you drop off the prescription and come back later? No, you do not. You sit in the blood-pressure chair while they slide ninety tiny little chill pills into a bottle.

A few months later, you're calm enough to see the truth: you are not ashamed of YOUR NEXT BOOK. You love it dearly, it's just that not everyone does, and if you can live with that, maybe you can write ANOTHER BOOK and THE BOOK AFTER THAT.

WE WILL ALWAYS READ TO KNOW
THAT WE ARE NOT ALONE

More years pass. Some things change. Some things don't. Somewhere in a Chicago exurb in northern Indiana, a woman named Pia lives alone—except for this particular weekend, because her daughter is home from college. "What are you reading in your English class?" Pia asks as she starts a load of laundry, and her daughter hands over her READER, a device that reminds Pia of the laptop computers she used as a girl—the screen half, anyway. Pia scrolls through the memory and sees a black-and-white image of an old couple standing in front of a house. Something about YOUR NAME rings a bell, so she watches the book trailer while she separates her daughter's dirty clothes into lights and darks.

"Is this a good book?" Pia asks.

"I have to read it for class," her daughter says, rolling her eyes. "It's all right."

Now that her daughter is in college and her husband is gone, Pia reads a lot. Two books a week, sometimes more. That night, she stays up reading YOUR FIRST BOOK. At six in the morning, she types this message into the READER:

> This will be brief. The sun is rising pink in the window, and I've been up all night with YOUR BOOK. In the last few years, I've experienced many losses, but this last long night didn't feel nearly as long or as dark, because I had the solace of YOUR BOOK. Thank you for the perfect weave, the grit and silk, for putting me squarely in downtown Wayland, New York, my grandfather's town, a mile south of the Erie Lackawanna RR. I know this book is about your roots, but it was as if you remembered mine, too. Thank you.

Pia searches for you on the internet so that she can send you the message, but instead, she finds your obituary. Her heart falls in her chest, and she wonders why she's mourning. She didn't even know you. Not really. Before she falls asleep, Pia orders YOUR NEXT BOOK, ANOTHER BOOK, and THE BOOK AFTER THAT.

The next time it's her turn to host book club, Pia chooses YOUR BOOK, and everyone holds up their READER and wonders aloud, "Why haven't I read this before?"

Pia shakes her head. "I blame television."

This story originally appeared in Ninth Letter, *Vol 6, No. 2.*

Cathy Day is the author of two books. Her most recent work is *Comeback Season* (Free Press, 2008), part memoir about life as a single woman and part sports story about the Indianapolis Colts Super Bowl season in 2006. Her first book was *The Circus in Winter* (Harcourt, 2004), a fictional history of her hometown, which was a finalist for the GLCA New Writers Award, the Great Lakes Book Award, and the Story Prize, and is being adapted into a musical. She lives in Muncie, Indiana and teaches at Ball State University, where she's currently serving as the Assistant Chair of Operations in the Department of English.

UNCLE TOM

JOHN GREEN

My parents named me after my great uncle, John Thomas Goodrich, whom I have always known as Uncle Tom. Like me, he was a Southerner who ended up in Chicago, where he wrote for the radio, as I do. He also wrote a novel, *Cotton Cavalier*, which was published in 1932, when he was 27 years old. My first novel came out in March, when I was 27. The author note of Tom's book lists his two passions as corn liquor and petite brunettes. I'm more of a wino, but as far as petite brunettes go—and the best among them will go pretty far—*Amen.*

And then it all went sour. When he was a couple years older than I am now, Uncle Tom ditched Chicago for Hollywood, hoping to make a fortune writing movies. He took to drinking, a fate to which my people are fairly accustomed, and he ended up divorced and bankrupt. Toward the end of his life, he sobered up, but he never wrote a second book. I wouldn't worry too much about the odd parallels between Uncle Tom and me, except for two troubling facts:

Fact 1: I have a deep, abiding affection for booze.

Fact 2: I am oddly drawn to the city of Los Angeles.

Now, I know a lot of writers who complain about how little writing pays, which is silly. Writers are in the business of putting the right words in the right order. It's plenty hard, but it ain't coal mining. To borrow a phrase from W. H. Auden, writing makes nothing happen, and jobs that make nothing happen don't tend to be terribly profitable. Still, it'd be nice to make a living writing. Hence my attraction to L.A. Sitcom writers make so much money that they go home every night, take off all their clothes, cover themselves in melted butter, and roll around in 100-dollar bills and rare postage stamps.

I got to thinking about L.A. in earnest a couple months ago, when I got drunk at a house party in Lincoln Square and made the acquaintance of a petite brunette named Sarah.

Within about five minutes of meeting Sarah, she expressed a fondness for southern California, and I became inalterably convinced that she and I needed to get married, preferably before we sobered up. And then we'd move to Hollywood together. She would work for an art gallery, and I would be a script doctor. We would drink after work in the moderate, responsible way couples do. And as I smiled down at her, I realized: That's how it happened. Tom took his girl to Hollywood, drank with her until she didn't want to drink anymore, and then he drank, as we will, without her.

I could see Uncle Tom at a Lincoln Square house party in 1932. Drunk but not yet fated to drunkenness, he smiles down at an olive-skinned brunette whose warm, boozy breath drifts up toward him as she leans forward, on her tiptoes, so that she can whisper a joke to him about Trotsky or iron lungs or whatever people told jokes about in 1932. And Tom could never have suspected that his best writing was behind him, that his coming failure would be so common and unspectacular that he, like his lone novel, would soon enough be forgotten.

A week after meeting Sarah, whom you will be surprised to learn I have not yet married, I flew to New York to meet the editor of my book. She took me out to lunch at a sushi restaurant and stunned me by offering to buy my as-yet-unfinished second novel. I went out that night and got fairly well trashed to celebrate, of course. But then I did what Tom couldn't do: I sobered up, returned to Chicago, and got back to work, struggling to put the right words in the right order, making nothing happen, trying to live past my name.

ROMANCING
THE BOOK

Lonely, a scrap of handwritten paper in a library book makes you long for connection to the body of another reader.

And then, you and an attractive stranger flirt in the stacks, searching for the same book. A week later, you meet at the library for a first date.

At each other's place the first time, you check out the books in the bookcases, on the kitchen table, at the bedside, and find you love and own many of the same.

You tell each other about learning to read, favorite first books, the books that freed you in high school, and those that lit your path ever since.

Falling in love, one with the cosmos, you quote the same poem, again and again: *Except for the point, the still point, there would be no dance, and there is only the dance.*

You give and receive books as presents. You borrow each other's books, read each other's old favorites, wanting to go back in time and fall in love at every age.

You move in together and neither complains that there are so many heavy boxes of books to load and unload from the U-Haul.

So sure that it will last, you mingle your books on the shelves, two collections becoming one.

You read together in bed, take turns reading aloud. You call just to share a poem.

The glow fades and real marriage begins, but you remind each other about the still point, and the dance.

On vacations, you spend time in hard-to-find small bookstores and old libraries, browsing together for hours.

Though you have your disagreements, when one of you urges, "You should read this book!" you still want to.

And you are also glad you both read books the other hasn't, because what is being read is like music—it fills your house, becomes part of the air you breathe.

When one goes away on a long trip, you read the same book to stay connected.

And yes, you repeat an old argument which won't be solved. But again and again you chose to stay, having read some truth that breaks through pain with balm for the heart.

SMALL PLANES, FLYING LOW

VICTORIA BARRETT

January, 2001

Rae bounded into the store and said, "Hey, Geezer, what's with the old-man music?"

"Are you high? It's the Ramones," Joel said, picking a Darth Vader eraser out of a bin next to the cash register.

Rae said, "Whatever," then, "Jeez, Psycho," as the eraser whizzed past her head. "What'd you do that for?"

"Because I'm a mean-spirited bastard. Go clock in."

Rae flung her backpack toward the stock room doorway and disappeared briefly, then joined Joel behind the register. "You are mean."

Rae figured that Joel, at her age, was probably a combination of the different boys who frequented Cosmo's Comics: geeky fact-collector, potentially violent artsy loner, aloof skater, Boy Scout.

Some of the boys could be pinned down as one or another, but most balanced all four personae in varying proportions. Although she did love the books, Rae had gotten the job primarily to meet boys, preferably the aloof skater-types, but she spent most of her Saturdays with Joel, who was closer to her mom's age than to her own, and Camille, who worked in another shop in the strip mall and spent all her breaks at Cosmo's mooning over Joel. Why anyone would moon over Joel, Rae couldn't figure.

"So," she said, "you were probably one of those skater-boys back in the dark ages, right? How come you don't have a little brother for me or something?"

Joel said, "Rae, if you keep teasing me I'm going to have to go cry in the stock room." Rae had no idea whether he was serious or not.

"No, really. What were you like when you were sixteen?"

"I was a dork who made pizzas for money to buy skateboards and records. I sat behind girls like you at school and drew pictures of the backs of their heads. What's with the interview?"

Rae grinned. "Got anything better to do?"

"Orders for next week."

"Okay. Just admit that there weren't any girls like me and I'll leave you alone."

"Rae, of course there weren't."

She nodded toward the door. "Ooh, look, here comes your girlfriend."

Camille stuck her head in the door and said, "Anybody here yet?" Joel threw Rae his meanest look, then said, "Come on in." Cosmo's had been open for all of seven minutes, and here she was already.

Rae said, "I need your job. Do you get paid for all these breaks?"

"Rae, be nice to Camille."

"I'm serious."

Camille had been dropping in for months. Joel had never defended her before, though he wasn't typically mean, either.

Joel told Camille to ignore Rae. Rae was sort of hoping to be unignorable. Camille seemed to find Rae completely ignorable, and propped her big chest up on her arms, leaned the whole mess on the counter, looked up at Joel. Joel was nice to Camille, but not that nice. Rae wondered why she kept coming back in. Joel wasn't any fun when Camille was in the shop, anyway, as though he put on a mask. He talked to Camille the way Rae talked to her father when he called on Sundays: grammatically proper, careful not to reveal too much, to stay a relative stranger. Rae would never want to come to work if Joel was always like that.

Rae headed straight for the old Spiderman books. Peter Parker, she had thought as a younger girl, was just her type: brainy and funny and always getting into trouble. She didn't think so much anymore that she could fall for somebody that uncomplicated, that loveable. She liked Spiderman now because it refuted the single-mother wisdom that boys equal danger, which she heard all too often at home, and sometimes from Joel. True, Rae knew girls younger than she who'd gotten messed up pretty badly, but some days she wanted to know what that was like. Could she be damaged? Would that make her bigger? Either way, the web and the red and blue spandex had by this point become as much a part of her as anything, and she went to the books like a home.

As Rae shuffled through boxes looking for one of her favorite issues, she could hear Camille whining over her boobs at Joel across the shop. She was at her usual, "I just don't know what to do about him," when Jackie and Devin, two guys Rae knew from school, came in. Rae had decided long before, with the help of some of the boys, that Camille's other man was a ruse to get Joel involved in her business. Joel would always say, "You know what's best, Camille."

As far as the local comic shops went, Cosmo's was a good one, mostly because of the geeky-collector side of Joel, who kept the stock up on anything you'd want to find, from *Love and Rockets* to *Sandman* to the really obscure shit. The whole of it took up one dim room in a strip mall plus a tiny stock closet in the back. The shop was bigger than your basic comic store setup: a maze of tables covered with double-strength cardboard boxes full of books in Mylar bags, one wall made up of shelves full of collections, one covered with collectors' toys. The counter that held up the cash register and guarded the door was lined with candy jars full of dork paraphernalia like the eraser Joel had flung at her. Cosmo's was organized categorically: superheroes covering two adjacent tables toward the back, punk rock stuff and really gory artsy shit nearer the register, since those drew in the most likely shoplifters. The store had lots of regulars, all of whom Rae classified by her four preconceived categories. Jackie and Devin leaned primarily toward the art-school group. They could definitely be creepy, especially Devin. The quiet ones were always creepier. Rae was sort of in a the-creepier-the-better-phase.

Jackie shot a gun-shaped hand at Joel and said, "Are you paying her to lay on the counter all the time, because I can do that even better," while still striding toward Rae. She put her hands on her hips as Jackie and Devin approached, cocked her head. Jackie flipped up Rae's skirt and hollered, "What up, girl?" He took the Spiderman book out of her hands and started leafing through it.

"Hey guys."

Devin raised one hand in greeting, then shoved both his hands deep into his pockets and hunched forward. His black t-shirt had the "Music for Mechanics" cover screened on it, and was tattered—an authentic relic. It hung loose, his skinny arms scarred, bony connectors between the sleeves and his pockets. When she felt up to it, Rae could imagine Devin with a crush on her, or more often, herself with a crush on him. He had a loose-limbed appeal, looked much taller than he actually was. He was constantly blowing his hair out of his eyes, squinting to read the comics he flipped through but never bought.

Jackie wrapped an arm around Rae's neck and said, "So you coming to my place when you get outta this hole?" Jackie didn't have a "place" except for his room at his parents' house, and Rae knew it, having been there for a perfectly harmless birthday party a couple of years before. Jackie, she thought, must get his lines from TV.

"What're you going to give me if I do?"

"Um," he said, "well," and grabbed the crotch of his saggy jeans. He would have to have hiked them up quite a bit in order to actually grab himself. Rae threw her head back laughing, flipped up the back of her plaid miniskirt herself as she sauntered away, and Jackie mock-panted, watched her walk. She flounced off thinking about Maggie, one of the girls on Devin's t-shirt, who could have a searing crush on some famous guy while shacking up with her gay girlfriend. While Rae and Jackie teased, Devin had sneaked away from the superhero stuff, was leafing through the Sin City trade where Marv falls in love with the hooker who just wants him to protect her, but they both get drunk and she gets killed after they pass out. Camille sighed long and slow, and slunk back to the office supply store which apparently didn't miss her much. Rae thought that's probably what Camille wanted most—to be missed.

Joel loaded up a couple more erasers and said, "Fucking delinquents. How am I not surprised to watch one of you trying to hump my employee while the other one gets greasy fingerprints all over one of the most violent books I sell?" He started pitching erasers, most of which Jackie caught and threw back. Devin put down *Sin City* and examined his fingernails. He shrugged, picked the book back up, dodged an eraser.

Rae ducked behind a table and watched the little black projectiles zinging across the shop. With so much boy-energy in the air she was afraid to stand up, like a mustard-gas cloud of it would swallow her. She had learned to draw a gas mask from thirteen circles after reading Captain America books and gotten sent to the school counselor. She would feel intoxicated in the middle of this fight, like she felt in the counselor's office, knowing what to tell them: just enough to scare them a little.

Devin moved around the shop, picking up erasers until he was crouched next to Rae, behind a box of classics, carefully catalogued. "Hey," he said, "you might want to watch out for Jackie. The guy's not always kidding."

"Who said I was kidding?"

"Whatever. Just thought somebody should look out for your well-being or some shit. See if I care."

"Fucking guys, always have to be watching out for somebody." Rae wanted Devin to know with no uncertainty that she could take care of herself. She also wanted—bad—to touch his wavy hair, to push it out of his line of vision, to tuck it gently behind his ear.

As she started to reach toward him, jittery from Devin's soap smell, his orange breath, he said, "Do whatever you fucking want," and looked down, the hair making a curtain around his face, muffling the end of the sentence.

"Okay, Mr. Blood and Guts. See you in art class." She jumped up, yelled "CEASEFIRE!"

For a minute everybody stood up from behind makeshift fortresses and looked at her. She was aware of herself standing very straight, bending one knee in a sort of pose. "What animal would you be?"

"Man," Jackie said. "We always do animals."

Rae said, "Jackie, you might do things to animals. We're just talking. Better idea?"

Joel said, "Chinese Zodiac?"

"Nope, has to be something you pick, not something that gets decided for you." They knew each other's favorite comics, favorite artists. They'd started on Rae's little personality tests long ago. "Bloody movie scene. One for Devin."

Jackie said, "That's easy, the basement stuff in *Fight Club*."

Joel drew back an eraser, then dropped it on the counter. "Jeez, you lose on the principle that *Fight Club* is just about the worst movie ever made. You're not even worth throwing this at. *Dracula*, Lucy and the wolf-thing in the garden."

"Ooh, that's a good one," Rae said. "Devin?"

"*Goodfellas.* Where Joe Pesci gets his head blown off and the camera stays on him with his blood spreading all over the tile floor. Rae?"

She wondered if Devin remembered the first time she'd seen that movie, at that birthday party at Jackie's house. She and Devin had sprawled on the rug near one another, and he had tried to explain the cinematography to her, but before the movie was over, she had fallen asleep. Jackie's mom had woken her up when it was over and sent her home.

"Hey—Rae!"

She shook off the memory. "Yuck, like I watch that shit."

"Cheater!"

"Whatever. At least I know none of you are suitable to take me to a movie."

Jackie said, "Like we'd fucking want to. Well, Devin might, but he'd probably scare you too much." Devin whipped an eraser at Jackie's ear.

"Fucker!"

The CD ended, and Joel switched on the radio. "...of Pan Am Flight 103. Al-Megrahi, a Libyan intelligence agent, was sentenced to life in a Scottish prison and will be eligible for parole in twenty years."

Jackie started to say, "Hey, what's up..." but Joel held up one finger and turned the radio up.

"The conviction confirms for many the suspected link between Libyan leader Moammar Gadhafi and the terrorist act. President Bush has stated that all sanctions against Libya will remain intact until Gadhafi accepts responsibility and compensates victims' families."

Joel said, "Are you kidding me? He killed like 300 people and he can get out in twenty years?"

"Never happen," Devin said. "He'll be dead within a year. Somebody in that prison will think it's worth it. Some guard will look away."

"What are you talking about?" Rae said.

"You don't remember? Christmas of 1988?"

"Joel, I was five."

"Right. A plane blew up over Scotland. Lots of people died."

"Shit." Everybody got a little quiet, stood a little stiller. Rae was sure she couldn't name 300 people. That was like her whole world multiplied by eleven.

Jackie said, "If you could be anything that flies, what? I'd be a six-foot fruit bat."

Rae shrugged. "Devin?"

"I don't' know. This is too depressing."

Joel said, "I'd maybe have been made for air shows a long time ago, one of those old-fashioned crop dusters."

Rae tipped her head and took a deep, dreamy breath. "Mmm. They do the best tricks."

Devin said, "Jackie. We gotta go."

"You're not even going to buy anything?" Rae said, leaning over a table of collector's books.

Jackie bumped up behind her full-on, a hand on each of her hips. "When do we ever buy anything in here?" Devin slouched over again, hands back in his pockets.

Joel started leafing through the catalogues. "Good. Get fucking lost."

"Later," Devin said, and followed Jackie out into the sunlight. Rae watched it filter in through the store's airborne dust, like slow motion in an action movie, like something significant might have just happened or was about to, but she would never be able to name what. She and Joel were on their own in the store again.

He slammed the book. "Why do you let Jackie treat you like that?"

"Like what?"

"You know what."

"Like you give a shit," Rae said, wondering what Joel expected.

"What if I did?"

"Then I'd say you're a sick old man and call you Geezer some more."

"Not like that, you little freak."

"Hey, isn't it time for your girlfriend's next break? Maybe you should go outside and join her, and I'll hold things down in here."

"I bet you will." Joel took the shop's cordless phone into the stock room and slammed the door. Rae followed him halfway, thinking to mock him some more. She stopped by the *Spiderman* boxes, re-bagged the book she'd flipped through, slipped it back into the box. She had suspected that Joel didn't have anyone to call, was punishing her for little indiscretions, letting her think he was mad, but she heard him dial, ask for Camille. She hoped he was just mad, that he wanted to shake her. She felt safer here than anywhere else. Three-hundred people were a whole universe, but so was Cosmo's.

Victoria Barrett's work has appeared in *Glimmer Train Stories, Colorado Review, Confrontation,* and *The Massachusetts Review.* She serves as the editor and publisher of boutique fiction press Engine Books. Victoria lives in Irvington, a neighborhood in Indianapolis where the streets are named after writers, with her husband, Andrew Scott, their two cats, and a dog named Mosley. Learn more about her work at *victoriabarrett.net.*

EL ESTOCADA

JOHN DAVID ANDERSON

The coffee was cold.

His fault, really. Sidetracked—predictably—by the covers of the weekly rags (he was only on one of them), he had left the lid off for too long, setting it on the windowsill beside the rack while he perused the new paperbacks.

He liked that word, *peruse*. In the past he hadn't been much of a peruser. It required a certain aimlessness, a languid imperturbability he didn't possess. He had always been more reactionary, instinctual; the job required it, honestly. You don't want the man who is supposed to catch you in midair missing his cue because he was distracted by a new billboard or musing over the way the sunlight splashed against the pavement. You wanted someone who was quick to act. A non-peruser. His mentor called him bullheaded, literally, rushing into every situation at full speed, horns sharp, ready to gore. At the time Harlan took it as a compliment. *El Matador* had been overly fond of bullfighting analogies. He was an immigrant, and had never bothered to fully tame the *bruja* he called English, so it was easier for him to stick with familiar turns of phrase. He probably wouldn't have appreciated the word peruse, but he would have appreciated Harlan's ability to do it. To take his time. To assess the situation for once.

Harlan assessed that his coffee was still cold. He could fix it, of course, easily, but there were rules against that sort of thing, unwritten but understood. Then again, you don't get where he was by working entirely within the system. He looked around. The bookstore wasn't crowded. He counted thirteen heat signatures, including the two in the storeroom and the one who, judging by the posture, had taken a book into the stall with him for a morning constitutional—also against the rules. The sign next to the bathroom expressly forbid bringing merchandise into the john.

Not that Harlan cared one way or the other.

He stared at his coffee. It would only take a second. Less than second. Still, it didn't pay to be sloppy. Harlan circled around the news racks toward the small, empty corner reserved for poetry and Dover Thrift classics. Under the watchful eyes of Dorian Gray and the Count of Monte Cristo, he stuck the tip of his finger in the cup, craning it just over the Styrofoam edge. It wouldn't take much, he knew. He was capable of manufacturing temperatures upwards of two thousand degrees. He just wanted it warmed.

He checked again to make sure nobody was watching and turned on the juice.

"Dammit!"

The contents of the cup boiled instantly, frothing up over the edge, dribbling down his hand, some of it—not too much, thankfully—splashing onto his boots, onto the carpet, dropping miniature brown bombs. He sucked on his hand, siphoning off now scalding coffee. He hadn't burned himself—that was technically impossible—just made a royal mess. He considered the spots by his feet, soaking into the beige carpet, looking like giant freckles. Whoever decided beige carpet was a good idea? He should notify someone. Maybe they could come spray it with something to keep the stain from setting.

Except he didn't want to call attention to himself.

Besides, what were a few coffee stains when set against the countless deeds he'd done for this city? Why suffer the embarrassment? He circled back around to the front of the store, keeping the lid off so that his coffee would cool back down faster. He passed an elderly couple arguing in clipped whispers over diabetic cookbooks. He could have heard every word if he'd wanted, but he learned a long time ago to stay out of other people's business. He wished they extended the same kindness sometimes.

Like that reporter who hounded him about the bridge incident last week. He knew it was wrong to clock a member of the press. He shouldn't have broken the man's nose, but the jerk wouldn't let up. Have you lost your edge? The man kept asking. Is the Sentinel no longer capable of protecting the city? We deserve to know. Harlan hit him with only a tenth of his strength. Still the blood had really stood out on that crisp white shirt. Like dark roast on a beige carpet. *What do you think?* Harlan had snarked back, watching the reporter crumple, waving away the camera. *Do you think I'm strong enough?*

It felt good. A little. Still, it was out of character, and he regretted it. A little.

Harlan took a tentative sip of coffee—still too hot—and decided he had probably wasted enough of the morning. *Enough perusing*, he whispered to himself. He should go. Get back on the streets. There was bound to be something happening. The city never stayed quiet for long, and he obviously still had something to prove, even after fifteen years. Inappreciative ingrates.

He made it all the way to the bargain bin with its oversized pictorial histories of American military weapons—several of which had been fired at him—and crossword puzzle collections before he saw her, sitting at the edge of the café, a copy of the day's *Herald* stretched out in front of her. She looked familiar. Like someone he had been introduced to in passing, at a fundraiser maybe, one of those Meet the Hero nights, or a charity luncheon. She wasn't part of the network, though. She wasn't law and she wasn't press, he had learned to sniff both out with ease. She wore a magenta dress with a gold swirls embroidered into the hem, the straps revealing sharp shoulders and toned arms. Her hair reminded him of tree bark, with its layers and undulations, its palpable topography. He wondered what it smelled like. He guessed honeysuckle. Or melon. He didn't have superhuman olfaction. A large cup sat on a red napkin in the space opposite her, the space where another person might be but clearly wasn't. A bag with books as thick as bricks, textbooks maybe, sat by her feet.

She was inexplicably arresting.

There wasn't anything particularly beautiful about her. If anything she seemed unbalanced, asymmetrical, with lips slightly larger than her face could ideally accommodate and eyebrows that threatened to spill over into dark brown eyes. And yet there was something about her that made him stop and take a deep breath. It had been so long.

He tried to catch those eyes over the horizon of her paper, carefully creased and held in one hand while the other twirled an ink pen. She was either too immersed in her reading or ignoring him on purpose. Harlan drifted over, careful to skim the hardcover new releases. Perusing. It had taken him a while to perfect this, his camouflage—his bumbling, unassuming, Everyday-Joe-walk. When he was first starting as town's champion he would strut everywhere. Strut to the dry cleaners. Strut around the produce department of the grocery store. Strut down his driveway to pick up the paper. Chest inflated, ready to rip his shirt off and flash his sign. It was almost like he wanted everyone to know that he could press a thousand kilos and melt steel with a touch. Matias had to convince him otherwise, to stay in the shadows, to protect his identity.

Of course what does a superhero who styles himself after a flamboyant Spanish bullfighter know about subtlety? El Matador had been outed long ago. Maybe Harlan wanted to be noticed again. He stood as close to her table as he dared.

She glanced over at him and smiled. Finally. Not an offhand smile. It lingered an extra second, he was sure of it. Was that an invitation? Over the last twenty years, countless women had swooned in his arms, pleading with him with their eyes, touching his shoulder, though admittedly he had always been wearing armor and couldn't feel it. There had been offers, some delicate, some not so. But even those had trailed off. He hadn't had a date in years. He understood how it worked, though, at least conceptually. She would smile. He would smile. He would think of something clever to say. They would introduce themselves. She would offer to have him sit. It was a *faena*. A series of steps, like a dance. Feint and flourish, designed to wear down the bull and put on a show for the crowd. He wondered what sort of clever thing Matias would say to this woman if he were here. All speculation, of course. *El Matador* was in a hospital in Saltillo, battling lung cancer and dementia. There was no chance of him scoring dates anymore.

The young woman had gone back to her paper. She had to be in her twenties. . .late twenties. Did that make her automatically out of his league? He wasn't sure. He had faced nearly insurmountable odds before. Like that army of genetically mutated giant ants. He caught sight of the headline again and puffed up his chest. He couldn't help himself any longer.

"It's not true, you know," he said.

"Excuse me?"

"What they are saying. About The Sentinel. He didn't just let that old couple die."

Maybe not the smoothest pick-up line. Probably should have led with something about her hair. But he was committed now. She was looking at him—alarmed? Just cautious. Or maybe intrigued. He pointed to the front page of the paper. It was a quote, presumably from one of the bystanders, or maybe from one of the surviving relatives. Harlan had sent flowers to the family of the deceased the very next day, anonymously of course. Fat lot of good that did.

"The incident. Last week. On the 34th Street Bridge?" he prompted.

"I'm sorry, do I know you?" the young woman asked, putting down the paper and pursing her lips. Her voice was quiet, or maybe Harlan was just used to people shouting at him, or mocking him mercilessly from behind steel masks.

"I doubt it," Harlan said.

"You look familiar," she said.

It was probably the mouth. The Sentinel's helmet covered

everything but the mouth. He had a pouty lip, he knew. "The name's Harlan," he said, extending his hand, careful to normalize his external body temperature, though her own hand still felt cold to him. He noticed her fingertips were calloused.

"Rose," she said. The name didn't trigger. She flipped the paper over to look at the headline in question. "So were you actually there, or are you just surmising?"

Harlan liked that word, too. Surmising. That's what he was doing now. Surmising that she might be interested in him. He held his coffee cup in both hands. "I was actually there," he said. "In the crowd, but I saw the whole thing. The Replicator forced the issue. It was either save the bus or rescue the old couple. The Sentinel had to choose."

That's what he told himself. And that's what he believed. He had to choose. No question. It was absolute chaos on that bridge. The bus was teetering off the edge, an entire high school marching band banging on the windows, sobbing and screaming. There were holograms of The Replicator everywhere, the sadistic freak, just teasing him. He knew the old couple was trapped, their VW mangled, the doors jammed. He saw the gasoline trail catch, the flames arcing towards the fuel tank. He had five, maybe ten seconds. Enough time to either pull the bus back onto the bridge or make a play for the couple in the car. Not both. Harlan had rehashed the moment a hundred time since. He choose the bus every time.

"Nobody could have saved them both," he added.

"That's not what the paper says," the young woman, Rose, replied. "It says that in his prime, The Sentinel would have been quick enough to rescue everybody."

"You can't believe everything you read in the paper," Harlan said. "And besides, that reporter," he bent down to pretend to read the name, even though he knew full well who it was, even though he could still see the man's nose spritzing like a water sprinkler, "Davidson? He's a big blowhard. He never gets any of his facts right."

Rose smiled again. Then looked across the table and down. She was looking at his crotch. "Looks like you had a little accident yourself," she said.

Harlan followed her eyes and cursed silently. He wasn't sure how he missed it before. Too worried about the carpet stains to notice the splotch on his pants, just a drip, but nicely blossoming there on his inner thigh. "Spilled my coffee," he said.

"Maybe you should sit down and drink it."

Was that an invitation? It had been so long, he couldn't be sure. She reached over and slid her own cup closer to make room, removing all doubt. He slid into the empty seat. She folded the paper so that it sat flat between them, half hanging off the table, the picture of the bus dangling over the side. "I'm sure you're right," she said. "It was a no win situation."

"I wouldn't say 'no win.' He saved thirty-two kids. Plus the other bystanders on the bridge."

"Like you,"

Harlan paused. It took him a moment. "Right. Like me." That was sloppy. He needed to be more careful. It had been a while since he had actually sat down and had a conversation with a normal human being. Just a regular conversation in a bookstore over a cup of coffee with an asymmetrically beautiful woman.

"Well, he probably shouldn't have been the one to deal with it anyways," she added. "From what I've read, The Replicator's hardcore—a little much for just one guy, any guy, to handle."

"I wouldn't say *that*," Harlan began, perhaps a little too defensively. The young woman backtracked.

"I'm not saying The Sentinel's not amazing. Just that, you know, he's been doing this for a while, what, ten years?"

"I'm not sure," Harlan said.

It was seventeen, actually. Ten alongside The Matador and another seven solo. Maybe he *had* lost his edge. Maybe his reaction time was slower. He knew his recovery time was longer; his back still ached from dragging that bus twenty feet. But that wasn't the point.

The point was she thought the Sentinel was amazing.

"And then to just have the villain get away," Rose said. "After all of that. It must be frustrating for him. That endless cycle. Battle after battle with no resolution."

"No *tercio de muerte*," Harlan said absently.

"Excuse me?"

"Sorry," he said. "*Tercio de muerte*. It's the third act in a bullfight. The one where the matador delivers the final blow, thrusting his estoque, his sword, into the wounded creature's heart. And you're right. It never seems to come to that. The bad guy always gets away. But what's the Sentinel supposed to do? Just let all those kids drop so that he can take a shot at capturing some psychopath?"

"He can't," she insisted.

"Exactly."

"It would be unethical."

He nods. You don't leave the bystanders hanging.

Not that the thought didn't cross his mind.

Standing there on the bridge, filled with abandoned shells of burning cars, plumes of smoke clawing their way up to the sky, everything literally hanging in the balance, Harlan had hesitated. A second. Maybe two. He considered not saving either of them.

He considered running down The Replicator instead. Tackling him and grinding him into the pavement. Just ending it, finally. Of course, if he had, then the old couple would still be dead and the bus would be stuck at the bottom of the river right now, a sunken yellow torpedo loaded with thirty-two teenage bodies.

Harlan shook his head, regretting saying anything about it in the first place. He fished for another topic, considered saying something about her eyes this time. Instead he pointed to the bag by her feet. "You always bring so much reading to a bookstore?"

Rose nudged the bag with her foot, wrapped in strappy gold sandals to match her dress. "I'm working on my Master's degree. I come here to study, but I'm procrastinating."

That makes two of us, he thought. "Master's degree in..."

"Chemistry," she said. "I'm in pharmaceuticals. But I'm also kind of into psychology. I like to study people. To know what makes them tick. What their strengths and weaknesses are."

"What if they don't have any weaknesses?"

"Everybody has a weakness."

"Not everybody."

"Everybody," she said.

"Then what's yours?" Harlan leaned across the table. He could be wrong, but it seemed like she leaned forward a little as well. She started to say something, but he was suddenly distracted by noises from outside.

Sirens. Police sirens.

They all have their own discordant melody—police, fire, ambulance—and these were clearly law enforcement, coming from several blocks away, two miles at least. Three or four car's worth. Harlan leaned back and looked at Rose. She probably couldn't hear it. Nobody else in here could. He glanced out the window at the mostly empty street. If it's not one thing…

He should go. He knew he should go. But then he would have to make up some kind of lame excuse. Pardon me miss, but I've got an important call to make. Excuse me, but I just realized, I've got a meeting that I'm late for. You can't just leap out of your chair and run for the door, popping the buttons off of your shirt. Rose was giving him a strange look. He didn't know what he would tell her.

He couldn't think of a good enough reason to leave.

The sirens started to fade, turning away. It was probably nothing. A robbery. A couple of purse-snatchers. He didn't hear rotors. If it were serious, they would have sent the chopper. He didn't hear gunshots. He could hear Matias's voice in his head, chiding him in Spanish, telling him to get up off of his *culo* and save the day, but Matias wasn't here. He couldn't see the way she was looking at him. If he could, he would understand.

"Everything all right?" she asked.

"Yeah. Sorry. So a Master's degree? I think that's great," he said, then he listened while she explained the thesis she was working on. Something about computational biomodeling and toxicology. It was all beyond him, the kind of stuff the nerds over at headquarters would eat up, but he listened anyways. Her voice was silky, purrish, if that was even a word. He could fall asleep listening to that voice. It had been so long since he got a good night's sleep.

"In fact," she said abruptly, leaning back, breaking the connection. "I've got a big test tomorrow. Which means I should probably go. Turns out there are too many easy distractions here."

Now he was a distraction. It was time for a bold gesture. A signature move. He picked up the red napkin from the table, the one her coffee had been sitting on and asked to borrow her pen.

"This one doesn't work so well," she said. She fished in her bag and pulled out another, handing it to him. He quickly scrawled his number. His regular number. The one he used to order take out Chinese; not the one he used in case of emergency. He wrote his name above it.

"I'm just surmising here, but maybe, if you get a free night away from those books, you'll want to grab coffee again. We could just meet here. Or go somewhere else."

It was the *estocada*. Harlan held his breath.

"I'd like that," she said.

He sighed audibly. He couldn't help it. Finally a clear cut victory.

The young woman named Rose stood up and reached for her coffee, accidentally knocking her newspaper to the floor, the bus plummeting off the edge. Harlan reached down to get it and felt her hand on his shoulder. It wasn't accidental. She meant to do it. He sat back up and handed the paper to her along with her good pen. She stuffed them both and the napkin in her bag, then tucked the other pen, the broken one, behind her ear. Her hair, he noticed, actually smelled like lilacs.

"It was nice meeting you," she said. "I have your number." She patted her bag.

He knew something else was called for. A final gesture. But he couldn't think of what to say. So he said the only thing that came to mind. "Until we meet again."

Harlan watched her through the store window and then, for an extra second, through the store walls, until there were too many layers between them for his somewhat spotty x-ray vision to penetrate. From outside he could hear the plaintive wail of more sirens again. Not just police this time. The whole brigade. That meant somebody got hurt. Which meant he should go. He took a sip of his coffee—lukewarm—then dumped it in the trash. As he walked to the door he noticed one of the bookstore employees down on his hands and knees, furiously scrubbing at the carpet.

★

It took her an extra twenty minutes to get home, taking a circuitous route to make sure she wasn't followed. She tossed her bag of books in the corner and took a moment to check her messages. There were four, three of them from Mom, almost frantic now, begging her to call back. She had been out of touch for three days, which was obviously too much for the woman, even with her Xanax. The last message was from her employer checking in to make sure she was still on schedule. She would have to call him back tonight. But first she had chemistry homework to do.

She went straight to the shower, layered with soap scum—she really needed to spend some time cleaning house—and pulled away the bathmat lining the tub, exposing the steel porthole cover underneath. With some effort the seal slid open, revealing a ladder down into a basement that nobody else—not even her doting mother—knew existed. Probably shouldn't have spent all that money on a secret entrance, she knew. Probably shouldn't have dry-walled over the perfectly suitable door that led to the perfectly suitable stairs that led to said basement. But it seemed so mundane, opening a door and walking down a set of stairs into your hidden lair. The secret ladder in the bathtub was infinitely cooler.

She climbed down and flipped the lights, then sat at the desk with all of her gear. At least a million dollars' worth of high tech lab equipment here—most of it on loan from her employer, some of it "on permanent sabbatical" from the university she used to study at.

After all, pharmaceuticals was nice. Lots of job openings. Excellent benefits. But there was so much more money to be had in assassinating superheroes.

She could be pulling down seventy, eighty grand developing drugs to lower high blood pressure or combat erectile dysfunction. Or she could make seven figures in a matter of days. All she needed was a drop of blood. She pulled the ink pen from its little nest in her ear and slowly dismantled it, revealing the delicate glass tubing inside. He hadn't even felt it. That was the thing about having supernatural pain tolerance and abnormally thick skin: You don't notice when someone pricks you with a titanium reinforced twenty gauge needle disguised as a broken writing utensil. She had gotten three drops at most, but that was all right. She only needed one.

Of course there was the chance that she was wrong. That it wasn't even him after all. She had been working from unreliable sources, and even though she had spent a week trailing him, she had never actually seen him make the switch. He had been so careful, or at least careful enough.

Until today. Today she was almost certain. One conversation was all it took. And Rose was nothing if not an excellent judge of character. Read deep enough, you find what you're looking for, and he hadn't done much to hide his true identity. He even gave her his number. Poor fool, she almost felt sorry for him.

She smeared a drop of blood on a clean slide and placed it in the analyzer, then looked at the red napkin that she had set on the desk. She would give it a couple of days—it would take that long to properly formulate a poison strong enough to kill him anyways, one that could circumvent all of his supernatural defenses, which were considerable. A couple of days, and then she would call. Suggest an evening. Dinner. Drinks. Something spicy—Thai maybe. She still had to figure out how to slip him the poison, but she didn't think that would be a problem. Her employer was right. He was slowing down. Losing his edge. She could take him. And then she would make a name for herself. The Recluse. The woman who finally brought the Sentinel to his knees. She even had her costume planned out. Brown and black with a blood red spider on the front. She would have to sew it herself.

The analyzer had warmed up and was starting its breakdown of the superhero's blood sample, lines of code marching across the screen. Nothing to do now but wait patiently—another thing spiders are good at. Just sit and wait for him to come to you. She would take this time to call her mother back. Explain that she was studying. Maybe even that she met someone. Her mother always said that a bookstore was a great place to pick up guys of a certain moral character.

John David Anderson is hardly ever called John David Anderson. He is called Dave by most people who know him, John by most people who don't, and Poppy by his daughter. His cat calls him yeowl and his mother calls him at least once a week. If he was a Star Wars character he would want to be a Jedi named Raith Starglider, but knows he would more likely be a used Bantha salesman named Bobba Twinklebeans.

In 2008, he published his first novel *Standard Hero Behavior* which garnered starred reviews, went on to be nominated for stuff, and helped him buy a new couch. That was followed none-too-quickly by *Sidekicked* in 2013, which landed him on the pages of the *New York Times* Book Review (if not on its bestseller list), and the recently released *Minion*.

Dave believes in the power of books to enrich lives and ask (and answer) the complex questions that drive our existence...or at the very least keep readers entertained and occasionally make them laugh so hard they snarf soda through their noses. When he grows up he wants to be Indiana Jones. Till then, he wants to be a writer and a root beer connoisseur. He lives with his wife, two kids, one cat, two gerbils, and lonely couch in Indianapolis, Indiana.

KAREN KOVACIK

READING THE BOYS' COMPLETE SHERLOCK HOLMES

When Holmes looked at me, I felt
    my body being shuffled
        like a stack of index cards:
            Button Missing, Weak Eyesight,
                Conversational Faux Pas.
But I too knew to observe
    if not brands of cigar ash
        then at least the caprices
            of men: my father sipping
                brandy and saying nothing,
Nixon blinking on TV,
    or Sherlock himself, my first
        flawed detective, whose coked out
            concertos in the dark flat
                shook beakers and test tubes,
revealing the violin
    to be its own strange kind of lab
        where sadness was catalyzed
            into math. Sometimes I still
                drift into that music, dense

as rain after fog, when I
    feel like a man, when words seem
        dull as buttons and knowledge
            a bin of coal, and my will
                a velvety specimen
pinned to the wall.

Karen Kovacik is the author of several collections of poetry, including *Metropolis Burning, Beyond the Velvet Curtain* and *Nixon and I.* Her work as a poet and translator has received numerous honors, including the Charity Randall Citation from the International Poetry Forum, a fellowship in literary translation from the National Endowment for the Arts, and a Fulbright Research Grant to Poland. In 2013, her booklength translation of Agnieszka Kuciak's *Distant Lands: An Anthology of Poets Who Don't Exist* appeared from White Pine Press, and in 2016, her anthology of Polish women poets *Calling Out to Yeti* is also forthcoming from White Pine. Professor of English at IUPUI, she served as Indiana's Poet Laureate from 2012-2014.

A LITTLE KNOWLEDGE

TERENCE FAHERTY

You could call it Rensselaer's first law of crime detection: A person's criminal imagination is limited by his or her profession. I'm not speaking here of career criminals, whose profession is crime itself. I mean the ordinary Joe or Jane contemplating a detour from the straight path. That kind of amateur crook is as constrained by work experience as a hamster is by its wheel. A teller will naturally daydream about robbing banks, an actuary about insurance fraud, and a cowboy about rustling cattle. It stands to reason.

If you're wondering who the Rensselaer cited above is, you're probably not a resident of Indianapolis, Indiana. Those happy few know me, Harley Rensselaer, the Hoosier Eye, from the television ads I run during *Cheers* repeats on Channel 4. The commercials have done wonders for my name recognition, if not my bottom line. They've made my blond pompadour—a distinguished gray at the temples—and my sharkskin suits as familiar as Larry Bird's squint, or almost so.

Naturally, when the members of the Ithaca Street Business Association—or ISBA—wanted a private investigator, they thought of me. And the case they handed me tested Rensselaer's first law of crime detection to the absolute breaking point. But that's getting ahead of myself a tad.

I was briefed by the president of the ISBA, Michael Meighan, at his place of business, the Four Leaf Jewelry Store on Indy's east side. His store was the first in a short string of stores set opposite an old movie theater in the middle of an otherwise residential stretch of Ithaca Street. The block was a holdover from the days when folks did their shopping afoot. Despite its name, the Four Leaf was as much a hock shop as a jewelers, a hock shop that specialized in what Meighan called "estate jewelry." I decided, based on the pieces on display, that the estates in question had been vinyl-sided. Modest or not, the Four Leaf had been the first victim of what Meighan insisted on calling the "crime wave."

"They broke in two weeks ago Tuesday. Got through my security system like it wasn't there. Opened my safe without leaving a scratch on it."

"I see," I said, trying to sound as impressed as Meighan was by the burglars' skill but falling short. I'd already checked out his "security system." It'd been state-of-the-art around the time Bill Clinton was president. And Meighan's safe was even older. I was pretty sure I could open it myself, given a quiet ten minutes. Not that I mentioned that, not wanting to lend my name to an all-points bulletin. That thought prompted a question.

"And the police said what?"

"The police," Meighan repeated with so much scorn you'd think I'd asked about the Girl Scouts. "The police don't give small businesses like us the time of day. That's why we have to band together to protect ourselves from the hoodlum element."

"Okay," I said. "What did these hoodlums take?"

"That's another mystery," Meighan said. "They ignored trays of rings and bracelets and necklaces. Ignored anything set with stones. They took a box of plain gold chains. A big box."

I'd already noted the prominent "cash for gold" sign in Meighan's front window. Since the price of gold went through the roof, everyone's gotten used to similar signs and roadside displays and even television commercials. Most people think of those as byproducts of a bad economy, if they think about them at all. To the police— and to us private eyes—the cash-for-gold come-ons are engraved invitations to crime. They've sired a whole new kind of burglary, one in which the thieves ignore televisions, electronics, and guns—the traditional targets of smalltime hoods—and focus entirely on pieces of nondescript gold and silver jewelry. No need to deal with a fence or even a pawn shop then. Just take your haul right to a legitimate jewelry store and pocket your cash, safe in the knowledge that the swag will be melted down almost overnight, making it untraceable.

Some jewelers turn away from the cash-for-gold idol, knowing all about its clay feet. Others hold their noses and bow down to it to stay in business. And still others—by no means many—join the clergy. Listening to Meighan mourn his "big box" of gold chains, I decided he had to be a deacon at least.

So one possibility was that one of the Four Leaf's customers had decided to steal back his stolen gold and had taken a bunch more as a bonus. I broached that possibility—diplomatically, of course—with Meighan. He responded euphemistically.

"The people who sell me gold are simple souls. I doubt they could finesse a burglar alarm."

I translated that to mean that his gold sources were mostly kids looking for drug or gas money. They were up to breaking a window or slicing through a screen door, but not much else. That fit with what I'd heard about the cash-for-gold perps, so I moved on, asking Meighan about his staff.

"I've just the one employee," the jeweler told me. "Bob Wilson. Nice kid."

Nice or not, I had myself a suspect. According to Rensselaer's first law of crime detection, Wilson was the most likely person to have coveted Meighan's goods. Plus, he had to know the security system and safe almost as well as his employer. But there was an objection to my theory, as Meighan's next remark reminded me.

"For the details on the other businesses that were broken into, you'd best talk to the other owners in person."

Yep, that was the rub. Bob Wilson might have been a specialist in the jewelry line, but not in two others. Still, I made a note to come back to the Four Leaf at three o'clock, when Wilson reported for duty.

Taking my leave of Meighan, I hoofed it east on Ithaca Street in the direction of the Tap Time Tavern. The first door I passed on the way belonged to a used bookstore, the Idle Hours Bookshop. It definitely wasn't one of the businesses Meighan had told me about, but, on an impulse, I opened its door, setting a little tin bell dancing and drawing the gimlet eye of a Persian cat seated on the front counter. Seated behind the counter, reading, was a man of about thirty with heavy black glasses and wavy hair to match.

"Excuse me, partner," I said. "But have you had any break-ins recently?"

The assistant professor gestured toward the crammed shelves all around us. "The only valuables I keep are truth and beauty. I can't even give those away."

His gesture had invited an inspection of his stock, so I made one. Specifically, I scanned the mystery section, which I could just make out from where I stood.

"Got any Travis Magee books?" I asked. The novels of John D. MacDonald had been favorites of mine growing up and maybe one of the reasons I became a private eye.

The proprietor actually sniffed. "A little sexist for this century, don't you think?"

So much for his judgment of "truth and beauty." I started to apologize for bothering him, but he interrupted me.

"Haven't I seen you on the television? Aren't you the guy who 'lives to sell guns'?"

The reference was to another late-night advertiser, a prominent local gun shop owner, maybe twenty years my senior. Maybe thirty. I couldn't tell whether the bookworm was genuinely confused or razzing me, so I forgot all about the apology.

The Tap Time might've had a German name in an earlier incarnation. Its façade was a little bit of old Heidelberg: heavy hand-hewn beams darkened by age and diamond-paned windows darkened by Ithaca Street traffic. The inside of the place wasn't much brighter than the exterior, except for the bar itself, behind which stood a woman who seemed to carry a light within her. If I was guessing right, she'd been voted the most beautiful girl of her high school class about ten years earlier, and she hadn't lost much ground since. I'd been voted most likely to spot the main chance by my high school class—longer ago than I care to remember—so I hitched up my alligator belt and ambled over.

The barkeep's name was Angela and she had a single stray hair, a touch more golden than its extended family, that fell across her big blue eyes while she talked, no matter how many times she brushed it away. After I'd IDed myself as the man hired by the ISBA, Angela told me she was authorized to speak for the owner, who was currently fishing down at Patoka Lake. She further told me that the Tap Time had been broken into five days after Meighan's Four Leaf Jewelry Store. A cigar box containing five hundred in cash had been taken.

When I observed that a cigar box was a place where kids kept interesting buttons and broken pen knives and not where bars kept hundreds of dollars, Angela shrugged and brushed at that golden hair for maybe the fifth time. It seemed to me then that the stray hair functioned like a hypnotist's watch and that I was way too close to going under. To rouse myself, I asked a more pointed question.

"Why wasn't that cash taken to some bank's night box?"

"Guess they forgot," Angela said, her blue eyes noticeably narrower.

Just then a door off the main room opened and a waitress came through carrying a tray. The room beyond the door seemed to have multiple sources of illumination, all of which flickered rhythmically. I pictured about five video poker machines, of the illegal variety.

"How much do you pay a point, darlin'?" I asked, conversationally.

"You sure you're not Excise?"

Meaning an officer of the Indiana Excise Police, the ones who'd be breaking the door down if they heard about those games of chance. I smiled disarmingly by way of an answer while brushing at some imaginary lint on one shark-skinned sleeve.

"Five cents a point," Angela said.

So the gamblers in that back room were paid five cents for every point they racked up on the illegal machines. Of course, they paid for the privilege of playing and, of course, they lost way more than they won. Which explained the five hundred dollars in the cigar box. It wasn't money that could go into a night depository because it wasn't money that would ever appear on the Tap Time's tax return.

I told Angela I'd be in touch and headed out. Headed out thoughtful, too. According to Rensselaer's first law of crime detection, Angela should be a suspect in the great Tap Time knockover. But how could she have known anything about the Four Leaf's cash-for-gold business or about its burglar alarms, for that matter? Could Bob Wilson, apprentice jeweler, and Angela be in cahoots? It wasn't hard to imagine. I'd be in cahoots with Angela myself, given half a chance.

The last business on Meighan's short list was Priority Tobacco. On my walk there, I passed a two-chair beauty parlor, the Prime Cuts Salon. I looked in, as I had at the Idle Hour Bookshop, to ask about a break-in and received the same negative reply. Then, resisting the temptation to borrow a can of hairspray and double back to corral Angela's hypnotic hair, I pressed on.

Priority Tobacco, a tiny brown brick building with a single front window, was the last door in the line. Just beyond it was a cross street, Priority Street, that was ironically named, as it was little more than an alley. As I left the Prime Cuts Salon, two teens emerged from that alley, took one look at me, and headed the other way. Before I reached the tobacco shop's door, a third kid, not quite as old as the first two, popped out of the same little street, lighting up a cigarette as he came. He must've been bolder than the earlier pair, because he stared me down as he passed by. This tough guy wore jeans and a T-shirt, both so tight there was no safe place for a pack of cigarettes, hard or soft. But the shirt had a pocket and in that pocket were six coffin nails, loose.

They're called "loosies" on the street when they're sold like that, which is as illegal as video poker, because the loosie seller almost never remembers to charge the tax. Of course, selling any tobacco products to minors is illegal. It's also as close to an immoral act as our amoral society has left. So I was very curious about who and what I'd find in Priority Tobacco.

The who was an older woman perched so high behind a glass counter that I found myself looking up at her chin whiskers. The counter between us held a flyblown display card for Dr. Grabow pipes, but not the pipes themselves. No cigars, either, which I might have sampled. Just cans of smokeless tobacco, safe behind the counter's well scarred glass face, and, on the back wall, shelves of cigarettes.

The guardian of those shelves declined to give me a name, even after I'd given her mine and described my relationship to the ISBA. So I decided to call her Mrs. Grabow after the doctor— not to her whiskered face, of course. She did admit to a break-in, about a week after the one at the Tap Time. She surprised me by naming her loss: nine hundred dollars. That was about twenty-seven hundred loosies, at the current Indy street prices.

I knew by then that Priority Tobacco did a brisk backdoor business. In the short time I'd been in the premises, two more teens, both female, had poked heads through the curtains that closed off the back of the shop. After spotting me, neither had tarried.

Perhaps because I was putting a crimp in her business, Mrs. Grabow seemed anxious for me to be off sleuthing. I hung on long enough to ask her two questions. Number one: Did the thieves take any of her stock? Number Two: Did the shop have any other employees? She replied with a no to my first question and a snort to my second, and I was free to go.

That final question was a last nod to Rensselaer's first law. I'd still been clinging to the notion that the burglaries were the work of a disgruntled employee or a team of disgruntled employees. But that idea was floating belly up by the time I was once again on Ithaca Street. As I'd feared from the start, no one employee would know the secrets and security arrangements of all three businesses, and the team I'd speculated on earlier—Bob Wilson, Angela, and a player to be named later—was now permanently incomplete, as there was no junior tobacconist to join it.

I'd held on to that theory a lot longer than I should have, because once you eliminated an inside job requiring inside knowledge, you went from a small pool of suspects to an ocean of them, by which I mean the population of greater Indianapolis.

Now, I'd noticed by then, as I'm sure you have by now, that the three break-ins had certain interesting things in common. For instance, each targeted business was engaged in shady or outright illegal activity. That explained why the ISBA had decided not to call in the police. It also reminded me of an earlier idea I'd had, when I'd suggested to Michael Meighan that the culprit might be a customer of his. It wasn't hard to picture some teenage housebreaker trading his stolen gold for cash at the Four Leaf and then buying himself some celebration ciggies at Priority Tobacco. And recognizing both businesses as ripe fruit while he was about it. As far as the Tap Time's side business went, a teen could easily have heard about it from a parent or older acquaintance. Against all that was Meighan's earlier objection: How does a smash-and-grab punk learn how to finagle alarm systems and safes?

I'd thought of another objection to the teen-thief idea while I'd been questioning Mrs. Grabow. In fact, one of my questions to her had borne on it directly. I poked my head into the Tap Time now and repeated that question to Angela.

"Did the burglar take any of your stock?"

She looked at the bottles on the shelves behind her. "Any booze? Not a pint."

"Thank you, darlin'."

You see what I was getting at. No teenager with the run of a bar or a tobacco shop would leave without an illicit souvenir or an armload of them. I wouldn't have, back in my wild oats days.

I crossed Ithaca Street—illegally, which seemed in keeping with the local ambience—and sat myself down on the bench in front of the old movie theater. The move afforded me a chance to think and a view of the storefronts I'd just visited. I considered first the possibility that my burglar was a professional cracksman. Right away I saw a problem with that. The take in each case was way too small to interest a true professional. Remarkably small, in fact. It was almost as though the thief had only needed enough to make ends meet, to supplement some other source of income.

Sitting there pondering, it occurred to me that the need for a little extra income had probably been what had pushed all three victimized businesses, the Four Leaf and the Tap Time and Priority Tobacco, across the line from respectable to not so. Being a small businessman myself, I knew the pinch and the temptation. You had to pay the rent, even the rent on crumbling storefronts on crumbling Ithaca Street.

At the moment I had that insight, I happen to be staring at one of those storefronts, the one belonging to the Idle Hour Bookshop. And I saw an answer to the problem I was having reconciling my case with Rensselaer's first law of crime detection.

What if what I was after wasn't an employee with inside knowledge of all three businesses or a team of employees, each of whom knew one business? What if all I needed was a man whose business was knowledge itself? Who had on his shelves books to teach him how to disable security systems and even open a safe? How-to manuals maybe, or maybe just whodunits, which, when you think about it, are really how-to manuals on crime?

Plus, the man I had in mind had a window on this particular stretch of Ithaca Street. If he was the observant type I took him for, he knew exactly what was happening on his block, the good, the bad, and the under-the-table.

I recrossed Ithaca and marched into the Idle Hour, slamming the door behind me. I wasn't bluffing exactly, but I was certainly playing a weak hand emphatically, as I always like to do. The Persian cat lit out before the front door's tin bell had stopped dancing its jig. And before the man in the black cheaters had recovered his sangfroid.

"Forgot to introduce myself when I was in here a minute ago. My name's Harley Rensselaer. What's yours?"

Only ten minutes earlier, the book merchant might've told me to guess and be damned, but he wasn't near as cocky now. He said, "Robert Watts."

"Sure it's not Robin Hood? Reckon not. That would make me the Sheriff of Nottingham, and I'm nowhere near that official. Good news for you."

That was me playing my weak hand again. All Mr. Watts had to do was point me to the street, and I'd be pushing a boulder uphill trying to convince the police he was guilty on the little I had. I'd be more likely to get the leading lights of the Ithaca Street Business Association locked up when the police gave their losses a careful look.

"I'm interested in recovery, not arrests."

I couldn't say it any plainer than that. As it happened, I didn't have to try. Watts reached under the counter and produced a well filled manila envelope.

"How much is left?"

"All of it. Not the gold, but the money I got for the gold from several of Meighan's competitors. He lost his markup, but that's all.

"I need the money, don't get me wrong. But I think I was more interested in the challenge of stealing it. As a research exercise. Once I had it, I couldn't bring myself to spend it."

The scruple set Watts apart from his victims, for whatever that was worth. He was interested in knowing its value himself.

"Do you have to say where you got it?" he asked.

I'd already made up my mind not to, to preserve the local peace and quiet. But I pretended to think it over, which resulted in a windfall of sorts. Watts reached under the counter again and produced a small blue bribe.

I knew it before he'd taken his hand away. It was a copy of the original Fawcett Gold Medal edition of the first Travis Magee novel *The Deep Blue Good-by*. On its cover, a young woman in hip huggers and high heels and nothing else was giving me the come hither over one bare shoulder. I obliged her by picking up the book—carefully—and opening it. I held a first edition, from 1964.

"How'd you come by this so fast?"

Watts shrugged. "I read MacDonald, too."

And collected him to boot. I said, "Your name won't come into it, not unless I hear about another crime wave."

He assured me I wouldn't. I tucked the book and the manila envelope under my suit coat to keep my part of the bargain. An hour or so away from Ithaca Street was also indicated, so Meighan wouldn't guess that the loot had never left the block. I decided to drive over to the Steer Inn for a tenderloin before reporting my success.

On the walk to my Caddy, I thought about my finder's fee, wondering if I could get away with asking for fifty percent.

Old Travis Magee always did.

Terence Faherty is an Indianapolis-based mystery writer. His Edgar-nominated Owen Keane series follows the adventures of a failed seminarian turned metaphysical detective. Terry also writes the Shamus-winning Scott Elliott private eye series, set in the golden age of Hollywood. His short fiction regularly appears in *Ellery Queen Mystery Magazine* and *Alfred Hitchcock Mystery Magazine*. His latest book is the stand-alone mystery *The Quiet Woman*.

THE PHARMACIST FROM JENA

MICHAEL DAHLIE

In the summer of 1912 I was sent from Stockholm by my father to work for an elderly uncle who was a pharmacist in the town of Winslow, Indiana. The nature of my job, a junior pharmacist, required a license from Indiana's Board of Health, and since the board had a system to monitor such things, my father paid to have forged a certificate of academic completion stating that I'd finished my studies at the University of Jena with honors and that I was entitled to practice pharmacy in "all regular and known nations." Counting on the unlikelihood of an inspector being able to tell a real certificate from a forgery, I was soon dispensing medicines in Winslow and taking cues from my uncle concerning my new life in America.

And such cues were not hard to follow. My uncle was a passionate lover of cocaine and had situated himself in such a way that he supplied nearly all the nearby interested parties—the brothels of Fort Wayne and Muncie in particular—with the drug. Thus it was no small thing for me to be the nephew of Johannes Lundquist, a man who, even in his seventies, was known as a great voluptuary and eroticist.

I lived then in a small room behind the kitchen in my uncle's house. My aunt had decorated it especially for me, as she told me several times when I first arrived from Sweden, although my uncle found the decorations upsetting. Even though he had accumulated quite a bit of money over the years and the decorations were clearly not very expensive, my uncle hated anything to do with the world of homemaking, and he became particularly outraged when this kind of effort was expended on behalf of a male.

In defense of my uncle, I will admit that the decorations were unusual in that they were astonishingly feminine. My aunt had no children of her own, and while such efforts on a younger person's behalf might logically have helped with some emotional desire on her part, it was evident that what she had most wanted was not just a child but a daughter. The bedding was pink and lavender and the wallpaper depicted light and amorous scenes from Walter Scott novels—that is, more forlorn Saxon princesses than errant knights, and certainly no battle depictions. On the day of my arrival, my aunt pointed out the likes of Rowena and Rebecca and Euphemia with deep affection, and she kept touching my neck and my back, and watched my face to see if I was happy.

Unfortunately for my aunt, in the fourth week of my stay something happened that led to drastic changes to the room's decor. My uncle came home early one morning, quite drunk, just as I was leaving for the pharmacy, and he brought with him, attached by the nose to a long chain, a large black bear, a bear that was, my uncle announced several times, "entirely tame!" Each time my uncle said this he jerked the chain, forcing the bear's head up and down at increasingly awkward angles. And it was true that the bear showed no resistance at all. Apparently a brothel owner owed my uncle money and this tamed bear was meant to serve as partial repayment while he raised other funds. My uncle ran his fingers through the bear's coat as he explained this to me, adding that this was simply the kind of thing pharmacists had to put up with these days. He then led the bear into my room, saying he'd keep it there for the day while he figured out what to do with it. After that, he mounted the stairs to his bedroom, saying that he was extremely tired and that he would be up by noon.

And I had just returned home for lunch and was taking my seat at the dining room table when my uncle reappeared, immaculately dressed and freshly shaven, complaining that he had been in to see the bear just half an hour earlier and that it had tried to bite him. My uncle was carrying a 16-gauge Kremling fowler, and after he passed through the dining room, he entered the kitchen and (I was now following) opened the door to my bedroom. The Kremling was not capable of killing a bear in a single shot, so my uncle stood at the door, loading and reloading for some time as he emptied nearly thirty shells into the animal. My uncle fired into its face the first two shells, and although the shots didn't penetrate the skull, the bear was blinded and its nose destroyed, and thus it lashed out with no sense of where its tormentor was. The subsequent shells slowed the bear bit by bit, and after it finally stopped breathing and ceased to move, my uncle removed the last empty shell from his Kremling and announced to my aunt that lunch had to be served immediately because he had an important meeting at the Winslow Rotary Club.

Lunch, however, was extremely unpleasant because my uncle and aunt got into a terrible fight over how to deal with the repairs my bedroom now needed—the fabrics and wall coverings had been ruined with the blood and the tissue of the bear, as well as the shot sprayed throughout the quarters. As soon as she took her seat, my aunt insisted on restoring the room to what it had looked like before the bear arrived—with the lavender ruffles and the pink linens and the wallpaper depicting Saxon romances. But my uncle declared that such a recurring expense was out of the question, and he became so angry with my aunt's assertions that he finally threatened to do to her what "I did to that supposedly tame bear!" After this, my aunt relinquished her point, and the next morning workmen arrived to cart off the ripped and blood-soaked decorations. They replaced them with white paint and a simple cedar bed and white sheets and a gray wool blanket, and I have to say that I was much more comfortable in my surroundings after these changes were made.

At the time I was living in Winslow it was fashionable for wives of wealthy men to suffer from mental disorders—a custom brought back from Europe, went the explanation in Winslow. My uncle took on something of the role of therapist for these women, the doctors in Winslow all attributing emotional distress to inadequate religious observance. Certainly the doctors were unwilling to offer medication for such problems.

In his work, my uncle most often used papaverine, although he gave his wards other opiates as well, and it was not uncommon to find in the morning one or two women anxiously waiting outside the pharmacy's front door to renew their treatment and replenish their stores of medication. I myself never took advantage of their condition, but my uncle often disappeared with them into the expansive back rooms he used for his offices, only to return half an hour later with a pleased look and a very relieved woman rushing past me with her medicines.

It was in light of this role as psychological counsel that my uncle began to experiment with other forms of emotional intervention, and I will say that this was not a passing or exploitative interest but something that really did consume his intellectual life. He assessed the merits of several treatments, including large amounts of mescaline, but, in the third month of my stay in Winslow, he became fascinated by the uses of electricity and electric shock for curing his patients. He did not endorse the heavy doses that were then commonly used (most notably in the clinics of Regensburg and Linz). There were numerous reasons for this, but the most important had to do with the possible catastrophic injury that might result—an acceptable and easily explainable hurdle in Regensburg, but an end to a man's practice in Indiana.

The results of his shock therapy were not what my uncle had hoped for. The women he treated never showed measurable improvement. But during this time my uncle did begin to develop an interest in the erotic properties of electric shock, and in this respect he claimed to have achieved quite a bit. Among his favorite exploits (he often told me as we drank our glass of vodka before lunch) was to strap my aunt to the cables and have one of his female cohort shock her while he had intercourse with another.

"Your aunt despises this," he always said, laughing, but he also insisted that afterward, after being unlashed, "she takes off her own dress soon enough, and very eagerly." "Whatever your aunt hates," he once added, "she always loves just as much."

An end finally came to my uncle's experimenting when a woman he'd involved in one of his sexual trysts ended up in the Marion County Hospital with severe electrical burns along her forehead, neck, and ears—my uncle had been using a new set of contact points he had read about in a medical journal from Leiden. She was the wife of a retired alderman and the sister of a state senator, and before long they paid my uncle a visit.

My uncle didn't seem at all bothered by their arrival. He didn't ask them to sit down, and when the alderman asked just what exactly he thought he was doing with this "horseshit electric cure," my uncle responded by saying, "This has nothing to do with me curing anyone. I just happen to enjoy watching your wife in pain while I fuck my own. And I know too much about the things *you* like, alderman, for me really to be afraid of you doing anything about it."

The alderman and the state senator told my uncle that he wasn't as immune to retribution as he thought, and my uncle again dismissed their threats. All the same, he did move his equipment to the basement of the pharmacy and, as far as I know, never used it again.

Interestingly, when the alderman's wife was treated for her electrical burns, she was given large quantities of morphine in the hospital, and while she had always refused my uncle's offers of opiates before, she quickly became attached to the medication and began to pay him regular visits in his back offices in exchange for her supplies.

It didn't take me much time to develop friendships with peers in Winslow, and I was soon involved in a string quartet, for which I played the violin, with three other young Swedish men. We were given space to practice at a place called Társas Magyar, or the Hungarian Social Club. It was an institution where my uncle was well known, and after our twice-weekly rehearsals we'd usually mount the stairs from the basement to join whatever events were transpiring above, often spending the following hours eating salted meats and drinking plum brandy and sleeping with the women who also visited the club. And in this way I quickly became quite close to my three friends, and we had many adventures together (albeit adventures in the confines of a four-story brick building in downtown Winslow).

We spoke English at all times, not just because it was the only way to communicate with the Hungarians but also out of a sense of custom, since every other Swede did the same. My English was the most natural in our quartet. I had spent several years as a boy in the city of Hull at a time when my father was trying to become a distributor of bedding (eiderdown, in particular) to the British market. His business failed in the end and we moved back to Stockholm when I was twelve, but my English was entirely fluent by that point and remained so, although with the customary eccentricities of the outsider.

One particular advantage of my polished language skills was that I was able to move more freely among the others at the club, and I came to know very well a young woman named Sarah Morrison, who frequented the establishment with a number of friends. We'd befriended Sarah and her gang one evening after my uncle had given me a present of cocaine—enough for many people for many nights—and that first night we slept not at all, passing our time in one of the club's many rooms with gin and cocaine and, at several points throughout the night, without our clothes.

While the women were all of the same spirit and temperament, Sarah's background was different from that of her comrades. They were all students at the secretarial school in nearby Fort Wayne, but Sarah had been bred for different things. Her father was chairman of the city council in Hudson and managed the circulation of potash to regions surrounding the Great Lakes. Secretarial school had not been part of his plans for his daughter, but she'd disgraced him when she'd broken off her engagement to a boy she'd grown up with, and he'd largely cut her off. She had a small trust of her own, however, with which she paid her tuition and rent and found interesting ways to distract herself.

The friendship between my quartet and the young women (their numbers changed from day to day) developed quickly, and three or four nights a week we'd play music for two or three hours and then find our way upstairs to join in the activities, often bringing our instruments and continuing to play for the girls and for the other guests.

One event, though, changed our arrangement. I had then been in Indiana for four months when our viola player, a young man named Brynnar Eliasson, unexpectedly fell in love with Sarah, love beyond what normally happened late at night at the Társas Magyar. Despite the fact that Brynnar was quite handsome and made a good income as a junior actuary for an insurance company, Sarah had no interest in anything at all permanent (Brynnar insisted he wanted to get married), and this is something she told him over and over.

The problem was that she continued to sleep with him, and in early November of that year she became pregnant. This was something of a rarity at the Hungarian Social Club, since methods of avoiding such things were common knowledge. But Sarah was a reckless person, and certainly even the safest methods had their flaws. Whether or not it was Brynnar's was another question. It could have been almost anyone's. But Brynnar became convinced that it was his, and following this conclusion, his obsession grew.

Sarah had no intention of having the baby, though, and soon she was in my uncle's back offices preparing for a procedure that he alone carried out in the town of Winslow. By this time Brynnar was keeping a close watch on Sarah, and when he saw her enter the pharmacy's back door—let in by my uncle—he knew the reason for the visit. Brynnar had a knife with him and apparently took some time to gather the courage to enter, but at last made his way into the pharmacy (through the front), rushed past me, and burst into my uncle's back rooms. Sarah was there, entirely undressed, and my uncle was washing his hands. He was quite surprised to see Brynnar, but when he saw the knife he acted swiftly. He grabbed a flask of sulfuric acid (with which he prepared barbiturates) and threw the contents in Brynnar's face.

The screaming that ensued was astonishing. Brynnar staggered back through the pharmacy, his hands over his eyes and in a state of pain that I had never quite seen before. My uncle and I quickly grabbed hold of him and held him down and injected him with morphine, and before long he slipped out of consciousness. The pain relieved, however, the real devastation became clear. His eyelids had been burned away and his eyes were abraded beyond recognition. Brynnar had lost his vision forever—this was immediately evident, and it was confirmed by the doctor several hours later, although such an official diagnosis was hardly necessary. After Brynnar was bandaged and began to regain some kind of awareness of his surroundings, he knew his fate as well, and just as soon as he could walk, he was out the door (the doctor escorting him) and on his way to the rooms he rented on the other side of town. He seemed entirely bewildered as he left, but less in anguish than you might imagine, especially given the pain that was now returning. He seemed determined and resolute, rather, and we all discovered the next day that this was, in fact, the case. Once he returned home he found his Baker .38 and shot himself in the head, dying as instantly as a person might expect to die from such an act.

It was of course heartbreaking for all of us, and the remaining members of the quartet played selections from Grieg's *Holberg Suite* at Brynnar's funeral. Sarah attended as well, and seemed entirely lost to the emotion of the moment. My uncle was there, too, and was so grief-stricken that he wept through the entire service and burial. Afterward he went directly home and stayed in bed for all of the next day, explaining himself to my aunt by stating that he could hardly believe what he had "done to that poor boy." The following day, however, he seemed to regain his composure, and that afternoon, as I dispensed medicines in the front of the pharmacy, he at last performed the procedure on Sarah that had been interrupted in such tragic fashion by my friend Brynnar.

Nearly six months after my arrival in Winslow a man named Christoph Reimann appeared at the Hungarian Social Club. He was a professor of German literature at the University of Chicago, but, as he explained on the night I first met him, he'd had a nervous breakdown and subsequently struck a graduate student during a heated argument about Schleiermacher's *Über den Wert des Lebens*. The terms of his rehabilitation involved a year of leave for "rest and thinking" in Winslow, where his sister lived and where he could get the kind of peace and quiet the faculty doctor insisted was necessary.

My interactions with Dr. Reimann were formal at first, aside from his occasional declarations of passions for Novalis and Schiller, but when he found out my uncle was Johannes Lundquist, he quickly warmed to me and told me that he had planned to seek my uncle's help with his current malaise. I told Dr. Reimann that my uncle had entirely renounced any interest in curing the mentally ill, but I soon learned this was not what Dr. Reimann was looking for. Rather, he told me, he had a deep interest in stimulants, and he'd heard my uncle might be able to help him in this regard.

This was how their association began, but it was clear from the moment of their meeting that my uncle would become something more than a merchant to Reimann, and before long my uncle commenced what he imagined would be precisely the kind of mental and pharmaceutical regimen that would restore his new comrade to full mental health. Every third day for the following month, the two men met at seven in the morning in a large shed behind the house and, following breakfasts of yogurt and large pieces of hard rye bread, they took peyote together and embarked on small adventures around our yard and the larger neighborhood. And their interaction was charming. My uncle was clearly in charge, and he simply led Reimann around, telling him what to do. His commands involved such things as eating boiled pinecones, undressing and then rolling in the snow, and once, incredibly, he chained Reimann to a railing on the house's back stairs and had my aunt beat him for nearly two hours with branches cut from one of the maple trees in the yard. They carried on like this while I ran the pharmacy and took care of my uncle's various ancillary businesses, until, at last, my uncle declared Reimann cured and told him it was time for them to go their separate ways.

Reimann was quite disconsolate at being thrown off like this, but my uncle said the cure had worked and that there was no need to continue. And to everyone's surprise, Reimann really was a changed man. After a day of fasting following the treatment (my uncle's final instruction, and the bridge between the therapy and the real world), Reimann arrived at the Hungarian Social Club having gained nearly ten pounds since I'd first met him and looking happy and flush. He ordered a lavish lunch and drank a bottle of burgundy on his own, and then spent the afternoon with three new prostitutes who had just arrived from Graz. And at dinner that evening—my now-smaller-by-one quartet had agreed to play during the meal at Reimann's insistence—he led the entire dining room in several Hessian folk songs, all having to do with exuberant love and the more vulgar appetites of youth. It was an extraordinary change, and he was so charming that evening that he even persuaded Sarah to join him in a suite where they did enormous amounts of cocaine and, as I heard later, even called up the new Austrian women to join them. Unfortunately, after Reimann finally fell asleep—he'd been up for well over twenty-four hours—Sarah continued to amuse herself on her own, and eventually consumed so much cocaine that she suffered a heart attack, and at eleven o'clock the next morning, when Reimann awoke, he found her slumped over in a Hoffenberg love seat, having died several hours earlier.

The funeral was held four days later, and we all planned to attend—I'd even proposed that our quartet play at the event. But on the morning Sarah was to be buried we were informed by the family that no one who knew her at the Hungarian Social Club was welcome. Reimann attended anyway, and since he was not known to the family and was, after all, a professor at the University of Chicago, no one asked him to leave. He did not come back to the social club again, and none of us saw him after the funeral, although he did write my uncle from Chicago to say that he had met with the administration and would be welcomed back the following semester, adding that the provost and the dean of humanities indicated that they had always sided with him concerning his opinions of Schleiermacher, and that, all things considered, the student he'd struck had had it coming.

It was no small thing in Winslow to die from using too much cocaine, in particular because just describing what such a substance was to the average person involved an elaborate act of articulation. It was also no small thing for a nineteen-year-old woman from a prominent family to die at all, and so, given the mysterious circumstances, there was no easy or obvious way through. My uncle, of course, had enough money to ensure some kind of safety, especially since so many of the people he bribed he could just as easily blackmail. But Sarah's father had a cousin who lived in Washington, D.C.—a State Department official who was an aide to Secretary Hayward—and he assured Mr. Morrison that he would certainly alert federal authorities to his daughter's death. And while my uncle was capable of managing what went on in Indiana and its border states, federal officials were beyond his expertise. Thus it was that he woke me up several mornings after Sarah's death with a pistol to my neck, and told me that he was turning me in for the death of Sarah Morrison. He was sorry, he said, but the situation allowed him no alternative.

Needless to say, I pleaded my case as a family member—one who had come to love him over the past year. And as I dressed at gunpoint, my uncle did look very unhappy as I spoke about my father and his sisters and their distress over the fact that I'd surely be hanged before a month had passed if he did this. But at last he picked up a large bronze paperweight that was on my bedside table—one of the few things that survived the slaughter of the bear—and struck me across my forehead. He then worked a pair of handcuffs around my wrists, and soon he and I were walking out the back door on our way to the Winslow courthouse.

The walk was only about a mile, but it was surprisingly cold that morning and I remember wishing that my uncle had at least thrown a blanket over my shoulders. (He was wearing a knee-length beaver-skin coat that he had just received from a furrier in Guelph.) But I decided not to complain, although certainly any kind of deference and compliance on my part was not going to cause my uncle to show me any pity.

The proceedings at the courthouse took less than forty-five minutes. Clearly the policemen had been waiting for me, as had a judge and two so-called state's advocates, although they were both arguing for my swift transfer to federal custody so they could be done with the matter as quickly as possible. And before long I was in the back of a car being driven to Fort Wayne, where a federal marshal was waiting to take me into custody.

It so happened, though, that the circumstances of my transportation proved to have advantages. Of the two guards escorting me, I knew one quite well from the Hungarian Social Club. His name was Alexi Margolis, and he and I had once embarked on a two-day adventure involving cocaine and mescaline and a prostitute from Duluth. Alexi was of course sorry to be the one to have to transport me, but the way he apologized let me know that he would be taking his duties seriously and that he would certainly not be complicit in any sort of escape. All the same, I explained to Alexi and the other guard (a person named Patrick who appeared to be about seventeen years old) that my uncle had just received a large cache of opium and that if we went to his house on the way out of town we might share a pipe together before heading north.

"My uncle will be at the pharmacy, and my aunt is spending the day at her sister's in Hanover," I said to Alexi. "No one will know, and it won't take long. I don't think I can face what's ahead of me without this." I also explained to Alexi that he could help himself to what he liked of my uncle's supply.

Alexi considered the proposal and then asked Patrick what he thought. Patrick was not a regular at the Hungarian Social Club, or a patron of my uncle's various businesses, but it was clear that he'd heard stories about our lives and was interested in what was being offered to him. Soon we were in my uncle's basement, sitting on three old wooden desk chairs, smoking what turned out to be very strong and pure opium. I should say that my knowledge of the opium's quality was secondary, however, since the pipe came to me last and, at that point, once Alexi and Patrick's shoulders had slumped and their pupils had dilated, I picked up a broken iron rod from a gate my uncle had torn out of the front yard and struck Alexi in the face, wheeling then to my right and hitting Patrick in the neck. Neither blow was incapacitating, but they caused enough pain and confusion to allow me to issue another series of blows before they could defend themselves. I did stop before I killed them, but I beat them to the point where they were unconscious and no longer a threat to me.

I was still handcuffed at this time, but the keys were easy to find in Alexi's pocket, and, after I bound and gagged my former captors, I was soon mounting the basement stairs and planning my escape from Winslow. There was one matter, though, that I decided I wanted to address, namely my uncle and his betrayal. As I passed through the kitchen, I noticed my aunt had placed beneath a cheesecloth a small meat pie made from veal kidneys and celery root, left there for my uncle's lunch. And after seeing the pie (and considering my circumstances for a moment), I decided to wait at the house for my uncle's return so that I could exact some kind of revenge for what he had done to me. And, in fact, two hours later, just as he lifted the cheesecloth from his pie and wedged his thumb between the crust and the china plate, I shot him from behind in the right shoulder with the same 16-gauge Kremling fowler he'd used to kill the bear. I said his name just before I fired, and I could see him arch in astonishment.

He quickly turned to look at me after I shot him, at which point I shot him again, this time in the face (blinding him as he had the bear), and then reloaded and shot him in the stomach with eight subsequent shells. Naturally, he was quite distressed by all this, but he seemed more angry than frightened and was able to express this somewhat as I continued to shoot him. He gasped several times (blood filling his mouth) that I had always been an ungrateful nephew and that he should have expected something like this all along.

Unlike my two guards, my uncle was entirely dead when I finally left him, although his death certainly lasted longer than a person might expect. The shells were packed for grouse and the charges were weak. Thus, I waited until he had mostly emptied of blood and there was no longer a pulse before beginning my journey out of Winslow.

Remarkably, I encountered no pursuit as I made my way south to Mexico—I was sure I'd be arrested at any of the major eastern ports, and the Texas border seemed the best destination for me. After a weeklong stay in Monterrey, where I sold my uncle's opium supply for 8,000 British pounds, I left for Sweden to rejoin my family. Needless to say, they were very happy to see me, particularly my father, and after he asked for news of my uncle, I told him about my uncle's life there in Winslow, and of my own life there as well, and then described how our association had come to a troubling end. My father listened in silence and seemed quite upset by what he heard. But as I finally concluded my story, and then came to a pause, my father leaned forward, put his hand on my shoulder, and said I had done the only thing I could. And over the next day, and over the following weeks, my father and I set about finding a place at a pharmacy in Stockholm, thinking that, perhaps, using the money I'd made in Monterrey with the opium sale, in a year or so I could establish a pharmacy of my own.

Michael Dahlie's most recent novel is *The Best of youth*. He's won the PEN/Hemingway Award, a Pushcart Prize, and a Whiting Award. "The Pharmacist from Jena" first appeared in *Harper's* in 2012.

BONNIE MAURER

*L*OVE AND WAR AND THE NEWS, 2002

I am brushing my hair in the mirror
for the chance meeting
with my lover at the dentist's office.
And I am thinking of pulling him
into the stairwell
before the dentist's door
and kissing him in the corner
and he will have no part of this and I will be
stuck standing on the Midwest flats
of the stairwell in my own film-noir fantasy.

The man I am passing on the way to the dentist
is picking his nose enthusiastically
and I am reading a poem in my car
about Midwest romantic bullshit. (I still want love
and still don't know how to get it.)
Love always wags
its betrayal tossing up fools—
gold and dust behind

and you can quote me
on that for your country song.

My mouth open: wide, wider, widest.
I leave before my lover's appointment.
It is January 2002: India stuffs land mines
into the patchwork of their Pakistan border,
batting for the newest peace quilt,
and the sad lion,
and his zookeeper, Mr. Omar,
in Kabul, stare back.
Mr. Omar must decide who
is going to eat,
he and his seven children
or this lion,
one-eyed from a grenade blast,
king of all of us, beasts.

Originally appeared in The Wabash Watershed, *March 2014.*

Bonnie Maurer, MFA in poetry from IU, is author of *Reconfigured* by Finishing Line Press, 2009; *Ms Lily Jane Babbitt Before the Ten O'clock Bus from Memphis Ran Over Her*, Raintree Press and Ink Press (2nd edition), 1979; *Old 37: The Mason Cows*, Barnwood Press, 1981; and *Bloodletting: A Ritual Poem for Women's Voices*, Ink Press, 1983. As a result of the 1999-2000 Creative Renewal Fellowship from the Arts Council of Indianapolis, she authored *The Reconfigured Goddess: Poems of a Breast Cancer Survivor*, 2013.

Currently, Maurer works as a poet for Arts for Learning, as a copyeditor for the *Indianapolis Business Journal*, and as an Ai Chi (aquatic flowing energy) instructor at the Arthur M. Glick Jewish Community Center.

WHAT ONCE WAS

FRANK BILL

The boy questioned how much longer he could live this existence of hand to mouth with his father, scavenging through the rural areas of Tennessee and Kentucky, where in the wee hours of night they ripped and cut bronzed wiring and piping from the walls and floors of foreclosed homes and traded the weight for tender at salvage yards.

After more than a year of travel their frames sketched into the truck seats like two skeletons from a past with no future. Maps lined the busted dash with the father and the boy's routes highlighted, addresses of houses seized by banks they'd written down from the county sheriff's bulletin boards in the towns they'd visited.

The boy longed for a life with kids his own age to fish with, talk about books and girls. Something more than the wiring of a home or the best price of copper per pound. He ran a hand through his reams of hair that were the width of a brick from forehead to neck, unable to restrain his thoughts from the father and said, "Tired of this shit. Wanna go back home."

When the economy went to snuff the boy was fourteen. He remembered stepping from the Ritalin shouts of children who lined the green vinyl seating of the school bus and walking the long stretch of gravel to a heat-bleached trailer and a pole barn the father worked from, a stretch of land they'd resided upon since the boy's birth.

The mother had ran off with another man when the boy was nine on what the father called the chemical path, rumor was she got clasped into a world of trading skin in truck stop diners to afford her and her new fellow's next fix.

Entering the living room, the boy found the father sunk into the couch lipping a bottle of black label Evan Williams, two backpacks expanded and laid out on the wooden coffee table and the boy questioned, "Where we goin'?"

The father swallowed hard and capped the bottle, knowing that other than the one-hundred dollars in his wallet, he was flat broke. Employment had dried up, no one was spending. The furniture restoration and handy man business where he'd strip and restore antique dressers and hutches, remodel a room, build a new deck or rewire a home, had sunk. He was left with nothing but splinters, tools collecting dust and a mouth to feed. He'd procured an idea from a regular down at the tavern who'd yammered about homes being built quicker than they could be inhabited. Their worth imploded and now they were unable to be afforded, the materials that constructed them lay in rot, a person would be better off looting the metallic conductors from the structures and burning the rest. From there the wheels of continuation turned in the father's mind, knowing what he could do and how he could do it.

Planting his palms on his knees, the father stood up, leveled his singed red eyes on the boy and said, "Into the wilds of life."

"What about school? Our home?"

The boy sensed the father's tension as he grabbed one of the packs, handed it to the boy like an uppercut to the gut.

"The road will provide each of those."

And without contemplating consequence for his words the boy asked, "What if I don't wanna go?"

It was the first time the father had laid skin to the boy. Bringing the calluses of his right palm to the boy's face, telling him, "You have no say in the tutelage I'm giving."

And they left that day with the clothes on their backs, a tent, a gun, some tools, fishing equipment and a few books the father and the boy favored. *For Whom the Bell Tolls, Old Man and the Sea, Tobacco Road, Wise Blood* and *The Sound and the Fury.*

Now, the boy's words brought the lurch of guilt for this way of life to the father, he'd questioned the boy's quietness as of late. His rolling of the eyes when talking scrap prices, distant stares at others kids hanging out in the mom and pop groceries when gathering provisions. But the father would not show this weakness. To him it meant failure as a provider and a sire. He replaced it with anger. Coaled the remaining tobacco from his cigarette, flicked the butt out the window where dark passed warm and rashy as a wool blanket. Took the steering with his left, teetered his right fist into the peak of the boy's left jaw. The boy's right side skulled the window. "Dammit!" the boy yelled. The truck swerved off then back onto the road.

Pointing out the insect-spatted windshield the father said, "All this here is your home."

Pushing the hair from his eyes, the boy rubbed his cheek. Felt the balm of heat. Held back the water that weighted his sight.

"I seen enough of this home. I want friends, to go back to school. I want it to be like it once was."

Over the past year they'd took shelter amongst the dilapidated houses within the hollers of shunned vehicles on cinder blocks, where dry-rotted tires hung from limbs and un-raked leaves piled to the shade of bourbon and replaced the grass. They'd back down rutted drive-ways that held no hint of movement, hoping for a few hours of shuteye. Sometimes they were met by half-mongrel hounds barking, then the father would shift from reverse to drive and speed away as the mixed-breeds gave chase. Other times they'd find a stream, set up a camp where they could bathe and fish. Cat hit at night while bluegill or bass struck at the break of morning. They'd scale, gut and then sear the opal meat in a cast-iron pan over an open flame. Fingering and spitting out the needlelike bones.

In the father's eyes he'd educated and ministered for he and the boy the only way he knew. Passing on his skills of how a house was blueprinted, where the wiring and piping ran, and knowing where to begin cutting the bronze colored metal. Then loading and hauling their wares to a place where they could burn the insulation from the Romex to trade weight for coin. To the father, these learnings were an apprenticeship for survival.

The father slowed the truck as they rounded a lake, a few houses were plotted across what looked to have once been un-trespassed acreage, more than likely willed to a family member after kin had died, then sold and sectioned off for new construction. At least that's what the father believed.

"Friends?" the father questioned, "You got me. What used to be has been banked into lies, squandered at the price of person's like us, the working. Tell me this, how else we suppose to earn our keep?"

When money was flowing well, the father'd splurge on a hotel, buy the boy a book from a grocery, offer a good night of comfort, cable TV and lamp light to read by. While the father swam in a twenty or thirty dollar bottle of whiskey and their battery-powered tools charged.

"Couldn't we get us jobs somewhere's, move back into our trailer?"

The father chuckled. "Your mouth pleads my ears with ignorance boy. You know they's no such foolishness being offered. And we rent our skin for no man."

They'd heard the stories when fueling up the Ford and grabbing a local paper, jobs had become scarce. Even getting part-time work washin' down the lot at a McDonalds was competitive. They'd spoken with families like them who'd become homeless and camped beneath overpasses in cities or within parks.

"How we know if we don't look?"

They were closer to home than they'd ever been, had crossed over the Ohio River from Kentucky to Indiana two days ago, paid a visit to the justice center, scribbled down some residences and pitched their tent at the Stage Stop Campgrounds, mapped out their digression. They'd been driving somewhere between Laconia and Elizabeth. Had entered a private area of housing, one road in and the same road out. Maybe this return to familiarity had brought on the boy's discourse, the father thought as he lashed back with his trail-worn wisdom.

"I've taught you better'n that boy. Never let you starve nor freeze."

"No we just lurk among the streams of decay, take company with human crustaceans."

The father hung a right, pictured himself stomping the brake, laying a tread of knuckles upside the boy's hard head, but he knew the boy had a venomous tongue. Would grow sharper than he'd ever be. And for this the father was proud.

Killing the truck lights, the father let the moon navigate him into a half circle driveway, rolling the boy's words around in his mind, believing that was no reason for the boy to wield him with disrespect. The miles they'd traveled wasn't easy for either of them. The father missed planing and staining wood, hammering nails or driving screws into treated-boards to frame a deck or an addition, to create something of substance. And he'd not laid with a female in over twelve months or better. But the whiskey helped to numb those emotions of want.

The brick home sat alone, devoid of vehicle or light, with others over a football field away. Shifting into reverse, the father backed down the rutted soil. Tucked the truck up next to the house and turned the ignition off. The boy grabbed his flashlight, unlatched the passenger side door. The father reached for the boy's arm. Strained for words to better all that had been said, but he found none and the boy jerked free.

The father stood opposite the boy fastening his tool belt. The boy pouted and stared out into the night from which they'd traveled and the father told him, "Quit wasting the dark, get your cutter and bar, go round back, they's supporting walls, looks to be a walk-out, try the doors, start on the pipes."

From the Ford's bed, the boy pulled a battery powered saw and hexagonal crowbar and said, "Yes, master," disappearing around the corner of the house before the father could acknowledge the reply.

Tasting the bitterness of truth, the father knew there was no reward for the struggling. Seemed the harder one tried the harder life came, and all one could do was keep dredging forward.

Trying the side door before committing to prying, the knob turned and the door opened.

Scents of mildewed lumber and chalky walls engulfed the father's inhale. Shining a light on the kitchen floor, tile and grout lay in pieces, had been plied or broken, tea stains dotted the ceiling with jellyfish outlines, the counter tops were scuffed to the particle board beneath them. Cabinet doors had been rent from hinges.

Kneeling down, the father looked beneath the sink, a foul odor decorated the square space, he checked the piping, how it was connected, whether it was hard or flex. It was neither; it'd been gutted.

In its place lay the chalky bones of a small animal. Pieces of hide. Specks of piss ants and shells of dead flies. "The hell?" The father muttered. Standing up, he walked to a set of doors, opened them expecting to find the water heater. It was gone.

Following the warped walls from the kitchen to the dining area, the father glanced around the open areas of shadow. Decay lingered in the air and the father listened for the boy, could hear no jarring of metal teeth against mineral. Took in the sheetrock that held smears of hand prints, had been pebbled to the floor from wire being ripped out but not finished. Just frayed ends of wire hanging, as if some scrappers had been halted of their actions.

From the far left corner next to a curtainless window, a yoke hung balanced in its center from above. It held medium sized hooks on each end where two hinds had been attached, now shriveled, the carcass they'd been connected to was no more, only sticky splotches of matted pelt and blood lay on the floor. Looked to have been from a deer, the father thought. Steps printed from the mess tracked toward a hallway where shapes flicked and strobed. Worry stirred within the father. He wanted to find the boy and be rid of this place. Stepped down the hall and into a windowless room on the right that reeked of urine, a candle sat on the carpet creating a static haze. He shined over the blots of shag, blankets lay twisted and piled. A doorless opening to the left descended down with a set of stairs. *Basement*, the father thought. In the corner, worn boots were attached to faded denim. The father guided the light up legs, made out the two silhouettes. A voice came in a sparking screech. "Dim that there light."

The shape of a man held a length of steel pressed to the boy's throat. He'd a face that looked cooked and split. One eye stared. The other was bare skin the shade of a cherry flavored slushie.

In the boy's right he gripped the reciprocating saw. The other was empty.

"Don't be quaking that edge to my boy's throat, we've no yearn for trouble."

Thoughts of dying entered the boy's mind. Of all that he'd seen and all that he'd not done. They'd crossed some unruly types on their journey but nothing that made him question his expectancy.

"This here is our squat."

"Release your clutch from the boy and we'll be a memory."

The words "our squat" had not registered in the father's understanding till the aroma of dated-cottage cheese suffused by humidity came all at once and the boy's white's metered wide.

Two feet of lumber angled into the father's nape. The flashlight dropped. The father palmed at the throb in his neck, hollered, "Shit!" Took another hit from the wood. A voice clanked overtop of the father with warning, "All your kind do is cripple the foundation of its worth. Teach you not to carve and steal for density."

Tense, the boy's gut knotted with the blows that descended upon the father. Knowing he should've turned back the same way he'd entered, seeing where the plumbing had been stripped, animal carcasses and human feces littered the basement walls and floor. The blade came from nowhere, threatened him with, "Yell and it'll be yur last. Walk." A hand pressed and led him up the steps. The heathen and the boy waited as they listened to the father walk from room to room.

Now the boy spasmed forward but was stopped by the sharpness against his throat. The laugh of words sprayed over the boy's shoulder. "Hold steady young man, Elsner's gettin' his groove on your pops."

The father's outline wilted to the carpet. The boy felt the man's chest in his back, a hand rubbed at the arch of muscle that connected to his hamstring. The other man laid a boot into the father's ribs. Some space came between the boy's Adam's apple and the knife as the man began sniffing the boy's lobe. The father grunted. The boy wanted to vomit. His hand steeped around the rubber handle of the instrument. Thoughts of what to do and how to do it came all at once like severing the heft of alloy from walls and floors of uninhabited homes. Gauging the man's right knee pressed into the bend his own, the boy did the one thing the father'd honed in him.

The boy raised his left hand up his body, fingered the sharp line below his chin, squeezed the trigger in his right, turned and slanted a cross-cut into the meat of the man's leg. The man belled, "Awe, awe, awe!" Hot specks peppered the boy's hand as he watched the man reach and pat at the dark that spread from his thigh like a busted transmission.

The one called Elsner looked to the screams. Then came the crack. The separation of foot. Then another crack and the discomfort that blistered up Elsner's shin and knee. Caused the release of the rectangular length of wood. Elsner squealed and bent forward at the split and give of his calcified metatarsal's tissue as the father worked his way from the floor with a hammer, stood heaving and leveled the straight claw into Elsner's scalp, silenced his agony. Fingers raked at the boy's shoulder with adrenaline. "Help your ole man." The boy leaned, supported the father's mass and the father panted, "Lead us from this layer of filth."

The boy guided them down the hall, into the dining room where several outlines emerged, the boy raised the tool, mashed the trigger and swung at the air. A man groaned, "Bastard." The boy'd clipped human rind, bodies backed away barking, "No, stop, stop!" The boy rushed, dragging the father into the kitchen and out the door. At the truck, the father swung his arm from the boy, reached for the driver's side door and said, "I can navigate."

Firing the engine, the father shifted into drive and stomped the gas. Tires flung dirt till they bit hard surface. The father drove out the same way he'd entered, questioned what had just taken place, trying to make sense of what they'd walked into, some unknown juncture of hell.

The father pondered what he'd spoken to the boy, the clenched digits he'd belted him with. This life of salvage. Maybe he'd traveled so long that he'd lost sight of change. He felt the rhythm pounding behind his breast, knowing what caused this beat was blood. It was the same that pulsed within the boy and as they disappeared into the raven of morning the father spoke.

"Maybe it's time we looked to settle, rebuild what once was."

This story originally appeared in Midwestern Gothic.

Frank Bill has been published in *Granta, Playboy, Oxford American, The New York Times, The Daily Beast, PANK,* FSG's *Work in Progress, New Haven Review, Talking River Review, Plots With Guns, Thuglit, Beat to a Pulp* and many other outlets. His first book *Crimes in Southern Indiana* was released by Farrar, Straus & Giroux in September 2011, and his first novel *Donnybrook* hit in March of 2013. He is currently at work on his third book and follow-up *The Salvaged & The Savage* for release in late 2015.

BONNIE MAURER

FIFTH MONTH

Up early reading a book of poems
I hear the neighbor's son
leave for school with his mother's goodbyes.
I listen for his steps
down the rocky drive. By now
he must be at the corner stop.
Did he grab his jacket?
Does he like his name?
Do his feet dance on the side walk
waiting for the yellow machine?
I consider how glad
I will be in my secret heart
to send a child off to school,
bend at the doorway issuing byes,
turn back to a small cereal bowl.

The bus heaves and hums to a halt,
opens its hungry mouth.
The persistent arrival of fortune.
The baby kicks in my belly.

THIS BITTER PILL

FRANK BILL

"Heroin, sometimes called Dope, H, Mud, Smack, Mexican Horse, Hell Dust, and Junk, is a highly addictive and rapidly acting opiate. Heroin is produced from morphine, a principal component of opium, a natural occurring substance that is extracted from the seedpod of the opium poppy. As of 2003, nearly 3,091,000 US residents aged 12 and older have used heroin at least once in their lifetime." — *National Drug Intelligence Center*

Cleaving the pockets of her denim, Tar Baby needs more than the lint that lines the cotton to pay back a debt to the heroin pipeline of Harrison County, a liability that satisfied the screams reaming her and her boyfriend's insides so they could swim in the feeling of heated foam last week.

She stands behind the counter of the English Mini-Mart, jagged and tactile, her arms scarred like graffiti on bathroom stalls, watching the 78 Thunderbird with a Bit-O-Honey-colored top pull up to one of two gas pumps through the smeared glass. From it steps a man linked with cellophane muscle beneath a sleeveless V-neck, his pants hang half off his ass, the stitch of boxers rimming his lower back.

The bell above the door jingles and the obligation of her addiction weighs heavy on her eighteen-year old conscience. Deuce bows his head to get through the opening, he's tatted with the numeral two about his neck and shoulders in the font of Roman, Franklin Gothic and Courier. His teeth glow white, some bordered with gold, and his serpentine eyes cut into Tar Baby.

The low croon of coolers that wall the left side of the shoebox-store where colas, teas, juices and sports drinks are refrigerated is the only sound heard. She stares into some thought he cannot see but fathoms all too well, one where she dissolves the cumin colored powder in liquid, heats it in a spoon, ties off an appendage, flicks and breaks her pigment with a needle.

Deuce tells her, "You and yur boyfriend Patch Work got credit that need recompensated."

Weeks ago, after birthing their baby boy Ezekiel into the world, the new wore off and that yearn to have their cavities waxed came calling. Tar Baby and Patch Boy went slumming, got their eyes rolled into their skulls and drooled down their chins til the cash given by relatives for the newborn dried up. They'd bought enough H from Deuce to get it fronted, thinking her pay from the mart and Patch's scrap money would settle up the barter and it would have if they'd not bought formula, diapers, some Oxy, and Patch's truck hadn't broken down. Now, every nerve ending in Tar Baby's frame shrieked with the fright of owing this man while craving what he pushed.

"We gonna pay," she says.

"Don't be playin' me fo some dumb shit redneck."

Her shoulders and knees belt as she imagines a tiny rivulet of blood expanding around the dissolve of the rig, the Hell Dust sizzling inside her like heated grease, frying the endorphins, dropping her back to a state of the perished.

"We ain't playin' you. Money been tight with us raisin' a newborn. Livin' at Patch's mama and stepdaddy's trailer."

Her tongue ovals her lips, she wants to feel her vanilla tissue beneath her nails. Deuce leans down, still taller than her, and rests his forearms on the counter, "One of you's gonna pay me notes, or—" he pauses and reaches a sharpie-thick digit toward her chin, runs it over her ear and finishes with, "by skin."

Smelling Deuce's saltine cracker and ashtray-stubbed body sickens her. Deuce stands and her whites are sunken lines of mascara that meet the fist of his crotch, she knows how he treats females, cuffs them, mars them and strobes them with shanks and syringes for days on end in the back bedroom of his trailer. She's heard testaments to the horror he calls payment.

Deuce sucks on the enamel of his teeth, takes in the shapes beneath her Rob Zombie concert T-shirt, looks to a door by the coolers. Behind it is the storage room, and he says "Maybe I make you lay down what you owe now."

She sees it in his face, him imagining her bent over the boxes of canned goods or potato chips and a chord of terror gauges her like a razor and she says, "No, Patch and me get whut we owe you."

"When?" he demands, slamming his hand on the register.

"Tomorrow," she lies.

Before she can blink Deuce's palm fills her vision. Meshes her lower lip against the marrow rooted in her gums. The taste of ore warms her taste buds and he tells her, "They's more of that, you and yo boy don't pay up."

Tar Baby stutter steps into the wall behind her, wrist dabbing at her mouth, she watches Deuce reach for a carton of Newports that are stacked above where she stood.

"I take these and some gas, call it interest on what I front you two junkies." Tracking over the floor, he pauses and says, "Be back tomorrow for my coin or yo husk."

He exits out the glass framed by scuffed steel and Tar Baby dams her sight, battles the impulse to scream at Deuce to stop, take her into the back, use her til she and Patch Boy are no longer indebted and maybe even a little extra if he'll give her some Mud to silence her ache.

★

Before the barnacled truck door slams, Elmer shakes his head and tells Tar Baby, "Won't be stoppin' to give you a lift no more." Then the truck goes left at the T and she walks the opposite direction along the right flank of the road.

Every evening since Patch Boy's truck broke down this has been her getting back and forth to work. Elmer not driving the extra mile to the trailer. But stopping, offering her a ride on his way home from the chicken plant when he sees her, he flirts with her and preaches his words of scripture.

Elmer's got bloodhound cheeks, flecks of tobacco in his teeth and smells of spoiled fowl. "God got a plan for us all, you'll see," he told her this evening, after questioning the swell of her lip. She told him she'd hit it on a cooler door at the mart.

And Tar Baby fights her body's pleas for a fix and says, "How you reckon the savior tastes?"

"How he tastes? Girl, what serpent has infested your tongue?"

"None," she says, "but the way you speak of him shapin' lands, formin' oceans, turning water to wine, even a grain of him would appease one's needs. I bet some'd pay top dollar."

"Girl, you has got to kick that sin-talk to a sinkhole, cover it over with answers from the good book."

All she could do was push her bony knee closer to the curious calluses of his hand that patted it in-between his spiritual oration. She wanted to ask does the Lord's plan involve fifty-year old men and eighteen-year-old girls who cannot pay a heroin-peddling sadist except with her hide. Desperate, she asked Elmer, "How much would you pay to get down my pants, for me to spill your gravy?"

And like that her transit from the mart had ended. Now she'd have to do as she did in the mornings, thumb a ride to work from the vehicles in the holler that zoomed past with the rusted squeak of axles and the cough of exhaust soot.

★

The dented tin trailer with a red stripe that's been bleached to pink by the sun sits with a couch the color of a coyote's hide in the dirt yard by two pine trees. A Chevy S10 with a blown head gasket sits parked with rungs of copper wire, an aluminum screen door and a stovetop in the bed. Tar Baby takes the steps up the warped deck, turns the doorknob that's actually a screwdriver handle, smelling chemical smoke and hearing Ezekiel crying over the thump of rustic Americana music before the door is opened.

Inside, the room has been mugged of all that is good, replaced by every shade of what's wrong with Tar Baby's world. Of wants and needs that shouldn't be. Things others pretend no longer exist. But this bitter pill called the truth of un-salvaged lives does endure.

Patch Boy's stepfather sits like a Crisco stain on the kitchen counter, oily and slick. He's shirtless, his ribs poke out like elongated fingers. He sometimes touches her, calls her his daughter-in-law, but she reads his affection, his accidental walking in when she's toweling the beads from her stretch marked breasts, hips and stomach after showering. His saying "I sorry" but still smiling with teeth that are broken shards of lactose dipped in Hersey syrup, taking in a final glimpse of her shapes before closing the bathroom door.

In the kitchen sits Patch Boy, he's still-brained and stutters but scores good drugs. He cries some nights about his real father, a man who loved him wrong, gave him the same love his father, Patch's grandfather, gave him.

The mother sits across from Patch Boy, not paying any mind to Tar Baby, passing a clear pipe that's the size of a baseball to the son. He presses it to his lips. Fires a lighter. The resin pot bubbles with water as he huffs the smoke.

The mother's robust with fish-batter curls and an eyeshot of pink glaze. She exhales toxins and says, "Bout time you got home. Can change that damn squealer of yours. Been barkin' fur near an hour."

Tar Baby wants some of what they're sharing, something to sear this edge off of what must be paid to Deuce, but Ezekiel's crying beckons her. The stereo blares with Ray Wylie Hubbard's tune "Opium" as the stepfather stomps the floor and slaps his knee. She speaks over all of this to Patch. "He come by the mart today."

Patch turns to her with a scalp nicked by shears, knuckles and barbed wire, he blinks and stammers, "Who...who...who come—" and he stops short, noticing Tar Baby's puffed lip.

"Deuce." She says.

A tear forms within Patch Boy's vision and he says, "He...he...he be touchin' you."

She thought of Deuce's finger rounding her ear, his eyeing her chest, the carton of smokes he took and the gas.

"He want his coin for the junk."

"We...we...dddon't...got it."

"Deuce gonna be payin' another visit to the mart tomorrow."

"You...you...don't wwwork tomorrow."

"I know, buyin' us some space." She hesitates and tells Patch Boy, "He say I can pay with myself."

"He bbbest st...st...step back."

The stepfather barks, "Ain't no sable be beddin' my boy's female less he wanna a mouth full of gunpowder and pellets."

Patch Boy scratches the stub of his crown, dandruff flakes and falls to his shoulders and he asks, "When...when you...you get yur check?"

"Friday."

"Th...then he...he gonna have tttuh wait."

The stepfather grazes Tar Baby's neck. She wants to smoke her lungs or roast her inner wadding. She spins, swats the stepfather's wormy clasp, and demands, "Whut about you?"

His façade pinches and draws and he says, "Whut about me?"

"Tender, you got any we can barrow?"

"Got none til Friday. Me and the queen tossed our last dime on a eight ball of crankshaft-candy."

Tar Baby mumbles, "That do us no damn good." and brushes past him.

"Hold on a damn minute girl. You's family and family caters to its own," the stepfather says as he watches her walk down the hallway to the squall of her child.

Ezekiel's heaves churn off the panel board walls. Grabbing him from the crate where he lays in unrest, he is warm but not from body temperature, it's from his tainted diaper that has leaked onto his Tigger and Pooh blanket. Laying him on a dresser to be changed, his face wrinkles, she rips the sides of the diaper, his hands crimp to his mouth, tiny fingers the size of bloated maggots curl, his eyes wide and ocean blue, she wads the heft into a lump. Reaches for a baby wipe, cleans the smears from his bottom, clasps a fresh absorbent around him. And Deuce's offer hangs over her like another layer of skin.

★

One morning passes as her day off, when the next comes she sits on the rotted and mildewed front porch, a blanket burrowed around her, a cigarette between her crusty lips watching the sun lift over a mess of cedar across the road. It is a Wednesday and a cordless phone rests next to a line of empty Miller High Life bottles on the deck's railing. Smoke pipes from her mouth. She has phoned Mr. Reece, the owner of the mart, tells him she's not feeling well. Mr. Reece questions her about fuel and a carton of smokes, nearly seventy dollars of combined sales that were inventoried on Tuesday but unaccounted for. Tar Baby has no answers and the owner tells her she is fired. Tar Baby does not argue, says, "I be in on Friday to get my check." The owner tells her the gas and cigarettes will be deducted from her pay.

Gravel crimps beneath rubber as a maroon Lincoln stops in the driveway, the thump of bass rattles the trunk, then goes deaf with the engine. The driver's side opens and a wheelbarrow of weight plants his feet on the ground. His complexion is a face of infected pores and a chaff of hair that appears singed and mangled.

Tar Baby knows not who this man is but why he has come. Behind her, there is the punch of feet and the trailer rocks, voices are drowned out until the door whistles open. From it the stepfather and Patch Boy step, they're bugging from two pots of coffee and a few lines of amphetamine. One holds a .22 revolver the other a dated .12 gauge pump. "You lost?" the stepfather yells.

The car's passenger side unlatches, out steps another man who appears hard as an oak fence post with a crooked ball cap and spurred lips, he points over the door at Tar Baby. "She know why we here. Settle her and Patch Boy debt to Deuce."

Tar Baby takes a final drag from her Camel Wide, flicks it out into the dewy yard and hears the faint beginnings of Ezekiel's wailing.

Patch Boy moves past Tar Baby and trains the .22 on the one man. "Sh...sh...she ain't go...go...goin' nnnooo...where's. Deuce get his when he ggget it."

Each of the men reach and raise 9mm Glocks. The driver aims his at the stepfather, the passenger points his at Patch and says, "Yo Porky the Pig speakin' ass best put that pea-shoota' down."

Tar Baby comes from sitting, her hand quakes as she pushes the barrel of the .22 toward their feet and says, "I am goin'. Deuce got tuh be paid. Go in yonder, Ezekiel needs changed and fed."

She'd phoned Deuce before Mr. Reece, after thinking about her life. About the gummy buds she started rolling at age fifteen, the man-made crank that she snorted at sixteen and the smack she began bruising her veins with at seventeen, then became broken-kneed and went to rehab, stayed clean until birthing Ezekiel, moved out of her parents' home and in with Patch Boy.

She does not want her child to see this life that she cannot grasp. One that never holds enough money to afford anything more than struggle and privation. She has inventoried this knowledge and takes the creaking deck boards one bare foot at a time to the yard. Walks to the car, glances back at Patch Boy who grapples for syllables to sound off the word 'no.'

Tar Baby squeals across the vinyl backseat, smelling the sweat and soured beer cans that are crunched about the floor. The two men get in, close the doors and the car fires to life, rhythms rime from speakers and shake her bones. She sits remembering what an addict once told her after seeing the track marks on her arms, that even after the swells of pus heal and scab, the pang of want never subsides. It's there tucked away like the blood kin that embarrasses one with a wondering orb and split-speech and is closet hid till the day you die.

This story originally appeared in PANK.

LIZA HYATT

TRILOGY

BOOK ONE

It starts in a garden, rose-petals, thorns, the heroine waking, a doorless circle of stone and mortar. An eagle flies over, calling, and she digs out, follows. Comes to quartz and cliff-dwelling mountains, a dream of an ancient poet, moon dancing. It is the last summer of an old magic, dying. The fading sound of Anasazi footsteps, the strings of a lyre played high in golden aspens, thunder, the maenads drumming, a dagger of light at solstice dawn, a sundial, planeteria, orrery. She, a student at a school of philosophy, alchemy, mystery, sexual awakening, translating ancient teachings about eidos, the Good, the soul, the moon, the One. There is a great conjunction of planets, a prairie triple rainbow. She meets Pan, an old bum sleeping under a bridge beside a desert river, a river flowing into all rivers, the milky night, the changing universe. She drinks this water and sees a dragon of new magic clawing its way from her womb.

BOOK TWO

This one starts with betrayal, the false ones, danger. She has to flee and begin again and the old magic, dying, dying, draws its last breath and those who know don't know what to do. She dreams she is being buried alive, is in the ground, exploding. In a hide-away on a distant coast, she learns to speak the language of moss and crows and the hunted deer and storm cloud and tides. She reads the words written by seaweed and foam on the shore, the long lonely prayer, and an impregnating wind blown from the fringes of the most distant stars chooses her. She makes her way back to where her life began. Her father, the usurped king, has become a monk. Her mother, the one who imprisoned her, now the leader of armies. She tries to tell mother, father, poet, midwife, that new magic is growing inside her. They hear the whisper of leaves, the howls of wolves, the drone of old roots, and believe she is crazy.

BOOK THREE

Is not finished being written. Claws keep ripping through the pages. It is being written in a cave, with ink made of woad, obsidian, blood, each rune written with a vulture feather quill. Outside the cave is a forest where the old magic has begun decomposing, and an old woman who has befriended death, tends both it, and our heroine as she gives birth to...the story does not yet say. In places, the pages of this book are turning indigo, cobalt, and the only word, the only symbol, is a white oval, like a closing eye, or an egg, a galaxy, opening. It is a dark book, the beginning of a new way, an old story in a new language, a new story in an old language, a myth, a songline being sung, animus mundi turning and settling deeper into this compost of dream-time, leaf rot, star dust, this bone shard cosmos, this big bang, sea spray singing, this seed sprout, sun flare, cell dance. Deep forgetting. Deep remembering. No self. No time. No end.

KAREN KOVACIK

READING THE BROTHERS GRIMM

She'd never seen a raven or a flounder.
No musician ever charmed her out of speech,
nor had she lost her way in a forest.
Thus, no woodcutter rescued her,
and her little sister did not become a magpie.
No prince shimmied up her short ponytail,
no tyrant ordered her to spin flax
till her fingers bled. She had many wishes
but no talking fish made them come true.
She did not have seven brothers, no one
kissed her awake, she didn't dance
till her soles were paper-thin.
Her parents never built her a coffin,
though once she wanted to die,
not like a princess on a bier of glass,
but like a servant cast down a well.
Still, she lived on in thorn-covered bowers.
Daily she foraged in thickets of ink.

And when the giants smelled her blood,
she fled not to a gingerbread house
studded with poisoned sugarplums
but to strongholds of sharp, black words.

LECTOR

DIANNE MONEYPENNY
GORDON R. STRAIN

¿Se podría decir que a un lector no le gustan otras personas? ¿No es un libro una persona, o mejor dicho, veinte personajes que sienten, comparten, bailan, aman, odian y mueren entre las páginas rectangulares?

El, de verdad, no sabía la respuesta.

Pero el debate siempre surgía dentro de él en medio de los polvorientos estantes de la librería que se combaban, pesados por los varios libros de diversas pátinas, temas y tamaños. Entrecruzaban y encarcelaban, estas estanterías inclinadas, con sus brazos inundados por la pulpa boscosa; pero la trampa de los libros era más difícil de ver.

Al coger un libro y liberar un lomo, una red de hilos plateados de los ensueños le esperaba.

Cuánto más leía, más se liaba.

Perderse.

Lentamente.

Palabra por palabra, línea por línea.

La vuelta de las páginas llegaba a ser automática. Inconsciente.

Y poco a poco se reducía la distancia entre el predador y su víctima.

El estridente sonido de una campanillita de plata sonaba en las orejas suyas.

"Hola," le dijo una voz preciosamente infantil.

"Red encantadora."

READER

DIANNE MONEYPENNY
GORDON R. STRAIN

Could you say that a person who reads doesn't like other people? Isn't a book a person, or better yet, 20 personages who feel, share, dance, love, hate, and die between the rectangular pages?

He truly did not know the answer.

But the debate always surged inside of him in the middle of the dusty shelves of the bookstore that bent, weighed down by the various books of diverse patinas, themes, and sizes. They intercross and imprison, the leaning bookcases, with their arms inundated by woody pulp; but the trap of the books themselves was more difficult to see.

Upon plucking a book and liberating its spine, a web of silvered threads of revelry awaited him.

To read more is to further entangle oneself…

To lose one's self…

Slowly.

Word by word; line by line.

The turning of pages becomes automatic.

Unconscious.

And the distance between the predator and victim closes.

The jarring discordant little silver bell sounds in his ears.

"Hello," says a preciously child-like voice.

"Lovely web."

Dianne Moneypenny was raised in southern Indiana and currently resides in Franklin, Indiana with her family. She is an Assistant Professor of Spanish at Indiana University East in Richmond, Indiana and has worked there since 2011. Moneypenny's writing usually takes the form of the scholarship of teaching and learning or Medieval Spanish literature, but being creative in various ways has always been a source of renewal. Professor Moneypenny and her Spanish students use bilingual books to promote literacy in the Richmond Hispanic community by visiting local elementary schools, so melding her creative talents into bilingual stories was a natural choice for this project.

Gordon Strain was born and raised in Indianapolis and currently lives in Franklin, Indiana with his partner Dianne, his stepdaughter Lexi and his daughter Josephine. He is an Associate Professor of Theatre as well as the Chair of the Theatre Department at Franklin College. While Gordon normally works in three dimensions, he has always had a great love for creative writing. His latest project *The Diminutive Man* is a blend of sculptures, paintings, photographs, writings and performance pieces that attempt to show the scale of the world around us. He is so happy to be collaborating on this project to help promote literacy.

WILL SHORTZ

WRITER'S BLOCK

Each row and column in the grid below contains the five-letter last name of a famous writer. For example, the first row contains the letters of (Stephen) CRANE. Cross off the letters as you use them. When you're done, the 25 remaining letters in the grid, reading in order line by line, will spell a quotation by Virginia Woolf.

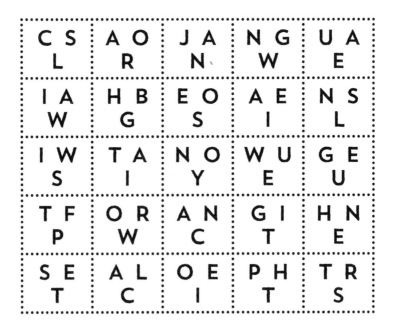

C S L	A O R	J A N	N G W	U A E
I A W	H B G	E O S	A E I	N S L
I W S	T A I	N O Y	W U E	G E U
T F P	O R W	A N C	G I T	H N E
S E T	A L C	O E I	P H T	T R S

What's an enigmatologist? It's Will Shortz, the world's only academically accredited puzzle master. He designed his own major program at Indiana University, which in 1974 led to his one-of-a-kind degree in Enigmatology, the study of puzzles. Will has been the puzzle master for NPR's "Weekend Edition Sunday" since the program's start in 1987, crossword editor of *The New York Times* since 1993, editor of *Games* magazine for 15 years, and the founder and director of the American Crossword Puzzle Tournament, which has been held annually since 1978. He also founded the World Puzzle Championship in 1992, and he co-founded the World Puzzle Federation in 1999.

Quotation: "Language is wine upon the lips." —*Virginia Woolf*
Down: *Swift, O'Hara, Joyce, Waugh, Alger*
Across: *Crane, Ibsen, Stowe, Twain, Scott*

LIZA HYATT

IMMRAM
CATHERINE MEEHAN
(The Voyage of Catherine Meehan)

She was seven when her family left Co. Cork
and for seven weeks and more they sailed
and on the first day they watched
the green hills of the West,
from the stories of heroes and magic she loved,
fade like a dream into the growing horizon.
And then it was into another west
beyond her imagination, no land in sight,
only the sky and sea and restless change.

Her Ma and Da told her other stories as they sailed,
to comfort her, to comfort themselves, to convince
their hearts, their bodies aching from separation,
that they were brave, not banished.
Stories about a better life where,
when they worked as hard as they always had,
they might achieve more than not drowning
in poverty's punishment, which is the most
they would achieve back home.

They told her stories of other voyagers,
of St. Brendan who sailed to the Land of Youth,
and of Bran mac Feabhail who sailed on and on
to lands unknown because he would turn to ash
if he set foot in Ireland again.
And on days when the sea did not toss them wildly
like an angry god, and they could emerge
from the belly of the ship into the sun,
and it was there that they opened their only book

and taught her to read the words *boat, sea,*
storm, rain, days, nights, dove and *leaf,*
and most nights she would fall asleep
curled into her mother's warmth,
spelling these words in her mind, knowing
that they were to be adrift as long, longer than Noah,
feeling her mother and father's faith
in some god-given promise of a future
wrapped around her like a blanket,

learning from them how to make hope
grow out of fear, how to carry it with her
like a scrap of green in the beak
of her strong, winged heart,
how to trust in flowing currents and wind and time
and their voyage toward an unsettled land
where life could grow
out of the ashes of their grief
and begin anew.

THE INDIANAPOLIS GAZETTE
Indianapolis' First Newspaper

RAY E. BOOMHOWER

About two weeks before Christmas in 1821, a family, after an arduous journey from Jeffersonville, Indiana, finally stopped their wagon before their home in the new state capital of Indianapolis. Inside the four-horse wagon in which they had made the trip were the family's meager possessions and the items upon which they would depend for their livelihood—the type, cases, press and other materials necessary for equipping a printing office. From a one-room cabin, George Smith, with assistance from his daughter Elizabeth and a recently hired journeyman printer lodged in a nearby cabin, on January 28, 1822, published the inaugural issue of the first newspaper ever printed in Indianapolis—the *Indianapolis Gazette*. For the next year, until the appearance of the *Western Censor and Emigrant's Guide*, the *Gazette* served as one of the few means of state, national, and international news for the fledgling state capital.

In addition to his important role as newspaper editor, Smith during his life also opened one of the first real estate agencies in Indianapolis and served two terms as an associate judge of the circuit court. John H. B. Nowland, describing Smith in his sketches of prominent citizens of the city, noted that he "was a man of warm feeling and devotion to his friends, and would go any length to serve and accommodate one. He cared nothing for money or property further than to make himself and his family comfortable." Smith also stood out in the community by the way he wore his hair, braided, hanging down his back in a queue. His choice of hairstyle got him in trouble one day with a lawyer named Gabriel Johnson. During an argument between the two men, Johnson grabbed the judge by queue and seemed to have the upper hand for a time. Nowland noted, however, that Smith managed to rally and "administered to the lawyer a sound trashing."

By the time Smith, with the assistance of his stepson and partner Nathaniel Bolton, placed the *Gazette* before the public, newspapers were well entrenched on the Hoosier scene. In 1804 Elihu Stout had printed the first newspaper in what was then the Indiana Territory, the *Indiana Gazette* at Vincennes. Other newspaper editors set up shop as settlements grew: Madison had the *Western Eagle* in 1813, Brookville the *Enquirer* and *Indiana Telegraph* in 1815 and shortly thereafter the *Indiana Register* in Vevay. Between Indiana's admission as a state in 1816 and 1829, papers were also established in Greencastle, Centerville, New Albany, Richmond, Salem, Terre Haute, and, of course, Indianapolis.

Smith was born in Lancaster, Pennsylvania in 1784. There are differing accounts on where Smith first learned the printing trade. Some historians have him serving as an apprentice with the Bradfords, colonial printers in Pennsylvania, another with the *Lexington Observer* in Lexington, Kentucky. Wherever he started, Smith, as did many other apprentices, underwent a painful initiation into the printing world. As the low man on the totem pole, apprentices were expected to run errands for the shop owner and his family, sweep the shop, keep the fires kindled, wash type, carry water for cleaning and wetting paper, and other onerous tasks. The chore dreaded most by printing apprentices involved the pelts used for ink balls. These pelts were soaked in chamber lye and gave the entire shop "a characteristic reeking smell."

After completing his apprenticeship, Smith worked for a number of printing shops, including one that produced the *Liberty Hall and Cincinnati Gazette* newspaper. While working in Chillicothe, Ohio in the early 1800s, he met and married Nancy Bolton, a widow with one son, Nathaniel. George and Nancy Smith eventually had a daughter, Elizabeth, born in Chillicothe on February 17, 1809. Elizabeth's earliest memories centered on the printing office, which often was located in the house the family occupied. Both children helped out by doing small jobs in Smith's print shop.

In 1820 the Smith family, which also included Nancy Smith's brother, Uncle Nat Cox, well-known for his skill as a hunter, carpenter, and practical joker, was "seized with the fever of emigration" and decided to move to the young state of Indiana. According to Elizabeth, her father had originally booked passage for the family down the Ohio River on board the steam packet *General Pike*. Nancy, however, upon seeing the steamboat, flatly refused to travel on what was to her an obviously dangerous craft. Instead, the family made the journey to Jeffersonville, Indiana, on a timber boat that was steered by Nat Cox. Upon reaching Jeffersonville the family hired a wagon for the trip to Corydon, then the state capital. Displeased with Corydon (what upset Smith about the area is unclear), the family returned to Jeffersonville, and there Smith opened a print shop.

The business in Jeffersonville, however, was merely a short stop for Smith, who in moving to Indiana had his eye set on establishing his printing trade in the newly established capital of Indianapolis. Perhaps as Stout had in picking Vincennes as the home for his newspaper, Smith looked forward to winning a contract with Indiana government as the official state printer, a distinction the Gazette later achieved. With the sale of lots in Indianapolis set for the fall of 1821, Smith left Jeffersonville and walked the 111 miles north for the sale. Upon reaching Indianapolis, he bought two lots at the corner of Maryland and West Streets at the intersection of Missouri Street. One of these lots included on it a cabin built by a Kentucky squatter who had deserted it and went back to his native state. Returning to Jeffersonville, again on foot, Smith prepared his family for the move north, all except Nathaniel Bolton, who remained behind to finish some printing work for the state. It was a rough trip; the only settlements the family passed through on their journey were Paoli, Bedford, and Brownstown. They also had to endure a heavy snowstorm, which stopped them dead in their tracks for two days.

Upon reaching Indianapolis, Smith, as he had in other locations, set up a print shop in the family home, a one-room cabin that also served as bedroom, dining room, and kitchen. Recalling those early days in Indianapolis, Elizabeth noted that her bed consisted of "two old sugar troughs with rails and short board laid crossways, on which was placed a good feather bed 'made up nice.'" Her father and mother slept on a bed made with buckeye logs and rails, overlaid with brush. Uncle Nat Cox and a journeyman printer hired to help with work at the fledgling newspaper slept in a neighboring cabin owned by Doctor Kenneth A. Scudder.

In spite of the cramped conditions, Smith, with thirteen-year-old Elizabeth's help (she had learned how to set type that winter) issued the first edition of the *Indianapolis Gazette* on January 28, 1822. Jacob Piatt Dunn Jr., in his history of the city, *Greater Indianapolis*, said that the *Gazette* was printed on "an old-fashioned, two-pull, Ramage hand press." Such a primitive press limited a printer's production to approximately seventy-five impressions per hour. After setting type, forms were hand-inked by Smith and Bolton with buckskin balls stuffed with wool. When not in use, these balls were kept soft with liberal doses of raccoon oil. The two outside pages of the four-page newspaper were usually printed early in the week, according to Dunn, with the inside pages on Friday and the whole paper released to subscribers on Saturday.

A subscription to the *Gazette* cost two dollars if paid within two months after subscribing, two dollars and fifty cents if within six months, or three dollars thereafter. In lieu of cash—often in short supply in pioneer days—the newspaper accepted for payment "produce of every description...if delivered at the office." Rags, a vital substance for the production of newspapers in those days, were also taken in lieu of cash. This barter system for purchasing newspapers continued in Indiana for many years. All the way up until the late nineteenth century, small-town newspapers took produce and livestock for payment.

In that first issue of the *Gazette*, Smith issued the following statement of purpose for his periodical:

> We, this day, issue the first number of the Indianapolis
> Gazette, without comment: believing that we shall receive

a generous support so long as we continue to publish it on principle consonant to the government and the times we live under. The Gazette will be enlarged to a sheet not inferior to any in the state as soon as the support will justify it.

Smith had all the confidence in the world that such support would be forthcoming. Although local news was often lacking in pioneer newspapers, Smith did in that first issue expound a bit on the bright future facing Indianapolis:

> The improvement of this town since the sale of lots in October last has surpassed the expectations of those who entertained the greatest hopes of its future prosperity. There have been erected forty dwelling houses and several workshops since that period, and many other buildings are now in contemplation. One grist and two saw-mills are now in operation, within one mile of the centre of the town, and several others are nearly ready to be put into operation, equally as near. Business is comparatively lively at this time. We have, already, mechanics and professional men of the following description and number, to wit: 13 carpenters and joiners, 4 cabinet makers, 8 blacksmiths, 4 boot and shoe makers, 2 tailors, 1 hatter, 2 tanners, 1 saddler, 1 cooper, 4 bricklayers, 2 merchants, 7 houses of entertainment, 3 groceries, 1 school master, 4 physicians, one minister of the gospel and 3 counselors at law.

There were numerous problems to be faced, however, by anyone foolhardy enough to attempt publishing a newspaper on the frontier during the early nineteenth century. "The first problem of the printer," noted one Indiana newspaper historian, "was to get paper, the second to get news, and the third to get paid." Securing the necessary paper for printing a newspaper proved to be a difficult task for any Indiana publisher at this time. Until 1826, when one was opened north of Madison, there were no paper mills in the state. According to Justin H. Brown, an early chronicler of Smith's life, the paper for the *Gazette*'s first issue was brought by wagon from Springfield, Ohio by George Smith's father. Inadequate paper supplies sometimes led to the newspaper suspending publication for a week or two.

For news to fill the *Gazette*'s columns, Smith and Bolton did not have the luxury of turning to a newsroom of trained reporters, ready at a moment's notice to scour the countryside, unearthing interesting tidbits for readers. Instead, they had to rely on a unpredictable source—the mail. At a time when local news was "all over town," noted Dunn, by the time it made its way to an editor, national and international news dominated newspaper columns. In fact, one scholar has noted, the "more exotic the location, the more news value an item seemed to possess in the minds of pioneer editors." To relay this kind of information to his readers, Smith, and other publishers, relied on mail dispatches concerning messages from the federal government and items of interest culled from other newspapers scattered throughout the country. Speeches and other messages from the president and Congress were related to readers in their entirety, without the news analysis that is commonplace today—a boon to politicians wanting to communicate their ideas and plans directly to their constituents.

There was one problem: Indianapolis had no post office, nor any regular mail service, at the time the *Gazette* started publication.

Smith set out to remedy the situation. On January 30, 1822, a meeting was held at Hawkins' tavern to arrange a private mail service. Under this system, all the mail for the community would be gathered at one post office and brought back to the city by a rider hired especially for that task. Those attending the meeting hired Aaron Drake as carrier and arranged with him to bring the mail from Connersville once a month. Drake issued a circular to postmasters requesting that they forward all mail for Indianapolis to the Connersville office. Drake's first distribution of the mail was very dramatic. "He returned from his...trip after nightfall," according to Brown, "his horn sounding far through the woods, arousing the people who turned out in the bright moonlight to greet him and learn the news." An Indianapolis post office finally opened for business on March 7, 1822, putting Drake out of a job. Even with a post office in the community, the flow of news could be halted by everything from bad weather to incompetent post riders, who sometimes fortified themselves with alcohol before setting out on their journeys.

Even with adequate paper supplies and fresh news from the mails, the *Gazette*'s owners faced a never-ending struggle to make ends meet. George Cottman, *Indiana Magazine of History* founder and a printer himself, noted that in the early days of Indiana statehood "the sentiment seemed to prevail that the newspaper man and the doctor could wait for their pay a little longer than any one else." Along with subscriptions, Smith relied for income on classified advertising (Calvin Fletcher was a frequent advertiser on behalf of his law practice) and printing such items as pamphlets, handbills, cards and blank forms of every description, which, Smith and Bolton claimed, would be "executed at this office on a short notice and on moderate terms."

To help keep their business solvent, Smith and Bolton also printed and offered for sale through advertisements in the *Gazette* books and almanacs. One of the first books the Indianapolis printers offered to the public was one titled *The Indiana Justice and Farmers Scrivener*, which contained information on the office and duties of justices of the peace, sheriffs, clerks, coroners, constables, township officers, jurymen, and jailers. Also, the book included a number of examples of written contracts that a farmer, mechanic or trader would have occasion to use during their life. Even in pioneer days, lawyers had to contend with a do-it-yourself ethic. An 1831 almanac printed by Smith and Bolton offered information not only on the phases of the moon and aspects of the planets, but also listings of federal and state officials and helpful advice for Indianapolis gardeners.

Smith and Bolton published the *Gazette* together until July 1829, when politics came between them. Until that time, the newspaper had been politically neutral, a path that Bolton wished to continue. His stepfather, however, wanted the paper to support Andrew Jackson and his policies. Bolton remained in charge of the *Gazette* while Smith announced his intentions to start a new paper to be known as *The Jacksonian*. In an August 6, 1829, letter printed in the *Gazette*, Smith proclaimed to readers that materials for *The Jacksonian* "are now ready and will shortly be here from Cincinnati." Unfortunately, if any such newspaper was published, there is no record of it today.

Smith's dream of a pro-Jackson newspaper did come true. On October 22, 1829, George L. Kinnard took over as part owner of the Gazette, changed its name to the *Indiana State Gazette*, turned the newspaper's politics to pro-Democratic, and staunchly supported Jackson. In late March 1830 the newspaper's last ties to the Smith family dissolved, as Bolton sold his interest to Alexander F. Morrison and the paper's name was changed again, to the *Indiana Democrat and State Gazette.*

After leaving the printing business, Smith retired to his farm, called Mount Jackson, which was located on Indianapolis's near west side. After what was described as a long illness, Smith died on April 10, 1836. His stepson Bolton took over the Mount Jackson farm and lived there with his wife, the poet Sarah Bolton. The two operated a tavern on the site until 1845, when the Boltons sold the property to the state as the new home for the Central Hospital for the Insane. In 1851 Bolton was elected as state librarian and four years later was named as consul to Geneva, Switzerland by President Franklin Pierce. He remained in Switzerland until 1857, when ill health forced him to return to Indianapolis. He died on November 26, 1858.

Most Indiana historians would probably agree that Smith was not an outstanding newspaper man. But he typified the pioneer editor and provided through the pages of his newspaper a valuable resource to his readers. As R. C. Buley noted in his classic *The Old Northwest,* the *Gazette* and other newspapers of its type played a vital role in pioneer society, furnishing "the bulk of the knowledge of the essentials of representative government," a task still being undertaken by newspapers today.

Ray E. Boomhower is senior editor at the Indiana Historical Society Press. He is the author of numerous books and articles on Indiana history, including *Robert F. Kennedy and the 1968 Indiana Primary* (2008) and *The People's Choice: Congressman Jim Jontz of Indiana* (2012). In addition, he has written biographies on such notable figures as Gus Grissom, Ernie Pyle, John Bartlow Martin, and Lew Wallace. In 2010 he received the Regional Author Award in the annual Eugene and Marilyn Glick Indiana Authors Awards.

NORBERT KRAPF

WHAT MY UNCLE ASKED

Don't remember exactly when he asked
but still feel the force with which
he did. Uncle Fritz, my dad's brother

who, like my dad, never made it
to high school, was one helluva
squirrel hunter who worked

in a wood factory. He was as short
as my dad. They loved to share a beer.
Maybe I was still in college, maybe

in graduate school home for a visit.
We three were sitting together sipping
a brew in lawn chairs in the evening

watching a softball game across
the street on the parish ball diamond.
Uncle Fritz looked at me over the top

of his Schlitz bottle with the eye
of a man who would teach a young
whippersnapper a thing or two.

He and my dad grew up in the little
village of St. Henry, not far west
of the somewhat bigger Ferdinand,

south of the town of Huntingburg.
"Did you happen to know," he began,
"that once upon a time in Ferdinand

there was a black woman named
Ida Hagen who was the postmaster?"
He could have added, "Did they

teach you that in your fancy classes?"
but he did and didn't at the same time.
He knew they didn't talk about that

in the schools we attended, knew that
if I was honest I would have to say No!
He looked me right in the eye and waited.

I think maybe I shook my head
and mumbled, "Huh uh." But I
never forgot Uncle Fritz's lesson.

He put you in my mind, Ida Hagen.
It has taken me decades to find my way,
but now I knock at Doc Wollenmann's door.

I come to call on the black young woman
who was the first to graduate from grade
school in the county. Became a clerk

in the post office, worked in the apothecary
and passed the exam to be certified
by the state to run your own pharmacy.

Became fluent in the German spoken
by my ancestors. Converted to Catholicism.
Ida, it's time to educate myself about you.

NORBERT KRAPF

IDA HAGEN IN THE FERDINAND PO, 1904

Miss Ida, Miss Ida, you have two open ears.
You look and see with two beautiful ears.
You know well what you want to hear.

You stand behind the counter in the PO.
You are the black clerk in a white PO.
At sixteen you know how it must go.

You put heart & soul into what you hear.
You give all of yourself to what you hear.
Somebody asks you, *Wie geht es mit Dir?*

Jawohl, you are here to learn.
Their language you want to learn.
Their language is what you earn.

You are a black girl in a little German town,
an African American in a German American town.
You listen to how their every word goes down.

Ida, you work for the Swiss doctor man.
Your boss is the Swiss doctor postman.
Folks here call him Doc. Wollenmann.

Mr. Doc Wollenmann stands behind you.
He is the white Republican who hired you.
Doc Wollenmann is proud of what you do.

Doc Wollenmann is of the party of Abe.
Doc is a proud member of the party of Abe.
He carries his Lincoln loyalty into the grave.

Es geht mir ganz gut! is what you say.
You stamp & send their letters on their way.
The Germans smile. You make their day.

NORBERT KRAPF

ANOTHER DOCTOR'S SON
ON MAIN STREET, FERDINAND
in memory of Pat Backer

Ida, there is a Main Street neighbor
I want you to meet, Pat Backer.
His daddy, father of ten children,
was town doctor well after you left.

Pat was a lover of the written word.
He loved literature, quoted poetry,
admired the phrase well turned,
as Germans love fine woodworking.

When I was a freshman in college,
struggling with composition,
he took me in hand, showed me
how to red ink excess words,

burn them out, cut to the heart
of any matter I wanted to express.
Pat gave me quiet encouragement
mixed with a model of concentration.

By the end of that year he was gone
from the Catholic college for men
isolated in the middle of corn fields
at the edge of the northern prairie.

After graduating from Marquette,
Pat came back home to Main Street.
An illness of the mind was not kind
to the young man who mentored me.

Miss Ida, Pat Backer led me to you.
He got on your trail, followed you
back to the Freedom Settlement,
dug up facts, praised your mind,

took the measure of your accomplishment
despite the odds stacked against you.
He sang the praises of how your family
and community made the sweet potato

flourish like never before in the hills
where both of you were born. He praised
your success in school, your determination.
He put a portrait of you in the town paper.

It was as though he painted you in full color
and framed that portrait and hung it on
the wall of a small room in Doctor
Alois Wollenmann's Swiss Chalet.

Pat Backer wanted us to know about
his Main Street neighbor Ida Hagen.
Pat came calling on you, Miss Ida.
The best of himself he gave to you.

He left you for me to sing in words.
He had a sharp eye for local treasure.
Even when his illness held him down,
he looked up to you, his neighbor.

Pat Backer would love a woman of words.
He admired spirit and determination
and dedication to learning and growth,
someone who set goals and overcame

the obstacles against achieving them.
A man who knew struggle, he saw you
as a woman of spirit who never gave up.
Pat left you for me to find and sing.

NORBERT KRAPF

WHEN IDA HAGEN WOKE IN A SWISS CHALET ON MAIN STREET, FERDINAND

Ida, descendant of one free black
and some slaves, what did you
wake hearing in this house
a hundred years ago?

Did you hear the voice
of Doc Wollenman's wife,
whom you must have met
before she died giving birth
to the stillborn daughter
whose cries he never heard?

Did the late Mrs. W send you
messages about how to care
for the boys she left behind?

Did you wake hearing the voice
of your mama Millie? Was Millie
always on your mind when you
stamped letters in the little post
office in the same building
in which you also helped out
in the apothecary before
and after you passed the state
exam certifying you as a registered
pharmacist in Indiana?

Did you ever wake speaking
German to yourself, as you
spoke it to the Germans,
some of whom were my
relatives? I think you could
have been my tutor. By the time
I was born in 1943, you were
fifty-five and long gone from
Indiana to Detroit, Michigan.
You could have taught me
how to speak the language
of my Franconian ancestors
they say came out of your
mouth ever so fluently on
your African American tongue.
You could have shown me
how to round-shape my mouth
to make the umlaut sounds
that made us laugh together.

I'm thinking, Miss Ida, that
you must have hummed spirituals
in Doc Wollenmann's Swiss chalet
on the Main Street of this little
German town founded by Croatian
missionary priest Rev. Josef Kundek
in 1840, the same year your great-
grandfather Emanuel Pinkston,
a free black from Georgia, founded
the Freedom Settlement in which
you were born in 1888.

I have read that you became
a Catholic one Christmas Eve
in Gary. Did the choir sing
Stille Nacht, heilige Nacht,
Silent Night, holy night,
when you took this step?

Did you like Gegorian chant?
How about the sound of Latin?
I got to think you must have later
loved Ma Rainey and Bessie Smith.
And what about the New Orleans
trumpet of Little Louie Armstrong?

In Doc Wollenman's chalet,
did you wake up hearing
work songs and field hollers

coming out of the mouths
of your brothers and sisters
and aunts and uncles
and grand- and great-grandparents
remembered from the days of slavery
in Kentucky and Georgia
as they tended the vegetables
and melons they grew in the fields
of the Freedom Settlement where
you were born and hauled them
on wagons pulled by mules
and sold them on the streets
of Main Street, Ferdinand,
Dubois County, Indiana?

Ida, I write at a desk in downtown,
Indianapolis, where you lived
and worked for a time as a pharmacist.
I'm staring into your deep and dark eyes
in a photo taken of you as a beautiful
young woman elegantly dressed
with a satin collar around your neck
and small circles hanging from your ears.

I feel you see into me more than I
can see into you. You know me
better than I can ever know you.
It's so clear your eyes could heal.
The way your lush lips come
together say you know what

to say and when to say it
but that you always know
more than you usually say.

I want to listen, hear your voice.
My ears are open to your music.
My eyes are open to your vision.
I'm ready for you to sing me
some bars of the country blues,
unless you prefer to scat sing
some downtown or uptown jazz.
Maybe you would dive deep into
dark love the way soulful Billie did.
Maybe we could even pray together.
I'd be glad to read you some Rilke.

WILLIAM HERSCHELL

THE OTHER HOOSIER POET

RAY E. BOOMHOWER

Upon awaking one day in May 1919 at his home at 958 Tecumseh Place near Woodruff Place in Indianapolis, a longtime feature reporter for the *Indianapolis News* trudged wearily to breakfast. Turning to his wife, Josephine, the journalist complained that he had no idea what to write about for that day's issue. Unsure of what to do, he picked up his typewriter and traveled out of town, finally ending his sojourn in the countryside at Brandywine Creek in Greenfield, Indiana. At the creek he spied an older man fishing while sitting on a log. When the reporter commented on the area's beauty, the fisherman responded, "I can't complain, after all God's been pretty good to Indiana, ain't he?"

The offhand remark on this lonely stretch of water inspired the reporter, William Herschell, to write his masterpiece, "Ain't

God Good to Indiana?" The poem proved popular with not only with Hoosiers (the work is inscribed on a bronze plaque in the rotunda of the Indiana Statehouse), but with readers from around the country who clamored for copies. The demand grew so great that Herschell's wife had to issue special printed facsimiles of the poem.

During his career at the *News*, which started in 1902 and ended with his death at age sixty-six in 1939, Herschell contributed countless poems and feature articles for the newspaper's Saturday edition. In addition, his World War I song "Long Boy" contributed the doughboy refrain, "Goodbye Ma! Goodbye Pa! Goodbye mule with your old heehaw!" to the nation's vocabulary. Herschell, a close companion of famed Hoosier Poet James Whitcomb Riley, worked in a corner of the newspaper's ninth floor that came to be known as the Idle Ward. Along with Herschell, other members of that delightful company included cartoonists Gaar Williams and Frank McKinney "Kin" Hubbard, creator of the renowned cracker-barrel philosopher Abe Martin. The three men were all quite productive when it came to producing copy and illustrations, but they seemed idle to other newspaper employees because they always seemed to be able to find time to discuss and gossip about the issues of the day.

Born in Spencer, Indiana on November 17, 1873, Herschell was the eldest of six children born to Scottish immigrants John and Martha (Leitch) Herschell. Trained as a blacksmith in his native Scotland, John worked for the Indianapolis and Vincennes Railroad and later served as foreman for a quarry near Spencer that supplied limestone for the state capitol in Indianapolis. One of William's earliest memories involved his father sitting by lamplight to recite to his family the poems of Robert Burns. John's work with the

Evansville, Rockport, and Eastern Railroad took him and his family to a succession of communities in southwestern Indiana, including Rockport, Evansville, Huntingburg, and Princeton.

Although at best an unfocused student, Herschell did display some of the writing talent he later used during his newspaper career. While in the Huntingburg school system he was falsely accused of running away with the teacher's pet dog. An unabashed Herschell penned the following in reply: "Teacher says I stole his dog / But why should I steal Jim, / When teacher's with me all day long / And I can look at him?" Herschell's talent for thumbing his nose at the school's authorities proved to be his undoing. As a seventh-grader, Herschell, already a solid supporter of the Republican Party, played hooky from school to carry in a political parade a banner that proclaimed, "A Vote for [Grover] Cleveland Means Souphouses." The school's principal found out about Herschell's truancy—and political persuasion—and expelled him from school, noting, "Inasmuch as William Herschell had gone into politics he could not possibly wish further education."

With the assistance of his father, Herschell found work as an apprentice railroad machinist. In 1894, when Eugene Debs's American Railway Union told its members to refuse to handle Pullman cars in support of striking workers at the Pullman plants in Illinois, Herschell allied himself closely with the union cause. With the strike's failure, Herschell found himself out of a job. Leaving the Hoosier State, Herschell toiled at a succession of jobs, including stints in Chicago, Buffalo, and Canada. Returning to the United States, he worked at an electric-light plant in North Tonawanda, New York. He eventually found his way back to his native state, where he worked as a night machinist for the Monon Railroad.

On a visit to his family in Princeton in 1896, Herschell met James McCormick, who just three years before had started the *Princeton Evening News*, an independent Republican Party daily. McCormick offered Herschell a job, telling him, "I'll give you $9 a week, if you can get it." Herschell did not discover what his editor had meant until the end of his first week at the newspaper. After everyone else on the paper had received his wages, there remained only $4.00 left for Herschell. Week after week there never seemed to be enough funds to pay Herschell his full salary. On one occasion, McCormick even had to borrow brown wrapping paper from a local butcher in order to publish his afternoon newspaper. An editorial dedicated the issue as "A Souvenir Edition to Our Creditors." To supplement his meager income, Herschell served as the Princeton correspondent for several larger newspapers, including the *Indianapolis News*. Herschell sometimes used his money from other publications to buy enough newsprint for McCormick to print his paper.

Although McCormick and Herschell became close friends, the publisher did not stand in his protégé's way when, in 1898, Herschell received a job offer from the *Evansville Journal*. Before Herschell left for his new duties, he found waiting for him in the newspaper's editorial office a gold watch—a going-away present from McCormick. Later, Herschell dedicated his 1922 book *Howdy All: And Other Care-Free Rhymes* to McCormick, noting that the editor taught him it was "easier to swing a pencil than a hammer." A year after starting at the Evansville newspaper, Herschell left to join the staff of the *Indianapolis Press* as a police reporter. With the folding of the *Press* after only sixteen months, Herschell moved to the *Terre Haute Tribune*. He returned to Indianapolis in 1902 for a position with the *Indianapolis Journal*.

Herschell's work at the *Journal* soon caught the attention of Dick Herrick, secretary to *Indianapolis News* editor Hilton U. Brown. Herrick told his boss that Herschell was "full of fun, can write rhymes and can make the dullest story read like a novel. He belongs here and ought to make a top feature man." Taking his secretary's advice, Brown hired Herschell in April 1902, beginning the reporter's thirty-seven-year association with the newspaper. In his early years on the *News*, Herschell served as a police and court reporter and won the lasting respect of the Indianapolis police department. At slack times, members of the department and local media conducted mock trials at an old bicycle barn. Conducted by the newspapermen, these trials often concluded with the officers having to pay a cigar or two in fines. Herschell presided over the proceedings as judge. His wife, Josephine, who also worked at the *News*, noted that her husband acted like "a regular roughneck when he came home at night after hanging around the police station all day. But he changed a lot after he became a feature writer." Josephine also noted that her husband used to jokingly scold a clock that he had been given as a boy, especially when he arrived home at a later time than he had told her to expect him. "We had a lovely life together," she said.

In 1911 *News* editor Richard Smith, impressed with Herschell's poetry, assigned him to write poems and feature articles for the newspaper's Saturday edition. Herschell's poems about such staples of city life as policemen, firemen, street urchins, and other characters appeared in a series titled "Songs of the City Streets." Later, his paeans to rural life were highlighted in the series "Ballads of the Byways." A fellow *News* employee noted that Herschell was a true democrat, a friend to everyone from bank presidents to truckers, and a person who could "rub elbows with prominent men at some important banquet, and the next day revel in a picnic at [Indianapolis's] Douglass park." The poetry Herschell wrote for the newspaper was collected and published in a number of books during his lifetime, including *Songs of the Streets and Byways* (1915), *The Kid Has Gone to the Colors and Other Verse* (1917), *The Smile Bringer and Other Bits of Cheer* (1919), *Meet the Folks* (1924), and *Hitch and Come In* (1928). A posthumous collection, *Song of the Morning and Other Poems*, which was put together by his widow, appeared in 1940.

Known simply as Bill to his friends inside and outside the newspaper, Herschell won the esteem of readers through his simple verses, flavored as they were with the dialect style pioneered so successfully by Riley. "There was no dullness where he was and there were no dead lines in what he wrote," Brown said of Herschell, who became well known for his laugh, described by Brown as a "musical roar" and which "preceded him wherever he appeared." Profiling Herschell for a biographical pamphlet produced by the *News* in 1926, B. Wallace Lewis described Herschell as looking "more like the manager of a successful retail store than a poet. He is big, with the kind of bigness that goes clear through. A round head, hair trimmed close, joins to a massive trunk with a powerful neck. The hands that once wielded a machinist's hammer are strong and grip yours as if they meant it."

With America's entry into World War I, the subject of Herschell's writing began to turn more and more to wartime matters. He produced for the *News* such poems as "The Service Flag" and "The Kid Has Gone to the Colors." His most successful effort, however, came after he spent time at Indianapolis's Fort Benjamin Harrison, which then served as an officers' training camp. Herschell became close friends with the camp's commander,

Major General Edwin F. Glenn. The two men often spent a part of each morning discussing news about the war and what was going on at the camp. During one meeting on May 18, 1917, Glenn asked Herschell to use his talents to write a war song. "These boys out here," Glenn said, "are sick of singing about 'Mother Dear' and 'Broken Hearts' and 'Gentle Eyes of Blue.' Give us something that will keep down homesickness, the curse of an army camp."

As he crossed the parade ground on his way to return to the office, Herschell spied a company of tall soldiers passing by, which gave him the inspiration to write about the army's "long boys." Driving back to downtown Indianapolis, he began to formulate the song's words and sang them to *News* photographer Paul Schideler. Charles Dennis, who worked just a few desks down from Herschell at the newspaper, remembered the day the reporter came back from Fort Harrison to work on the song "with pursed lips and corrugated brow, his blue eyes in a fine frenzy rolling." After seeing Herschell finish his writing, Dennis slipped into a chair next to the poet to view and hear the final result. "As he voiced the verses the workers in this hive of industry gathered about him," said Dennis. "Other workers from various parts of the building came in. He was obliged to sing it over and over again and though his throat became raw and raucous he kept his good humor through seventeen recalls, and the curtain went down amid the most appreciative applause."

The next day, Herschell submitted his work, titled "Long Boy," for Glenn's review. The general took an immediate liking to the song, especially the chorus line "I may not know what th' war's about, / But you bet, by gosh, I'll soon find out." Several members of Glenn's staff also expressed their satisfaction with the song, and the general asked Herschell to find someone to set the words to music so his troops could sing it on parade. Herschell responded by turning the lyrics over to Bradley Walker, an Indianapolis composer, who produced the music for the song. Just a week later, the troops at Fort Harrison sang "Long Boy" as they passed in review before Ohio governor James M. Cox. The song became an instant success, selling more than a million copies. Wabash College honored Herschell for his war verse by awarding him an honorary degree.

Herschell died on December 2, 1939 at his Indianapolis home. His last words to his wife were: "I'll whip it yet, Jo." Reminiscing about Herschell's life, the newspaper he served for so many years said that he had been a part of Indianapolis as much as the Indiana Soldiers and Sailors Monument. "He loved writing," said the *News*, "he loved to compose his sincere verse, but most of all he loved people. Otherwise he could not have written so inspiringly of their lives."

★

Ain't God Good to Indiana?
William Herschell

Ain't God good to Indiana?
Folks, a feller never knows
Just how close he is to Eden
Till, sometime, he ups an' goes
Seekin' fairer, greener pastures
Than he has right here at home,
Where there's sunshine in the clover
An' honey in th' comb;

Where the ripples on th' river

Kinda chuckles as they flow—

Ain't God good to Indiana?

Ain't He, fellers? Ain't He, though?

Ain't God good to Indiana?

Seems to me He has a way

Gittin' me all outta humor

Just to see how long I'll stay

When I git th' gypsy feelin'

That I'd like to find a spot

Where th' clouds ain't quite so restless,

Or th' sun don't shine so hot.

But, I don't git far, I'll tell you,

Till I'm whisperin' soft an' low:

Ain't God good to Indiana?

Ain't He, fellers? Ain't He, though?

Ain't God good to Indiana?

Other spots may look as fair,

But they lack th' soothin' somethin'

In th' Hoosier sky and air.

They don't have that snug-up feelin'

Like a mother gives a child;

They don't soothe you, soul an' body,

With their breezes soft an' mild.

They don't know th' joys of Heaven

Have their birthplace here below;

Ain't God good to Indiana?

Ain' He, fellers? Ain't He, though?

ASSEMBLING A POEM

after Joseph Cornell

Begin with this box, common as a star chart,
and blow into it till something shows up:
maybe the dim clarinets of Standard Oil with their flaming bells,
or the rows of white storage tanks like hatboxes for giants,
each with a curling staircase dangling from one side like a ribbon.

Build boxcars and tiny houses, your grandmother
hovering in a doorway like a witch,
your elfin grandfather painting wooden ducks
on stakes to poke into a lawn.

Add your mother in a red headband, who just lost a baby,
and your father drinking a shot and a beer, probably bored,
though you wouldn't have guessed it then—
all the elements you thought were frozen forever like the plot
        of a fairy tale,
with death a gory ornament, maybe a frame,
instead of the unhappy end.

Time lurched slow like the freight trains behind the house,
marked by whipped cream birthday cakes and tabletop Christmas trees.
In the Chevy's backseat you'd shut your eyes over the humming
       bridges of East Chicago
and open them only at the Sinclair dinosaur guarding the oilfield.
You wanted to run up a staircase like Cinderella
and spin like a weathervane over that concrete forest.

Now poetry arranges the black car, white tanks,
paper stars on a circle of blue
and you in a skirt like a cocktail umbrella on the windy top.

Poetry restores the mother and father
and old folks whose story you couldn't understand.
Poetry brings back even seven-year-old you,
now your grandma's age and waving from a different door
as the cars and bikes and children of the world stream past.

This poem originally appeared on Indiana Humanities' poem-a-day feature, curated by Indiana Poet Laureate George Kalamaras, in April 2014.

BONNIE MAURER

THE POEM STANDS
ON ITS HEAD
BY THE
WINDOW

Even so, the poem cannot reverse the order of things.
The fruit bowl on the table spills plums,
blue and speckled, still ready to split their skins.
Brains still blow up at markets and blood rains the beach.
Coins knock and jangle, clocks collide, and a buckeye,
polished as childhood, slides from the poem's pocket
into the rivered shag. Guns, bombs, missiles still fly in its head.
The poem's feet flex a silent beat. Can the poem move a line
of soldiers aimed to kill? Change a word to stop the genocide?
The poem sighs, heaves, utters the moans and sputters
of earth, the lost vowels groaning—hearts jettisoning
from daily life. The poem has seen the blue marble fully lit from space.
So, what gives, the poem asks, rearranging roots, hands and
      feet and blood and
breath to accommodate a world of violence and wonder? The poem
floats on a blue scribbled ground and ochre sky, reaches like Jacob's ladder.

When can the poem come down, walk among the pineapple groves,

tupelo trees, the coasts of Maine and Madagascar,

under the mottled green leaves safe again to marvel at you and me?

From War, Literature & the Arts *and* So It Goes, The Literary Magazine of the Kurt Vonnegut Memorial Library (Third Edition).

JUMBLE®

that scrambled word game

by JEFF KNUREK and DAVID L. HOYT

Unscramble these six Jumbles,
one letter to each square,
to form six ordinary words.

TOLINO

CABLEH

NAMREN

TEERLT

RONELL

KRAMTE

LIKE us @ facebook.com/Jumble

INDY READS:
THE MOVIE,
take one.
Quiet on the set!

INDY READS BOOKS

Leo can't
make it.
Have you
ever acted?

Me? Wow, Mr.
Scorsese. I've
done some
local theater.
May I call you,
"Marty?"

WHEN THE BOOKSTORE
WAS THE SETTING FOR A
NEW MOVIE, IT HAD A ---

Now arrange the circled letters
to form the surprise answer, as
suggested by the above cartoon.

Answer:

◯◯◯◯◯◯   ◯◯◯◯

JUMBLE
60
Years of
That Scrambled
Word Game
1954   2014

David L. Hoyt and Jeff Knurek began inventing toys and games together back at the turn of the century (the year 2000). David lives in Chicago and he authors puzzles for 20+ daily word games. As this nation's most syndicated puzzle creator, he is often called *The Man Who Puzzles America.* For more about David L. Hoyt, visit *www.dlhoyt.com*

Jeff lives near Indianapolis and is an award-winning toy and game inventor, consumer product developer, puzzle creator, cartoonist and musician. Together, David and Jeff create the world's favorite puzzles, including Jumble which is celebrating its 60th anniversary this year. For more about Jeff Knurek, *visit www.brainstorm-designs.com*

KAREN KOVACIK

FLOODING
THE HOUSE

Roll up the sunshine and clean wood floors—
boom out the low notes in baritone hymns
for my loved house without windows or doors.

Fashion a rowboat with soup spoons for oars.
Hack holes in the roof, let the rain pour in
then roll up the sunshine and clean wood floors.

Imagine old Noah with no view of shore.
Dispatch Gulliver and the Brothers Grimm
to my strange house without windows or doors.

Empty the cupboards, the tall chest of drawers.
Cull bookshelves of rendezvous, wild and prim.
Roll up the sunshine and clean wood floors.

Then turn on the hoses and let them pour:
bring buckets of catfish to root and swim
in my drowned house without windows or doors.

Let teacups cascade on the stream's corridor,

the bedroom's pond now swampy and dim.

The sun rides the rapids over wood floors

in my blurred house without windows or doors.

This poem originally appeared in Valparaiso Poetry Review.

HOW TO SWIM

LARRY D. SWEAZY

The door handle was cold and wet, and at that very moment, Tom Wilson regretted not wearing gloves. The thought quickly passed as soon as he entered the dry store. It was warm and comfortable inside, and once the door was fully closed behind him, the outside world and the dreary spring weather affecting it vanished completely. The only sign of rain dripped from Tom's hat onto the black floor mat. He stared at the little puddle for a long second before wiping his feet. A lake was starting to grow underneath him.

At first sight, it seemed as if no one was working in the store. The lights were on, the shelves fully stocked. Most of them overflowed to piles on the floor; books dutifully waiting to be put in their rightful place. There was no apparent sign of a resident cat, which Tom was glad of. He was horribly allergic to cats.

A regulator clock ticked from somewhere close by, unseen like a heartbeat, and the fluorescent lights hummed overhead, offering the only interior sound. A white orchid with a fading purple stamen drooped next to the sleeping cash register.

The not so subtle aroma of books, old and new, permeated from every direction—like there was a fan blowing on a scented wax air freshener, spreading the smell of slow-rotting pulp around the room on purpose. Tom found the smell comforting, like coming home to a favorite stew simmering on the stove in winter. He had read once that the mold in old books was addicting, could cause hallucinations. He'd never researched that specific type of mold any further to see if such a thing was true, but it made sense to him. He especially loved the smell of old books; tattered yellow pages written in the style of language that no longer existed. That smell could change a man if he breathed it in deeply, touched it in just the right way.

Oddly, Tom was uncomfortable standing alone in the bookstore; it almost felt like he had let himself into a stranger's house unannounced. He looked over his shoulder just to make sure the OPEN sign was flipped the right way in the door. It was. Along with a list of the operating hours. It was getting toward the end of the day; the gloom from outside reached in and made it feel later, grayer. He had forty-minutes. That would be plenty of time—if there was anyone around.

"May I help you?" The voice, female, came from behind a bookshelf to his left.

"I'm looking for a book," Tom said, standing in his place, calling out with a lift of his chin. Then he scanned the room, relaxed, took in as much as he could from where he was standing.

The store was small, maybe seven hundred square feet, crammed with books ceiling to floor, and not much else. These days other bookstores, mostly the chains, were stocked with a plethora of other merchandise to pad their bottom lines; toys, games, art, bright colored doodads to attract the kids—who can say no to a kid in bookstore? Books were like an afterthought. But not here—they were everywhere. He was encouraged, and amazed, as always, that there were so many writers in the world.

The woman stepped out from behind the bookshelf, offering a puff of air out of the corner of her mouth to vanquish a strand of stray hairs that obscured her line of sight. Her hands were cradled full of books. "You came to the right place."

There was no hint of a smile on her plain face. She was in her early forties with untouched gray hair just starting to show at her formerly blonde temples, and wore comfortable casual clothes; not quite a Birkenstock hippie, but close. Thin turquoise earrings dangled from her ears, and her faded smock would have been called a dashiki once upon a time.

Tom stood still, and watched the woman move effortlessly toward the front counter. She didn't look like she needed help, or would be glad to accept it, so he restrained the urge to offer any assistance.

With as much ease and care as she could muster, the woman unloaded the books on the counter next to the doomed orchid. "Returns," she offered sadly.

"I'm sorry?"

"The books. They're returns. Can't sell them. The covers are stripped, and sent back to the publisher for credit. It's a consignment racket." There was a hard edge to the woman's voice; a sudden show of bitterness fell over her face, wrinkles above her lips grew deeper, then disappeared as suddenly as it had appeared.

Tom never broke eye contact with her. He didn't know what to say.

"Oh," she paused, "right, you're here for a book, not a business lesson. Sorry about that. I get carried away sometimes. I hate to send back books. I'd just as soon leave them on the shelves forever until that perfect reader walks in the door and finds one, but I have to eat don't I? There's only so much shelf space in this place, and new books come out all of the time."

"I suppose they do," Tom said. He had never thought about books rolling in and out of a store like cars or other widgets being spit out from a factory press.

The woman shook her head. "I'm sorry. Really. Have you been here before?"

"No. I've driven by a thousand times. I just had no reason to stop in, until now."

"You're looking for a book?"

"I am. Do you have something on swimming?"

"Swimming? I wasn't expecting that."

"Well," Tom said, "something more specific. Like how to swim?"

The woman started to say something, then restrained herself. She looked at Tom Wilson from head to toe, like she was seeing him for the first time. He knew that he didn't look much like a swimmer. He was a little round these days, and his temples had gone white instead of gray. He'd never been much of an athlete, but he watched what he ate, walked the dog when the weather was decent. Still, there was no mistaking him for one of those lean old guys who refused to give into aging, ran fifty marathons a year and had the body of a forty year old.

A slow smile grew on the bookseller's face, and then she shrugged. "I might have something. I don't know. Maybe you can tell me a little bit more about what you're after."

★

There was no sandy shore at the edge of the lake, only a bed of white limestone rocks that were all the size of sharp pointy baby heads. The rocks were pristine like they had just been chunked out of the earth and recently dumped there. Algae, or plants of any kind, had yet to form, and weeds were nothing more than seeds trying to find a place to take root. It was a new lake, primal in its intention, built for the coming modern age as a water supply. They had passed a broken-down steam shovel on the way in. If there was any rust growing, it was underneath where it couldn't be seen.

The sky overhead was clear. The moon was perfectly round, glowing brilliantly, threatening to hang in the July sky forever. There was no need for a fire to stay warm, or a flashlight to make a path from the camp to the water. Time had to be taken, though, slowly, carefully, with ease. The white rocks were damp with midnight dew. One slip would tear the skin off an ankle, or worse, twist it, break it in the middle of nowhere. The thirsty city was fifty miles south of them, out of sight, like it didn't exist.

"Where was it?" Tom asked.

"Just over there." The man pointed across the water, then lowered his head a bit. He was in his early thirties, with a razor-sharp flattop haircut that saw the barber every Friday, every pay day, after work, and eyes as blue as the ocean; different than Tom's dirty brown eyes. He still wore his second-shift uniform: black work boots scuffed with oil, blue jeans folded at the cuff, and a white T-shirt with a pack of Winstons rolled up in the right sleeve. He smelled of Aqua Velva and metal shavings. "I started coming here when I was a little older than you, Tom." His voice was hushed. Everyone else was asleep.

Tom leaned in to hear better. They sat shoulder to shoulder on the front of the camper, a 1956 Chevrolet panel truck that had belonged to Roger's father, a butcher by trade, dead and gone now. You could still see the outline of a cow on the side, underneath the fresh paint, in the bright sun, just under the ghost letters that said Morelow and Sons Meats in proud block letters. From a distance, the truck looked like it was supposed to now; a customized camper, built and assembled in the backyard garage. Roger had a knack with mechanical things; he was tinkerer, took things apart and put them back together so they suited his needs. Up close, the dings of time and the rust on the fenders couldn't be hidden. The truck had been retrofitted for pleasure, but the fact that it had once been used to cart around sides of beef and pig parts couldn't be missed, and didn't matter much to Roger. The old truck was a weekend getaway; a cheap pleasure.

"My grandparents had a shack next to the creek for as long as anyone could remember," Roger said. "There were lots of them. Simple places for folks to come up from the city and get away from the heat and swelter in the summer. Nobody ever thought they'd come along and build a dam, flood out half the town, but they did." A tinge of anger hung in the air like it was permanently tethered to the tip of Roger's tongue.

"Why'd they do that?" Tom asked.

Roger shrugged. "They call it progress. A reservoir for the future."

"What do you call it?"

"Theft."

Tom looked at Roger curiously, and Roger answered back with a shrug, slid off the front of the Chevrolet, lit a cigarette, and made his way slowly, carefully, over the rocks, to the edge of the water. He stood there staring out in the direction where his grandparents' shack had once stood, bathed in the glow from the moon, and the occasional red glow from the cigarette.

Tom liked Roger Morelow. He had filled a void that Tom thought was permanent, his fault somehow. The mechanics of the relationship between Roger and his mother was a mystery to Tom's eight year old mind. One day, Roger showed up, a single man with no children of his own, and assumed the head of the table where there previously had been none. It was a role the lanky factory worker, son of a butcher whose business collapsed for reasons unknown, took on easily, at least for Tom. His brother and sister were less than thrilled with a new routine, new house, and a new set of rules that were strictly enforced, but rewarded if followed. The two of them were older, and had a living father of their own (even though he had been physically and financially absent since Tom had been born). Tom had never known his real father; the story was that the man was a wanderer who wandered off when his mother's belly started to grow, never to be seen or spoken of since. Roger Morelow was a new hope, a comfortable step toward a normal life that had never belonged to Tom. His mother called Tom "Roger's shadow." He liked that, too, but he wasn't sure that she did.

Roger came back from the edge of the water slowly, careful at every step.

"Could you see it?" Tom asked.

"It's not there. It's gone forever." Roger smiled, tussled Tom's hair. "Come on, time for bed. We're gonna have lots of fun tomorrow."

★

The bookseller didn't wear a name tag, and there was no clue given in the bookstore's sign: CITY BOOKS. She carried herself with authority and Tom assumed that she was the owner, but he didn't know for sure, and knowing really wasn't important to him. He didn't know how to address her if he needed to, so he avoided speaking to her directly, just followed her as she zigzagged through the store. It was like he was in a labyrinth, an optical illusion; the rain outside was lost to him.

The woman stopped in front of a shelf that was neatly organized with no room for another book. Her turquoise earrings jingled, and for some reason that made Tom smile, relax a little bit.

"So you don't know how to swim?" she said. She had deep, expressive crevices in her face that she did nothing to hide. Tom felt like he was about to be asked to recite the Gettysburg Address. It was more a demand than a question.

"I can swim short distances. Dog-paddle, float on my back," he said. "It's not like I'm a rock and would sink to the bottom. But I can't swim like Mark Spitz or Diana Nyad."

"They're professionals."

"Exactly. They understand the foundational requirements of swimming," Tom said. "A wise man once said to me that if you master the basics of anything, you'll be head and shoulders above the rest. That's really all you ever need. The fundamentals. Without that, everything is lost."

"Ah, yes, a very wise man," the bookseller said. "We're in the wrong section. Follow me." She spun her flat heels like a sergeant off to battle, stalked off in the opposite direction from Tom. He'd barely had time to take a step to follow. Ten feet away, she stopped abruptly and turned back to him. "Who was the man?"

"My stepfather," Tom said.

★

A cove had been cut into the shore directly across the lake from the camper. Even in the soft glow from the morning sun, Tom could still see the claw marks left behind by the steam shovel. It would take time, erosion, or human effort of some kind to smooth the presence of a man-made cut in the earth.

A thick grove of trees stood beyond the edge of the cove, mature leaves in a high hardwood canopy that would offer shade and shadows below, once the summer sun reached its peak in the cloudless sky. The water was smooth as the bottom of an iron. It was dirty brown, muddy like the aftermath of a flood. The lake was creek-fed, controlled by a dam on the south end and the rise and fall of rain at the north end, where the creek drained in. There was no wind, and the air was almost dry; all of the humidity had been wrung out of it, but it was already warm, making it the perfect kind of July morning that only required a bathing suit, no shirt or shoes. No other boats had made their way out onto the water. Only a cloud of bugs that hovered and shifted casually over the water offered any sign of life. It was like they were the only family in the world.

Roger had built a fire on the land side of the camper, made a circle with rocks and put a grate over it. A coffeepot simmered, and a big iron skillet sat heating up, readying for sausage and eggs that had been packed into a dark green ice chest that had seen more than one camping trip. It was dinged up like the fenders of the Chevy truck, but there had been no attempt to restore it, or change it into something it wasn't.

His brother Lee and sister Donna had awakened not long after Tom. Donna was always slow to wake, slow to lose the scowl on her face, if ever. A smile was even rarer lately, especially when Roger was around. She was fifteen, and camping was not her idea of fun. Tom was never sure what was fun for her. Even though they shared a mother and the same brown eyes, she was a mystery to him. His brother didn't seem to mind Roger being around. Lee was a year younger than Donna, and all he wanted to do was be off by himself. He'd already grabbed a fishing pole and cottage cheese container full of worms and made his way wordlessly to the water. His back was to the camp, focused on the red and white bobber that sat perfectly still on the water.

The only one who hadn't come out of the camper was Tom's mother, but that wasn't unusual, she was always the last to arrive, and the first to leave.

Tom sat on a fold-out stool in front of the makeshift stove. The canvas sagged underneath him. It looked like a row of faded rainbow stripes that were near the first stage of rot. He studied every move Roger made. Camping of any kind was a new adventure, out of the house, away from the TV, that required new skills, new rules. They had never been to anyplace like the reservoir before.

Roger moved the logs around in the fire with focused intention. They crumbled into pieces. Once the flames died away, the coals pulsed orange like they had hearts, were alive. A poof of magic smoke billowed upwards into the clear blue sky, then thinned to a ribbon. A look of satisfaction crossed Roger's face. He got up and made his way to the cooler, fetched a package of freshly made sausage wrapped in white butcher's paper, then tossed it into the skillet and began to break it into smaller pieces.

The sizzle of meat was a foreign noise to the rocky shore. It echoed across the flat water like the first note of a movie soundtrack announcing something to come. Lee turned away from his bobber to see what the sound was. Donna didn't flinch. She hated sausage. She hated everything that Roger cooked.

Every move Roger made from that moment on seemed like it was even more choreographed, a practiced ballet of creation that would produce sausage gravy, biscuits baked in a Dutch oven buried in the coals, and scrambled eggs. They would suit every taste bud that needed pleased. One of the new pleasures in Tom's life was the enthusiasm Roger showed for cooking, for good food. His mother was the Master of the Fish Stick.

Tom, Lee, and Roger ate heartily while Donna pushed her eggs around and tried to keep from gagging at every little bite. Finally, when they were all nearly done eating, the door to the camper pushed open, and Tom's mother eased out into the sunlight.

At that moment, everything ceased to exist for Roger. He let out a slow almost silent whistle. Donna rolled her eyes and scowled. Lee got back up and cautiously made his way back to his fishing pole. Tom remained seated and finished up his gravy, watching them both with a little confusion—but it didn't make him uncomfortable. He liked how they looked at each other.

Tom's mother was a tall brunette without the first hint of gray or a wrinkle on her face. She was in her mid-thirties, but with a little effort on her part she looked ten years younger. People, always men, said Donna and his mother looked like sisters. Her hair, just put up and fixed at the local beauty shop the day before, was covered by a simple white headscarf. Her eyes were shaded with a pair of brand new Ray Ban Wayfarer sunglasses, the kind Marilyn Monroe wore. She had on a black one-piece bathing suit that could be seen underneath a sheer white coverup. Her legs were shapely, something she was always complimented on, and her skin was tanned dark brown, stained with baby oil, iodine, and hours of basking in the sun on the cement porch behind their house. She had to step with care out of the camper or she would twist an ankle in the white high heel sandals she wore.

Roger stood up, and wiped his hands on his jeans. "Don't you look pretty."

Tom's mother stopped once both heels were solidly planted on the rocky ground. "Why thank you." A smile beamed broadly across her face, threatening to outshine the sun.

"We should have bought you a pair of flip-flops," Roger said.

Tom's mother shrugged. Before she could utter a word, though, Donna stood up, and said, "I hate this place."

"Donna!" Her mother snapped. The smile disappeared, replaced by a look that meant that the dark cloud of trouble had just pushed in front of the sun.

"Well, I do hate it here. The truck smells. You can't walk anywhere without scraping your ankle, or breaking it. And I didn't want to come in the first place. Nobody asked me!"

"That'll be enough, Donna." Tom's mother hadn't moved an inch. If she would have been a dog, all of her hackles would have been raised as high as they could go.

"It's all right," Roger said in his normal, calm voice. "She's right."

The look didn't disappear from Tom's mother's face. "Well that may be true, but she should appreciate what..." Roger put up his index finger mid-air, stopping her mid-sentence.

"We'll go across, to the other side. It's smooth there. We'll have a picnic on soft ground. That's why I brought the canoe." He glanced up to the roof of the camper to the beat-up canoe that was still tied down with new rope. "We'll just have to go one at a time."

★

The bookseller scanned the shelf, then stopped. "I know it's here. I just saw it the other day. I know I haven't sent it back. Some days, I swear there are imps in this store that come out and play at night, rearrange things so I can't find them, just to entertain themselves."

Tom forced a smile, then glanced quickly at his wristwatch. His wife was expecting him home anytime. He was as reliable as Big Ben. She would start to worry if he didn't show up soon.

"Ah, here it is." The woman smiled for the first time since Tom had walked into the store. She reached to the shelf, and pulled out a slim hardbound volume with a red and gold spine. It looked older than the other books, didn't have a slipcover on it to protect the binding. She handed the book to Tom without hesitation. "I think you'll like it."

He looked at the book, and was immediately surprised by the title, *Swimming Away*. "Are you sure? This looks like a memoir." Tom was tempted to crack open the book and take a deep whiff of the pages, but he restrained himself.

The bookseller nodded. "It is. Julius Goldfeld was taken to a concentration camp, Neuengamme, when he was just a boy. During the evacuation, as the war was coming to an end, on a death march, Julius escaped and swam up the river Elbe in Hamburg. He had never swam before in his life, but he knew if he was caught by the Nazis, they would kill him right then and there. He decided he would rather drown a free boy than face that kind of death, that kind of life. He couldn't take it anymore. So he made the decision between life and death at eight years old. He became a swimming coach at a university in Poland, and lived to be ninety-six. It's a really good story. There's more to it, of course, than just swimming, but there's that, too. Things Julius learned along the way."

"Eight. That's how old I was when..." Tom stopped, girded himself by holding onto the book as tight as he could. He knew this was going to be hard, but he hadn't been prepared for the depths of pain he suddenly felt. His mouth drained of any moisture, and it felt like he was about to have an allergy attack. He was certain there was no cat in the bookstore, but he should have asked. He should have kept on driving. *This was a stupid idea, Tom.*

"Are you all right?"

"I'm fine."

"You don't look fine to me." The woman stared at Tom with concern in her eyes. "Come on," she said, "I have something else in mind, something more instructional." She wasn't so sharp in her turn this time. She waited for Tom to follow along, so they were shoulder to shoulder, like she was prepared to catch him if he fell.

★

By the time Roger had pulled the canoe off the roof of the Chevy, with the help of Lee and Tom, a few speedboats had made their way out onto the water. The lake looked like a giant mixing bowl, waves lapping against the rocks, churning the water, making it muddier than it was before. The future drinking water was so brown that it could have been mistaken for thin chocolate cake batter.

"Take the kids first," Tom's mother said.

Roger shook his head no. "Ladies first."

She leaned in and pecked him on the cheek with a quick kiss, leaving bright red lipstick behind. "You're sweet. I'll be fine."

"You're sure?" He made no effort to wipe away the lipstick, left it there.

"I'm sure."

"All right."

They made their way to the edge of the water slowly; one man and two boys carrying the canoe, a woman and her angry daughter close behind.

Roger put Donna in the canoe first, launched it and paddled across the growing waves to the cove. It took him a minute to steady the craft, and find a comfortable place for Donna to disembark, but he did. It didn't look like the two of them said one word the entire trip.

Lee was next, carting along his fishing pole, dragging his fingers in the water as they went. Roger talked. Lee nodded, never took his eyes off the murky brown water.

The trips back and forth didn't take long. Tom was glad for a long minute alone with his mother.

"You do everything Roger tells you to do, okay honey?"

"Sure, mom."

"I'm serious." She stared down at him, her face void of any expression.

"It'll be all right," Tom said as he slipped his hand into his mother's. She glanced down to their hands, smiled, then looked back to Roger, never taking her eyes off him until he landed back on their side of the lake.

Roger got out of the canoe, grabbed an orange life preserver, and helped Tom put it on. "It's called a Mae West," Roger said as he cinched the belt at Tom's waist, just above his butt.

"Why do I have to wear this, and they didn't have to?"

"They know how to swim."

Tom didn't like how the vest felt. It was tight, and he thought it looked stupid. He glanced up to his mother, and the look on her face warned him off arguing. He wanted to go to the other side with Donna and Lee, so he didn't push it. Sometimes, he hated being the youngest.

The canoe swayed backed and forth, and Roger tried to hit the wakes of the speedboats head-on, but a few times he was unable to. Tom hung onto the sides of the boat with both hands. His knuckles were white, and he thought he was going to lose his gravy more than once.

"We might have to wait until the boats go in before we go back across," Roger said as they landed, and he helped Tom out of the boat.

Tom found a spot on the shore, just above a claw mark, and watched Roger make his way back to fetch his mother.

She climbed into the canoe with uncertainty, but settled in across from Roger, facing him. Roger offered her Tom's Mae West, but she shook her head no. They talked for a second—Tom couldn't hear them, but he was certain that Roger was trying to convince her to wear it. Roger kept pointing to the speedboats, coming closer and closer, rounding in circles, making the wakes grow as high as they could.

Roger lost the argument, and paddled away from the rocky shore.

The world moved in slow motion then.

A boat full of laughing, drinking men headed straight for the canoe. Tom started screaming, trying to get to their attention.

Roger, too. The alarm got Lee and Donna's attention, and they ran over to Tom, stood next to him, and joined in. It was a chorus of pleas that no one but them could hear.

By the time the driver of the boat saw the canoe, it was nearly too late. He cut the steering wheel, spun the boat around ten feet from the canoe. There was no crash. But the big wave dumped the canoe, sent it over on its side.

Roger and Tom's mother disappeared under the swirling ugly brown water.

There were screams and shouts. The boat came back. People dove in to the water to help. Roger surfaced, went under again, and again, and again. The three kids screamed and cried, stood there alone, and watched helplessly. Donna wouldn't let them in the water. She assumed control of them, like some kind of natural rule kicked in and told her to.

They never saw their mother alive again. Her high heel shoe had gotten caught in an old chain-link fence, next to the foundation of an old shack. It had once stood in front of a creek where a generation of little boys learned to swim and paddle a canoe.

★

The bookseller rang up the two books, and handed Tom the receipt. "If you don't like the Goldfeld book, bring it back. I'll give you a refund."

He nodded, stuffed the receipt into his wallet, and grabbed up the books. "Thanks. I'm sure I'll enjoy it."

"The YMCA is right down the street. They give lessons. It's never too late to learn, you know."

"I've been thinking about that. Thanks, again." Tom headed for the door.

"What happened to your step-father?" the woman asked.

Tom stopped, his hand on the door handle. It was warm and dry. The water he had brought in with him had disappeared, evaporated. "He died a few weeks ago. Lung cancer."

"I'm sorry, that must have been hard."

"I saw the obituary in the newspaper. He had started a new family after...Well, just after. I didn't blame him though. He needed a family. I learned a lot from him. He tried to save us all. He just couldn't. That's all. He just couldn't."

"I hope he found some happiness."

"Me, too." He pushed open the door. "My wife's waiting." Then he walked out, heard the woman say, "Come again," and kept on walking, holding onto the books as tight as he could.

The rain had stopped, and Tom was glad of that. He settled into the car, started the engine, called his wife on his cell phone and told her that he was fine, that he'd stopped by the bookstore. She was happy that he was going to finally learn how to swim.

He decided to take the long way home. He wanted to drive to up to the lake, see the houses, the water, the cove. He hadn't been there for a really long time. He was sure that it had changed, that he wouldn't recognize any of it.

Larry D. Sweazy is a two-time WWA Spur award winner, a two-time, back-to-back, winner of the Will Rogers Medallion Award, a Best Books of Indiana award winner, and the inaugural winner of the 2013 Elmer Kelton Book Award. He was also nominated for a Short Mystery Fiction Society (SMFS) Derringer award in 2007. Larry has published over 50 non-fiction articles and short stories, and is the author of the Josiah Wolfe, Texas Ranger western series (Berkley), the Lucas Fume western series (Berkley) and a thriller set in Indiana, *The Devil's Bones* (Five Star). A new mystery from Seventh Street Books will debut in 2015.

He lives in Noblesville, Indiana, with his wife, Rose, a dog and a cat. *www.larrydsweazy.com*

BONNIE MAURER

WHAT AN AFTERNOON IS HERE
Cape Cod

We have found this Sunday afternoon,
you on the couch reading baseball statistics—hits,
runs, RBIs—and I, twenty love poems by Neruda.

We have come to the edge of the sea. We love
and lick the salt from shoulders and cheeks and
the nameless channel above the lips,
the silver mica sand

fallen on our thighs, stardust
blessed by accidents. I am not longing.
Yet my soul flies out over this sand and sea.

Let the cormorants
pitch it back to the rocks where
I stand ready—your catcher,
your soft glove.

I am not longing.
I only wish you would shout
your desire.

You, who love baseball,
look at me making this up to you
while the whales are being sighted
only an hour away.

Only an hour away, the Albanians
are calling Boston for the right way
to speak to God.

Only yesterday another
worm crawled through Walt Whitman's
bones. (Who can call up the world for
love or despair?)

It makes no difference to me
who hits and runs. The sea is
infamous for winning every inning.

From Reconfigured, Finishing Line Press, 2009.

ANNA'S WINGS

ANGELA JACKSON-BROWN

When the phone rang, Sheriff Leo Skinner jumped and then reached for it, knocking over the stacks of criminal files that were stacked on his desk. He cursed under his breath. He had been sitting all day in his basement office with a box fan whirring in the window, trying to get through the mounds of paperwork his secretary had given to him that morning, but he hadn't gotten any significant work done. All he'd really been doing was biding time until he could go home and check on his wife Anna. Leo glanced at the Caller ID. Jimbo Smart, the Assistant Manager at the Winn Dixie was on the line.

Leo sighed. "Hey, Jimbo. What's going on?"

"Howdy do, Sheriff," Jimbo said cheerfully. It always irritated Leo that Jimbo could sound so upbeat all the time. It didn't matter if he was calling to report a break in or letting Leo know that Del Monte peaches were on sale two cans for a dollar—Jimbo was always in an annoyingly chirpy mood.

"Can I help you, Jimbo?" Leo asked.

"Well Sheriff, I hate to be the bearer of bad news," Jimbo said, each word coming across the phone line with the painstaking slowness of syrup getting poured onto a plate of biscuits. Leo ran his fingers through his hair that was now nearly all white. He looked like he had fine, white porcupine bristles on his head. He knew it was the stress. Three years ago his hair had been dark with only specks of gray. Three years ago his friends and colleagues said he resembled a slightly older Denzel Washington. Three years ago, his wife had not been a butterfly retreating into a cocoon.

"It's Miss Anna, Sheriff. I'm afraid she was at it again today," Jimbo said. A lump formed in Leo's throat. A few months ago, Jimbo had cornered him after church to tell him that Anna had stolen a notebook, a picture frame and some W-D 40 from the store. Leo had stuffed a twenty in Jimbo's hands and told him to keep the information to himself. Now, it was happening again.

"What did she take this time?" Leo asked.

"Oh, not much really. My stockboy stayed behind her the whole time like before."

Leo winced. "What did she take?"

"A pack of Saltines, some Red Devil potted meat, and a bottle of hot sauce," Jimbo answered. "Like I said, she didn't take much at all today."

Leo closed his eyes. He could see his beautiful Anna in his head the way she used to be. Anna. Body thin like a dancer, hair tightly cropped to her head, and a smile that seemed to radiate all the wisdom of the universe. Anna. His Anna.

By day, Anna had been the librarian and Yearbook staff advisor at Ariton High School, and by night she taught ESL classes after school to members of the local immigrant community. One of her French students named her *La Bibliothèque*, because Anna was never at a loss for words, and she always knew just the right words to say at any given time. When her Spanish-speaking students needed help figuring out how to translate some word or phrase, she knew exactly what they were trying to say. She proudly held these positions for over 30 years, but all of her abilities to communicate had started to slip away, like dew drops in late morning.

Now Anna could not even make out a simple grocery list and remember to pay for her purchases.

"I'll be in to make good on Anna's purchases," Leo finally said, allowing his memories of his past Anna to fade to black.

"Oh, I know you're good for it, Sheriff. I just thought you'd want to know, that's all," Jimbo said, still in that chirpy, high pitched voice. "And Sheriff," Jimbo said with dramatic flair. "I'm sorry about your wife and all. Don't none of this change the fact that Miss Anna was a good woman."

"Is."

"Pardon, Sheriff?"

"I said 'is.' Anna is a good woman." Leo hated when people referred to Anna in the past tense. He hated it more when he did it.

"Right, Sheriff. Well, I'll be seeing you later." Jimbo hung up. Leo slowly returned the phone to its cradle. Suddenly, more than anything, he wanted to go to Anna. He chided himself for not hiring someone to look after her while he worked.

Leo pushed back from his seat and got up quickly. He walked to the front desk where his top deputy B.J. Larkins was catching up on some paperwork. B.J. looked up.

"Need something, Sheriff?" B.J. asked.

"I'm going home, B.J. Page me if you need me."

"Is everything alright, Sheriff?"

Leo nodded. "Yeah. Just need to go home for a while."

B.J. appeared to be about to say something, but cleared his throat instead. Leo nodded again and went out to his car. Leo got into his Sherriff's car and pulled out of his parking space, being careful not to hit any of the many pedestrians who were going in and out of the courthouse where he worked. As he turned left at the stop sign, he turned the radio to one of the local country stations. Tim McGraw was singing "My Best Friend." Leo thought about how B.J. had found Anna two weeks before when she had gotten lost.

B.J. had been out patrolling Highway 123, which ran between Ariton and Ozark, when he found Anna sitting on the side of the road beside her car, crying. The sun was shining but it was also drizzling rain, something that often happened during the month of June in southern Alabama. When B.J. finally got a drenched Anna into his squad car, she admitted that she had forgotten where she was going and had become frightened. B.J. radioed for Leo, who drove out to pick her up.

"I'm disappearing, Leo," she had said once Leo got her settled in his car.

"I'm not going to let you disappear, Anna," he had said, stroking Anna's damp hair.

But if the truth be known, Anna was disappearing and there was nothing he could do to stop it. Little by little, piece by piece, segments of Anna's personality were slipping away, like birds during the onset of winter.

As Leo drove into his yard, he choked back a sob. Looking out over his and Anna's property, which stretched out nearly 150 acres off Highway 123 on Jernigan Road, he saw her in the distance, standing by the duck pond. Most days, Leo would find Anna somewhere near the ducks. It had been Anna who first noticed them five years ago.

"We have a family of ducks, Leo," Anna had said excitedly, pulling him from his comfortable seat in front of the television, insisting they go down to the pond so she could show him their new visitors.

"American Wigeons," she'd said excitedly. "I looked them up. They whistle, Leo. Isn't that darling?"

Leo had agreed. Since she'd gotten sick, he'd been afraid they would fly off. In order to make certain that they did not, Leo had clipped their wings. When Anna found out what he had done, she'd become livid.

"How could you, Leo? How could you clip their wings?" she had cried hysterically, pounding her fists against his chest.

They had been standing out by the pond, watching the ducks scurry about, when Anna had wondered out loud why the birds never seemed to fly anymore.

"I didn't want them to fly away from you, Anna," Leo had said to her, as he'd tried to pull her close to him, but she jerked away.

"What about me, Leo? Is that what you'll do to me?" she exclaimed, her eyes shining brightly with tears. "When it's my time to fly away, will you clip my wings too? Will you? Will you, Leo?"

He didn't have an answer.

Leo pulled into the driveway and parked his car. The back door of their house was open, so he knew Anna had gone down the hill to the duck pond. He walked with a pronounced limp. His hip hurt and his head was throbbing.

"God, I'm getting old," he mumbled under his breath as he slowly got out of the car. He stood for a moment, taking a deep breath, and then he started walking down the hill that led to the duck pond.

It was a sunny afternoon. Not a cloud in the sky. As he turned the corner he saw her standing in her usual spot.

"Anna. Anna, darling," Leo called out. He waited for her to turn. She continued to throw breadcrumbs to the ducks.

"Anna. Anna, darling," Leo called out again as he walked towards his wife, whose back was still turned to him. She was completely engrossed in the wild antics of the ducks, who seemed to be involved in some bizarre bird game that bore a striking resemblance to the game of tag. Leo did not want to startle her. Finally, Anna turned around. Although it was nearly a hundred degrees outside, she was dressed in gray sweat pants and a black turtleneck sweater. Her hair was a mass of grayish, black curls that framed her cocoa-brown face, which was now lined with fine wrinkles. Anna looked old. And tired.

"Hi, Leo," she said. Leo sucked in his breath; thankful to hear her say his name.

"Hi, beautiful girl. How are our ducks?"

"Frightened."

Leo walked over and carefully put his arms around Anna's waist. She was so thin. Anna had always been small, but now, holding her was like holding a wisp of air.

"Oh baby, I don't think they're frightened. Look," he said pointing. "They're playing and having a good time."

Anna looked up at Leo. "That's what they want you to believe.

But inside," she said, placing her hand on her heart. "Inside they are frightened."

"What are they frightened of, my darling?" he asked, as he stroked her hair, burying his nose into her soft curls, trying to memorize her woodsy, fruity scent.

Anna looked at Leo with dark, penetrating eyes. For the first time in a long time, her eyes did not seem to have a thin film of confusion clouding them. "They're frightened because they are afraid they have forgotten how to fly. They know they will never fly again, and they have accepted that fact, but they don't want to forget how to do it. It is the forgetting that is so frightening."

"Are you forgetting how to fly, my Anna?" Leo asked.

Anna turned her back towards Leo. "Why are you home so early? Did I do something wrong today?"

Leo rubbed her back in a wide circular motion. "I just wanted to come home and see my beautiful wife. That's all. Is anything wrong with that, my love?"

"My students are looking for me, I suspect," she said, raking her fingers through her hair. "I'm not sure what to tell them if they find me."

"You don't have to tell them anything, darling, because you retired a few years ago," Leo said, hoping his words would bring her comfort this one time. He hated when she would get upset and cry over students whose well-being still worried her, even though she had not taught in several years.

"Leo, do you remember?" she whispered.

Leo closed his eyes. "Yes," he answered, his voice throaty with emotion. "I remember." He could have played off her question but he knew what she was talking about. They had made the vow years before the disease started ravaging her mind. Now, it was time for him to make good on his promise to her.

"It's time," she said in a strong voice.

"No," Leo said, shaking his head.

Anna turned around and stroked Leo's face with the palm of her hand. "You promised."

"How? How do I do...that?" he said with anguish, pulling away.

Anna tugged on Leo's arm until he turned back towards her. "Birds should never have their wings clipped, Leo. But if it happens, if their wings are clipped and they are forced to forget the very thing that makes them birds, then someone has to step in and give them wings again. Please, give me wings again, Leo."

Leo didn't answer her, he simply pulled her into his arms and held her tightly. For several hours he and Anna alternated between standing and sitting, not saying a word, just holding each other as they watched the ducks skim across the water and occasionally call out in their game of bird tag.

When the afternoon shadows began to gather and form a gentle cocoon around Leo and Anna, they knew that it was time to go inside. Leo bent down and kissed Anna on the mouth.

"You will get your wings, my Anna," he whispered in her ear.

Anna looked at Leo, smiled, and then reached out her hand for his. Leo took Anna's hand and they both walked slowly up the hill to their house.

It was close to midnight before Leo and Anna turned in. They had spent their last evening holding each other; not really talking, just touching and breathing each other in. Leo got Anna settled in the bed under their favorite down comforter just like he always did.

He was about to walk to their bathroom, when she reached for his arm, gripping it tightly.

"Don't leave me, Leo," she said, a single tear sliding down her left cheek. He brushed the tear away.

"We don't have to do— "

"Yes, we do. I'm just frightened."

"I'll be right here," he told her, a solemn look on his face. "I won't leave you. Not even for a second. Just let me go get—let me go get what we need. Then, I'll be back, and I won't leave you again. Okay?"

Anna nodded and let his arm go. Leo stood without talking for a moment and just looked at her. He watched as her breathing began to slow. He patted her shoulder. It felt thin and fragile.

"It's okay, sweetheart," he said. Leo then went to the bathroom, unlocked the medicine cabinet, and took down her prescription Xanax.

Leo looked at the pill bottle for a moment, then he squeezed it like a stress ball, his eyes closed, body shaking slightly. He took several slow breaths. Trying to bring calm to himself. Trying to remember that crazy yoga breathing Anna had taught him. A half-laugh, half-sob escaped his throat.

"You can do this," he whispered. "You can do this."

Once calm, he walked back out to the bedroom and sat on the side of the bed beside Anna. Her face looked weary. Her eyes were bloodshot. She had fought so hard to stay with him. Every day he could see how much it was a struggle for her to just be present—to not withdraw completely, and he knew that she had done all of that for him. He knew he had to do this for her. She sat up in the bed and gingerly held out her hand. He prayed for a moment that her hesitation meant that she was not ready to do this. Maybe on another day, he hoped.

"Baby, are you sure? I mean—"

She nodded. He looked away, still gripping the pill bottle tightly in his hands. *Goddammit to hell*, he thought. Anna touched his arm. He looked at her. Her eyes spoke to him. He could tell she knew his inner turmoil. He tried to smile at her. Tried to reassure her with his eyes that he would be okay.

They could always say everything they needed to say to one another with just a glance. He would keep this promise to her. He had never broken a promise to her before. Not even a small one. So, he put the pills in her hand. Silently cursing each and every one of the tiny blue pills. She swallowed them one by one, taking large gulps of water. After a moment, she looked up at him with huge eyes.

"It won't be long will it, Leo?"

Leo shook his head, climbing under the comforter with her, pulling her towards him, letting her head rest on his shoulder. His body was tired and achy. His head was throbbing, but all he could think about was Anna and this moment. "No, baby. You'll just go—" he cleared his throat. "You'll just go to sleep. That's all."

She sighed, closed her eyes, and snuggled closer to him. "I love you, Leo Skinner."

Leo couldn't speak. He pulled her closer.

After a few minutes, he couldn't bear not looking at her. He propped up on one arm, looking down at her face as her breathing became shallower and shallower. He tried to memorize every part of her face—the little crinkly laugh lines around her eyes, the teardrop-shaped scar near the right corner of her mouth from some injury she got as a child, climbing trees with her cousins, and that beautiful, curly hair that always seemed wild, untamed and free.

"Leo," she whimpered, taking a sharp breath, eyes still shut tight. He could feel that her spirit was beginning to slip away. He almost wavered. All it would take would be one 911 phone call and him administering CPR until the paramedics arrived. They could pump her stomach and bring her back.

That's what a man who had spent his life upholding the law would do. Should do. But he knew he had to do what Anna asked. He knew she would have done the same for him, had the circumstances been identical. She squirmed restlessly. Fighting the effects of the pills. Anna moaned as if in pain, but Leo knew that she wasn't. She was just frightened.

"Shhhhhh," he said, and pressed his lips to hers, kissing her until he felt her body relax.

Close to 2 AM, Anna took a long breath that filled her lungs, exhaled deep, and that was it. She was gone. For a while, Leo just lay there looking at her. Then he stroked her face with the back of his hand. She always said the inside of his hands were too rough, so he would always stroke her face with the back of his hand.

"Only you—my beautiful girl," he started, then paused when emotion overtook him. The tears started to trickle down his face, "Only you could make death look so beautiful." Leo kissed her face slowly and deliberately, making sure there was no part that he didn't allow his lips to touch. The worry lines on Anna's face had smoothed out. Leo pressed his nose against her hair and drank in her smell one last time.

★

The next morning, shortly after daybreak, Leo called Sam Levins, the local coroner. Sam lived only a few miles from Leo and Anna's house, so it took him just a few minutes to arrive. After a quick assessment of the situation, Sam announced that he was ruling Anna's death an accidental overdose of sleeping pills. Nearly overcome with emotion, Leo only nodded. While Sam prepared the necessary paperwork, Leo walked down to the duck pond, carrying his rifle.

For a while, Leo stood and watched the ducks swim, then he aimed his rifle and, one by one, shot each of the ducks. Strangely, they barely made a sound, even when the shots pierced the early morning air, ringing out like a final benediction. The only recognizable sounds that could truly be heard were the firing of Leo's rifle and his loud, mournful sobs. When the last duck had fallen, Leo dropped his rifle to the ground, and allowed himself to be enveloped by the overwhelming sense of peace that had begun to permeate the air. Breathing in deeply, Leo looked upward, smiled through his tears, and then slowly walked back the hill leading to his and Anna's home.

Angela Jackson-Brown is an English Professor at Ball State University in Muncie, IN. She graduated from Troy University in Troy, AL (B.S. in Business Administration), Auburn University in Auburn, AL (M.A. in English), and Spalding University in Louisville, KY (MFA in Creative Writing). Her work has appeared in literary journals such as *Pet Milk*, *Uptown Mosaic Magazine*, *New Southerner*, *The Louisville Review*, *Muscadine Lines*, *Blue Lake Review*, *Identity Theory*, *Toe Good Poetry*, and *94 Creations*. Her short story, "Something in the Wash" was awarded the 2009 fiction prize by *New Southerner* and was nominated for a Pushcart Prize in Fiction. Her debut novel *Drinking from a Bitter Cup* was published by WiDo Publishing in January of 2014.

NORBERT KRAPF

EMPTY UNDERGROUND SHELVES
Humbolt University, Berlin

I stand on the spot where the Nazis
burned books at this university in 1933,
look through a Plexiglass window

in the cobblestones and stare
at a hollow underground room
where walls of empty shelves stand.

The longer I look, the more I hear
the silence of those whose pages
fed that fire and whose words were

released into the elements to climb
like small stars into the sky and look
back down and shine like sparks

when we gaze into the night sky.
The voices of those who were
burned begin to moan, then murmur

like a sad choir that has not yet
found its collective voice, but the longer
I listen the more I hear the murmur

approach the right resonance. I stand
in the presence of those who were
burned and they rise in me as I walk

away with a hum in my ears and
a hurt in my heart, an animal howl
escapes from the hollow room

I carry away with me, and I leave part
of myself squatting in silence on empty
shelves where pages of books should be.

Originally appeared in Looking for God's Country *(Time Being Books, 2005).*

THE DEAD

SUSAN NEVILLE

It was an informal wake, in a restaurant next to an art gallery on a busy corner of the city. Binkley's was the name of the restaurant. It was also the name of the drugstore that had occupied the site in the fifties. The druggist's name had been Binkley, though no one at our table knew this, not in any profound sense of the word knowing. Nothing was left of the old place except the footprint of the building, and since no one had written a book about the druggist and he had left no record of his interior life, the restaurant's name seemed to be the pharmacist's only verifiable resurrection. It's doubtful he could have imagined the gas fireplace, the minimalist black tables with their candles, the waiters in their white shirts, life going on without him.

There were pictures of the old drugstore in sepia on the walls, but they were purely decorative and not many people really looked at them. They could have been photographs of some other place, purchased at an antique mall, for all we knew.

Whenever I came to this restaurant, I had a vague sense of having walked to Binkley's drugstore from my grandmother's house when I was a child and ordering a chocolate soda, but it may have been a dream of some sort. I couldn't look at the place now and say where the fountain had been, where the pharmaceuticals. And the restaurant seemed to be miles away from where my grandmother had lived.

It was the first day of the New Year, 2013. One of our colleagues had died two days earlier. The eve of New Year's Eve, in fact. We were in shock, and grieving. The gathering was in his remembrance. We felt drawn together by this death. It wasn't called a wake in the emails, just an opportunity to lift a glass and mark a colleague's passing. Nothing else could have brought us together on this day, a day reserved for families.

Despite our sadness, it felt oddly festive in the restaurant, as such things do. We were teachers, and we hadn't seen each other since the semester ended. We'd had a chance to relax over the holidays. We'd been released from our obsessions, our student papers and our grievances. Everyone from the Department had come out at the last minute for this. There had been thirteen of us and now there were only twelve.

There would not be a funeral for several weeks, we were told by the department chair. One of the dead man's daughters was in the last stage of pregnancy and couldn't travel.

The waiter brought our waters as we asked each other questions. Was he at home or the hospital when he died and if the former, was his wife alone with him or was the hospice nurse there? How awful, we agreed, if the wife had been alone with him.

And apparently, according to our chairman, our colleague's death at the end of the year left the widow in a quandary over whether she still had health insurance, something she herself desperately needed.

Late capitalism is cruel to widows, one of the colleagues, a Marxist critic, said.

Life has always been cruel to widows, our Medievalist said. Not in this way, the Marxist said. It'll be hours on the phone, a stack of death certificates fed-exed to insurance companies, government agencies, credit cards with his name on them and not hers, all the grieving time spent in bureaucratic capitalist tangles.

Remember your Dickens, the dead man, a Victorianist, might have said, had he been there.

Who would teach Dickens now? I wondered. Or rather, who would love Dickens enough to teach him? Who would there be to pass on that passion to the students? No one could say. In the house of literature there was a light flickering out in the room of Dickens, a slight power outage for a day or two, since our colleague's passing. Any one of us could bring out the flashlights and candles, but no one could provide the illumination he had provided. It took years of reading to provide that illumination. It originated in the heart, and the mind followed.

Still, our Modernist said, so sad that it makes a difference whether it's the last day of the old year or the first of the new when he died.

Perhaps the widow should have hidden the body until tomorrow.

This from a Poe scholar, said in jest. He knew as soon as he said it that it was inappropriate. We veered quickly away from that thought or from asking where he was now, the body, if it had been donated or cremated or embalmed or was in some cold waiting station. We wondered how much our colleague had suffered at the end.

So here we all are, the department chair said. We made it through the end of the world once again.

It was 2013 and the world was to have ended in December, along with the year, but it hadn't. The approach of the Mayan calendar's end was the second or third end-of-the-world scenario most of us had lived through. Y2K, earthquakes and rumors of earthquakes, wars and rumors of wars. Apocalyptic fears seemed to cluster around the change in centuries and particularly millennia. Our students are fascinated with things blowing up and the world beginning again with them: against all odds, they would find a need for their bravery, a secret power they carried and had never been called upon to find. Each one would be an Adam and an Eve. Put the words 'utopia' and 'dystopia' or 'zombie apocalypse' in a course description, and the course would fill. One of our rhetoricians, in fact, specialized in zombie studies. The coming plague, terrorism, climate change. We all fear it.

We all agreed 2012 hadn't been a particularly good year. In part because the colleague whose informal wake we had gathered for had been dying for much of it and we had to go on all year as if this were not true. One or two of us had spent the year dropping by his house with food and watching his slow decline. The others had spent the year feeling guilty that we watched from afar, just asking for news. The occasional email, phone call, or card. What do you do in a situation like this? He was a serious, sincere man, at times a great man, living in a time of irony. What do you talk to a dying man about? What was good enough to say?

When all was well, department or college politics drew us together. Even when you talked about department politics among the well, it was a panacea, a quick rush of gossip followed by guilt. The sides were constantly shifting.

Gone were the times when you assumed everyone knew all of Milton, Shakespeare or Virgil. You could mourn this or celebrate it. Most of us did both. You couldn't even be sure that each of us labored in one small unlit corner of that house of literature—an obscure poet, an untranslated Slovenian. Most of us still labored in that house, some of us one of the only ones in the room of John Clare or Iris Murdoch or Jean Rhys or Trolloppe: keeping the floor swept, the fixtures shining, waiting for some passionate young person to walk in and trigger the blazing lights. Come in! The shelves are full! And one room leads quite naturally to another!

But what did we have to talk about with each other? We had no passions in common, really, aside from the golden age of television—who was binge watching which boxed set. *Deadwood, The Wire, House of Cards.* We could go on about television and film for hours. We had passions for teaching and reading, but our passions outside the classroom were wide-spread, too separate to provide a basis for conversation. One brewed craft beer and one made homemade mead from local wildflowers. One rescued mastiffs. One of us rode everywhere by bicycle and was constantly slipping on the ice or in rain puddles, breaking this or that. He was fresh off a concussion and was leaving in a few days for a six hundred mile ride through the Everglades.

But it all seemed so silly now compared to illness and death, things taking place on a different planet. Our dead colleague had loved Jane Austen as well as Dickens. He had taught Austen for the past few years because students lacked the patience for his beloved Dickens. He was 72 when he died, was wearing a leather vest and hat the last time I saw him leave the office. He was an early adopter of technology. He had a beautiful wife, beautiful successful daughters.

I had been his suite-mate. For years he had hired a student to help him file his papers. Every afternoon the murmur of their voices talking about the student's future, about books, about art and music and the purpose of education; that perfect domestic murmur, familiar and comforting, came from the office and offered the type of calm I have only felt when I listened to the similar sound of my parents' voices, at night, when I was a child. That easy shift from subject to subject, born of true intimacy, though more father and daughter or son than husband and wife. He and his assistant would take breaks and walk to the student union for coffee. They would bring back plates of sweets for his afternoon classes, though he himself was diabetic and could not eat them.

After years of the young men and women graduating and a new one taking on the job, I had begun to wish that at some point in my life I'd had a surrogate father like that. It would have made me feel less lonely about the whole endeavor, shown a way. My parents read, and there were always books in the house, but we didn't talk about them. As a child I had read so ravenously but in such a solitary way.

This is what we have in common, I thought. I look around the table at my colleagues. How to express what it meant to work that closely to someone, yet not intimately, and to have that person, suddenly, gone. It was in the books, someplace. If called upon, I'm sure we all would have a poem, a line from a novel that might express it.

Should I, as his suite mate, put a sign on his office door? Will Annie, the administrative assistant, do this? Should I take down the sign with his office hours, the photos of his family in our shared outer office, his New Yorker clippings? Will his children want the clippings? The files and files of lecture notes? He was working on his autobiography when he died. How far along was he? Would anyone finish it? And how would I talk to the former students who, not having heard the news, would come by and knock, asking after him or those who, having heard, would come by his office door weeping, as to a memorial. It did not seem real to me yet. And what about all the books?

We had worked in such close proximity for over twenty years. It was an easy relationship, as we were both good natured, though perhaps not a relationship at all in any real sense, not any more than the relationship between this restaurant and the drugstore. At some point he had withdrawn into his own work, the role of remote dispenser of wisdom, and that easy camaraderie with the brightest students. He was kind. I always felt I disappointed him when I opened my mouth to speak. Not his fault, but a lack I felt in my own education. I am a voracious reader, still, but an autodidact. I went to public school. I have read all of Chekhov and Willa Cather and Eudora Welty and a lot of contemporary poets and novelists but I have not read Thucidydes, for instance. Never read Ovid. I'm always googling classical references. I have read as much in my life as I have had the hours for, but I read without a plan, moving from one shiny thing to another. Drop me a line and say I must read Thucydides, and I will do it I'm sure with passion but then I will worry because I have yet to read *The Faerie Queen* or *Paradise Lost*, and I need to look once more at *Leaves of Grass* and for some reason feel the need, right now, to read about the history of agriculture.

My suite mate had a classical education, University of Chicago. He knew Greek and Latin. He knew French. He knew Middle and Old English.

And here is my confession. I did not go by to see my colleague in his illness. I called him on the phone. I exchanged emails.

Illness removed the one ill to a battlefield, and I am afraid of battles. Reports from scouts at the front came back with horror stories of a hand too weak to lift a spoonful of soup, gallons of fluid removed from the abdomen. He had worked up until the day of his diagnosis, which came at the beginning of summer break. That was the last time I'd seen him, the day of the leather vest and hat. He planned on working on his book over the summer and had every intention of coming back in the fall to teach but was too weak by then. Just as I had every intention of seeing him until the end.

And he had handled that end, to all accounts, with his customary grace, even sending out a message to all of us explaining that he knew we would not know how to act and that he knew us to be fine people and however we approached his illness was exactly the way we were meant to approach it. He tried to relinquish us from guilt. I have never done anything with that much grace.

And so we went on with our teaching, our forming and re-forming of alliances, our *next* day I will call him, the *next* I will stop by. I never had the sense of crisis. All of life is like this, I know from reading, but it didn't help. It was the sudden cutting off of those possibilities that seemed so difficult to take in.

So let me say now what I remember about him. When he was younger and his girls were still young and at home, he had given parties and his beautiful princess daughters had greeted his guests and given tours of the house and bookshelves. He had planted a holly bush by the front door when his daughter was born, and in kindergarten she was fond of standing by the bush and saying I'm Holly and I'm named after this tree. His oldest daughter took after her father and became an Austen scholar.

I remember most the stories of his southern Indiana childhood: the stories of abuse and beatings, religiosity and fraud, that went back generations. He worked his way through college as a fireman on a railroad. I remember him saying he was saved by reading, was given a scholarship to graduate school, and then after his marriage (which also saved him) and the birth of his first daughter, he experienced a conversion. The conversion was this: when he looked down at his first-born daughter's form he had begun this cathartic weeping that was, he said in later years, almost a mystical experience. He heard a voice, and it was his own voice saying 'It all stops here, with you.' The horror of his family's story. And it did. He stopped it, changed the course of all of it.

If he was sometimes too aware of his intelligence, it was a minor flaw.

Earlier on, our Modernist said, he had a tough time of it. Remember when he was department chair? Everyone was angry with him.

He wasn't born into sainthood then? A young Romanticist asked. There were the criticism wars early on, an older colleague said. We spent an entire year trying to agree on the Great Books list and finally gave it up.

And it was the beginning of the whole postmodern thing, he said. And creative writing as a discipline, I said.

I know, I said, that we were, the creative writers, at times insufferable. We demanded special offices, reduced teaching loads, better computers and carried, sometimes, an aura of revelation, as though we received all our words directly from the mountaintop. It wasn't an easy time to be department chair.

But at least we kept close reading alive, our poet said. Novels and poems are cultural studies. It's the writer's job to pull together the popular culture and people's lives and combs and brushes and *sidewalks*.

We'd had someone apply for a job recently whose dissertation was on sidewalks and strolling in early 20th century France. It was weirdly fascinating, I'd thought, but more as a detail about our times.

Would you put that dissertation in your house of literature? someone had asked me after her job talk, knowing I was fond of that metaphor.

If the dissertation's any good, I said, it can go in the room with dissertations on urban studies, but not Baudelaire. If it is, in other words, a book to be read.

And what does *good* have to do with it? he might have said. Luckily, we'd already had that argument.

So. Here we all are, the department chair said again. Let's lift a glass.

Irish coffee, water, soda, a few wines, a few beers. Should we order some appetizers? It was late afternoon, mid-winter. No difference in the quality or direction of the light from sunrise to sunset, as though the gray landscape was lit from within, on some kind of dimmer switch that made the day visible late in the morning and invisible again at night.

So yes, it was agreed that 2012 had not been a good year and that it had ended badly. A photographer somewhere had taken a photo of a wired garland shaped into 2013 from some small town's New Year's parade, and from the back it spelled Eros. We had all seen it on the internet. Every one of us had seen it! We were happy to be entering the year of Eros. What is it called? someone asked. That phobia, the fear of 13. Tri something, someone said. Three. Fear. Phobia. Triskaidekaphobia, a Postcolonialist said, pulling it out from a dark recess in the brain.

I'll bet there are people who came out from under their beds after the Mayan Calendar passed and dove back under when they realized they'd be living for one whole year in 2013, the poet said. Even skyscrapers skip that floor number.

But here we all are, the department chair said again, all of us here together. It seemed important to him to say this.

We talked about bad TV shows we had caught up on over break.

The oldest one of us, the Shakespearean, tuned out during this conversation. When it was his turn to toast our former colleague, all he could think of to say is that he and his colleague had always been in competition for everything. They were the same age. It was the first time any of us realized that the two hadn't talked in years, that perhaps there was even some resentment there.

There was a two-sided glass fireplace separating the restaurant from the bar. The fire was going. The restaurant was warm. It was a gray New Years, two feet or so of snow on the ground, beginning to turn sooty at the edges of the cleared streets.

So here we all are, the chair said again.

We talked about the musical tastes of the departed. Classical mostly, a lot of opera, but also some Diana Krall and Nancy Griffith. Sometimes his students would recommend music to him. He had been heard having a very serious intellectual conversation about Mumford and Sons, one where he asked questions and then placed them in context musically and culturally but was ultimately a bit dismissive.

You know when Amy Winesap died, I thought that was it, I said to my friend, the rhetorician. There would never be another somewhat contemporary / cool / hip / heroin-addicted bluesey, smokey-voiced person I could listen to over and over again on my playlist. It would be all really old and then really dead singers, like it was for my father. Frank Sinatra, Miles Davis, Glenn Miller for him. Mick Jagger and Bruce Springsteen and the Indigo Girls until they keel over for me.

But no more new ones. No more romances for me, I said. Just passion remembered, nothing fresh.

Then along came Adele, I said, and she sounds just like Winesap to me. I mean, I've been married for years and I find myself screaming out "Someone Like You" when I'm on the treadmill.

Is it Winesap? I asked. It wasn't Winesap was it?

Winehouse, my friend said.

Yes, that's it. I knew that! How soon we forget, right? Winehouse. But there's Adele, and she's her own person, only she sounds like Winehouse. Like Winehouse sounded like someone before her and on back and on back.

Who knows what fresh hell this year will bring? The Marxist said.

Dorothy Parker! I said. That's how she answered her telephone: What fresh hell is this?

How do we know these things?

I was babbling. No wonder the dead man hadn't had conversations with me. There was some hope for the young women in his office. They were malleable, smarter than I had ever been.

I looked around the place.

When I was a kid I used to come here, I said to my friend, the rhetorician. Those pictures on the wall over there, I said, the ones that look so old-timey. I swear I was here when it all looked old-timey and it didn't feel that way, you know? It felt like a *now*, only I was a kid and this was a drugstore, not a restaurant.

I think there was a soda fountain over there, I said, and I pointed to a row of tables underneath a window. I would walk down here from my grandmother's house and order a chocolate soda, I said.

There had to have been some mistake in my hiring, I said. No one who was born here works here without moving far away first.

I know there was a mistake in mine, she said. They never hire anyone from Texas.

And I remembered right then the taste of the sodas, remembered most coming in here with my cousins and buying lined notepads in the summers. On the front there would be pictures of movie stars. Those summers I spent with my cousins writing secret thoughts in the notebooks and talking in secret languages and sucking nectar directly out of phlox blossoms. How long had it been a drugstore? A couple of decades?

It was rude, I know, but I looked it up on my phone while the others talked.

The phone took me to the history of pharmacy in Indianapolis. It was all there on my phone. It was in my hand, all the information. There wasn't a book, but there were primary sources. So easily accessible! What an amazing year 2013 was proving to be.

Charles Binkley opened his first drugstore in 1910, I read.

I wondered where he got his training, if it had been at Butler where we all taught. We had the only pharmacy school in the city now. I wondered if there was a connection.

In that same decade, I discovered, the city's first school of pharmacy opened then closed down briefly then opened again. Mr. Binkley opened the second incarnation of his store in 1915 and moved to the location that was now a restaurant in the thirties. The Indianapolis School of Pharmacy and the school of pharmacy at Butler merged in 1945, the year a man named Lill (whose recent obituary came up first in the google search for The Indianapolis School of Pharmacy) would get his diploma and begin working at Binkley's drugstore. At the time of Lill's recent death he was the oldest pharmacist in Indiana. He died within days of our colleague. Two families mourning, the story of their lives brought together here in this one place in this one simple search.

All of this information was available online, but randomly, to be brought together in something like this. An essay, a story.

Everything in the world means something. Everything in the universe is connected. That's the real labor in the house of literature.

The appetizers were delivered by a young man with curly hair. Calamari, hummus. I put my phone away.

The older ones talked about colleagues who had left. Remember when so and so was chair? She was awful to the women under her and then she became a feminist when she didn't get a grant. And that other chair, the one who became a provost at some college? We had a drink when he was gone. The conversation went in this sort of direction, into gossip and jokes.

The untenured colleagues listened to this, folk tales of people from some unreal time. Names they had never heard before. They could not possibly have existed and the stories were not interesting enough, not really, to record or to outlast the memories of the tellers. These people had been here and then they were gone.

Still, we all felt close, oddly closer than we had ever felt, like we were huddled together in a cave, a big wind swirling around us from all sides. One by one we would turn and walk into that wind. But not now. Not now.

And what I want to say is that it felt good to be there together in that place in the dying light, but we couldn't stay too long. It felt in those moments like we were in the same story at the same time. We held onto it for a moment or two like a breath, a prayer. We couldn't hold onto it longer than that. Only art could do that.

The youngest of us had children to get to. This has never happened before, of course, in the history of humanity, the oldest of us thought. Children to get to. Let's get another drink! The oldest of us had four children, grown, and not one of his colleagues ever asked about them, though he listened to their endless stories as someone had listened to his.

But why is it the bitterness that lasts sometimes? he wondered. Toward whom is it directed? There were times he hated the man who had just died, that aura of greatness, his need for an assistant when his own papers piled willy nilly on the floor, the tops of every surface. The stories of greatness that would continue whenever his name was mentioned. And how long would that be? Would he too become a caricature? Would he be remembered as the kindly punster, the one who loved Shakespeare and a good joke? Would they all go from human being to caricature to forgotten?

We were all thinking the same things from our own points of view. I could see the thoughts on the Shakespearean's face. Behind his whimsical smile.

And how do people know when it's time to leave a gathering? How do you end a story properly?

The waiter brought the check for our drinks and appetizers. The chair brought out his credit card.

While I was sitting at the table with the candles, the remains of hummus and crabcakes, craft beers and gourmet pizzas, I thought about the pharmacy. Underneath the now or within it or existing in some ghostlike parallel past there had been another place: jars of medicines that looked medicinal because of their packaging or preparation; medicines that were in fact only tree bark, ash, lilac, poplar, ginseng, rhubarb, ephedra from China, fatty oils pressed by seeds, animal glands and dried blood, alcohol and distilled water; essential elements like oxygen, chlorine; prussic acid, tartaric acid, tungsten, glycerin, nitroglycerin, camphor, morphine and alkaloids. Ordinary things, taken for granted. Culture and history behind it. The Shakers dispensing over 200 varieties of herbs while waiting for their own endtimes, explorers dispensed to jungles where they return with tens of thousands of herbs, chemists testing compounds on their own bodies, a system for coloring poisons, systems for inhaling oxygen, the glass ampoules for sterilization, and eventually the biological preparations, the toxins and compounds and antibiotics—taken for granted but somehow magical. All of these things had existed and they existed still to slow it down, the ending of each story, to relieve the pain of passing.

Chemotherapy gave our friend the extra months that allowed him to make it to the end of the year, a year that had opened with such hope.

The word apocalypse, I had read in a student paper, is connected etymologically to the word "uncovering." We look at the world for signs that it all is ending. We change our sense of what a story means as we go along, testing hypothesis, and only in the ending does that meaning reveal itself, the possible meanings collapsing into one. Until then we make and revise guesses about the encoded meaning of it all. Those guesses won't be satisfied until an ending reveals that meaning and retrospectively illuminates those experiences, "frankly transfigur[ing] the events in which they were immanent." Who am I quoting? The student? A rhetorician? At times it all merged together. At times all the books and all the stories and all the words and voices were part of one whole. There was no house with separate rooms. There was a swirling world of words and images.

And so. Here we are all were together minus one, the department chair said as we began to gather our coats. Soon we were standing in a broken circle by the table. The Shakespearean and I, the oldest now, stood slightly outside the circle, like crooked teeth, like ghosts. We were on opposites sides of the table, would leave by two different doors. The Shakespearean tried to catch someone's eye, someone to say goodbye to. No one saw the gesture but me and I couldn't hear him over the sound of talking. Goodbye goodbye! I waved at the Shakespearean. Same time next year, in different circumstances, the department chairman said.

And we turned from the fire, left the restaurant one by one. Outside, in the twilight, the cold was bitter. And the snow fell on all of us, of course. On all of us, the living and the dead.

Susan Neville's collections of short fiction won the Flannery O'Connor Award for Short Fiction and the Richard Sullivan Prize. Two of her stories have appeared in Pushcart Prize anthologies. She is also the author of four books of nonfiction, and she teaches at Butler University in Indianapolis. As a child, she was known for reading six Nancy Drew books in one day, bringing bags of books on vacations, and being told by her father that she had to go outside and do something that wasn't sitting and reading for at least part of the summer. Most of the contributors to this volume have, she guesses, very similar life stories.

SITTING AT THE FEET OF MY FLANNER HOUSE ELDERS

A Lesson After Dying

DAROLYN JONES

Norman Cousins, celebrated American essayist, long-time editor of the *Saturday Review*, and author of *Anatomy of an Illness* is quoted as saying, "Death is not the greatest loss in life. The greatest loss is what dies inside us while we live."

Anyone who has experienced death—particularly an unexpected death, a life taken too soon, a child—lives this quote daily. Grief never dies.

But here in the Midwest, this truth is rarely spoken or acknowledged and it certainly isn't made visible. Grief is hidden, not revealed, and certainly not welcomed or celebrated. Unlike early American women, we don't wear black for a year to show we are still in mourning; unlike the players in the NBA or the NFL, we don't wear black armbands to symbolize and remember a tragic event; and unlike a country, there are no flags to wave at half-mast. After a brief mourning period, we archive our grief; we don't exhibit it.

I speak this truth as a lifelong Hoosier. When I travel outside of the state, I am a mouthpiece for Visit Indy. I resemble a barker inviting folks to come, come and watch the World's greatest spectacle in racing, come and walk through the 100 Acre Park at the Indianapolis Museum of Art, which includes the bones from John Green's novel and movie *The Fault in our Stars*, come and experience a vibrant food and art and cultural scene. Our city is friendly and clean and full of amazing history.

But what I don't say is that we are also conservative, reserved, and private. We portray a "pull yourself up, work harder, keep a stiff upper lip, don't let them see you cry" attitude. When someone dies, after the big church funeral and at the grave side, you can cry, and we will even sympathetically share our catch comfort phrases like "Death is just part of life." Or "He had a good life," or "He would want you to be strong." But, after that, the mourning period is over.

I don't know if that's because of the immigrant stock that brought our early families here in the first place, in hope of a better life. Brought our families to a state that might well have been better than where we came from, but has always been mired in difficult physical, social, and economic terrain. But what's true of us in Indiana is that we are survivors. And after we bury our dead, our upper lips are stiff and we move on. Some find comfort in prayer, some find comfort in support groups or therapy, and some never find comfort and welcome their own death so they can stop this half-life. They speak of not being afraid of death because they look forward to being reunited with the one who died.

The living dead are offered the famous Elisabeth Kubler-Ross' grief cycle and are told that they can expect to experience denial, anger, bargaining, depression, and acceptance. Some support and some contest Kubler-Ross' model. I find it overly simplistic, part of the hegemony of what we are supposed to do. And if we don't find a solution in "working the program," then there is something wrong with us. Death should change us. Death should make us never the same again. Death is the great equalizer. Everyone has or will experience death. It's our greatest common denominator.

My own son, Will, was born dead 11 years ago. Born dead, revived, dead again, revived and currently living. He lives now as a very different boy than the one who was born. He lived 39 days in critical condition in a Neonatal Intensive Care Unit. He has lived through 33 surgeries and procedures. He lives because of the medical care of 9 pediatric doctors, multiple therapists, a host of specialized equipment, suspended and highly formulized medications and formula, and a surgically placed pump and feeding tube that keep him alive. He lives with Cerebral Palsy and autism. He lives as a boy who is both nonverbal and non-ambulatory. He lives with round the clock care from my husband, nurses, and myself. He lives, but a part of him died. And a part of me did too. The death of the boy who should have been born instead of the boy who lived, and the death of the dream of having more children. I still live that death. Those experiences don't leave you; they don't dull, nor should they.

After his death, I became immersed in memoir. When Will was only three months old and we were in yet another appointment with his neurologist, Dr. James Pappas, asking again for a diagnosis, a prognosis, a life expectancy—what will he do, what won't he know, what should we do? He sat down, part weary from our questions and part from the complexity of Will's case, and simply replied, "I can't tell you. Will is writing his own story." I wrote that down in the notebook that I always carried, went home and began to write down everything Will did or didn't do, recording his story. I would write his story.

I even began several writing groups with women who had children who had died or who, like my son, were now living with special needs. I said we were writing to heal, but every time we wrote, we laid down new scar tissue, picking at the scab. My friend, Indiana author and Executive Director of the Indiana Writers Center, Barbara Shoup, took notice. Together, we created the Memoir Project with the Center and decided to take writing out of the center. The women in my writing groups wrote with such intensity and detail and authenticity that we thought maybe others would do the same with their own stories. And while grief wasn't our prompt or muse, it always showed up. When you ask someone to write about what they remember and to make memoirs and to make sense, you will hear about death over and over and over again.

With our grant outreach programs, courses, and CityWrite memoir project, we have worked with over 50 sites in the greater Indianapolis community and served close to 1,500 youth, seniors, and every age in between. We serve those marginalized voices that we believe should be heard, whose stories should be told and written down. We have worked with girls in prison, veterans of war at the former Indianapolis Senior Center, youth with the Saint Florian Youth Leadership Camp, homeless seniors at the John H. Boner Center, adults with intellectual disabilities at Outside the

Box and Noble of Indiana, and individuals who come to our center because they want to make sense of a life lived, whether that's growing up on a farm, living with cancer, or a husband's suicide. They come with a story to write and lay down.

But, what shows up every time is death. Like Justice's poem, "Incident in a Rose Garden," death is there. Every writer I have worked with through the Center shares a story of how HE [death] came and beckoned a loved one. And like Dickinson's "Because I Could Not Stop for Death—He kindly stopped for me—" every writer explains how they too could not and did not want to stop for that death, but now they can't seem to find the momentum to move the same, or to move at all.

In 2006, I began working with seniors at the Flanner House. A proud and historically significant African American community in Indianapolis, the seniors were skeptical of this white, middle class woman standing in front of them excitedly gesturing and telling them, "Let your voices be heard; Write down your stories!" Standing next to the very brilliant, powerful, and sometimes intimidating then director Myron Richardson, I gave my spiel about why we were there and what we were going to do. One of the seniors looked at me with furled brow, leaned in, took a sip of her coffee, and questioned me honestly, cautiously, and pessimistically, "Why would I do that for you? Why would I tell you my story?"

Excellent question, for which I had no answer. Of course, Myron helped me make the transition, and my colleague and friend Mark Latta and I learned that arriving early, making fresh coffee, bringing sweet rolls, and playing some cards and talking with them first went a lot further than my very planned and articulated curriculum. We talked and they warmed to me, recognizing that I was for real and not there to exploit. They shared and revealed and found their stories to write.

On our first writing day, after talking about what how memory is a funny thing, poignant and infallible, we began with a simple exercise of completing the sentence "I Remember..."

The seniors wrote their one to two sentence responses. One by one, as we moved around the writing circlem reading our responses aloud, the following refrain was repeated: "I remember when my son died."

Death had once again shown up to the writing table.

Below read three excerpts developed from that sentence:

1

I remember February 3, 1973 when my son got killed. He were 18 years old, his senior year in high school. It were about six o'clock in the evening and I had just got home from work.

Telephone ring. I went upstairs to answer it. The voice on the phone say, "Harris just got shot." I scream. My husband is comin' in the door. He grab me and asked what was wrong. I could hardly talk. Somebody call and say Harris just got shot. He said where and they say 30th and Central.

We got in the car and drove to 30th and Central. There was a big crowd and we had to push through the crowd. I took a running start and jumped over people to get to him. I touched his face and checked his pulse. A medic asked for a sheet. I thought it was to keep him warm. They put the sheet over his face. That's when I knew.

One detective say it was self-defense and another say it was just a mad white man who killed a black kid.

I never got the chance to say goodbye. I have learned to deal with it, but it's been hard.

2

I remember the day my son was born in Indianapolis, Indiana. He was a beautiful baby boy. He always had a smile on his face. His name was Kevin. He attended School #83 and Warren Central High School. He enjoyed track and basketball.

I remember the day when he was killed. His life was taken October 29, 1994 at 6:37 p.m. at the age of twenty-six year and five months.

My son left behind two beautiful daughters, Keonya and Jane and a very good friend Marsha, their mother. He loved them so much. The last time I saw my son was that morning, October 29. He came over and cut my grass. He said, "Mom, I am getting' ready to go."

I said, "Okay."

Then, later that evening, I saw the news. I did not know that they were talking about my son. As I was watchin', the police came on my door. My brother went to the door and they asked for Mary Joyner. But I did not go right then cause I know something wrong. But I heard the police tell my brother, "I hope she got Christ in her life."

My brother said, "Yes, she do."

3

I remember August 10, 1998, my son came to my house. He came in the front door and went out of the back door. He spoke to me, but I was in the bedroom. I didn't get to see him.

The next time I saw him, he was dead. We had his funeral that Saturday. His birthday was the next Wednesday. He was 31 years old so I gave him a birthday party and invited all of the family and his friends to celebrate his life when he was living.

I still love talking about him, it makes me happy instead of being sad. He was a good son. I love me like I love him. It was been 20 years ago and to talk about him makes me happy and remember every little thing about him.

The police never did find out who killed him. But I know they will suffer more.

Those memories and stories told are hard to hear, hard to process, hard to take in. I would leave thinking, "What do I do with this? Where do I put these senseless deaths of young men and their mourning mothers left behind?" Like the main character John Coffey in the movie *The Green Mile*, I would often have to leave Flanner House and spew out the stories I had heard the seniors tell that day because they made me sad and sick and heavy. And my own son's death/birth was still very raw.

I never shared my son's story with the seniors, but I know the seniors knew that death had also shown up in my own story. Susan

Zimmerman describes in her book *Writing to Heal: Transforming Grief and Loss Through Writing* about feeling like one open large seething wound covered with a hundred Band-Aids, attempting to cover up the gaping hole so visible to everyone else.

Ironic since I was asking them to reveal the most deeply profound and personal parts of their autobiographic life, yet I couldn't or wouldn't reciprocate. I have learned a lot since then about building community. I should have been telling that story all along. I'm writing this piece now to not only share powerful memories of Indianapolis people, places, and events intersected in a strange and serendipitous way, but also to now share my story with the seniors.

As part of our practice at the Center, I took the Flanner House seniors out of their own center, to spaces that would trigger memories, remind them of their own people, places, and events. We visited Crispus Attucks museum, where they talked and wrote about the impact the school programs and basketball glory had in their lives and in the community. We visited the Lily House and gardens and talked about our grandmother's, mother's, and our own gardens. Our final field trip was to the Indianapolis Museum of Art to see African art. I wanted them to experience the artifacts and art in the hopes that a guided docent tour might inspire stories of ancestry, ritual, and legacy.

But we much more than inspired, we were burdened and then exalted. And in sitting at the feet of my elders in a corner of that exhibit, I found the answer to my grief. I learned a powerful lesson about dying and living.

What happened in that small moment and in that small space has left a memory scar for me. Not a scratch or a scab that heals but a scar. Like the ones I bear on my right wrist from falling over in an unfolded lawn chair and landing on a small piece of barbed wire fencing in my grandmother's garden, or the burn scar on my left calf I got from crash landing on the exhaust pipe of a Suzuki 50. Or the hip-to-hip, crooked scar I have from doctors trying to rip my baby out. I can see it. I can feel it. I can show it. I can talk about its origin. I can tell its story. It's a memory that as writer Christopher Poulos explains, "Shows up, unbidden, and demands attention." It can't be ignored.

As we walked and stopped throughout our tour, the seniors asked questions, shared connections, pointed out garbs, images, and artifacts that reminded them or appealed to them. The memory cues were working. I asked the docent if we could find a space in the exhibit where there extra benches to allow the seniors an opportunity to sit a spell. My feet were tired, and I knew many of them were struggling with the amount of mobility and standing required for such a tour. She obliged, leading us to a small corner in the exhibit where there was maybe a 20 by 24 color image of a woman carrying a wooden doll on her back. And another smaller image of a woman and her children, sitting on the floor of a primitive African home, with the same wooden doll sitting at the table, a bowl of food in front of the doll. Finally, in between those two images, tucked into this low corner, was a small plastic museum box holding a carved wooden doll, fully dressed and standing alone, staring back at us.

The docent said that while we were sitting, she could talk with us about this part of the exhibit. Immediately, one of the seniors asked why the doll was being fed. And, "Why was the mother carrying this doll on her back?" The Ibeji doll, according to the docent, represents a Yoruba twin. The Yoruba people are from the southwestern region of Nigeria and the Yoruban women disproportionally birth twins. The average twin birth rate worldwide is 4 per 1000 and in Yoruba, it's 150 per 1000, the highest in the world.

Understandably, twins are considered very special, as are their mothers. Twins are considered the children of the King Shango, the God of Thunder. The Yoruba people believe that all twin children are spirited, unpredictable, and fearless, much like Shango. If a twin dies, which happens often because of the high infant mortality rate, the mother must appease the spirit of the dead child, because neglect of that spirit could cause the dead twin to tempt its surviving sibling to join him.

So, an Ibeji doll is carved in the same gender as the deceased twin to serve as a dwelling place for that dead child's spirit. Ibeji are cared for, revered, and even celebrated their entire life and beyond. They are dressed in traditional garb, they wear the beads of their nation and deities, and their bodies are rubbed with cosmetics and indigo. And just like any Yoruban, they sleep in a bed, and they sit at the table to eat with the family. The mother carries her dead twin with her when she leaves with her other children. The Ibeji are handled gingerly and with great reverence. Mothers with Ibeji are asked to perform rituals because of their sacred abilities. When the mother dies, the Ibeji doll is passed on to the surviving twin or to another family member. The child lives on. The child is dead, but lives on through this spirit doll.

We learned that in the African spirit world, the lines between living and dead remain blurred, yet connected, not disconnected. While the story of the Yoruba and the Ibeji doll is laden in death, it made me feel alive for the first time in a long time.

When the docent completed her explanation of what was the smallest exhibit in the space, you could see the weight sink under the bench as we all sat heavier, as if our hearts were tired of trying to keep themselves in their cavity, tired of trying to hold that heaviness in. Heads lowered. You could hear involuntary deep sighs, see hands clasped together near the mouth, and hear the humming of one senior saying, "Mmmmmm." Those sounds and motions our bodies do when we have to let out the overflow of emotions that we can't control or keep inside. I had to walk away, step around the corner for a moment to compose myself. I stood there holding back tears, again not publically showing my grief.

I kept hearing a stanza from Seamus Heaney's "The Poplar" running through my head:

> *Wind shakes the big poplar,*
> *quicksilvering*
> *The whole tree in a single sweep.*
> *What bright scale fell and left this needle quivering?*
> *What loaded balances have come to grief?*

"What loaded balances have come to grief?" All these years I had searched for a way to grieve and here it was—finally revealed. I wanted an Ibeji doll to hold, an Ibeji doll to carry, an Ibeji doll to remind me of the son I had lost.

I returned and sat down while we all moved in closer to examine the intricate beauty of the Ibeji son doll. Carved as an adult and an idealized form depicting who he would have grown up to be, he wore a beautifully crafted shell tunic and beads, his wood form was worn from being handled and loved so much, and his sweet and soft eyes stared back at all of us. We felt his spirit and no doubt his mother gained the same comfort from his presence as we were in that silent moment.

After backing away, we all sat back down, unable to continue to the next part of the tour. It was a communal grief that rendered our feet rocks. I raised my head and asked the seniors how they remembered, how they honored, and how they revered their dead. Some immediately opened up their purses and shared pictures or copies of obituaries of their dead sons that always remained with them, some recited Bible verses and prayers said daily, some pulled out necklaces with their son's initials, and some explained how they kept their son's clothes, school items, or images at home in a box and sometimes visited that box to feel closer.

But even after that sharing, there was a common resolution that the primitive Yoruban people were far more equipped to mourn than we were. All of us with dead sons wished we had a doll. We wished we could carry that doll out with us. We wished people wouldn't look at us as someone who had a son who got killed or who had died, but as someone special who has special powers, as someone with a child to celebrate not grieve. As a child who could live on beyond us, instead of being mourned and buried, left behind.

The docent was on a schedule, but she could feel we were not ready to move on, so she shared that the doll, along with most of the pieces in the exhibit of The Eiteljorg Suite of African and Oceanic Art, were donated by Indianapolis native, art collector, and museum supporter Harrison Eiteljorg, who collected and kept these pieces in a small office until it came to the IMA. She revealed an image of him nearby.

"A white man?" said one of the seniors surprised. Everyone chuckled, and with that said the tension eased. We were finally able to stand up and walk forward to continue our tour.

I took one look back at that boy and thought of my boy, who is living and breathing. Differently? Yes. But, generously? Yes. My amazing boy, Will, is my sunshine, my joymaker, my muse. He has taught me the most important and simplest lesson of life—live your joy. He proves his name because his will is the greatest I have ever known. Regardless of my grief, I know that I am grateful that I was chosen to care for his spirit.

My son's birth was a death. He was never born. He came out dead. There was no happy delivery, no photos, no taking the baby out to see the grandparents with a blue or pink hat on, wrapped in a striped hospital baby blanket. He was born emergently and prematurely at 33 weeks. And while he weighed 6 pounds, he was not alive. The ethical line for saving a hypoxied baby is 15 minutes, as the ability for a newborn to make a meaningful recovery with no oxygen source for 15 minutes is rarely possible. Because the doctors were unclear of how long Will had been deprived of oxygen, dead in utero, they proceeded to attempt to save his life. Had my husband been present (he was on assignment for the military, desperately trying to get to the hospital) or had I been conscious, we would have been asked whether or not we wanted this dead baby to be revived.

Will was born with an Apgar score of 0 and was given two blood transfusions before he could be revived. Apgar stands for appearance, pulse, grimace, activity, and respiration, and is the standard criteria used to assess a newborn's health at delivery. Will had bled out in utero and had lost 75% of his blood into his mother. His blood crit level was only 16; normal is within the range of 82-98. Will was on full life support, an oscillating vent, and intubated. His initial brain scan showed Burst Suppression

Syndrome, meaning no brain activity. Wavering between life and death for 12 days, he crossed over and miraculously did survive, regain brain activity, and while significantly challenged has thrived more than anyone thought possible, but his birth will always be framed and sit on my memory mantle as a death.

He is now 11, a tall, curly blond-haired and joyful boy who loves everyone that loves him back. He stands in much opposition to his parents who are short, dark-haired, cynical people suspect of kindness.

Looking back at the Ibeji one last time that day, I decided that Will was embodying both the boy he should have been before his brain died and the boy he is now. He carries the spirit of his twin self, and unlike the mother carrying her dead twin, I get both boys in this one boy. And it was at this shrine, at this alter, sitting at the feet of my Flanner House elders, that I laid down my own heavy burden, that I decided to stop grieving the boy who had died and embrace the one that had lived.

Like Auden's famous poem, "Funeral Blues," my son Will is "my talk, my song." He changed my world, my thinking, and my speak. But it took those elders and our gathering to make me hear that song and talk that talk.

A lesson after dying.

This piece is dedicated to the Flanner House seniors.
It was an honor to be taught and trusted with your tales.

WORKS CITED

Auden, William. "Funeral Blues." AllPoetry.com. n.d. Web. 13 June 2014.

Celenko, Theodore and Harrison Eiteljorg. *A Treasury of African Art: From the Harrison Eiteljorg Collection.* Bloomington, Indiana: Indiana University Press, 1983. Print.

Dickinson, Emily. "Because I Could Not Stop for Death (712)." Poets.org. American Academy of Poets. n.d. Web. 13 June 2014.

Frank Darabont. Dir. *The Green Mile.* Warner Home Video, 2000. DVD.

Gaines, Ernest J. *A Lesson Before Dying.* New York: Alfred A. Knopf, 1993. Print.

Green, John. *The Fault in our Stars.* New York: Dutton Books, 2012. Print.

Heany, Seamus. "The Poplar." The Spirit Level: Poems. New York: Farrar, Strauss, and Giroux, 1996. Print.

Ibeji Twin Figure. 20th century. Wood, Pigment, Glass, Fiber, Iron, Cowrie shells. Gift of Mr. and Mrs. Harrison Eiteljorg 1989. Indianapolis Museum of Art.

Jones, Darolyn. (2011). *The Joyful Experiences of Mothers of Special Needs Children: An Authoethnographic Study.* Diss. Ball State University, 2011. Muncie, IN: Proquest. Print.

Jones, Darolyn, and Mark Latta. Eds. *Sitting at the Feet of our Elders: Flanner House Speaks.* Indianapolis: Writers' Center of Indiana Press, 2009. Print.

Justice, Donald. "Incident in a Rose Garden." Ronnow
    Poetry.com. Robert Ronnow: Poetry. n.d. Web. 13 June
    2014.

Poulos, Christopher. "Writing Through the Memories:
    Autoethnography as a Path to Transcendence." *International
    Review of Qualitative Research*. 5.3 (2012): 313-324. Print.

Visonà, Monica Blackmun, Robin Roynor, Herbert M. Cole,
    Susanne Preston Blier, and Rowland Abiodun. *A History of
    Art in Africa*. Upper Saddle River, NJ: Pearson/Prentice Hall,
    2008. Print.

Zimmerman, Susan. *Writing to Heal: Transforming Grief and Loss
    Through Writing*. New York: Three Rivers Press, 2002. Print

Darolyn "Lyn" Jones is a mom to a son with a disability, a wife, a teacher, a writer, a sister friend, and a social activist. She is an Assistant Professor in the Department of English at Ball State University and the Education Outreach Director of the Indiana Writers Center, where she has facilitated several urban outreach writing programs, including Girls in Prison Speak, Sitting at the Feet of our Elders, Building a Rainbow, Recording War Memories, CityWrite, and Special Needs Moms Write. Lyn is passionate about literacy and has devoted her personal and professional life to teaching and writing with writers both in and out of the classroom. Check out her website, publications, and blog at *www.darolynlynjones.com*

BLACK LIKE...ME?
Thoughts on Reading, Teaching, and Literacy of the Heart

BARBARA SHOUP

My first personal encounter with a black person, or "Negro," as we said in the 1950s, occurred when I was five years old. My dad had picked me up from Sunday school, and it was just the two of us in the car, so I got to sit in the front seat beside him. We hadn't gone too far when he pulled over to the curb, and leaned across me to call out to a black man on the street. The man stopped, beamed at the sight of my dad, walked toward the car and bent to look inside. He was a big man, his face filled the window.

"This is my friend, Albert Cherry," my dad said to me.

I have no memory other than that moment. I have no idea how my dad and Albert Cherry had come to be friends. But many years later, it occurred to me that this encounter had subconsciously taught me that such friendships were normal. *What's the problem,* I thought, from the time I understood there was such a thing as racism. Some people have light skin, some dark. Why do we care?

As a little girl, it upset me to watch black school children walk the gauntlet of snarling white people on the television news. As the 1960's commenced, I was horrified again and again by beatings and murders that occurred in the South. By watching Watts burned. I grieved for the black people who suffered at the hands of those who hated them; it hurt my heart. But it wasn't until I was sixteen and read *Black Like Me* that I felt the profound difference between being a black person and a white one.

In the book, published in 1961, John Howard Griffin, a white man, decided to see what it was like to be a Negro in America. He starts his experiment in New Orleans, where he explores the community for several weeks, creating casual acquaintances, both black and white, along the way. Then, with the help of a physician, he undergoes treatments to darken his skin—and the world turns upside down. Traveling from New Orleans through Mississippi, Alabama and Georgia, alternating his skin color, the difference between the way white and black people are treated becomes painfully real. As a white man, he is treated by other whites with respect and dignity; as the same man, with dark skin, the treatment he receives from (sometimes the very same) white people ranges from rudeness to cruelty. He is often threatened, sometimes treated as if he were invisible. Denied the most basic rights, it frightens him to realize how quickly he abandons the assumption that he will be treated humanely and even begins to regard himself as unworthy.

I remember the book itself, a battered paperback. On the cover was a stark black and white photograph of a man walking away from the viewer down a wide corridor of what looks like a government building. The title is centered above his head, Black Like Me, in big lime green letters. An arrow formed by the left side of the "M" points down at him. I remember being lost in the book for days, living in it. I remember turning the pages with real fear, and the visceral shift of my perspective about that abstract issue, race, that occurred because for a little while I was a black person, just as John Howard Griffin had been.

I was forever changed. It wasn't just that I felt as if I had experienced the cruelty of whites toward blacks first-hand, though that was powerful. It was that I experienced the sheer stupidity of racism. John Howard Griffin was exactly the same person, black or white. But the world in which he lived as one could not have been more different from the world of the other.

William James, the psychologist, is said to have observed, "The greatest gap in nature is between two minds." He was right. Each one of us experiences the world from an utterly different point of view. At times, a sibling's point of view, her memories of your shared childhood, can seem as unlikely, as foreign as the point of view of a person you've never known and will never know and who comes from a world in no apparent way like your own. When reasonable people disagree on issues of importance to them, they often conclude, "I don't see it that way, but I respect your point of view." Rarely, in my experience, do they ask each other, "What shaped you? What made you see racism or capital punishment or divorce or your daughter's new tattoo the way you do?" Rarely do they ask it of themselves.

There's another gap, too: the one between the true self inside us that knows our shortcomings and yearns to be better and braver than we are and the self we present to others. We know that gap in ourselves all too well. But if we don't read stories that wrestle with the way life is, we might never even realize that such a gap exists in everyone. We might assume that there's nothing more to a person that what he does and what he says.

Which is why books matter so much: the good ones ask questions of their readers. They take us into the hearts and minds and worlds of people unlike ourselves, shifting our perceptions and quietly asking when we emerge, "What do you think now?"

Learning about the death of Holden Caldwell's brother near the end of *The Catcher in the Rye* shocked me into understanding that there are things we don't know about people that cause us to judge them harshly, when in fact they may be acting from hopelessness or despair. *All Quiet on the Western Front* made me see that, regardless of what side they're fighting for and how much they believe in the cause, most soldiers are just scared, lonely, exhausted boys, far away from their loved ones, longing for war to be over so they can go home. Lisa Alther's novel *Kinflicks* showed me, in a single exchange of dialogue between an estranged mother and daughter, that memory is infallible: people who have had exactly the same experiences may remember them in very different ways—and neither is lying. Reading Ann Tyler's *Dinner at the Homesick Restaurant*, I understood that there is no such thing as a perfect family, but we all long for one nonetheless—and felt less lonely in my own longing.

The best books explore the complexity of the human condition. They offer the privilege of living in the heads of people who are not us, freeing us briefly from our own point of view to see and experience the world in new way and to be changed by it. Characters may think and behave in ways that are completely alien and even repugnant to our own sensibilities, but we can feel compassionate toward them because, privy to their inner lives, we can know them in a way we can never know real people, even the ones we're closest to and love the most. Reading good books makes us less judgmental in our real lives, less certain, less inclined to make rigid pronouncements about right and wrong. It makes us curious, particularly about what makes people tick—and curiosity mitigates hurt and anger. It trumps hatred every single time.

I think of the benefit of this kind of reading as literacy of the heart.

★

Ann Patchett's *Bel Canto* opens with a horrific scene in which a group of terrorists interrupt a performance by a world-renowned opera singer and take her and the audience of international dignitaries hostage. But as the weeks go by, as the group lives together in close quarters, the terrorists are slowly revealed as individuals and the line between good and evil begins to blur. You know how it will end, you know it has to end that way—the act the terrorists engaged in was wrong. But you mourn for them, and for the world that shaped them toward believing they were right.

I read the book in the direct aftermath of 9/11, a time when people were deeply enraged by what had happened and hungry for revenge. The nineteen Al Qaeda terrorists were depicted simply: as evil incarnate. There was little curiosity about who they were, individually, or what had brought them to see the world in such a way that they believed flying the planes into the World Trade Towers and the Pentagon was the right, even holy thing to do— and made them willing to sacrifice their own lives in the cause.

Though I dared not admit it except to a few, at the same time I was aghast and heartsick at what those men had done, I thought a lot about the courage it had taken them to do it, wondered about the experiences that had shaped them toward that moment, grieved for the families they had left behind. 9/11 seemed to me tragic in every possible way, not the least of which was the Bush Administration's stubborn refusal to acknowledge the personal and political complexity of the act, stoking the rage of the American people, fueling hatred, and creating an atmosphere of fear. If we didn't try to understand the personal and cultural experiences that had delivered those young men to the morning of September 11, how could we hope to keep similar, even worse incidents from happening again?

Bel Canto exactly expressed what I wished I could say about 9/11. Conflicts and estrangements, large and small, happen for a reason and the reason is always directly related to the people involved: who they are, how they think, why they think the way they do. Could we please start there when we talk about the horrible thing that happened to us?

"You have to read this book," I said to fellow readers, again and again.

I said it about Andre Dubus III's *The Garden of Last Days* a few years later. A master at depicting the tangle of human frailty that leads to fatal miscommunication and tragedy, Dubus tracks a fictional 9/11 terrorist over the last days of his life, making him fully human, allowing the reader access to the beliefs, rationalizations, fears and misgivings that bring him to the moment he passes through airport security in Boston and "...joins his brothers who await him in the crowd."

I regularly recommend the book to aspiring writers because of the way Dubus succeeded at the supreme challenge of creating a character whose despicable act is complicated for the reader for having had access to the character's mind and heart for a little while.

★

One of the great pleasures of teaching literature is witnessing the moment when a book makes a student's world crack open and you witness something shift, visibly, causing him to reconsider something he thought he knew. Teaching *The Adventures of Huckleberry Finn* to high school sophomores every spring for many years, I posed this essay question: "Did Huckleberry Finn believe that his relationship with Jim was right or wrong? Support your conclusion with examples from the text." Throughout the book, Huck observes that he is sinful and wrong to have befriended and protected Jim. He'll go to hell for it, he finally concludes. There's no other choice because "…you can't live a lie."

Yet year after year, students would argue, "…in his heart of hearts he knew that he was right."

"Where do you find that in the text?" I'd ask.

They couldn't tell me. It wasn't there.

More than a hundred years beyond the world that shaped Huck's beliefs, students simply couldn't get their heads around it. Ours was an integrated school, an integrated community. There were racial tensions, sure. But even those with negative feelings about African Americans couldn't imagine a world in which it would be morally wrong to befriend one.

So I'd ask them, "What if a hundred years from now people look back at how our culture treats gay people with the same incomprehension you feel about how black people were treated a hundred years ago? What if, over time, the world comes to see that whether a person is gay or straight doesn't matter any more than whether he's black or white?" I'd just leave it at that. But in the silence that invariably fell, I sensed the whisper of little windows opening in their minds.

Once I visited a high school English class that had read my YA novel *Stranded in Harmony*, in which the main character is struggling with a variety of issues, one of which is the fear that his girlfriend might be pregnant. One student asked why I put sex scenes in the book. "I don't think it's right," she said. "It's like you're condoning it."

"It's a writer's job to tell the truth about life," I replied. "And the truth is, right or wrong, lots of teenagers are involved in sexual relationships. Those who aren't are probably wondering about it, possibly considering it—and worrying about what the consequences might be. It's hard to talk about sex with your parents or other adults, no matter how close you are to them. Experiencing sexual relationships by way of books is a safe way to learn about what they feel like. Not to mention the repercussions that come from the decision to have sex at your age."

A spirited discussion ensued. Some thought what I said made sense, some argued on the side of the student who believed that sex in books for teenagers was immoral. One student said she thought sex in YA books was okay, but only if the characters were punished so readers would know it was wrong. Near the end of the class period, a girl in a seat near the door raised her hand. "I'm pregnant," she said in a quiet voice. "This book helped me see why my boyfriend acted the way he did when I told him."

The bell rang. She was gone.

It was an amazing thing to me, a great gift, to know that my book had made life a little more bearable for someone who had read it. It was all I could do not to run after her.

Beloved, One Flew Over the Cuckoo's Nest, The Things They Carried, Slaughterhouse 5 and *Catch 22* are among the books I teach and recommend over and over for the way the points of view from which they're written often bring insights that make us more deeply human. "I never thought about slaves looking for their families after the Civil War," one student marveled. "I never realized what it meant to be in a mental institution, how you have no control over your own life once you go there," said a troubled kid, adding that he never, ever wanted to end up in a place like that himself. Stories change, depending on who's telling them; time is fluid; war is on some level absurd. By reading, we gather these slivers of light, each one slicing open a peek-hole through which we can contemplate the world.

"It's all true," Hemingway said. It is.

The great lesson reading good books teaches us is to acknowledge, celebrate, and learn to live with the fact that each of us lives in our own universe, with our own unique view of planet Earth. What I see may be invisible to you. But that doesn't mean it isn't there. Reading with an open heart, you might catch a glimpse of it and narrow the gap between us.

Barbara Shoup is the author eight novels, including four for young adults, and the co-author of *Novel Ideas: Contemporary Authors Share the Creative Process* and *Story Matters.* Her books have received numerous awards, including ALA Best Books for Young Adults. She was the 2006 recipient of the PEN Phyllis Reynolds Naylor Working Writer Fellowship. Currently, she is the Executive Director of the Indiana Writers Center. Visit her at *www.barbarashoup.com*

AMERICAN HISTORY

DAN WAKEFIELD

My goddaughter and I are in our favorite booth at McDonald's, studying for her eighth grade midterm in American History. This is Miami, and American history is taught in Spanish. Liti (her childhood nickname is pronounced "Leetee") has to translate questions in her class workbook for me so I can look them up in the hefty English version I bought online that must weigh about five pounds. It is called *The American Journey, Florida Edition*, by Appleby, Brinkley, and McPherson. (I have come to think of the authors as "The Three *Gringos*." I am the fourth.) What we have to cover for tomorrow's test is simply American history from *Cristobal Colon* and *Ponce de Leon* to the end of the Revolutionary War.

I mainly try to hit the names and events that are printed in boldface type, like "The Iroquois Confederacy."

"Is that like in Iraq?" Liti asks.

"No, it's in our own country—or it was. It's Indian tribes—I mean, that's what they used to be called, 'Indians.' Now I guess we call them 'Native American tribes.'"

(I think it's all right to say 'tribes,' unless they're now called 'extended families.')

Liti looks puzzled.

"You know," I say, "the guys with feathers in their hair."

"Oh yeah—and they dance around a fire!"

"You got it."

That takes care of the Indians. We need to press on to Bunker Hill, The Boston Tea Party, The Boston Massacre, Valley Forge, and George Washington crossing the Delaware.

"What about 'The Green Mountain Boys?'" she asks.

"I think they were from Vermont. What about them?"

"Miss Humarra is always taking about them."

I say in my awkward, Indiana Spanish—"*Los Ninos de las Montanas Verde?*"

"Yes—what did they do?"

"I don't remember—I think they attacked somebody. They didn't come up that much when I was in school. I don't think they're that big a deal."

"So why is Miss Humarra always talking about them?"

"Maybe she just likes to say '*Los Ninos de las Montanas Verde.*'"

I like to say it too, since it's probably one of the few events in American history I am able to say in Spanish. I have to look it up, so I heave the history tome up to my lap, scan the index, and turn to the pages cited.

It says Benedict Arnold, then a captain in the Connecticut militia, was planning to attack the British at Fort Ticonderoga. He "learned that Ethan Allen was also mounting an expedition in Vermont to attack the fort. Arnold joined with Allen's force, known as The Green Mountain Boys, and together they caught the British by surprise."

The book gives no further explanation of who Ethan Allen was or who his "Boys" were. All I can contribute is that Allen and his boys were from Vermont, which is called "The Green Mountain State" and that must be how they got their name.

We both are at a loss as to why "The Boys" are so important to Miss Humarra. Anyway, we've nailed them; they captured a fort.

"Does Miss Humarra ever talk about *Los Hombres Minutos?*"

"Yes!—didn't they have to get dressed real quick?"

"Right—and grab their guns—I mean 'muskets.'"

Hitting on all the high points—at least most of the people and events in boldface—takes us until 7:30. We've been at the books for three hours, fueled by several orders of "apple dippers" and Liti's standard meal—a cheeseburger with catsup only—when we finally pack up and return to her house. Abuela (grandmother) is sitting on the couch with little Rey beside her. Little Rey (spelled "R-e-y" as in Spanish for "King"), is twelve years old but he will never walk or talk. When he was a year old he was diagnosed as "hypotonic," more commonly called "floppy baby," and meaning "lack of muscle tone." He can crawl and make sounds, laugh and cry, but that's all. Little Rey has been sick with a bad cold for about a week now. At least he is sitting up, rather than leaning his head down in front of him like he's been doing.

Alina, the mother of Liti and Little Rey is standing in front of the couch, talking to Abuela. I heft up the American History tome and Liti holds up the notebook she's been writing in to show Abuela "proof" that we've been working, studying for tomorrow's test. Abuela looks, smiles, nods, gives us "Ahhhs" of approval, and adds "Yes, yes!" She hands the notes to Alina, and I display the book, but Alina brushes them aside, turning to her daughter.

"Liti! Take your brother into his bed and fall him asleep."

"But Mom—he still has a cold!"

"You won't get sick—you're in the same room with him right now, breathing the same air."

"Mom, I don't want to get a cold."

"Do what I tell you to do! You've been slacking off lately, and I don't like it."

Alina turns and clicks out of the room in her high-heeled boots.

I know I can't say anything. It won't help. I look at Abuela, and little Rey, and Liti, and no one moves or speaks. My mind seems frozen, a blank slate. All I know is I don't want Liti to get a cold, especially now, when she has her midterms all week, starting tomorrow. Without thought, I bend down and pick up little Rey. I haven't lifted or carried him since he was six years old. He is twice as old now, and even though his arms and legs are as thin as strings, he must weigh at least twice as much as he did since the days when I used to carry him around the yard. I am one triple-by-pass and one new heart valve older, but I manage to hoist him up and get his legs under my arms to carry him. I start toward his mattress room, and I take a step, then another. All at once I feel my legs about to fold as I tilt toward the big TV on the living room table, little Rey in my arms.

I am wordless with fear as my body fights the falling; everything I am is in the trembling effort to stay upright, and in that hung moment Liti calls "Danny!" and the weight is lifted as Abuela is beside me and takes the boy from my arms. For a moment it feels I am still in the fall, the blank TV screen blurring before me, and I think I may be sick. It seems a wonder I can stand, and when I do, I go carefully to the couch and sit, and we all start talking at once. The nausea passes but the fear takes a longer time to subside, and my hands grip the wheel hard as I drive back home.

Dan Wakefield, author of the bestselling novels *Going All the Way* and *Starting Over*, edited and wrote the introduction to *The Letters of Kurt Vonnegut* and *If This Isn't Nice, What Is?: Kurt Vonnegut's Advice to the Young*. Mr. Wakefield moved back to his hometown of Indianapolis three years ago, and hopes that his years of living in Greenwich Village (1955-63) will not disqualify him as an "Indiana author."

"American History" is excerpted from *Liti*, a memoir-in-progress, copyright Dan Wakefield.

READING, WRITING, AND OTHER LIFE LESSONS

A Fairy Tale Romance Between a Boy and a Stand-in Grandmother

LORENE BURKHART

Jamear was 8 years old and I was 76 when we met. I had volunteered to tutor once a week at an elementary school and was assigned to his second-grade class.

He didn't stand out to me at first; many of the children in the class needed help with their school work. Yet, when we began our one-on-one sessions, I realized that what Jamear needed was someone who would pay attention to him.

And I realized that what I needed was to know if I was capable of meeting such a challenge, and that my heart was big enough to embrace what this disadvantaged young person had to offer.

★

For the first half of the school year, I was in Jamear's classroom just one hour a week. With that limited time, it took a while to sort the better performers from those who needed some help. But it did not take long to see that these children needed more from me.

They all wore worn uniforms—some clean, some dirty, some hand-me-downs. Most were chatty and uninhibited. The girls' personalities were reflected in their hair adornments, while the boys "showed their shoes," as they said. At first I knew nothing about their home lives, but that didn't last long. The outstanding student, a little girl, came from a home with both parents and a brother. It was obvious she received loving attention: She was well-behaved, self-assured, and a good student.

Then there was Jamear. For our first meeting, the teacher asked me to help him with his printing. He became frustrated and agitated when he couldn't do the work, and he wandered the classroom and wouldn't look me in the eye.

It was not a successful session.

The next session went better; we completed the assignment, but his behavior irritated the teacher enough for her to place his desk facing the front wall. His humiliation only added to his problems.

That's when I asked if I could spend more time in the classroom.

The teacher and the students had issues. She was in her first teaching position and unprepared for the challenges of an urban classroom. She couldn't get control of the class. (Midway through the year, she was told she would be fired when the school year ended; meanwhile, she had to keep teaching. I'm not sure I could have survived any better than she did under such circumstances!) I wanted to help her, and rather than resent my presence as an intrusion, she appreciated that I was willing to devote more time to students like Jamear.

One afternoon, as I complied with the daily security check-in protocol, this teacher rushed up to me with a stricken face. The class was in the gym for a special program featuring a clown—and, Jamear was hysterical. She asked me to take him.

This was the beginning of our fairy-tale relationship. I hugged this crying, terrified little boy until he calmed down, then we talked about his fears. Eventually, we began on his school work, and the situation was behind us.

From that day on, Jamear was "my boy."

He began sobbing again later that same week when the teacher distributed grades. As I held him, he showed me three Fs. After all our hard work!

The teacher told me the problem: Jamear never turned in homework. I went back and knelt close to ask gently if there was anyone at home who could help him. With tearful eyes and a scrunched-up little face, he replied, "No, mommy is at work and grandma watches TV."

Armed with this information, so easily obtained, I asked the teacher what we were going to do about the problem. She agreed that I could help Jamear with his homework before he left school. He would be allowed to turn it in with the other children to avoid being noticed.

We began to work together consistently. I complimented him on how well he was doing and how proud I was of him, and I always sat on one of the small chairs to avoid being above his eye level. And he slowly began to trust me.

It was amazing to see his progress. I felt a moment of parental pride the day Jamear quickly grasped a concept and went on to complete his work with little assistance from me. When another child came to our work area complaining that she didn't understand the assignment, Jamear piped up with, "I know how to do it and I'll help you." I was thrilled to see his self-confidence and pride in his own accomplishments.

Every day became a new adventure with Jamear. He asked countless questions and wanted me to reassure him that I would be there the next day. When I entered the room, he was the first to run to me for a hug. He loved to hold my hand when we walked with the class. I could tell he felt a sense of "one-upmanship" over the other children because he thought I was helping him more than the others.

As the other students noticed this relationship, they too became more trustful of me. One day, a little girl near us had her head down on her desk, sobbing. I went to her and asked if she'd feel better if she sat on my lap while I assisted Jamear. She thought she would, so there I was, a girl on my lap, Jamear at his desk beside me, and others crowded around to ask if I would help them, too. In the midst of all this, a child walked by and said, "You really are a grandmother."

Of course, life with "my kids" continued to be a rollercoaster. One day they would be well-behaved, and the next day—or the next hour—would be chaos.

Then I had an idea, and the teacher agreed to let me try a little experiment.

The boys and I gathered our chairs in a circle and I presented my idea: A good behavior club. The basics were this: Each Friday, a boy and a girl would be selected to receive a prize because of good behavior. There would be no repeat winners. The boys loved that they could name their group and decide on the rules. And when I said good behavior would win prizes, they really got into it! One of the boys selected himself leader, and they began working on their rules.

They obviously were very familiar with behaviors they knew were a problem. They asked how to spell certain words (cussin') and proclaimed that "the b and f words" should never be said. I helped make sure all the boys participated and typed up their notes to keep in their lockers.

Here's what they came up with. (Since the girls couldn't get organized, they followed the boys' rules.)

BOYS' CLUB RULES

CLASS:
Sit to do your work.
Do what you are supposed to do.
Stay in your seat.
Raise your hand to speak.
Keep your hands and feet to yourself.
Help the teacher.
No hitting.
Don't yell.
No cursing.
No being nasty.

PLAYGROUND:
Do your best.
No choking.
No pushing off slide.
No pushing down the stairs.
No pushing off the monkey bars.

HALLWAY:
Don't run.
Don't push anybody down.
Don't talk because it is a Quiet Zone.
Don't put stuff in the drinking fountain.

LUNCH ROOM:

No talking. (The school principal did not allow talking in the cafeteria.)

No spitting food.

Stay in your seat.

SPECIAL:

Do not run.

Do not throw the chairs.

Do not take pens or pencils.

Do not steal.

Do not joke.

BUS:

Don't get out of the seat unless it's your bus stop.

Don't fight.

Don't sit or step on people.

Don't stand up.

Don't kick or smack people.

RESTROOM:

Don't do it on the floor.

Don't climb on the door.

Don't lock the door.

Flush the toilet.

Don't use it like 30 times.

I reviewed the good behavior project the following Monday, read the rules and explained that on Friday, one boy and one girl would be selected as the best-behaved students based on their rules.

All week, I watched for changes in behavior but observed none. Until Friday. When I arrived, I thought I had walked into the wrong classroom. There was no noise. All day, everyone stayed in their seats doing their work. It was perfect!

Too perfect, it turns out. When it came time to select the winners, the teacher named the boy and the girl that everyone expected would win because they were always well-behaved. They walked proudly to the front of the room and selected a prize from the bag of gifts I had supplied. Everyone clapped. I was beaming that my project was working!

And then, children began to cry because they didn't win a prize. Hadn't they behaved all day?

The next Monday, we started over. I explained that the good behavior had to be every day and that, eventually, everyone would have a prize. The week saw a small improvement in behaviors. When the first winners selected this week's winners, we heard no outcry of disappointment. They seemed to understand they had to follow the rules all the time and that it was OK to have different winners.

The incentive didn't solve all the problems, of course. The children still faced challenges outside the classroom. The self-proclaimed leader of the "boys club" had difficulty staying on an even keel. The worst day was when he told me he planned to kill himself with either a gun or a knife. I tried to reason with him, but he didn't budge. Sadly, when his father arrived for an emergency meeting with the teacher, he was furious. He declared he wasn't coming back for any more discussions and that the boy would either be in jail or dead by the time he was 18.

It was heartbreaking. Here was a child with tremendous leadership potential who would likely become a serious problem for society one day.

Then there was the new girl. She was 9 years old but looked 12. She was very quiet. After the first good behavior prizes had been awarded, she had burst into tears because she didn't win;

when I tried to comfort her, she said that she had nothing at home. I later learned she had never been to a movie and had very little contact with the outside world.

Another troubled girl spent a lot of time sobbing in a corner of the room. I learned that she wanted to live with her mother, but the court had placed her with her father. I also learned that as a small child she had witnessed two murders in her home. She became extremely distraught one day and tried to choke herself with her necklace, becoming so violent that a second teacher was called to help. The children I was gathering to line up for the bus didn't even react.

One of the taller girls sat on the floor one day with her back to the wall and began to sob, unusual behavior for her. I leaned down to talk to her when one of the other girls dragged over a chair and said, "Here, Ms. Burkhart. Sit down and talk to her." I ended up cradling this distraught girl like an infant while stroking her cheek and whispering that she was a wonderful person. After a few minutes, she stopped crying, said that she felt better and went back to her desk. I can only imagine what was bothering her.

Like the girl who brought me the chair, the children could be kind. A small girl who was bright but inclined to pester others snuggled up next to me, sniffed my sweater and asked knowingly, "JC Penney or Macy's?" Another day we were walking to the gym with her little hand tucked into mine when a teacher commented on what I was wearing. The girl looked up at me and said, "That was really a nice compliment, wasn't it?" Yet, her behavior could quickly change from sweet and willing to uncooperative and outright refusals to complete her work.

Jamear continued having his own set of problems. He once earned in-school suspension for having a conversation with a female classmate about masturbation. I asked him where he had obtained the information. "From my uncle," he replied. If my information was correct, the uncle was a high school student.

During spring break, I invited Jamear, his mother and his older brother to go with me to the Eiteljorg Museum. We had lunch and toured the museum, but my real purpose was to review admission forms for the boys to attend the 100 Black Men's summer school. It was obvious by then that Jamear would not be promoted to third grade (and he shouldn't have been), so summer school would allow him to catch up and be a good repeat second-grader. I gladly offered to take care of tuition, and Jamear's mom agreed to provide transportation for the seven-week, five-days-a-week program that began at 7:30 a.m.

Back at school after spring break, our "captain" called a meeting of the boys club to review the rules and make sure the boys were going to follow them. The boys talked about not smoking or drinking. One told about how hard his mother was trying to get a job; another, a boy who had arrived midterm and seemed to be shrinking before our eyes, confided that his mother might not come home from the hospital. The captain had appointed a secretary and if I wanted to speak, I had to ask permission. (If only those leadership skills could be put to good use!) I asked the group which of them planned to go to college, and three or four hands went up. They wanted to go to college, they told me, to get a job and to make a lot of money for fancy cars and big houses.

These children, just 8 and 9 years old, already had mindsets about the importance of "things" in their lives. They had very little connection to the value of education, especially college. I talked to Jamear about the importance of graduating from high school and going to college, and then he shocked me by asking, "What is college?" He didn't know what I was talking about! He'd never known anyone who had been to college. Our very next adventure became a visit to the Butler and Marian campuses; another day, Jamear accompanied me to the University of Indianapolis, where I was taping a radio show.

The last few weeks of school were rewarding in many ways. As the good behavior club had settled down and seemed to be working, we decided that the names of all the children who had not yet received a prize would be put in an envelope, and all week the teacher would remove the names of the children who misbehaved. On Friday, she would draw a winner from the remaining names. One week, only one boy's name remained in the envelope: Jamear!

By the time the school year was finished, Jamear and I had begun to "hang out together" one Saturday a month. We called them our Enrichment Adventures. I would pick Jamear up at his mom's beauty shop and off we'd go. We visited the best Indy has to offer— museums, the Zoo, Conner Prairie, the library, the ISO Christmas concert, the IMAX—any place that was enriching. Over lunch, we would discuss our families, his schoolwork, any subject we found interesting. Everything we did became a learning experience, even when we didn't intend it. I was often surprised by this young boy's mature insights; after seeing panhandlers on a street corner one day, he asked me, "Why don't they just get a job?" That sparked another learning moment.

For this relationship to flourish, I set all judgments aside. I was an outsider watching the workings of a single-parent family plus the aunts, uncles, nieces, nephews and grandma who came and went. It became apparent that housing depended on how many people were living together at any given time. Jamear moved to a different location once or twice a year. When he told me they were moving to a five-bedroom house and I asked who would be living there, I counted up to 12 individuals; then, as they began moving out, Jamear explained that his family couldn't afford to live there anymore.

Of course, every move meant a different school. Yet he never complained. I could always count on him to be cheerful, articulate and grateful for what he had.

Most of us were born into homes where a "sense of place" was never an issue. Even if our family moved, we continued to feel secure and we knew our parents would keep us safe. For children like Jamear and his classmates who don't have that sense of security, they act out their fears and frustrations.

Through all the sudden moves and phone disconnections, I struggled to keep track of Jamear and his family. Once when I thought I'd lost him, my cell phone rang one day and I heard a small voice on the other end ask, "Is this Grandma?"

But the inevitable happened, and it breaks my heart that after three years I no longer know where my boy is. I think about him every day and wonder if I loved him enough to last through his ups and downs. Did our relationship provide him with the strength to survive his turbulent life?

I called this story "a fairy tale romance between a boy and a stand-in grandmother." But did we live happily ever after? I can only hope Jamear did, because my life is certainly richer for having known him.

★

When I think about the combined potential of these 20 children, I want to cry, because most of them will never have the opportunity to realize even a fraction of that potential. As much as I loved the experience of tutoring, it was very frustrating to see these children's possibilities and know that I could provide only a fraction of what they needed. I learned what they needed—far more than just extra help with writing or math—by giving them my attention. Sometimes I think we become so concerned about providing answers that we forget to listen. Asking the child is a start.

I saw that these children would have thrived if given responsibilities and control over activities. My efforts to organize the behavior club proved they were capable of handling difficult situations in the classroom. I found they could be comforting to each other when offered the opportunity; they copied my behavior of compassion and they began to care about what was bothering a classmate. I always dressed nicely, and I believe they learned about respect from the way I conducted myself and, as they said, "dressed up" for them.

There is a gap in these children's lives that could be filled with a variety of community services from schools, churches, social service organizations and individual volunteers. More could be done to teach good citizenship so that children could understand the role of individuals in a community. When they see powerlessness with entitlement as a virtue, it is not surprising that they are greedy and materialistic.

There is always hope and there is always faith but we, as individuals, have to light the fire.

Lorene McCormick Burkhart is an author and speaker best
known for her leadership and philanthropy throughout
Indiana and the Midwest. Burkhart has used these skills
and talents throughout her career as a teacher, broadcaster,
civic leader, and corporate executive. She continues to
educate, influence, and inspire others to advocate causes
for the betterment of education, the community, and the
human spirit.

COLLEGE

JOHN GREEN

Let me tell you the best-kept secret about college: It's easy. The two hardest things I did in college were, in order of difficulty: 1. Beat *Tony Hawk's Pro Skater* on the PlayStation, and 2. Explain to a very nice guy named Mike DiTullio how and why I came to urinate on his mattress. Reading *Ulysses* barely even cracks my Top 10.

I don't mean to imply that life in college is easy—it's not. But the classes themselves are pretty easy, whether you're at U of C or Depaul or the Devry Institute. My girlfriend, for instance, graduated *summa cum laude* from the renowned Medill School of Journalism at Northwestern, and the other day she called me to ask whether Yemen was in Asia or Africa. I didn't know either. If you can graduate, as we both did, from prestigious institutions of higher learning without knowing your continents, you can rest assured that college is not particularly arduous.

Because college is so easy, a lot of students go four years without learning or doing anything worthwhile. This is a mistake, because six months after you graduate, when you're living in an overpriced studio contemplating the idea of nighttime telemarketing to supplement your temping income so you can afford your college loan payments, you'll need an excellent answer to the question, "Why the hell did I go to college anyway?" I've collected a brief list of DOs and DON'Ts for college life to ensure that our current and future students won't be left with regrets the size of their student loans.

DO: Take classes in liberal arts departments, like anthropology and history. Not only will these classes give you invaluable knowledge about such confounding questions as the geographic location of Yemen, they will also make you seem smart at parties and job interviews. Seeming smart is much, much more important than being smart.

DON'T: Take science classes, unless for some strange reason you aspire to become a scientist. For one thing, science classes are hard. For another, science is always being reinvented, which means that everything you learn could become suddenly obsolete. Just think of those poor saps who got their degrees in biology just before Watson and Crick figured out the structure of DNA.

DO: Study some. College is the last chance you'll have to spend entire days reading good books, and anyway, it's a lot easier if you do your homework. I'm not saying stay up all night popping no-doz and drinking seventeen pots of coffee. I'm just saying that if nothing's going on some afternoon, you might as well read Kant.

DON'T: Turn down the opportunity to do something absolutely amazing because you need to study. My sophomore year, I passed on a chance to go to a casino in Indiana because I had a big test, and you know what happened? One of my friends won ten thousand dollars at the slots, got drunk, and gave each of his cohorts a thousand dollars. I did fine on that religion test, but I would have gladly failed it for a thousand bucks.

DO: Things you can't do anywhere else. If you want to really live in the Midwest and not just study there, you'll need to find something that makes you uniquely enamored with it. For my friend Dean, it's eating hot dogs with only mustard while loudly complaining that people who eat their hot dogs with ketchup are communists. For me, it's sitting on the corner of Huron and Wabash on windy winter afternoons and watching gusts of winds knock over pedestrians. Even if you grew up somewhere else, you'll need to make college a second home. Finding a distinctive interest will ease that transition.

DON'T: Start acting like you're suddenly sophisticated now that you're on campus, with its jazz festivals and ballet troupes. Take a lesson from the town and accept that you're exactly as cool and smart as you were back home in Iowa or where ever.

DO: Go on zany adventures you'll never be able to do as an actual grown-up, like for example driving 6000 miles to work in an ice cream shop in Moose Pass, Alaska for a summer even though you could have stayed here and interned at the Trib. But...

DON'T: For instance, drive to Moose Pass, Alaska with a girl you've been dating for two weeks and who will soon dump you for a balding 33-year-old divorcee named Clarence. Just an example.

And finally, DO: Take a moment as you're driving down Halsted at four in the morning on a Tuesday with five of your best friends piled into the back seat to realize your tremendous good fortune to be young, bright, and free to skip your morning classes.

But for the love of everything holy DON'T: Buy into all that talk about how college is supposed to be the best years of your life. College is like any other phase of your life—except much, much easier.

FINDING EUDORA

AMY SORRELLS

"It had been startling and disappointing to me to find out that story books had been written by people, that books were not natural wonders, coming up of themselves like grass." — Eudora Welty

DUE DATE: 11 APR 14

The slow death of words began for Zoe sometime between *Watership Down* in fourth grade and the completion of her college senior thesis on Walt Whitman. She'd read and studied hundreds of stories, books and poems in between, but her enthusiasm for words fell like a helium balloon, at first full and red, tugging against its tether, then hovering low, until it fell wrinkled and limp to the floor. As far as Zoe was concerned, Faulkner could take his pipe and smoke it. Hemingway was a selfish bastard for killing off so much raw talent. The words of T.S. Eliot fell flat and hard like the stony rubbish of "The Waste Land." And Kurt Vonnegut, she was so over him. The guy deserved accolades about as much as he deserved the Purple Heart he got for suffering from frostbite during WWII. She knew her old professors and classmates would chastise her for her unjust haughtiness, but she couldn't help it. Years of dissecting the arrangement of morphemes and homonyms, vernacular and verbs hardened Zoe's heart to the magic, the same way a seasoned homicide detective can smoke and laugh over a bludgeoned corpse. Letters on pages had become nothing more than fonts, rounded serifs tumbling over each other, lost.

Zoe pushed the last of the books retrieved from the night drop—Danielle Steele's *Fine Things* and JB Stanley's *Carbs and Cadavers* among them—through the library's automated scanner until the computer screen bleeped an acknowledgement next to the lending patron's name. She shook her head and mumbled, "Well who'dve thought," when the crotchety, and very married, Mrs. Spilker's name popped up after scanning Jackie Collins' *The World Is Full of Divorced Women*. If books weren't to be judged by their covers, then neither were patrons' reading habits.

The patrons of Whitcomb Street Library, Zoe's first job after graduating *summa cum laude* with a Creative Writing degree, evidently shared her current disdain for quality literature. The covers of bodice rippers and cheap, bloody mysteries wore thin well before any quality literature, unless the local high school put a classic on their required reading list. *Fifty Shades of Gray* had a back hold list a dozen deep.

Zoe took the job in the downtown library because it was the only thing she could find, all the ivory tower illusions of working as a copywriter or editor shattering when it was the only job with benefits she could find, besides being a barista at Starbucks. She'd tried the local newspaper, but the twenty-something managing editor, Kelly Hurst, delivered the rejection via text message. She'd vetted Ms. Hurst and discovered the woman's Facebook profile picture was a full-on photo of her ass in a thong. Publishing houses, corporations, magazines, no one had a spot for her. She couldn't even find a job at a suburban library, where at least kids and teens attended programs and adults participated in book clubs.

Zoe's brief consideration of the altruistic possibilities of the Whitcomb Street Library soon perished. Missions only worked in places where people were hungry for the word, and the only thing residents near Whitcomb Street hungered for was something to eat and an hour's worth of decent heat or air conditioning. Situated near enough to downtown to be desperate for funding, but close enough to the revitalization districts to have a small but decent collection of what the central library deemed popular, Zoe passed neighborhood kids who clearly preferred loitering in the parking lots of Safeway and Rally's to any kind of gospel a library could offer. She knew, because she had been one of those kids a decade or so earlier. Only unlike other kids, books fell on her heart like grace, baptizing her away from the intrigue of sexual awareness in the backseat of a car with the smell of grease and onions wafting through the windows. The safety of the quiet nooks and crannies, the straight lines of letters on crisp, clean pages provided her salvation from furious tirades of her mother, who had been plagued by dueling demons of bipolar and borderline personality disorders.

Few kids came to the Whitcomb Street Library.

Few kids, except for Veronica Haynt.

DUE DATE: 2 MAY 14

Zoe watched the girl as she sat behind the children's circulation desk, cutting paper rabbits out of construction paper for the upcoming spring reading promotion that would, like the rest of them, be a flop. Veronica wore her usual attire: a T-shirt and mismatched shorts a size too small for even her too-thin frame, her shoulder blades like the buds of angel wings poking out from her back. By the time Zoe'd met her, she'd read all the way through the V's and started on the W's, well on her way toward fulfilling her quest to read every book in the library.

"Do you have anything by Welty?" Veronica asked, her voice small but determined as she approached Zoe.

"As in Eudora?" Zoe couldn't help grinning at the precocious request. If she had to be a librarian, she was determined not to become one of those picky old bags who'd redirect a similar request towards something "more readable" in the youth and young adult sections. Years of reordering disorder created by sloppy patrons stiffened the spines and pinched the countenances of tired librarians. Besides, Eudora Welty was one of Zoe's favorites. In fact, when it came time to decide on her senior thesis, she'd had a difficult time choosing between Welty and Whitman. She had eventually chosen Whitman, figuring she'd have a lifetime to focus on story, but that college might be the last time she could focus on poetry.

Spring sprouted a band of freckles across Veronica's elfish nose, and she smelled vaguely of pancake syrup and sweat. Humidity already hung in air, which meant by August they'd be melting, waves of heat ascending from the burning asphalt all around them.

"Yes, Eudora Welty," Veronica repeated. "She seems to be missing from the W's."

Zoe clicked her computer keyboard and found a short story collection. A bright red "CHECKED OUT" flashed next to it. She met Veronica's big, emerald green eyes. "I'm sorry. Do you want to put a hold on it? I could also order a copy from Central."

"No, I'll check for it later," Veronica sighed, pausing for a moment before heading back to the stacks. "Grandma doesn't feel well. I read to her every day. And she likes Eudora Welty. She said in one story a man's heart explodes."

"That's true. Death of a Traveling Salesman."

Veronica tilted her head slightly. "Why does his heart explode?"

"He'd had the flu, I think, which weakened it. But some people say it was broken by loneliness."

"Hmm."

"Your grandma's a lucky lady, you reading to her like you do."

The girl shrugged her shoulders. "I suppose. Not much else to do around here."

"What about your mom?"

Veronica's gleaming eyes turned stone cold. "Don't know where my mama is. Just me and Grandma and Grandpa."

Zoe watched the girl disappear into the W's to find a substitute.

DUE DATE: 23 MAY 14

The only thing the barren stacks and nooks of the Whitcomb Street Library had going for them were the visits Broady paid to Zoe. Zoe'd noticed his hard biceps, dimpled chin, and the slight curl of his messy blond hair the first time she bought gas at the Speedway next door. She knew anyone who worked at a combination gas station and mini mart lacked long-term relationship potential, but he was a nice distraction. Broady brought her cigarettes and beef jerky and an occasional chocolate rose, wrapped in red tin foil if he was feeling especially romantic. And he had a clean record. She'd checked that as soon as she'd learned his last name. He wasn't the first person she'd looked up on the library computers. She often passed the time vetting strange and suspicious patrons, especially guys she saw looking at porn on the computers and mothers who strutted in wearing Lululemon yoga pants, residents of the newly revitalized district a few blocks away who always demanded their child's overdue fees be waived.

"I've always wanted to do it in a library," Broady breathed hot into her ear that morning, pushing her up against the spines of *All of a Kind Family*, *Roll of Thunder Hear My Cry*, and *The Hobbit*. Since Zoe was often in charge of opening the library, they often took advantage of the half hour of quiet before the other librarians and patrons arrived. Out of the corner of her eye, she noticed someone forgot to shelve *Watership Down* the night before. Hazel and Fiver stared, nibbling on grass as they rested on their haunches on the front cover of the book. Zoe felt heat rise up her neck and into her cheeks.

"You need to leave." She pushed Broady away from her suddenly.

"But babe—"

"We can hang out after closing."

He zipped his pants just as Veronica skipped up the sidewalk. She was grateful the girl paused to pick a handful of dandelions from the poorly tended lawn, giving Zoe time to settle into her chair.

"Here," Veronica held a jar stuffed with the bright yellow dandelions under Zoe's nose. "Did you know the dandelion is the only flower that represents the 3 celestial bodies of the sun, moon and stars?"

"I didn't," Zoe replied.

"The yellow is sun, the poofy white ball is like the moon, and the seeds are like the stars." Veronica waved her hand over her head as if tossing brilliant seeds into the dark night sky. "And did you know dandelion flowers close at night to sleep, and open in the morning?"

"Nope."

"And," Veronica inhaled deeply, "Farmers grow dandelions as a crop in Belgium. One cup of dandelion can give a person more than one hundred percent of their daily requirement of Vitamin A, and one third of their daily requirement of Vitamin C."

"You don't say."

DUE DATE: 13 JUN 14

Zoe soon learned that as much as Veronica liked to recite facts, she liked to tell stories. At first the girl's constant chatter drove Zoe nuts, including her descriptions of frightening things she encountered on her way to the library. Though not impossible, sometimes her stories sounded a bit far-fetched, pit bulls chasing her, a trio of gang members following her home, a screech owl swooping down and plucking a Slim Jim Broady'd given her right out of her hand. Zoe remained suspect until the day Veronica, deadpan, told her of the man she walked by lying in the gutter, a bullet hole in his chest.

"Blood looked like a bright red ribbon streaming into the storm drain," Veronica said.

Moments later, the sirens of emergency vehicles shrieked by, and Zoe never doubted her stories again.

"Don't you have any friends? Someone to walk here with you?"

Zoe asked as Veronica set a stack of W books on the counter for check out.

"Not really," Veronica replied, a dreamy, unconcerned look on her face. "When I'm in school I do, but no one likes to come to my house much. I don't have a lot of toys and video games. But it's okay. I have my books. And besides, I'm not scared of much."

DUE DATE: 5 JUL 14

Veronica was into the Ys when Zoe began to worry about her. Her clothes, threadbare thrift store finds, hung on her frail arms. Her eyes had dark circles under them. She walked slowly and didn't skip nearly as much, if at all, anymore. She hadn't visited the library as much, either. Once a week, compared to her previously daily visits.

"Your grandma okay?" Zoe asked.

Veronica set Bart Yates' *The Distance between Us*, Christy Yorke's *Song of the Seals*, and Yevgeny Yevtushenko's *Don't Die Before You're Dead* on the desk. She did not look at Zoe. "She's taken a turn for the worse."

"I'm sorry to hear that."

Veronica lingered a moment after Zoe handed her the pale yellow checkout receipt. "Do you remember Beth in *Little Women?*"

Zoe did. She'd played the piano herself as a young girl, alone in a home she suspected was just as lonely as Veronica's. She'd identified more with Jo and her independence and devotion to books and education, but Beth's demise had devastated her. In hindsight, she'd wept more for the camaraderie, the cozy fires, the gently patient eyes of Marmie she'd never experienced in her own mother. She wondered if Veronica felt that, too. "Yes I do. Poor, sweet Beth."

"It's like that."

"I'm sorry."

After Veronica left, Zoe wondered where home was for the girl. The girl's file showed an address of 425 Yardley Street, which Zoe looked up on Google Maps. The camera showed an obviously once beautiful street featuring a center island with ornate, overgrown limestone urns and parched fountains. Zoe drove by Veronica's house as evening fell and hoped the girl wasn't outside to notice. Blighted, the neighborhood was boxed in on the east and west by streets notorious for late night gunshots and sirens, and on the north by an abandoned factory, "Cohen Tailoring Plant" letters still flaking from the brick above busted out windows. On the south side of Yardley Street sat a seedy strip mall, boarded up except for a lone check-cashing store, its windows covered in iron bars.

425 Yardley Street.

Parked in front was a late model Honda minivan with a large Visiting Nurse Service magnet slapped on the side of it. An old man sat on the brick wall of the brownstone porch and spoke to the nurse, dressed in sky blue scrubs. He noticed Zoe and waved. She blushed and drove on. As decrepit as he looked, if his wife, Veronica's grandma was sick, no wonder Veronica was failing, too.

What would happen to the girl if her grandmother died?

DUE DATE: 25 JUL 14

"This is it," Veronica said, thunking Timothy Zahn's *The Domino Pattern*, Anne Zourou's *The Doctor of Thessaly*, and Penny Zeller's *Kadie* on the circulation desk.

"What will you do when you've finished these?"

She thought for a moment, then her face brightened as if she'd realized the answer to the most puzzling story problem. "Start back over at the A's."

Zoe noticed the thinness of her frame, the way the bones of her spine stuck up as she bent to stuff the books into her library bag. Broady had said the girl and her grandfather bought their "groceries" at the Speedway, their diet consisting of chips and SpaghettiOs, non-refrigerated cheese wrapped in plastic, donuts and YooHoo.

"You ever been to the City Market?"

"What's City Market?"

"Where they sell fresh food, fruit, vegetables. It's not far from here. Maybe we could go sometime."

Veronica paused, one shoulder drooping from the weight of the bag of books hanging on it. "I'd like that."

Zoe watched Veronica push through the doors and set her bag full of books on the sidewalk to picked dandelions. She picked and picked until her fist couldn't hold anymore, then swung the bag on her shoulder and headed toward home.

5 SEP 14

The dandelions had all gone to seed—or had become stars, as Veronica might remind her—a few plumes of white remaining on the library lawn, the day Zoe heard the voice behind her as she scanned in the newest returns.

"Do you have anything by Eudora Welty?" the woman said.

Zoe turned and noticed the deep green eyes, which reminded her immediately of Veronica.

"Eudora Welty?"

"Yes. We was looking for some of her short stories awhile ago, but they was checked out or somethin'."

Zoe couldn't help notice the woman's meth-stained teeth, her bird-like frame, the way her yellowed skin hung from her cheeks before she pointed toward the stacks on the far right. "Should be down that aisle there, the W's. Alphabetical by author."

"Thank you."

"Pardon me for asking, but you said 'we' were looking for it awhile ago. Who else was looking with you?"

"My granddaughter."

"Veronica?"

"Yes, you knew her?" The woman's face brightened.

Knew.

"She was reading through the library in alphabetical order," Zoe explained. "She said she was reading to her grandmother who was sick, whose heart was giving out like Beth's in *Little Women*."

"Oh dear," the woman ran her nicotine-stained fingers through her disheveled hair. "She told you that? She was reading to me, yes. But it was her heart that gave out. She had a condition. We knew from the time she was born she wasn't long for this world. I couldn't even go to the funeral, damn slammer wouldn't give me leave. Let me talk to her on the phone every day which is when she read to me." The woman paused, sighed. "I was only two weeks away from getting out on parole. Can you believe that? They wouldn't let me outta there for nothin'."

It struck Zoe then that it was in the knowing and getting to know, through the bumping together of words and lives that hope rises. The writer has little to do with it. The person who matters is the reader, turning the words until the heart spawns the fullness of their meaning. That was why she knew Walt Whitman. Not because she wrote a thesis on him, but because of the exquisite realization of the bones and the marrow in the bones he described. She knew Hazel and Fiver not because Mrs. Thomas said she had to read about them in fourth grade, but because she felt the same fluttering within her chest as they fled the warren to find a safe place in the world.

After Veronica's grandmother left, more characters came to her. Colin and Mary. Charlotte and Wilbur. Opal and Winn-Dixie. Corduroy and his missing button. Naima and her rickshaw. Gatsby and Mr. Rochester, Carol Milford and Holden Caulfield. She moved among the ghosts of them as she straightened the stacks and thought about how, just like Phoenix Jackson's son in "The Worn Path," we all swallow a big dose of lye at some point, causing our throats to close up until we see how the beginnings of things often come at our ends.

She pushed the spine of *The Heart Is a Lonely Hunter* deeper into the shelf so it was even with the spines of those around it, turned out the lights, and locked the front door of the Whitcomb Avenue Library for the night.

And just like old Phoenix Jackson, Zoe's slow step began on the stairs, going down.

An Indianapolis native and graduate of DePauw University, Amy Sorrells lives with her husband, three boys and a gaggle of golden retrievers in central Indiana. She's a former weekly columnist of the *Zionsville Times Sentinel* newspaper and the award-winning author of the novel *How Sweet the Sound* (3/1/14, David C. Cook). Her sophomore novel *Then Sings My Soul* is scheduled to release 3/1/2015 (Cook). When she's not reading or writing, Amy loves spending time with her three teenage sons, spicy lunches and art gallery walks with her husband, digging in her garden sans gloves, walking her dogs, and up-cycling old furniture and junk.

THE JOURNEY

MARY SUSAN BUHNER

I braced my delicate hand on the nightstand to ease myself up and out of the deep featherbed from my childhood. As I leaned forward, the sun pierced the thin linen drapes my grandmother stitched by hand all those years ago. The sunlight reached out for my skin like a playmate trying to catch me through the sheer drapes. I closed my eyes to the warmth, letting it rest on my brow for just a moment. I slowly opened my eyes, taking in my reflection in the vintage mirror across the room.

Amazed, I caught a fleeting glimpse of the young woman I had once been in the mirror. The glistening sun filled my face with shadows of yellow and orange, restoring my youth. My cotton nightgown clung to my small frame, and my hair had escaped from the grasp of my hairpins and now rested loosely at the nape of my neck.

I whispered, "I'm a young girl again."

Again, I raised a whisper. "A gift. That is what this moment is, isn't it? It is a gift before I begin my journey."

I dressed myself. I skillfully pulled back my silky hair with a beautiful butterfly hair comb. A mischievous smile passed over my face, emphasizing the crevices in my countenance.

I hurried now, excited, dancing over to the mahogany dresser that once belonged to my mother. I pulled open the top drawer to find my best stockings, and when I did, the bureau let forth the sweet smell of summer flowers. My mother's perfume was embedded in the wood itself, reminding me of her love, a love that still surrounds me.

As the stockings glided over my somewhat shapely legs, my hands tingled in rhythm with my racing heart.

Overwhelmed with memories, I rested a moment.

Surprised by the rawness of emotions felt a half-century earlier, I forged on with my plan for today. Selecting a deep blue gabardine dress, I reached for my once-coveted spectator pumps and slipped them onto my narrow feet. Pleased by my appearance and eager for my journey, I did feel remarkably alive today. More importantly, I felt like Savannah Worthington, the woman I had worked so hard to become all the years ago.

With my legs crossed at the ankle and tucked primly beneath me, I sank into the ornately carved rocking chair that once belonged to my father. I recalled that it once stood guard in his den next to the fireplace. When I was a girl, I would wander into his den, and no matter what he was doing he would stop to give me his full attention to me. He lit up just seeing my face peek around the corner, and I was never more delighted than when he pulled me on his lap to recount the tales of his own mischief as a young boy.

I missed my father today. As I rocked back and forth I could faintly hear his laughter in the creaking of the wood, and could nearly smell the halo of his fine tobacco encircling me in the haze of the Georgia heat.

My chair was perched near the open window so the fragrance from the magnolia tree and the sun's shadow dancing on the wooden floor could join me like two old friends. I reached forward for the trunk next to me, turning the lock and cracking open the lid. Carefully, I lifted out a weathered book and gently laid it on my lap like the precious treasure it was.

The leather cover was cracked and the onionskin pages flimsy from turning them so many times.

I opened it and winced as the binding protested. I realized what all the moments, all the obstacles, in my life added up to over the years. Each one had been a separate adventure and awakening, but this particular moment was the one. It was my journey.

I was born Savannah Worthington Kincaid Miller on October 25, 1914 in the deep south of Georgia. My well-to-do family resided on a plantation that had withstood the war. It possessed everything a girl could want from stables teeming with the finest thoroughbreds to a swimming pool glistening with refreshing water. The ultimate indulgence for me was a hand-carved carousel on the south lawn. Like the exterior surroundings, my room was a fairytale with hand-painted murals depicting literature's greatest heroes and heroines, much to my liking. I spent hours before them imagining my own grand adventures like I had read in detail in all the books my father had given me.

While amused by these luxuries, I never allowed myself to think that it was real. Early on I realized that surroundings were only temporary and merely what they were created to be, a fairytale. My foreboding was never articulated, as I could not find the words to share these feelings. At age 12, an explanation was no longer necessary. I was in for the shock of my life, one that would profoundly affect the remainder of it. It would define my life's journey.

Miss Anne quietly knocked on my half-opened bedroom door. I lay across my bed reading *The Wind and the Willows*, one of my favorite books, and hesitated to put it down.

"Savannah—Sweetie, your mama wants to see you in her study, sugar," Miss Anne half-whispered.

Surprised, I asked, "Mother wants to see me? It's teatime. She never wants to visit with me during tea." When my presence was required, teatime was maddening for me. Ladies sitting around steeping in idle chatter and mint leaves was not this girl's idea of excitement, but my Mother thrived on it. I liked talking about things and not around things.

Mother says a lady never oversteps her place by directly addressing an issue. Instead, dancing around it during an agonizing hour over tea was much more appropriate in her mind. My outbursts were a stubborn wrinkle in her properly starched world.

My father, on the other hand, appreciated that I think for myself. In fact, he actually encouraged it. He called me his "little captain." He said a captain that is brave will sail through the storms of life showing courage. Father always had great admiration for sailors, with books and books on the subject neatly stacked in the den to prove it. He said that a sailor has to be one with God and Mother Nature, reading the wind and the water, respecting the journey. His boat is his refuge, his vessel to a successful journey.

None of that rang true with my mother. She was content to stay on the plantation, sipping sweet tea and embroidering pillowcases. True, she's a long way from her impoverished roots on a cotton farm in Camden, South Carolina, but her life's journey seemed to have ended here at the estate.

Once, I asked Mother about my Grandmother Parker, who passed on when I was a baby. Mother told me how hard she worked all the time—cooking, baking, washing, canning, sewing and mending. On a farm with nine kids, work was never done, yet there was little to show for her efforts. They scraped by to get just the basics.

A muddied portrait of Grandmother Parker guarded our front foyer and I studied it for clues. There wasn't much to draw from—sandy hair yanked into a painful bun, a stony look on her face and pale eyes that shared no story. I have studied her photograph many times, wondering if the fuzziness of her portrait was purposeful—somewhat symbolic of her life.

I came back to Mother and asked what Grandmother Parker was like as a woman. Was she rigid or carefree, funny or serious, warm and loving, or cold and distant? What were her interests—her passions? Mother looked me in the eyes—really right through me—and said brusquely, "I imagine Grandma Parker didn't have the time or energy to be her own person."

I sheepishly muttered, "Managing nine children and a farm would be a lot to handle." For a moment we were both lost in our own thoughts of the hardships women in our very own family had endured in days gone by.

Mother did take time to add one thought. "Each generation of women, Savannah, gets stronger and better. Don't forget that, dear. We have a duty to move forward, no matter how painful sometimes. There is no need to look back."

I don't see Mother's inadequacies as entirely her fault. She was, after all, only a girl herself when she had me. Now, at the age of thirty-three, she had all the luxuries one could ever dream of: diamonds, fashionable clothes, and linens. Everything except courage. I was about to discover how deep my courage ran and if she had any at all.

Miss Anne urged me to hurry and gave me a look that meant business.

"Well, if I have to dress for tea, couldn't you tell me what's on mother's agenda?" I pleaded.

"Don't sass me. Child, there is no tea today. Just come. Come now. Your mother needs to see you now—this instant, baby girl," her tone lightening.

Miss Anne had been my caretaker since the day I entered this world. She knew all my thoughts and dreams. Sometimes she told me that I was a "crazy child" for talking of such things, but I know deep down she listened to every word I say. Miss Anne, now there is a courageous woman. Not courage to do or see things that one only reads about in great books, but the courage to survive. Courage to leave her four children at home with her mother and live here with us to earn money to send back to them. Crazy really, to give up one's own children to raise another's, just to survive.

When I looked into Miss Anne's eyes I swore I could see her soul. She was a robust woman with an enormous bosom. When I was little and she would pull me tight and hug me I would call her "fluffy." I didn't know any better and it felt like being hugged by a big soft pillow. I still love getting hugged by Miss Anne. Her hair was coarse and dark and it showed that she never really had the time to give it any attention. She wore it short, which accentuated the gray around the temple. Her eyes were dark and deep like her hardships and heartbreak.

Her hands were calloused, belying her tender heart. When I was six I got the German Measles and nearly died. For days my fever ran high and my small body was limp from sickness. Mother and Father would sit with me all day stroking my hand and talking to me. At nightfall Miss Anne would come into my room and scoop my out of my bed as if I were a feather. She would rock me all night long singing spirituals in her sweet voice and read to me. All night long she would read to me. Read anything she had close by—a recipe she had scribbled on a scrap, the Bible, or would just make up a story she had in her mind. Her warm embrace was all the medicine I needed. I could hear her pray aloud, as if the Lord himself were standing right in my room.

"Lord, I know you surely already have a plan for this child. No doubt in my mind about that. I know you're listening and I am going to keep on praying that your will is the same as my prayer. Don't take this child yet, Lord. Not yet." Then she would go back to singing or reading from the Bible.

Miss Anne never put me down that night. She rocked, prayed and sang to me through the entire night, and by the next morning my fever had broken. After that night I never question Miss Anne or The Good Lord.

"Savannah, come on now. Hurry along," Miss Anne said. Her voice was shaking a bit and her eyes were filled with tears.

"Okay, okay, I am coming." Wondering what was troubling her, I tried to lighten her mood by making silly noises as we walked across the house to my parent's wing.

As I walked through Mother's study door the thick air immediately tugged on me. I never had liked this room, and that day it was dull and dim as ever. My mother slowly turned from her overstuffed chair and looked at me with pitiful eyes. "Savannah, my dear, come here."

I wasn't sure what to make of it all, but something wasn't right.

"Just tell me, Mother. Whatever is wrong, just tell me."

She began to cry softly into her perfectly pressed linen hanky. I decided to placate her by sitting next to her, comforting her, as our roles reversed.

"Your father...daddy...he has..." Now crying violently, she couldn't spit the words out.

I reached out and touched her head and brought it to my chest.

"It's okay mother, what happened?"

Before she even raised her head to look at me, I knew of only one thing that could be so terrible. Tears rolled down my face as I patted her back and rocked her back-and-forth.

"Shhh, mother it will be okay. Tell me what happened," I whispered.

She whimpered, "Your father—he is—dead."

She was crying so hysterically now I couldn't understand the rest of what she gurgled out. It didn't matter to me. I didn't need to know the sorrowful details. Father was gone, forever. The joyful fog that had graced my young life was lifted.

It started to sink in. Father was gone. The one who laughed at all my silliness, the one that believed in my dreams, and the one that called me his "little captain." Gone. At thirteen years old I was alone. I had nothing left except my courage and his books.

Four days later we buried him. Oddly, it was a perfect day for a funeral: a chilly day with clouds and whistling wind. My overwhelming grief circled me like vultures, just waiting for me to trip up so it could consume me.

Nothing consoled me. He was cut down, like a sturdy oak, by a massive heart attack at work. His partners at Worthington, Davis and James law firm said he went quietly. Mother received great comfort from this fact, but I didn't. I knew that if Father thought he was going to go, he would want to do it kicking and screaming.

Panic and fear punctuated my numbness. Everything felt so unsettled. Now that I had been cheated and betrayed, I couldn't trust anyone or anything. If something like this could happen and change my life in an instant, I wondered what else could happen. I didn't know where to look for my safe harbor.

I had always believed that there were angels around us, probably because Miss Anne talked so frequently about "guardian angels." Now I felt confused. They sure didn't stop my father from dying.

I began to sleepwalk at night. I couldn't stand the aloneness. Come morning, I would find myself in Miss Anne's room, curled up on the floor next to her bed.

Months went by and finally one morning Miss Anne grabbed my hand while I was picking at my breakfast. Food seemed so irrelevant. Nothing tasted good—nothing felt like it had life.

She rubbed my hand and said, "Child, what doesn't kill us makes us stronger. You will be sad for a long time, my dear. Your heart probably will never stop hurting over your Daddy. But I know this for sure, child, God will make good come from this. You've got to believe in that. Good will come from this sadness, sugar."

I sat there contemplating her words. They made sense, but I couldn't yet embrace them. I just wanted to be sad and wallow in my misery.

Mother must have sensed my retreat. That afternoon she came to my room with some toast and tea. Gingerly, she perched on the corner of my four-poster bed. What she was about to broach caught me totally off guard.

"Sweetheart, I was thinking that a change in scenery might be good for you," she said.

My eyes bulged open. "What do you mean change of scenery?" As I buttered my toast I felt increasingly annoyed.

"Well, you excel so much at school, it might be good for you to really focus and go away to a preparatory school."

I had now pierced my toast with the knife. All I could do was shout at her.

"You're kicking me out? You want me gone? I can't believe this, Mother."

Mother spoke calmly, "Savannah, this has been a difficult time, honey."

She moved beside me and extended her hand to brush my hair off my forehead as I steamed over her big plan.

"Sweetheart, healing from this loss is going to take time. We are going to hurt for a long time."

I began to sob. I mumbled, "Oh Lord, will things ever be back to normal?"

"Savannah, we are going to have to find a new normal now. He is gone and we are left to try to heal. Your Father would want you to be happy. You dreamed of becoming wonderfully educated, traveling and marrying someone you love and someday settling here on The Estate. He would want you to be brave."

I mumbled to myself, "little captain," and recalled Father's words. "A captain is brave and will sail through the storms of life showing courage. Respect the journey. Know the boat is your refuge, your vessel to a successful journey."

I decided I had to go on. I had to choose to not be a victim by this horrible tragedy in my life. I had to make good come from this circumstance. It was my choice.

That fall I left the sultry confines of The Worthington Estate for a small preparatory school on the East Coast. Sayren School was steeped in tradition, dotted with limestone buildings and guarded by thick trees. It was a conservative single-sex setting, but liberal learning was alive and well within the halls.

I came across all sorts of contemporary writings and came across a passage that rang true to me. It was an excerpt from Indiana poet Max Ehrmann's *Desiderata*. I quickly copied parts of it down and tacked it to my dormitory wall. I liked the essence of it and just started to scratched at the surface of its powerful meaning on life—my life.

"Do not compare yourself with others, you may become vain or bitter; for always there will be greater and lesser persons than yourself. And whatever your labors and aspirations, in the noisy confusion of life; keep peace in your soul; And to whether or not it is clear to you, no doubt the universe is unfolding as it should."

I excelled in all areas of school with ease. Literature was my favorite subject, because it was the only course that transported me to another place and time—an escape. Mathematics and science, boring. Something about requiring an exact answer arrived at it in precisely the right way frustrated me. I didn't care about subtracting a number just to add it to another number to come up with an exact other number. No adventure in that, no imagination, that is for certain.

On the other hand, literature opened up worlds that had so many different answers. Just like my bedroom murals and the books that lined my shelves, literature was my escape. The great works dare not be so arrogant to say what is right or wrong. There is no definite; there is always room for interpretation. Just like life, I guess. I suppose that is what I found so intriguing about these stories: never knowing what the answer was going to be until the end.

I decided early on that literature was what I liked best in school and made no bones about it from my teachers. My teachers found me completely frustrating, but my marks were high enough in each subject that they could not complain to the headmaster. I steered clear of trouble and was actually quite popular with my classmates.

I reveled in the freedom that school offered. I had no distractions. No boys to bother me. I didn't need them anyway. Father had seen to it that I could support myself and pursue whatever goals this little captain set for herself. I was ready for the next step: college.

I earned an academic scholarship to a small private liberal arts college near my boarding school and would be one of only a handful of women studying there. Even then, I knew my life would be different from theirs—they might go on to be teachers or secretaries or wives. I wouldn't have to. I could choose my path. Yes, my life would be different from theirs, and my mother's.

I attended college for 3 years, graduating early and with honors. While there I studied English Literature. I remembered each day how fortunate I was to be earning a college education. The country was in a depression and so many students had to drop out to go home to help their families. I studied hard, learned everything I could and waited for my day of complete freedom to come. I wanted things to move along more quickly than they ever could.

May of 1935 finally arrived. With my degree in one hand and my suitcase in the other, I boarded a train to head home to the Worthington Estate. As a college graduate, now I would travel the world. Mother was not going to approve, expecting me home to sip tea and sew, but it was time for me to ship out.

As I walked into the house a sea of hats, gloves and pearls enveloped me. I felt as if they were all moving in slow motion and speaking in strange tongues. My mother greeted me first and hugged me feverishly.

My return embrace was stiff and awkward. It was then the fog lifted and recognized the bustle that surrounded me. My old childhood friends were grown, my mother's socialite friends were even richer and Miss Anne was even poorer.

"Oh my precious daughter, welcome home! We are all so glad to have you back home in Georgia," Mother said.

The room began to clap, clamoring for my execution, I thought.

"Sweetheart, I know you must be tired, but there are so many reasons to celebrate."

I could not speak. My feet could not move. I was paralyzed with anger. The masses parted to reveal Jimmy Miller or more appropriately, James Wilson Miller IV.

Tall and lanky, with thoroughbred breeding and grooming, there was nothing wrong with his appearance or manners. I knew he really was a gentleman. He was also wealthy, highly regarded in the community, and sincere. Just the kind Mother would choose for me, with a family who had just endowed the Art Museum at the request of the Governor. All that annoyed me. Slick dark hair and icy blue eyes aside, that is.

James stepped forward and knelt in front of me. In my fog I looked over at Miss Anne.

She looked at me with such sad eyes and then bowed her head to stare at her feet.

James spoke deliberately and said, "Savannah, I know you have just returned and have had a long journey home. But I cannot wait to ask you this one question." He paused only for added drama, not to gain his courage.

"Will you be my wife?"

I wanted to run for help, but my Mother's whimpering cry interrupted my silent scream. "Oh, this is just what your father wanted."

That statement alone by the poor widow Worthington sent the crowd of executioners into a rousing cheer.

"To the memory of Charles!" one yelled. "To James and Savannah!" another exclaimed. Without even saying a word to James Wilson Miller IV I was marrying him.

I barricaded myself in my bedroom, staring at the walls of literature that used to stir my imagination. I felt comfort in my old room accompanied by my favorite books, but knew it could only serve as a temporary sanctuary. I sprawled across the bed, my dress a wrinkled mess, feeling weakened by the afternoon's events.

The leather binders stared at me from the bureau. I looked at myself in the gilded mirror across the room before picking one up. I carefully took the butterfly comb out of my long blond hair and clutched it in my hand. I remembered when father gave it to me on my tenth birthday. He held me close to him and said, "You are as beautiful as this butterfly, Savannah. Someday you too will fly."

That confirmed it. Father would never plan my life for me the way my mother claimed. I knew he wanted me to fly and find true love over monetary wealth. He wanted me to captain my own ship. He wanted me to travel and see wonderful places and experience different things. With strength from my own memories, I decided to read the journals and see for myself.

As I opened the first book, I could smell his familiar aroma. I could nearly feel his arms surround me, the scratch of his starched shirtsleeves on my bare arms. I was overwhelmed with fresh grief. With the comb still in hand I was consoled by his love and steady guidance. It was as though I could hear him whisper to me, "my little captain." Hot tears fell as I read the first page of my father's journal while surrounded by the books he loved. His words, penned only for my eyes only, would fill me with courage once again. I was about to embark on a journey that would change the course of my life forever.

Mary Susan is the author of *Mommy Magic: Tricks for Staying Sane in the Midst of Insanity* and a contributing author to several books including *Even Inmates Get Time Off for Good Behavior, Bye Bye Board Room: Confessions of a New Breed of Moms* and most recently the 2014 release *Nothing But The Truth So Help Me God: Women on Life's Transitions.*

Mary Susan's honest and humorous approach to motherhood has empowered and inspired thousands of moms around the country. She has created a community that encourages women and gives them permission to forgo the need to be the "perfect mom." She is also a trained Life Coach for Moms, but her most rewarding role is being a mom to her three girls.

Before staying home to raise her three girls, Mary Susan Buhner had a successful and rewarding career in the not-for-profit sector. With a degree in Speech Communication from Indiana University and a Management Certificate in Fundraising from the well-respected International Center on Philanthropy, she led fundraising efforts for several educational institutions including the Indiana University Foundation, Butler University and the Lawrence Township School Foundation.

BONNIE MAURER

CLEARING THE SEPTEMBER GARDEN

uncombed as my daughter's hair—
flowers appear, curls twist at her shoulders—
we pull the tangle of bean and squash vine.
Yarrow, sun-gold healers, burns brown, pungent
as the old herb books with stories
of women who knew how to heal, how to
bury the fingernails of a sick child or
advised to turn the picture against the mirror
of the lover gone sour.

Thick stems lean into the cool circle
the pines make, a place we sit,
and I tell her the tale of the Indian maiden
who ran from her false lover to the arms
of the evergreen offering peace.
"Yarrow, sweet yarrow..." begins
the chant the maidens sang
to ask a vision of their future lovers.

I cut daisies and the zinnias, faded
as summer dresses,
the dead yarrow blossoms,
and toss the stems
my daughter throws into the compost pile
casting another spring.

What of the wild cliome? she asks.
Sitcky white starlight wands,
wishes or my white hair,
all summer claiming the wind,
waving on long stems as if
risen from the ancient sea:

"Leave them," I say.

SENSUOUS ITALIAN 101

CAROL FAENZI

I grew up in the warm embrace of Italian grandparents, which meant all my senses were constantly being charmed to one degree or another. A deep connection was being fashioned between the lyrical sounds and meaning of the Italian words with what I was experiencing, although I did not fully awaken to it until much later in life.

My grandparents' backyard in Indianapolis was like stepping into a Tuscan garden. The herbs were dominated by the king of them all, *basilico*. The emerald green leaves, warmed by the sun and exuding their unmistakable aroma, filled my nostrils and hands. My *nonna* Olga pulled off sprigs of *rosmarino*, *mente* and *salvia*, teaching me their purposes, both medicinal and culinary. Inhaling their distinctive smells, she would add them to the collection growing in the palms of my hands.

As she taught me their Italian names, the vowels seemed to linger on my tongue as I pronounced them out loud, matching the longing in my soul to linger there with her.

My grandfather Ottavio cultivated Italian vegetables (*le vedure*), mostly lettuces. The bitterness of *radicchio* and the peppery nature of *rucola*, tempered by luscious green olive oil, were early trainers of my tastebuds. Rarely did bland-by-comparison iceberg lettuce make an appearance at the table.

Zucchini, another Italian staple, would frequently arrive *a tavola*, stuffed and baked. This was a favorite childhood dish, and one I attempt to make that measures up to Olga's. I am still trying.

But it was the flowers (*le fiore*) of the zucchini that seduced me. Bright, yellow-orange sirens which at the moment we removed them were rinsed, battered, fried, drained and showered with *parmigiano*. Morsels of pure bliss.

Ottavio meticulously looked after his garden tomatoes, the now well known *pomodoro* version. The literal translation is "golden apples," and indeed, their summer taste was fit for the gods. Their blood red juices mingled with creamy mozzarella, dark green olive oil and tender leaves of basil, creating a dance on the tongue of the four most iconic of all Italian ingredients. And not only the taste, but the texture. The density of the firm tomato, the smooth suppleness of softening cheese, the subtle detection of tender herb, the lush silkiness of oil...and perhaps just the slightest crunch of sea salt, all tantalizing your mouth at the same time. The word "texture" in Italian is "*tessitura.*"

More about texture, later.

There were also fruit trees in their garden, and none more evocative of Italian life than the fig, *la fica*.

Every year for fifty years, Ottavio nurtured that tree. After giving up its fruit for the season, he pruned and covered it to protect it against harsh Indiana winters. Olga prophesied doom. Ottavio believed in its resurrection.

Later in life, I learned (during a Roman "rite of passage" romance), that *"una fica"* is a metaphor for the vagina. It was a provocative revelation, but if you have ever opened up a fresh fig, you understand the correlation.

Adding *"issimo or issima"* to many an Italian word makes it a superlative. Hence, describing something or someone as *"ficchissima,"* can indeed refer to an extremely alluring woman (or really, anything that is ultra fabulous), but in its essence, it contains the meaning of a piece of fruit that is so beautiful, it is adorned with garlands.

The sensuous nature of the Italian soul is almost always connected to food. *Buonissimo.*

What Tuscan garden would not have a vineyard? Like any self-respecting Italian immigrant, Ottavio made his own wine (even during Prohibition, I am told). He built a sweet arbor for his grapes (*acino d'uva*), and as summer deepened, so did the ruby red glow of the juicy fruit, nestled among the dark green leaves. Production would go on in the cool damp confines of the basement.

Years later, when I serendipitously found my family's farm in Tuscany, my cousins took me into *la caverna del vino.* They told me that when Ottavio visited them in the early 1960s, after fifty years of being in America, he helped them build it.

Upon entering that stone cave, the smell of the fermentation and sensation of cool humidity clinging to my skin transported me to Otto's humble basement on Gladstone Street.

My childhood was saturated with food at my grandparents' table and with music as well: Italian grand opera, as sumptuous as a four-hour Italian meal.

When people tell me they do not like opera, I oftentimes sense a physical resistance, a pulling back from something unknown that might sweep them away. And they are not wrong.

I speak here only of Italian opera and its dazzling, otherworldly, delirious, unrestrained glory. . .acrobatic performers masquerading as voices that defy the heights and yet fall to a place where my breath and heart both just stop.

And the words that define the music! Italians don't use mundane words or phrases to accomplish that, like "fast, slow, song, singer, lyrics." Rather, *allegro* (cheerful/lively), *imbroglio* (with intrigue), *herzo* (a joke), *pizzicato* (pinch or sting), *capriccio* (whimsy or a temper tantrum), *diva* (goddess), *aria* (the air), *libretto* (little book), *ritornello* (a little return trip) and, yes, here it is again—*tessitura* (texture of voice).

One doesn't have to understand Italian to know how these words direct the music and voices: *tremolo, vibrato, espressivo, accelerando, coloratura.*

My personal favorite? *Sotto voce.* Meaning "under the voice," this is the moment when the *prima donna* takes a note to the heavens and lets it descend to barely a whisper. And that is when my heart stops. There is a brief moment of silence in the audience followed by a simultaneous surge of applause, standing and calling out for more. *Bravissima!*

This glittering music was almost always in the background, playing on the stereo in my grandparents' "front room," as they referred to it. Caruso, Callas and Pavarotti sang to Verdi's, Rossini's and Puccini's emotional music...and while I did not understand what they were saying, I could *feel* it...hearts that were lustful, longing, joyful or tragically breaking spoke to my young spirit in ways that left an imprint.

When a career move took me to New York City, I also took my love of opera and gorged myself on it at the Metropolitan Opera House.

For the first time, I was able to watch the performance as well as listen to the music, a kaleidoscope that mesmerized and delighted me. And not only see the performers, but the words of the *libretto*. The English subtitles showed up on a small screen on the back of the chair in front of me. In my line of vision, just below the stage view, I could simultaneously watch the stage, understand the words and listen to the music!

And it was the understanding of the words that flung open another door into the sensuous nature of the Italian soul, my soul.

The words, the words, the words.

The words to *Madama Butterfly*'s *"Un bel di"* ("One Beautiful Day") fuse betrayal and hope so powerfully, I always have to sit down, pull over or otherwise stop what I am doing when I hear it. Her stratospheric voice in this *aria* commands that kind of attention and so I surrender, tears streaming, still hoping she will somehow escape her fate.

The brilliant *"Bella Figlia dell'Amore"* (Beautiful Daughter of Love) from *Rigoletto*, a quartet of people embroiled in deception and revenge, is a masterpiece of conveying four different perspectives and two conversations simultaneously...the innocent young woman, Gilda, watches her manipulative lover, a Duke, seduce a commoner, Maddalena, who knows he is a player, while Gilda's father plots his death. Sound complicated? It is deliciously complex and stunning in its beauty.

Italian opera, like so many aspects of the culture, engages all the senses. In my favorite, Puccini's "*Tosca*," beyond the pleasure of sight and hearing, which alone would satisfy, I can also taste her desire for revenge, take in the palpable smell of fear as she contemplates the blade and the visceral blow at the moment she runs it through Scarpia's black heart...Tosca's Kiss, as she calls it.

I can never manage to eat dinner after seeing an opera performance. I am completely sated by what all my senses have absorbed. Yes, swept away, released, elated...*issimo*. I highly recommend it.

All through my life, I received letters and cards from Olga. She always signed them like this: "*non mi dimenticare e ti voglio bene.*" She did not write or say, "I love you."

The first part of the phrase I had no trouble understanding (think Nat King Cole). Don't forget me.

But, "*ti voglio bene*"? I did not understand that part until after Olga's death, when I made many more trips to my homeland, following in her footsteps...where she showed me what it meant.

"*Ti voglio bene*" literally means, "I want you well." It is the phrase Italians use to express to children, parents and close friends, "I love you." ("*Ti amo*" is reserved for lovers and married people).

Unlike American English, the word "love" is not used by Italians to describe a feeling for everything...*love your hair, love my car, love that movie*. Italians think it very strange that we use the word "love" to describe how we feel about experiences or possessions.

"*Ti voglio bene*" embraces so much more than a feeling. It's a desire for a person's total good. Yes, I want you well. I want you prosperous, fed, rested, blossoming, thriving, happy, radiant! "*issimo!*"

Now do you understand why Italians are so concerned about feeding you? Why they just keep bringing you more? Now do you understand why opera is so essential to how they live? Why food, sex and music are all wrapped up with garlands? Why Italians want you to take a nap, why they want you to not worry so much? Why they are evangelists for "*la dolce vita*"?

The sweet life, like *gelato*.

So, no, my grandmother did not say, "I love you." She wanted me well. She nurtured my mind, body and spirit, an infusion of all things Italian, including *la bellezza*. . .the beauty of the words.

Carol Faenzi is an award-winning author, speaker, contributor to the *Indianapolis Business Journal* and accomplished business consultant. Her popular historical novel *The Stonecutter's Aria* is based on the true stories of her Italian marble-carving, opera-singing ancestors who settled in Indianapolis. It won the "Book of the Year" award for historical fiction by both *ForeWord Magazine* and the Independent Publishers Group.

Faenzi took a sabbatical from a busy corporate career in New York when she bought a one-way ticket to live in Tuscany in search of her ancestral roots. Her time in Italy and writing the stories of her immigrant ancestors inspired her to change her life. Faenzi presents programs across the United States that inspire audiences to preserve their family legacies, stories and rituals.

In addition to her creative pursuits, Faenzi has a private practice, cultivating management and leadership development for women and is a consultant for organizational strategy. She splits her time between Indianapolis, New York City and her family farm in Tuscany.

KAREN KOVACIK

IN THE LETTER R

The wish to postpone arrival
the desire to be lost
begins in a wild box of crayons
when the child writes R A I N
in her drugstore calendar
and out the window
real silver is falling
and the word on the page
is more than the hinge and hook
of pressure on wax
the letters shooting open like parasols
or maples in slow motion
the calendar pages
March April May
dissolving into a city
the child has not yet seen
but she can smell its wet wool
its boulevards of neon and chocolate
the hexagons of sidewalk
that invite her in

and though her mother is cooking

veal pocket and green beans

maraschino tapioca for dessert

the child has booked a room

for the evening

in the letter R

where from its window

she watches the bracelet of lights

sway along the river

and beneath her sloping ceiling

beneath the roof of staccato rain

she undresses whole sentences

like paper dolls

turning TANG into TANGO

RIG into RIGOR

and though she can't foresee it

she will aim for the dazzle

of what her English will allow

its boroughs now her boroughs

with their intricate streets

its river the one she will fish in

beads of rain lighting the way overhead

This poem originally was published as "Liquid Syntax" in Metropolis Burning *(Cleveland: Cleveland State Poetry Center, 2005).*

BONNIE MAURER

ANOTHER STORY

Before bed, I sat
on father's lap
and handed him
my brush.
Unwinding
the day's work,
he brushed
the black sky
into my hair,
the stars
into my shine.
He brushed
one hundred
strokes,
rowing through
dark water.
Sparks,
he brushed
into the moon's path,
lighting his way,
crowning my head

hand over hand,
knotting
the story of earth
and heaven,
day and night,
father and daughter.

From Reconfigured, *Finishing Line Press, 2009*

BUENAS NOCHES, PAPÁ

DIANNE MONEYPENNY
GORDON R. STRAIN

Era una noche cualquiera. Ordinaria en cualquier forma. Aun así era especial. El trabajo pasó. La cena fue preparada y comida. La casita de ladrillo rojo era tranquila por la noche. Un papá se sentaba sobre el suelo de una recámara verde con su hija de cuatro años.

La lucha de la hora de dormir había empezado.

Bueno, al enfrentarse con un niño, los adultos se dan cuenta de algo; la magia se desvanece. La vida sigue pasando. Y todo el estrés nos curte. Como cada día, somos hormigas en la marcha del trabajo en un mundo de matices grises y negros que cubren todo. Lo que nos salva es que cada noche para un papá los colores del amor infantil pintan el mundo. A veces el contraste entre el día y la noche lo hace peor. Debido a la discordancia que se nota en la brecha.

Ella se batió al duelo. "Papá, leamos un librito más. Será el último. Te lo prometo," dijo empujando el libro hacia su papá.

El había pasado tanto tiempo intentando en esconderse en el mundo gris que cada vez que oía esa vocecita dulce, en su inocencia y asombro descarado, se le paraba el corazón.

"Es nada más una demora," él respondió alegremente.

Pero, ella sabía que lo tenía. Sonreía pícaramente y revelaba los hoyuelos para terminar el debate.

"Pero solo es uno. . .pero pequeñito. Porrrrr favorrrr, papá."

En las manitas abrazó una versión condensada del *Maravilloso Mago de Oz*. La tapa de la cartulina brillaba con zapatillas carmines rociadas con brillantina; adentro incluía el tornado, el Espantapájaros, el Hombre de Hojalata, la Bruja Verde y Mala y el Mago. Todos los demás estaban ilustrados, pero les faltaban las gran entradas de la versión original.

Flecha bien puesta. Nunca entendía cómo esta criatura, esta niña, esta hija perfecta lo había enredado tan rápidamente. Que con solo 4 años le pudo vencer con facilidad. Al papá le encantaba *El Maravilloso Mago de Oz*, incluso en forma corta y francamente, era aun más loco para ella.

"Bien, uno más, pero acuéstate primero. Lo leo cuando estés en la cama y debajo de la cobija," su voz una mezcla de dureza y culpa. Desesperadamente quería más tiempo con su hija, pero sabía la importancia del sueño para una niñita. Se acercó.

Ella sonrió y emocionadamente empezó a girar su pelo entre los deditos gorditos con esmalte descascarado mientras él abría el forro.

Antes de empezar a leer, él echó un vistazo por la habitación, la identidad de guagua estaba abarcada por las cuatro paredes. Colgada en una pared había una reproducción de Matisse con una niña sentada en un vestido amarillo. Ella lo escogió por sí misma en el museo. La Princesa Leia Organa, de tamaño real, pegaba en la pared y, finalmente, encima de un estante una hazaña de Lego en la forma de El Halcón de Milenio (que ella rogó que comprara en la tienda de juguetes) meticulosamente construido descansaba en el cuarto también. Darth Vador y Chewbaca jugaban felizmente al ajedrez en el espacio. Han Solo manejaba la cabina mientras Dora la exploradora montaba una gatita encima de la nave espacial.

En los otros estantes rebosaban rompecabezas, juegos, juguetes, animales y otras sorpresas. El viejo Conejo de Felpa, el cual era suyo, el Oso Baloo y Hello Kitty llenaban las manos enormes del Increíble Hulk. Todo le indicaba una versión miniatura de él. Una identidad reciclada por la próxima generación. Esta niña perfecta. Ella sería mejor que él en este mundo.

Con esta realización tenía miedo y se preocupaba por ella y esperaba lo mejor para ella. Esperaba que ella fuera todo lo que él no fue. Todo lo que no podía ser. Rogaba que fuera inteligente, simpática, confidente y saludable. Exitosa. Feliz. Le preocupaba que creciera como él. En un abrir y cerrar de ojos, se le inundaron todos los problemas de la madurez con todas las inseguridades de la paternidad.

Con esfuerzo, se liberó de estos pensamientos y se dirijo otra vez al libro y lo abrió. Antes de que empezara, ella interrumpió, "Papá, haz las voces, por favor," chirriaba con emoción.

Entretenido respondió, "Sí, cariño, haré las voces."

Había leído el libro más de 50 veces, pero todavía se concentraba en cada palabra e indicaba cada palabra con el dedo, por si acaso ella lo seguía.

Página tras página leía con las voces de los personajes y cantaban las canciones cuando era necesario. Cuando el cuento requería música de fondo contaba con ella. Y ella tenía cuidado de no ser ruidosa, por temor de que arruinará la historia.

"Me derrito, me derrito, O qué mundo, qué mundo," ella gritaba mientras que él señalaba cada palabra escrita.

Y, sí sabía cada una las palabras. Las sabía porque su papá las señalaba lentamente cada noche.

Con un suspiro contento, la niña se acostó en su almohada y se acurrucó con su monito. Miró por la habitación para asegurarse de que tuviera todo lo necesario: su linternita, una cobijita, agua y, claro, el libro para que pudiera leerlo unas veces más sola antes de dormirse.

Terminada su rutina de velada, la arropó bien y le dio un beso en la frente.

Mientras que las estrellas titilaban en un cielo hecho de azul oscuro afuera del cristal de la ventana amarilla, "Te amo, papá," susurraba mientras él cerraba la puerta. El sonreía mientras un dolor le pasaba por el corazón.

"Buenas noches, alma mía," respondió con un clic de la puerta y salió para vagar otra vez por su mundo gris.

GOOD NIGHT, DADDY

DIANNE MONEYPENNY
GORDON R. STRAIN

"Daddy, let's read just one more. I promise it's the last," the daughter said, pushing the small book back towards her father.

It was a night like any other. Ordinary in every way. And yet it was remarkable. Work had passed. Dinner had been prepared and eaten. The little brick house was quiet for the night. A father sat on the floor of a little green bedroom with his daughter. The struggle for bedtime had begun.

As a grownup, when the magic fades but life marches on, all the stress hardens us. Each day was the same at work, a wash of gray and black over everything, but each night the world was dappled with the colors of the love of a child. He spent so much time lost in the gray world that each time he heard that little voice, in all its innocence and unabashed wonder, his heart skipped a beat.

"You're stalling," he replied with a sigh.

She knew she had him. She grinned devilishly, revealing her dimples. "Just a short one, PAH-LEASE daddy!"

In her tiny hands she held a condensed version of *The Wizard of Oz*. The cardboard cover shone with ruby slippers covered in glitter; inside it included the tornado, Scarecrow, Tin Man, the Wicked Witch, and the Wizard. All of the other characters were in the illustrations, but lacked the grand entrances they had in the original version.

He never understood how this little creature, this girl, this perfect little daughter had figured him out so quickly. Is this what all children do to their parents? She knew that he was a sucker for *The Wizard of Oz*, even in short form and, frankly, an even bigger sucker for her.

"Fine, one more…but you need to lay down. I'll read it to you once you're in bed and under the covers," his voice a mixture of sternness and guilt. He desperately wanted more time with her, and yet he knew the importance of sleep for a four year old.

She smiled and excitedly climbed onto his back and started to twirl his hair between chubby fingers with chipped nail polish as he opened the book.

Before beginning he cast a furtive glance around her room, at her toddler identity encompassed by four walls…there was a Matisse print she had picked out at the museum hanging on the wall, a life-sized Princess Leia stuck to another wall, and a Lego Millennium Falcon she begged for one day at the store—perfectly constructed and sitting on her shelf. Darth Vader and Chewbacca happily playing space chess, Han Solo manned the cockpit while Dora the Explorer was mounted on a stuffed kitten perched on top of the ship.

Her other shelves brimmed with puzzles, games, toys, and stuffed animals. His old Velveteen Rabbit, a Baloo the Bear, a pair of large foam Hulk Hands with Hello Kitty dolls stuffed inside. It was all a miniature version of himself. A recycled identity. A projection of the things he liked, both as a child and as an adult, being adapted and repurposed by his little girl. This perfect little girl. She would be better than he in this world.

That realization startled him and he quickly worried for her and he hoped for her. He hoped she would be all the things he wasn't. All the things he couldn't be. He hoped she would be smart, kind, confident, beautiful, and healthy. Successful. Happy. He worried that she would become like him. All the worries of adulthood showered him along with all the insecurities of parenthood.

He quickly turned back to the book and opened the page. Before he began she interrupted, "Daddy, do the voices, OK? *Por favor,*" with a squeak of excitement.

Amused, "Yes, sweetie, of course I'll do the voices."

He had read the book well over 50 times and yet he focused in on each word and ran his finger under the oversized letters—in case she happened to be reading along.

Page by page he read in the character's voices and sang the songs when there were songs to be sung. When there was underscoring necessary, she took care of that. And yet she was careful not to be too loud, lest she disturb the story.

"I'm melting! Melting! Oh what a world! What a world!" she shrieked as he carefully pointed to each word.

She knew them all, every word. She knew them because her daddy pointed slowly to each one every night.

With a little sigh, completely content, she laid her head down on her pillow and snuggled in with a stuffed monkey. She glanced around to make sure everything she needed was there: her flashlight, blanket, cup of water, and of course the book, so she could read it to herself a few more times before falling asleep.

He tucked her in and kissed her softly on the forehead.

The stars twinkled in a dark blue sky outside of the yellow window panes. "I love you, daddy," she whispered as he closed her door. He smiled as a twinge of ache passed through his heart.

"Goodnight, sweetheart," he replied, as he wandered back into his gray world.

BONNIE MAURER

THE SNEEZE

Something delicious
in a sneeze
my husband's grandmother
Annie loved. The way she relished
cold butter on bread.
Satisfaction. I first heard
the sneeze at Thanksgiving.
Her sneeze clinching the family meal.
The End. Last page of the book.
The final sneeze, laughing
us toward digestion,
the migration
to the living room chairs.